DEAD IN
THE WATER

Books by Stuart Woods

Fiction
Dead in the Water
Dirt
Choke
Imperfect Strangers
Heat
Dead Eyes
L.A. Times
Santa Fe Rules
New York Dead
Palindrome
Grass Roots
White Cargo
Under the Lake
Deep Lie
Run Before the Wind
Chiefs

Travel
A Romantic's Guide to the Country Inns
of Britain and Ireland (1978)

Memoir
Blue Water, Green Skipper

DEAD IN THE WATER

A NOVEL

STUART WOODS

HarperCollins*Publishers*

HarperCollins books may be purchased for educational, business, or sales promotional use. For information please write: Special Markets Department, HarperCollins Publishers, Inc., 10 East 53rd Street, New York, NY 10022.

FIRST EDITION

Designed by Liane Fuji

Library of Congress Cataloging-in-Publication Data

Woods, Stuart.
    Dead in the water : a novel / by Stuart Woods. — 1st ed.
      p. cm.
    ISBN 0-06-018368-3
    I. Title.
PS3573.O642D394   1997
813'.54—dc21   97-14255

97 98 99 00 01 ❖/RRD 10 9 8 7 6 5

This book is for the saints
of Washington, Connecticut,
Paul and Joan Marks

CHAPTER

1

Stone Barrington slowly opened his eyes and stared blearily at the pattern of moving light above him. Disoriented, he tried to make sense of the light. Then it came to him: he was aboard a yacht, and the light was reflected off the water.

He sat up and rubbed his eyes. The night before had been the stuff of bad dreams; he never wanted to have another like it. The nightmare had started at Kennedy Airport, when his live-in girl-friend, Arrington Carter, had not shown up for the flight. She was supposed to come directly from the magazine office where she had been meeting with an editor, but she had not arrived.

Stone had found a phone and had tracked down Arrington, still at *The New Yorker.*

"Hello?" she said.

Stone glanced at his watch. "I guess you're not going to make the plane," he said. "It leaves in twenty minutes."

"Stone, I'm so sorry; I've been having you paged at the terminal. Didn't you hear the page?"

He tried to keep his voice calm. "No, I didn't."

"Everything has exploded here. I took the proposal for the profile on Vance Calder to Tina Brown, and she went for it instantly. Turns out she had tried and tried to do a piece with Vance when she was at *Vanity Fair,* and he would never cooperate."

"That's wonderful," he said tonelessly. "I'm happy for you."

"Look, darling, Vance is coming into New York tomorrow, and I've got to introduce him to Tina at lunch, there's just no getting around it."

"I see," he replied.

"Don't worry, I'm already booked on the same flight tomorrow. You go ahead to St. Marks, take delivery of the boat, put in some provisions, and get gloriously drunk. I'll be there by midnight."

"All right," he said.

"Oh," she sighed, "I'm so relieved you're not angry. I know you can see what a break this is for me. Vance hasn't sat still for an in-depth interview for more than twenty years. Tina says she'll bump up the printing for the anticipated increase in newsstand sales."

"That's great," he said, making an effort to sound glad for her. "I'll meet you at the St. Marks airport tomorrow night, then."

"Oh, don't do that; just sit tight, and I'll grab a cab." She lowered her voice. "And when I get there, sweetie, try and be well rested, because I'm going to bounce you off the bedsprings a whole lot; you read me?"

"I read you loud and clear. I'd better run; they've almost finished boarding. And remember, we've only got the boat for ten days; don't waste any more."

"I really am going to make it up to you in the best possible way, Stone," she said. "Bye-bye."

"Bye." Stone hung up the phone and ran for his plane. Moments later, he had settled into a comfortable leather seat and had in his hand a rum and tonic, in honor of his long-anticipated winter holiday. As the big jet taxied out to the runway he looked out the window and saw that it had started to snow. Good. Why have a tropical holiday if you can't gloat?

Vance Calder was, arguably, Hollywood's premier male star, often called the new Cary Grant, and he had played an important part in Stone's and Arrington's lives already. She had been in Calder's company when they had met at a dinner party at the home of a gossip columnist nearly a year earlier. Although

Stone had been struck by her beauty and had found her marvelous company, he had not bothered to call her, because he hadn't believed for a moment that he could take a girl away from Vance Calder. Instead, Arrington had called him. Vance, she had explained, was no more than an acquaintance who, when he was in New York, liked to have a pretty girl to squire around, especially at dinners like the one at Amanda Dart's apartment, which she would feature in her column.

Inside a few weeks they were living together, and Stone had never been happier. At forty-two, he was still a bachelor, and he liked it that way. Living with Arrington, though, had made a lack of freedom seem very attractive, and he was determined to hang on to her, even if it came to marriage. Marriage had been increasingly on his mind of late, especially since Arrington had been showing signs of feeling a lack of commitment on his part. On the plane down to St. Marks he had reached a decision. They would have a wonderful cruise on the chartered boat, and they would come back engaged, unless it turned out to be easy to be wed in St. Marks; in that case, they would come back married. He was looking forward to the prospect.

Then the night began to go wrong. In San Juan, their first stop, he learned that his flight to St. Martin, the next leg, had been delayed by two hours. In St. Martin, the connecting flight to Antigua had also been delayed, and by the time he had arrived there, the light twin that would take him to St. Marks had already left and had to be summoned back at great expense. He had reached St. Marks sometime after 3:00 A.M. Nevertheless, he had been met by the charter agent and taken to the boat, a Beneteau 36, a roomy French design, and had, without unpacking, fallen dead into the double berth in the little owner's cabin.

He got out of bed and stumbled naked into the little galley and found half a jar of instant coffee in a cupboard. Shortly he had found the gas tap in the cockpit, boiled a kettle, and made himself a really terrible cup of coffee. While he drank it he took a stroll around the interior of the little yacht, a very short stroll indeed. He was glad there would be only the two of them aboard.

There was a very nice dining table, some books, no doubt left by previous charterers, and a small television set. He wondered what he might receive on that. He turned it on and, to his surprise, found himself looking at CNN. The marina must have a satellite dish, he thought. He slid into the navigator's seat, the leather cool against his naked buttocks, and looked around the chart table. All the island charts were there, plus a small Global Positioning System (GPS) receiver, a VHF radio, and everything else they needed to navigate in the islands.

He found some stale cereal and ate some, watching CNN. A major snowstorm would reach the New York City area by evening, and travel was expected to be disrupted. *Thank God Arrington is getting out this afternoon,* he thought. He washed his dishes, then unpacked and put away his clothes. A swim might be nice, he thought; he got into some trunks and climbed into the cockpit.

As he did, a yacht of about forty-five feet hove into view, under engine. It had a dark blue hull and teak decks, and her name, *Expansive,* was lettered on her bow in gilt. Two other things about the yacht caught his eye: the mainsail was still up, and in tatters, and it was being steered by a quite beautiful young woman. She was small and blond, wearing a bikini bottom and a chambray shirt knotted under her breasts, leaving a fetching expanse of tanned midriff showing between the two. The yacht passed within twenty yards of Stone's boat, but she never looked at him. Oddly, no one came on deck to help her dock. He started to go and help, but a yellow flag was flying at the crosstrees, signaling that the yacht was arriving from a foreign port, and he saw a uniformed customs officer waiting to take her lines. Stone watched the somewhat clumsy operation and wished he had gone to help. He'd have liked a closer look at the woman.

He put down the boarding ladder, then dove off the stern into the bright blue water, which turned out to be exactly the right temperature—about eighty degrees, he reckoned. Maybe later today he'd call somebody in New York and gloat. He swam out about fifty yards into the little harbor, then sprinted back to his boat, hauling himself up the boarding ladder. He got a towel from below, made himself another cup of the awful coffee, and settled into the cockpit to get some sun on his all-too-white body. As he did, he saw the customs officer leave the yacht and, at a dead run, head for the little police shack fifty yards away. Odd.

A moment later, the customs officer emerged from the shack in the company of two police officers, one of them of rank, judging from his uniform. The three men marched rapidly back toward the blue yacht and went aboard, disappearing below. Stone watched with interest to see what would happen next. Ten minutes passed before the young woman skipper appeared on deck wearing a cotton dress. Accompanied by the three uniformed officers, one of them carrying a small nylon duffel, she walked toward the police shack and disappeared inside.

What the hell was going on? Stone wondered.

He kept an eye on the police shack all afternoon. Finally, sometime after five o'clock, the woman left the shack in the company of two uniformed policemen, got into a waiting car, and was driven away. Stone didn't know what sort of trouble she was in, but he felt for her, alone in a foreign place, at the mercy of the police. He had seen many people in custody, and he had never envied any of them.

2

Stone showered, shaved, and got into some of his new tropical clothing—a short-sleeved silk shirt, Italian cotton trousers, and woven leather loafers, no socks. He found it an unexpected pleasure to dress so lightly in January; there was much to be said for winter in the tropics.

As the sun set he wandered across a wide green lawn toward a wide thatched roof covering a bar and restaurant open to the breezes. It was early, and there were few customers. A black bartender stood behind an expanse of varnished mahogany, idly polishing a glass. A television set over the bar was tuned to CNN, the sound muted.

"Evening to you, boss," he said amiably, with what sounded to Stone like a Bahamian accent.

"Evening," Stone said.

"And what might be your pleasure this fine evening?"

"Oh, something tropical, I guess, to celebrate my first evening in warm weather."

"A piña colada, mebbe?"

"Sounds good." Stone looked up at the television and saw a woman in a heavy coat standing on what looked like a New York City street corner. A blizzard was raging about her. "Could you turn the sound up on the TV for a minute?" he asked the bartender.

"Sure thing, boss."

". . . was predicted for later this evening, but it started around noon, and we already have a foot of snow on the streets, with at least twenty inches expected by the wee hours of tomorrow morning. Kennedy, La Guardia, and Newark Airports closed at midafternoon, so nothing is flying into or out of the city until further notice. The Port Authority predicted that no flights would be moving until noon tomorrow."

"Shit," Stone said aloud. "Okay, you can turn the volume down again."

"What you care, boss?" the bartender asked, turning down the TV. "You already here."

"Yeah, but my girl isn't. She was due to leave at four this afternoon."

"Bad luck, boss," the man said.

"Where are you from?" Stone asked.

"Born right here on St. Marks, boss."

"Funny, you sound Bahamian. You shining me on with that accent?"

The man grinned. "You're too good for me, pal." He stuck out his hand. "I'm Thomas Hardy, like the writer." Now the accent was more island British, with an extra, familiar layer.

Stone shook his hand. "Do I hear a little New York in there somewhere?"

"Lived in Brooklyn a long time; worked all over the city."

"I'm Stone Barrington; I'm on a charter yacht over at the marina."

"That's kind of a familiar name," Thomas said.

"Don't know why; it's my first time in St. Marks."

"Were you ever a cop?"

Stone blinked in surprise. "I was, mostly in the Nineteenth Precinct. Have we ever met?"

Thomas shook his head. "No, but I heard about you. I was walking a beat in the Village when you left the force; everybody was talking about you, said you got a bad deal."

"I can't complain," Stone said. "I left with the full pension after fourteen years."

"Yeah, but you took some lead with you, huh?"

"They got it out. What are you doing in St. Marks?"

"I was born here, like I said. My mama moved to New York when I was a kid. I joined the force, did my twenty, and brought my savings and my pension down here and put it to work."

"This your place?"

"Lock, stock, and liquor license."

"How long you been at it?"

"Six and a half years."

"Business good?"

"Not bad; a little better every year. That blizzard in the Northeast is going to cost me, though. A lot of people will be in your girl's shoes."

"I guess so." Stone sighed. "I was looking forward to a more romantic week than this. Where can I make a phone call?"

Thomas reached under the bar, pulled out a phone, and set it on the bar. "I charge the tourists a buck a minute, but for an old cop, I'll just put what they charge me on your tab. Got a fax machine, too, if you should need one."

"Thanks." Stone called his home number.

"Hello?"

"I guess you're not going to make it tonight, huh?"

"You heard? I tried to call you at the charter office, but I didn't get an answer."

"They get CNN down here."

"I'm sorry, baby. It started to come down around midday, and let me tell you, it's really something. I'm a southern girl; I've never seen snow like this."

"CNN says the airlines will be flying again tomorrow afternoon. See what you can do."

"I'm already rebooked on tomorrow's flight, assuming it goes."

"Good. What are you up to now?"

"I'm having dinner with Vance and some friends of his. He actually found a Range Rover somewhere, and he's picking me up."

"Where are you dining?"

"Wherever's open, I guess."

"I miss you, babe."

"And I miss you, my darling. I was looking forward to that first piña colada."

"I'm drinking it for you right now. Say, let me give you this number."

Thomas shoved a card in front of him.

Stone read off both the phone and fax numbers. "Keep me posted on the flight situation, will you? The boat is moored no more than a hundred yards from this phone."

"I will, baby."

Stone said good-bye and hung up. "Well, Thomas, it looks like you and me." He sipped the piña colada. It was perfect—cold, sweet, and pineapply.

"Let me know when you're ready for dinner," Thomas said. "I'll keep a table for you." Customers were drifting in now, and a waiter was seating them.

Stone watched as a large black man dressed in a white linen suit, and in the company of a beautiful café-au-lait woman, entered and was shown to a prime table overlooking the harbor. "Impressive-looking fellow," he said.

"That's Sir Winston Sutherland, the minister of justice," Thomas said.

"A mover and shaker?"

"He both moves and shakes. And if his own opinion holds, he just might be the next prime minister."

Stone heard a car door slam and turned to look. The blond woman from the blue yacht, *Expansive,* had left a police car and, alone, was making her way across the lawn toward the marina.

"Very nice, huh?" Thomas said.

"Very nice indeed. She spent the afternoon with the local cops, though. I wonder why."

"Word is, the lady left Europe with a husband but arrived in St. Marks without him."

Stone turned and looked at the bartender. "I didn't see anybody else on board when she came into the harbor."

"That's because she was all alone on that big boat."

"You mean she sailed it all the way across the Atlantic?"

"Well, not all the way," Thomas said. "Her husband was along for part of the time."

"Is foul play suspected?"

"On this island, foul play is always suspected," Thomas replied. "That lady is going to have to convince a number of people"—he pointed at Sir Winston Sutherland—"that man first among them, that she is as innocent as a newborn lamb."

"And how difficult is that likely to be?" Stone asked.

"It could be very difficult indeed," Thomas said. "There's going to be a coroner's jury over at the town meeting house tomorrow morning. Word is, Sir Winston is asking the questions."

"Is that unusual?"

"Usually the coroner does it."

Stone looked over at Sir Winston Sutherland, who was digging into a bowl of something. "What's he eating?" he asked.

"Conch chowder."

"Well, I suppose you have to be careful of any man with enough daring to eat conch chowder in a white linen suit."

"Oh," Thomas said, "there's more reason than that to be careful of Sir Winston."

When Stone got back to his boat, late, there were lights on in the big blue yacht. He was tempted to call on the lady to offer his condolences, but he was a little drunker than he liked to be when he introduced himself to a beautiful woman.

3

Stone, a little worse for the wear, entered the Markstown Meeting Hall at ten o'clock the following morning, just as the coroner, a wizened little black man with snow white hair, was about to call the proceedings to order. A jury of five black men and one white sat on folding chairs along one side of the hall; the coroner sat on a folding chair at a card table at the front of the room, and the woman from the blue yacht sat in the front row of chairs, dressed in a trim black dress that set off her tan. The dress was not quite demure enough for mourning, but it bespoke a certain dignity. Stone took a seat in the front row, across the aisle from her, just as Sir Winston Sutherland made his entrance, carrying a large satchel briefcase and dressed in a double-breasted blue suit with chalk stripes. He looked very official.

"These proceedings will come to order," said the coroner. "We meet to hear testimony on the death of Paul Phillips Manning; we are pleased to have Sir Winston with us to conduct questioning."

Stone glanced at the woman, who sat, looking tired but somehow radiant, staring serenely at the coroner. She glanced briefly at Sir Winston. Stone wondered if she knew who he was and what was about to happen.

The coroner spoke again. "Call Mrs. Allison Manning."

The woman rose and walked toward a folding chair set next to the coroner's card table, between him and the jury. The scene resembled a rehearsal of a high school play set in a courtroom.

"Hold the book," the coroner said to her, extending a Bible. "Do you swear by Almighty God that the evidence you are about to give will be the truth?"

"I do," Allison Manning replied.

"State your full name and age for the record."

"Allison Ames Manning; I am twenty-nine years old."

Stone now noticed a stenographer seated near the jury, taking down the proceedings in shorthand.

Allison Manning gazed evenly at Sir Winston as he rose from his seat to his full height, which was a good six-three, and approached her.

"Mrs. Manning," Sir Winston said gently, "may I begin by expressing my condolences on the loss of your husband?"

"Thank you," she replied.

"Mrs. Manning, how long were you married to Paul Phillips Manning?"

"It would have been four years next month."

"And how old was your husband at his death?"

"Forty-two."

"And where did the two of you reside?"

"In Greenwich, Connecticut."

"Would you be kind enough to tell us of your last months with your husband?"

Allison Manning took a deep breath and spoke in a clear, well-modulated voice. "My husband and I left Newport, Rhode Island, last May and crossed the Atlantic to Plymouth, in England, just the two of us. Paul had had the yacht built in Finland and fitted out with some extra equipment after it was delivered to Newport. From Plymouth, we cruised up the English Channel to Cowes, on the Isle of Wight, then crossed the Channel and cruised the coast of Brittany, in France. We made a long passage to Bilbao, in northern Spain, then went on to Lisbon and Gibraltar. In the Mediterranean, we cruised the Greek islands and the Balearics and then sailed out to Madeira and the Canary Islands. We called at Las Palmas and did some refitting there, then at Puerto Rico, a port on the southernmost island of the Canaries, and our last port of call before starting across the Atlantic, bound for Antigua." She took a sip of water from a glass poured by the coroner.

"Please go on," Sir Winston said.

Allison Manning looked a little sadder. "We sailed southwest from the Canaries down to the latitude of Antigua, then turned west. We had picked up the trade winds by then, and we were making good time. We were ten days out of Puerto Rico, over halfway to Antigua, when the incident occurred."

"Tell us about the incident, with as much detail as you can recall."

"It was on the early afternoon of the tenth day," she said. "We had been in and out of squalls, then the wind dropped, and we were very nearly becalmed. The weather had been very changeable. We had been down to short sail in the squalls, using a roller-reefing headsail, which was like a big window blind, and when Paul began to unroll the sail in the light winds, the top swivel of the roller-reefing gear separated into two parts. The sail fell down with the bottom part, and the top part of the gear remained at the top of the mast, attached to the halyard. I hope I'm making this clear."

Sir Winston turned to the jury. "Gentlemen, do you understand?"

The jury nodded as one man.

"Please go on, Mrs. Manning," Sir Winston said.

"This wasn't the first time this had happened," she said, "and it meant that someone had to go up the mast and pull the top part of the swivel down to deck level so that it could be reattached to the bottom part."

"And who went up the mast?"

"I did."

"Was this usual? Did your husband often send you up the mast at sea?"

"No. I had done that a couple of times before, but when we were tied up alongside in port. It was easier for Paul to hoist me up the mast with a winch than for me to hoist him. He is . . .

•

13

was a large man. On this occasion he wanted to go himself, but he had woken up not feeling well that morning and was obviously not well. He had a thing about making good time at sea, and he didn't want to wait until he felt better, so I said I would go up the mast."

"And how did you accomplish that?"

"Paul lowered the mainsail; I got into the bosun's chair, which is a canvas sling, and Paul winched me to the top of the mast on the main halyard, then cleated the line while I hauled the genoa halyard down to deck level. There wasn't much wind, but there was a sea running from the last squall, and it was pretty uncomfortable at the top of the mast. I called to Paul to lower me to the deck, and that was when I saw him, sitting on a cockpit seat, holding his arm, near the shoulder." For the first time, her voice quavered. "His left arm."

"What happened then?"

She seemed to struggle to keep control of herself. "I called to him again, and he looked up at me. Then he seemed to be in terrible pain, and he sort of just lay down on his side on the cockpit seat." Tears appeared on her cheeks now. "I was very frightened. The wind began to get up again, and with no sail up, the boat was rolling very badly. I continued to call out to him in panic—panic that I was stuck at the top of the mast, and panic that he seemed to be having a heart attack, and I couldn't help him." Now she began to cry in earnest. Sutherland stood without speaking while she produced a tissue and dabbed at her eyes. Finally in control again, she continued. "A few minutes passed—I don't know how long—then Paul slid off the seat onto the cockpit sole. He just lay there, facedown. It was obvious that he was unconscious; he just sort of flopped about when the boat rolled."

"And then what did you do?"

"I just clung to the mast and cried."

"For how long?"

"A long time. Two hours, maybe three. I wasn't wearing a watch. Finally the sun got low in the sky; I realized that Paul wasn't going to help me, and that I had to do something to help myself."

"And what did you do?"

She took a deep breath and let it out. "I hugged the mast as tightly as I could, then I slipped out of the bosun's chair and began sliding down the mast, except I slid a lot faster than I meant to. I went down very quickly until I came to rest on the crosstrees, in a sitting position. That hurt, and I was sort of stunned for a minute, so I just stopped and collected myself for a few minutes. The rolling wasn't quite as bad, since I was farther down the mast. Finally I got up enough nerve to go the rest of the way down. I still don't know why I didn't fall and hurt myself."

"Then you went to help your husband?"

"No, not immediately. I was so terrified and so exhausted from clinging to the mast that I just lay there in a heap. I think I may have even fainted for a while; I don't know how long. When I could get up again, I made my way back to the cockpit. Paul was dead."

Stone found that he had been holding his breath. He let it out in a rush, and everyone in the room—the coroner, the jury, and Sir Winston—turned and looked at him. "Excuse me," he said sheepishly. He looked up and found Allison Manning staring at him. It seemed to be the first time she had been aware of his presence.

"Please go on," Sir Winston said. "What did you do next?"

"I tried to give him cardiopulmonary resuscitation," she said.

"Had you been trained in this technique?"

"I took a class once, at the yacht club at home."

"Did this have any effect?"

"No. I couldn't get a pulse at all, and Paul . . . I couldn't get him to breathe, and his body was growing quite cold by this time."

Stone marveled at how calmly she related all this.

"And then what did you do?"

"I sat and cried for a while and let the yacht take care of herself. When I finally got a grip, I started thinking about what to do next. It was dark by then, and it seemed so strange that Paul was dead. I kept expecting him to come up from below and adjust the sails or something."

•

"Did you move the body at all?"

"Not at first. Paul is . . . was a big man, and I'm quite small. I thought about moving him down below, to a berth, but then it occurred to me that if I did, I'd just have to get him up again, sooner or later. So I left him in the cockpit that night. I was exhausted, so I got some sleep. I couldn't eat anything, though. The boat took care of me; the wind dropped, and she lay fairly quietly."

"What did you finally do with the body?"

"When I woke up it was still dark, but there was about three-quarters of a moon, so the night was bright. It was clear to me that in that climate, I was going to have to bury Paul at sea. I went up into the cockpit and tried lifting the body, but I couldn't budge it. Finally I got the main halyard around him and winched him into a sort of standing position. When I let out on the line, he fell to leeward, and I was able to get him onto the side deck and undo the halyard. Then I released the lifelines and got him overboard."

"What did you do next?"

She swallowed hard, then continued calmly. "I said a prayer for Paul's soul, then I began to think about sailing the boat. Dawn came; I got the mainsail up with a winch and got us headed due west, and I repaired the headsail reefing swivel with a little steel clip. We had half a dozen spares, and we had already used half of them. Paul often talked about finding some more permanent solution to the problem, but he never did. Finally I got the headsail up again. I set the self-steering gear, as Paul had taught me, and I got a sleeping bag and slept in the cockpit through the morning. It was easy sailing, and with one or two direction changes as the wind came up, I got through the day. I slept in the cockpit that night, and by the second day, I was getting used to sailing the boat."

"So you just kept heading due west?"

"No, there was a book on board about celestial navigation; I couldn't find the manuals for the GPS or the high-frequency radio. I had never taken any real interest in the subject before—Paul had always done the navigating—but he had shown me how to use the sextant. From the book I learned how to find our latitude, and I just tried to keep us on the right latitude the rest of the way. We finished up a little farther south than I had tried for; our landfall was at St. Marks, instead of Antigua."

Sir Winston reached into his briefcase and brought out two books. He showed one to Allison Manning. "And you kept this logbook?"

"Yes, after Paul died I kept the log in a sort of abbreviated fashion. Paul was always very meticulous about recording everything, as you can see by reading the earlier entries."

Sir Winston held up the other book, a leather-bound volume. "And do you recognize this book?"

She looked at it. "Yes, he bought that in Las Palmas, and he wrote in it a lot."

"Did you ever read what he wrote in this book, Mrs. Manning?"

"No. He often made notes in such a book."

"Mrs. Manning, are you quite able to continue? Would you like a rest?"

"No, I'm fine; I'd like to go on."

"Good, good. Tell me, Mrs. Manning, how would you describe your relationship with your husband?"

"We had a good marriage; we were very content and happy."

Sir Winston looked surprised. "Really? You didn't have fights, arguments?"

"Rarely. Oh, I suppose anyone who's married has an argument now and then, but we got along well."

"No children?"

"No. Paul didn't want children."

"But you did?"

"Well, yes, but I suppose Paul was more important to me. I didn't want to ruin our marriage by having a child unless Paul wanted one, too."

"So you were deeply in love with your husband?"

She hesitated. "I loved him, yes," she said finally.

"Did you treat him well?"

"Yes, I did."

"You were a good wife at all times?"

•

"I tried to be," she replied. "Excuse me, sir, but what are you getting at?"

Sir Winston opened the leather-bound book and showed her a page. "Is this your husband's handwriting?"

"Yes, it is." Allison Manning was looking concerned for the first time.

"Let me read you some of what your husband wrote in this book," Sir Winston said, opening the book at a marked page. "I quote: 'They had been on the boat together for months now, and she had been the perfect bitch.'" Sir Winston paused, looked at the jury, then continued. "'She had always had a temper, but now she frightened him with the intensity of her anger.'" He looked at Allison Manning as if to elicit a response, but she said nothing; she looked stunned.

Sir Winston turned to another marked passage. "'They argued one day as she was making lunch. She had a chef's knife in her hand, and for a moment, he thought she might use it on him. He slept badly that night, waking often, expecting to feel the blade in his back.'"

Allison Manning was suddenly on her feet; her face was red and contorted with anger. "That's not about us, dammit! It's written in the third person, don't you see? What are you trying to do, you bastard?"

Sir Winston feigned shock at her outburst, but before he could speak, the coroner broke in. "Please compose yourself, Mrs. Manning; Sir Winston is only doing his duty." He looked at his watch. "I think we will stop now for lunch. We will resume in one hour. Gentlemen of the jury, please do not discuss these proceedings among yourselves during lunch." He stood, and the jurors stood with him.

Sir Winston collected the books and his briefcase and strode quickly from the room, leaving Allison Manning standing, staring after him. Finally she collected her purse and walked slowly toward the door.

Stone, nearly as shocked as she at the turn in Sir Winston's questioning, followed her from the building. "Mrs. Manning?" he called.

She stopped and turned. "Yes?"

"My name is Stone Barrington; I'm an American, too. My chartered boat is moored near yours."

"Oh, yes," she said absently. She turned to go.

"I wonder if I could speak with you for a moment?"

"What about?" she asked, looking puzzled.

"I was present at the inquest this morning, and I heard what took place. I think you may be in over your head."

"How do you mean?"

"Do you know who this Sir Winston is?"

"No."

"Nobody mentioned that, huh?"

"No. Just what is your interest in this, Mr. Barrington?"

"Back in New York, I'm a lawyer, and right now, I think you need a lawyer very much. Can I buy you lunch?"

CHAPTER

4

They walked quickly across the lawn to her boat and went down below. "Would you like some lunch?" Allison Manning asked. "I'm going to make a sandwich."

"Thank you, yes," Stone replied.

She went to the galley and began putting together some sandwiches. "Please tell me your name again," she said. "It always takes me a couple of times."

"Stone Barrington. If you'll forgive me, we only have an hour before the inquest resumes, and we should talk quickly."

"All right."

"First of all, let me explain the proceedings. A coroner's inquest is . . ."

"To make an official determination of the cause of death," she said.

"The cause and the circumstances. In this case, the jury could probably return one of three verdicts: death from natural causes, death by homicide, or an open verdict, which means the jury doesn't feel it has enough evidence to decide how your husband died."

"I understand," she said, handing him a sandwich. "Something to drink?"

"Anything diet," Stone said and accepted a soda.

"What are the consequences of these three possible verdicts?" she asked, then took a big bite of her sandwich.

"If the determination is natural causes, the coroner will give you a death certificate, and you can get on with your life. If it's an open verdict, maybe, but not certainly, the same. But if the verdict is death by homicide, then Sir Winston is going to be very nearly obliged to bring a charge of murder against you."

She gulped down the bite of sandwich. "Murder? I didn't murder Paul!"

"I don't believe you did," Stone said, "but Sir Winston may have a very different opinion. If you should be charged with murder, your alternatives would be to stand trial or to plead to a lesser charge for a reduced sentence or a suspended sentence, if the circumstances warranted."

"I have no intention of pleading to any charge," she said.

"I understand," Stone replied. "Now we have to talk about what's going to happen when the inquest resumes. My assumption is that Sir Winston has other kinds of evidence to present which might cast you in a bad light. I think that to adequately present your side of this, you need more time and a good local lawyer, so the best thing to do would be to ask for a recess of the inquest until such time as you are ready to present your case."

She shook her head vigorously. "I'm not going to hang around this godforsaken island for days or weeks. I want to get home, get Paul's estate settled, and get on with my life."

"That's certainly understandable," Stone said. "Alternatively, you can allow the inquest to resume on time and present the best case you can in the circumstances and take a chance on the outcome."

"What's your recommendation?"

"I think it's always a mistake to rush the legal process unless you're in a very strong position, and I'm not at all sure you are."

"If I go back to the hearing, will you represent me?"

"Yes, if the coroner will allow it. I'm not licensed to practice in St. Marks, but an inquest is less formal than a trial, and he might do it. But there's Sir Winston to consider, too."

"You asked me if I knew who he was. I don't."

"He's the minister of justice of this island country, and I'm told he aspires to be the next prime minister. If that's true, and if he sees some political advantage in pursuing this, he could be dangerous to your interests."

"I see," she said. She leaned against a galley counter and looked down at her feet, silent. Finally she spoke again. "I want to get this over with and get out of here. I can't believe he could possibly convince a jury that Paul's death was anything other than natural. After all, there were no witnesses; they'd have to take my word, wouldn't they?"

"No, they wouldn't, not if Sir Winston can present convincing evidence to the contrary. Your husband's diary, for instance."

She waved a hand. "I can explain that; it's no problem."

"I'm glad to hear it," Stone said. "Did the police remove anything else from the yacht besides the logbook and the diary?"

"Not that I'm aware of," she said.

"All right. First, let's talk about the diary, then let's see what else we can dig up that will react to your benefit." He glanced at his watch. "We have forty-five minutes to build our case."

Stone looked at his watch again. Five minutes to go, and she was in the head. "Better hurry," he called out.

"Won't be a minute," her muffled voice called back.

Stone took the opportunity to look around the interior of the yacht. It was gorgeous. The maker was Nautor of Finland, and the boat was a Swan, widely held to be the best production yacht in the world, and very close to being custom-built. She had obviously been built with little regard to cost; every piece of equipment aboard was the best that money could buy—the electronics, the sails, even the galley equipment. He reckoned the boat had cost between a million and a half and two million dollars.

She popped out of the head, her makeup redone, her long, blond hair combed. "Okay, let's go," she said.

Stone picked up the documents she had given him and followed her up the main companionway ladder.

Five minutes later, they were back in the Markstown meeting hall, and Sir Winston Sutherland was resuming his questioning of Allison Manning.

CHAPTER

5

Sir Winston rose to his full height and addressed Allison Manning. This time he was not bothering with charm. "Mrs. Manning," he said, "was your husband a wealthy man?"

"We're well off, I suppose," she replied, looking a bit nonplused. "Paul never really discussed money with me; he took care of that. I mean, on the boat, he tied the knots and spliced the wire and fixed the engine and navigated, and I did what I did at home—I kept house. I'm not a business executive or an entrepreneur or a stockbroker or a lady lawyer or a yachtswoman. I'm a housewife, and that was all I ever did. Paul made the money and invested it and, except for my clothes and the things in the house, he spent it; I hardly gave it a thought. We have a nice house, we drove nice cars, but the only really extravagant thing Paul ever bought was the boat, and I don't even know what it cost."

"I see," Sir Winston said, as if he didn't see at all. "You never give money a thought."

"I think I see what you're getting at," she said. "You're implying that I hit my husband over the head or stabbed him with a kitchen knife and dumped him overboard so I could have his money, right? Well, do you have any idea how big Paul was? He was as big as you!" She seemed to reconsider. "Well, almost as big."

The jury tittered at this. Allison Manning was becoming very assertive now, and it worried Stone a little. He had instructed her not to argue with Sir Winston, not to lose her temper again.

"Well, Mrs. Manning," Sir Winston continued, seeming to regroup, "let me ask you this: what were your husband's toilet arrangements on the yacht?"

She looked at him as if he were a raving lunatic. "What?"

Sir Winston looked flustered for a moment. "Let me rephrase, please. When your husband was on deck, and he felt the need to relieve himself, how did he do it?"

"In the usual way," she replied.

The jury began laughing, but a sharp look from the coroner subdued them.

"I mean, Mrs. Manning, did he go below and use the toilet, or like most men on a boat, did he just pass his water into the sea?"

"He stood on the stern of the boat, held onto the backstay with one hand, unzipped his fly with the other, and peed overboard."

"Ah," said Sir Winston, as if he had caught her in some monumental admission. "This large husband of yours made himself vulnerable for just a moment when he urinated. A small shove, even by a small woman, was all it would take, eh?"

She fixed him with a hard stare. "That speculation, Sir whatever-your-name-is, is not worthy of a reply."

Stone sensed his moment; he rose and addressed the coroner. "Pardon me, Your Honor," he said. "My name is Stone Barrington; I am an American attorney, and Mrs. Manning has asked me to represent her in these proceedings. I wonder if I might put a few questions to her?"

Sir Winston spun and looked at him. "Are you licensed to practice in St. Marks or in Britain?" he demanded.

"No, I am not," Stone said evenly, "but if these proceedings are so informal as to allow the minister of justice to question a witness at an inquest, then perhaps Mrs. Manning might be questioned by someone of her own choosing."

"Well . . ." the coroner began.

"Are you a barrister? A trial lawyer?"

"I wasn't aware that this was a trial," Stone replied.

The coroner asserted himself. "I will permit Mr. Barrington to put questions to Mrs. Manning, if he believes he can shed some light on this matter."

"I believe I can, Your Honor," Stone said. He hadn't the faintest idea how to address a coroner in a former British colony, but "Your Honor" seemed to do the trick. He picked up a manila folder, stepped forward, and addressed his new client. "Mrs. Manning, how did your husband earn his living?"

"He was a writer; he wrote spy and mystery novels, mostly; he had quite a following."

"And when your husband was preparing to write a book, was it his practice to make notes?"

"Yes, he made very extensive notes, sometimes writing almost the whole book in telegraphic form."

Stone picked up the leather-bound book from Sir Winston's table. "In a form like the contents of this diary?" he asked.

"Exactly like that. Paul bought that blank-paged book in Las Palmas specifically for the purpose of outlining a new novel. He mentioned it to me over dinner, and he wrote in it often. He liked to save his notes in a bound form, because the university he attended had asked to be the repository for his personal and professional papers."

"And why, when Sir Winston read you the passages from this outline, did you not mention your husband's usual practice?"

"He didn't give me a chance," she said, casting a withering look at Sir Winston.

"I see," Stone continued. "Mrs. Manning, what was your husband's state of health shortly before his death?"

"Well, Paul had never been seriously ill, but he wasn't in very good shape."

"How do you know this?"

"We both had thorough physical examinations before we set out across the Atlantic."

Stone removed a sheet of paper from the manila folder in his hand and presented it to her. "Is this a copy of your husband's examination results?"

She looked at the paper, then handed it back. "Yes, it is."

Stone looked at the jury and the coroner. "Please follow as I read from the doctor's report." He held up the paper and began to read. "'Paul Manning is a forty-two-year-old author who has come in for a physical examination prior to an extensive sea voyage. Mr. Manning has no complaints, but he is desirous of being examined and taking a copy of his medical records on his journey.

"'Mr. Manning is six feet, two inches tall and weighs two hundred and sixty-one pounds, rather too much for a man of his frame. The results of blood tests show a serum cholesterol count of 325 and serum triglycerides are 410. These are both dangerously elevated, the high end of normal being 220 for cholesterol and 150 for triglycerides. Because of these numbers, in conjunction with Mr. Manning's lack of regular exercise and a history of heart disease in his family, I have advised Mr. Manning to immediately undertake a program of exercise, a diet low in cholesterol and other fats, and to bring his weight down to a maximum of two hundred pounds.'"

Stone handed the coroner the page and turned to his client. "Mrs. Manning, did your husband take his doctor's advice and go on such a diet?"

"For about a week," she replied. "Paul was incapable of dieting for longer than that."

"Right," Stone said and addressed himself to the coroner and the jury. "Paul Manning was grossly overweight and had been clogging his coronary arteries with cholesterol for many years. He was, in short, a heart attack waiting to happen, and happen it did, in exactly the way Mrs. Manning has described. You have heard how she coped with this disaster at sea, and I put it to you that she could not have invented such a story. It is simply too heartrending not to be true. This brave woman has lost her husband under extraordinary circumstances and then mustered the fortitude to save their yacht and her own life. You cannot believe otherwise. Thank you for your time, Your Honor, gentlemen." Stone sat down.

The coroner turned to Sir Winston. "Do you have any further questions?"

"None," Sir Winston replied almost inaudibly, looking at his knees.

"Gentlemen," the coroner said to the jury, "do any of you have a question?"

The jury was mute.

"Then I will ask you to retire and consider your verdict."

Stone and Allison Manning sat at the bar of the Shipwright's Arms, as Thomas Hardy's restaurant and inn was called, and sipped piña coladas.

"I can't thank you enough," she said. "I'll give you my address in Connecticut, and you can send me your bill."

"For practicing law in a foreign country without a license?" Stone asked. "I'd be disbarred."

"What do you think the verdict will be?"

"You can never tell about a jury, even a coroner's jury, but I believe we answered every point Sir Winston made. I'm optimistic."

"So am I; you did a brilliant job."

"You're too kind. What are your plans now?"

"I suppose I'll go home and settle Paul's affairs. He had a lawyer and an accountant; I'm sure they'll help me. We both made wills before we left on the transatlantic—simple ones, each leaving everything to the other."

"What will you do with the yacht?"

"Sell it, I suppose; I've spent all the time on that boat I ever want to."

"I'd buy it myself—I've always admired Swans—but I think I'm a few years away from being able to afford one. My advice is to get it ferried back to the States—Fort Lauderdale, maybe—where there's a brisk market in expensive yachts."

Thomas tapped lightly on the bar and nodded in the direction of the meeting hall.

Stone turned and saw the coroner approaching, an envelope in his hand. They had not yet been out of the meeting hall for half an hour.

6

The coroner handed the envelope to Allison Manning. "Here is your husband's death certificate," he said. "Please accept my condolences."

"Thank you," Allison replied.

He turned toward Stone. "For what it's worth, I thought you did a very good job." He turned and walked away.

Allison handed the envelope to Stone. "You open it," she said.

Stone tore open the envelope and read the certificate.

"Well," Allison asked, "what was the verdict?"

"It's an open verdict," Stone said. "The jury felt it had insufficient information to assign a cause of death."

"And what does that mean to me, legally?"

"In my opinion," Stone said, "it means you should get the hell out of St. Marks right now."

"Do you mean you think Sir Winston might still come after me?"

"It's certainly possible," Stone replied.

"If you'll forgive me for butting in," Thomas Hardy said, "I think it's more than just possible."

"Thomas used to be a New York City policeman," Stone said, "and he knows how things work here. Thomas, do you have any idea what the airline schedule is?"

Thomas looked at his watch. "There's a daily flight out of Antigua for San Juan in an hour and a half, and you'll have to get Chester to fly her to Antigua."

"Who's Chester?" Allison asked.

"He flies a Cessna twin to Antigua, by arrangement," Thomas replied. "Would you like me to call him and the airlines?"

"Please," Stone said.

They sipped their drinks nervously while Thomas did his telephoning.

"You're on the flight from Antigua," Thomas said, hanging up. "Now let me see if I can raise Chester." He dialed another number. "Chester? You got room for one lady to Antigua, right smart? Good. She'll be along." He hung up. "You'd better get going," he said to Allison.

"I'll go get my things," she said, hopping off the barstool.

"Forget your things," Stone said. "I'm sure Sir Winston had the verdict before we did. If he wants you, the police could be here any minute."

Thomas put some car keys on the bar. "A cab could take a while to come; my car is out back."

"I've got to get my passport," Allison said. "And a few other things."

"Run," Stone said. "Don't take a second longer than absolutely necessary. I'll get the car."

She jogged off toward the marina.

"Thanks, Thomas," Stone said.

"You take the main road and turn right after about two miles," Thomas said. "There's a sign. Chester's airplane is white with blue stripes."

Stone ran to the rear of the restaurant, found the car, a new Toyota Camry, got it started, and drove around front. He looked toward the marina but saw nothing of Allison. "Jesus H. Christ!" he muttered, getting out of the car. He was halfway across the lawn when he saw Allison hurrying across toward him, carrying a duffel and a man's briefcase. Stone opened the door. "Let's go!"

Allison dived in and slammed the door. "I'm not accustomed to running from the law," she said.

"Don't say things like that," Stone replied, driving off. "As far as we know, the law has no interest in you. You've accomplished all the legal necessities in St. Marks, and you're leaving for home like any other tourist."

"Just in more of a hurry," Allison said. "Do you think they might come after me at home?"

"I think that if you were arrested, then ran, they probably would go for extradition, but since no charge has been made, well, there are no guarantees, but I think it's unlikely they'd come after you. If they do, my advice is to get the best lawyer you can and fight it tooth and nail. Would you like me to recommend a lawyer?"

"Yes, please."

"I'm of counsel to a firm in New York called Woodman and Weld."

"I've heard of it; very prestigious."

"Call Bill Eggers there. The firm probably has someone who specializes in this sort of thing, and if they don't, Bill can recommend the best man in town. If this happens, it's going to cost; how are you fixed for money?"

"I won't know that for sure until I've talked with Paul's lawyer and accountant, but I think I'll be all right. I can always sell the boat."

Stone turned right onto the airport road. "As soon as you get home, find a yacht broker and have him fly a ferry crew down here at the earliest possible moment to get the boat out of here."

"All right." She dug into her handbag and came up with a card. "Here's my number in Greenwich; will you call me when you get back? I'll buy you dinner."

"That might be tough to explain to the lady I live with," Stone said, "but I would like to know how things work out. I'll call you."

"So why isn't this lady with you?"

"She got snowed in. Oh, I hadn't thought of it, but the airports might still be closed up there. When you get to San Juan, check with the airlines. It might be best to spend a night there and wait for the weather in the Northeast to clear up."

"Thanks, I'll do that." She smiled at him. "Sure you don't want to come with me?"

•

30

"It's a lovely thought, but I've got a yacht charter here, and I hope Arrington will be here soon."

"My bad luck," she said.

God, Stone thought, *you're supposed to be the grieving widow!* He drove through the airport gates and toward a large hangar. The Cessna was parked in front of it, and the pilot who had flown him to St. Marks from Antigua was waiting. "There's Chester," Stone said.

"Thank God," she said.

Stone pulled up next to the plane, took her duffel and her briefcase, and stowed them in the baggage compartment. He walked back to the wing and held open the door for her. "You're on your way," he said.

An engine coughed to life, followed by another.

She slung an arm around his neck and gave him a much bigger and wetter kiss than he could have expected. "I'll never be able to thank you enough, but I'll try," she shouted over the roar of the engines. "Good-bye."

"Good-bye," Stone said. Then an unexpected sound reached his ears. He looked back toward the airport gate and saw a Jeep driving toward them, making some sort of strange siren noise.

The vehicle skidded to a halt next to the airplane, and two starched and pressed black policemen got out. The officer gave them a casual salute with a swagger stick. "Mrs. Allison Manning, I presume?"

"Yes," she said.

"Good afternoon," he said, smiling, then handed her a document. "You are under arrest for the crime of murder. You will be charged tomorrow morning at ten o'clock at the courthouse in St. Marks City. Do you have any luggage?"

"No," Stone said quickly, "Mrs. Manning does not have any luggage." He took the document and looked at it; it appeared to be a properly drawn warrant. He turned to Allison. "You'll have to go with them. I'll get you a local lawyer and see you at the hearing tomorrow morning. I doubt if I can get anything done until then."

Allison looked stunned. "All right," she said. She put a hand on his arm. "I'm so glad you're here." She got into the Jeep and was driven away.

•

Chester killed the engines. Stone watched until the Jeep had driven through the airport gates, then went and got her duffel and briefcase from the luggage compartment. He didn't know what was in that briefcase, but he knew that he didn't want Sir Winston Sutherland rooting around in there. *Poor Allison Manning,* he thought. *She's in for a rough time, and I suppose I'm going to have to help her.*

CHAPTER

7

Stone drove back to Markstown, mulling over what he might do to help Allison Manning. There wasn't a whole lot, he reckoned. He could find her a local lawyer, and that was about it. Then he recalled that Sir Winston had asked him, during the fateful coroner's jury, if he were licensed to practice in Britain. Maybe, with the help of Woodman and Weld in New York, he could get hold of some high-class British barrister and have him flown in, if Allison Manning could afford it. He parked the car behind Thomas Hardy's restaurant and walked in.

Thomas was alone at the bar, writing on a steno pad. He looked up as Stone came in. "I heard," he said. "Chester called me."

"It looks bad," Stone said, taking a stool and handing Thomas the arrest warrant. "I'm going to have to find her a first-class barrister."

Thomas shoved a pad across the bar. "I thought that might be the case. Here's a list of three who might—I stress, might— take her on."

Stone read four names. "What about the fourth name?"

"First we'd better call the first three. Shall I?"

"Please."

Thomas picked up the phone and dialed a number.

Ten minutes later, after the third call, Thomas hung up the phone.

"Well?" Stone said.

"No hope," Thomas replied. "The word is out that Sir Winston really wants this one—nobody knows exactly why—and nobody is going to go up against him right at this moment in time, with an election coming up soon. The consensus seems to be that a conviction would give him a lot of favorable publicity, and nobody wants to get between Sir Winston and publicity."

"What if Sir Winston should lose the case?"

"As far as I can tell from these phone conversations, nobody in the legal community thinks he's going to."

"How about somebody else?"

"Not a chance," Thomas said. "I eliminated most of them before I made my list. Those three were the only ones who might have opposed Sir Winston."

"What about the fourth name on the list?"

"Sir Leslie Hewitt," Thomas said.

"Yes, what about him?"

"He'll represent her," Thomas said. "He hates Sir Winston's guts, as his father before him did."

"Well, then, give him a call."

Thomas shook his head. "You don't understand."

"Explain it to me."

"Leslie was once a first-rate barrister, one of the best, in fact."

"And now?"

"He's well past eighty; he hasn't tried a case in at least fifteen years; and . . ."

"And?"

"And he's . . . failing, you know? I mean, he's bright as a new penny at times, but at other times . . ."

"I think I get the picture," Stone said. "You're suggesting that an eighty-year-old barrister who's half gaga should defend Allison Manning?"

"No, that's not what I'm suggesting. You've got a hearing tomorrow morning at ten, and somebody besides you has got to be there to go through the motions, to be the barrister of record until you can get somebody in here from out of the country."

"You mean from England?"

"Probably. You could go to Antigua, which is another former British colony and which has a similar legal system, but that's too close to home. Those people are going to have to get along with Sir Winston, too, if his political dreams come true, and they are very likely to."

"I thought about London. I do a lot of work for a firm in New York, and I can ask them to recommend somebody in London. But I don't know whether Allison can meet that kind of expense."

"Then she's between a rock and a hard place," Thomas said. "Right now, I think you and I had better go see Leslie Hewitt."

They drove along the coast road to the western end of the island and turned off toward the beach onto a rutted dirt road.

"Where are you taking me?" Stone asked.

"Leslie has a cottage down by the beach," Thomas replied. "It's been in his family since the seventeenth century."

"Is he black?"

"Yes."

"I would have thought that in the seventeenth century, any blacks on this island would have been slaves."

"You're not far off the mark there, but an ancestor of Leslie's bought his freedom and started a stevedoring business. They were a very prosperous family indeed until we got our freedom from Britain. Then the new government confiscated nearly everything Leslie had inherited. His wife died, his children fled the country, and he was left here with nothing but this cottage." He pulled up before a whitewashed building.

It was larger than Stone had imagined. He got out and, with Thomas leading the way, approached the Dutch front door, which was open at the top.

"Leslie!" Thomas called out. He beckoned to Stone and entered the cottage. They walked through a small foyer and into a comfortably if somewhat seedily furnished living room. "Leslie!" Thomas called out again, but there was no reply. "Let's take a look out back." They walked through a neat kitchen and through a pretty garden, then down to the beach. A tiny black man in faded shorts and a straw hat was pulling a dinghy up the beach from the water. "There he is," Thomas said, approaching. "Leslie, how you doing?" he asked.

"Thomas? Is that Thomas Hardy?" Leslie Hewitt asked, shielding his eyes from the light.

"Sure is," Thomas said. "Come to see you, and I brought a friend." He introduced the barrister to Stone.

"How do you do, Sir Leslie," Stone said.

"I'm very well, Mr. Barrington; and you?"

"Very well, thank you."

"Leslie, can we go into the house?" Thomas asked. "There's a matter we need to discuss with you."

"Do I owe you money?" Hewitt asked, removing his straw hat and mopping his brow with his forearm. He had short, snow white hair.

"Certainly not, Leslie."

"Then this is very surprising," he said. "It's been a very long time since anyone needed to discuss anything with me except a bill."

Sitting in a small study crowded with dusty books, Thomas Hardy explained the situation to Leslie Hewitt. "What do you think, Leslie?"

"Well, I certainly don't like the sound of it," Hewitt replied, crossing a bare leg over another and dusting off his foot. "All happening very quickly, isn't it?"

"Very quickly indeed," Thomas said.

"I shouldn't be surprised if, in the circumstances, Winston will ask for an early trial date. What is it you want of me? I don't know if I'm up to trying a murder case, not unless you enjoy a hanging."

Thomas and Stone laughed. "We need your help for the hearing, Leslie," Thomas said. "To hold the fort until we can get a barrister in from London."

"Ah, I see," Hewitt said. "Well, I can certainly help you to that extent."

"There's the matter of bail, too, Sir Leslie," Stone said.

"Please call me Leslie," the little man said. "Everyone does."

"Leslie, do you think there's a chance of bail?"

"It's not unheard of in such a case," Hewitt replied. "It's not an easy island to get off of, especially if you're a foreigner, so the judge might smile on such a request. Bail might be steep, though."

"How steep?"

"A hundred thousand dollars, perhaps twice that."

"Cash?"

"Does the lady have any property in St. Marks?"

"An expensive yacht."

"That might do very nicely, if the judge is sure she won't sail away."

"That's good news; I'll pass it on to Mrs. Manning."

"I shall want to meet her before the hearing," Hewitt said. "May we meet at the courthouse at, say, nine in the morning? That should give us time."

"Of course," Stone said. "Ah, you mentioned hanging; I hope that was in jest?"

"Oh, no," Sir Leslie said, shaking his head. "Certainly not in jest."

"St. Marks has capital punishment, then?"

"Oh, yes; it's quite easy to get hanged in St. Marks. You see, Mr. Barrington, there's no prison system to speak of on our lovely island. Crimes tend to get divided into three classes: first, there's anything from petty theft through assault and battery up to, say, multiple burglaries. These crimes are dealt with by fines and short sentences, up to about three months, in our local jail. If there's no room in the jail, then the fine is increased, and the Ministry of Justice is very scrupulous about collecting the fines. Then we have a second category of offenses, starting with armed robbery and running up through assault with intent to kill—virtually any crime involving violence but not death. These are dealt with by exile, permanent exile from our island. For natives of St. Marks, who love their island, this is a crueler punishment than you might imagine. Then, lastly, we have crimes involving death: voluntary manslaughter, any degree of murder, conspiracy to murder—these crimes are capital offenses, and death is by hanging. We have one or two hangings a year."

"You mean, then, that if Allison Manning is found guilty of any degree of homicide, she will be hanged? They would hang a woman?"

"Quite so. Only about one in ten persons hanged is a woman, but it happens."

"What about race? Would the fact that Mrs. Manning is white be a factor in a possible death sentence?"

"I should say that would increase her chances of hanging," Sir Leslie said, "especially since her jury is very likely to be all or nearly all black."

Stone swallowed hard. "I see."

"I should mention, too," Sir Leslie continued, "that in St. Marks, jury verdicts are by majority, not unanimous vote, so a white juror or two would not be able to cause a deadlock, and the judge elects the jury."

"Jesus Christ," Stone said quietly.

Sir Leslie smiled. "I'm glad to see you are taking this seriously."

"What is the appeals procedure?" Stone asked.

"There is only a single appeal," Sir Leslie replied. "All capital convictions are automatically referred to the prime minister, whose word is final. He generally responds the next day, and, should his decision be negative, the hanging takes place on the following day." He smiled. "Since our system is so efficient, we tend to think that capital punishment really is a deterrent to capital crime."

"Yes," Stone replied, "I can see how it might be."

Thomas turned to Stone. "You're going to be doing a lot of telephoning tomorrow, I should think. There's a room with a phone over the bar you can use."

"Thanks, Thomas," Stone said. "Maybe I should just take the room for the duration."

"That will be fine."

"Is there somewhere I can rent a printer for my laptop?"

"My bookkeeper is on vacation; I'll move hers in there for you."

They turned back to Leslie Hewitt, who seemed to have dozed off.

"Leslie?" Thomas said.

The little man opened his eyes. "Thomas? Is that Thomas Hardy?"

"Yes, Leslie."

"How very good of you to come and see me," he said, beaming at them. He turned toward Stone. "And who might this be?"

When they returned to the restaurant, Thomas handed Stone a fax. "This came for you while we were gone."

Dear Stone,

I cannot find a way to tell you how important this assignment has become, but the fact is, I have to spend as much time as possible with Vance Calder while he is in New York, which is for the rest of the week. I know how angry and disappointed you will be to read this, but there's simply no way I am going to be able to get to St. Marks in time to go sailing with you, no matter how hard I try, so we may as well both face it now. I ask your forgiveness, and I look forward to your return.

Love,
Arrington

Stone wadded up the paper and tossed it into a wastebasket.
"Bad news?" Thomas asked.
"Is there any other kind?" Stone replied.

CHAPTER

8

tone sweated through a nearly sleepless night, tossing in his berth, trying in vain to think of some tactic to abort this whole process. He rose at dawn, had a swim in the harbor and showered off the salt water, then forced down some breakfast. He left his chartered yacht, walked to the berth where *Expansive* lay, and went aboard. Below, he found a makeup kit in the head, and he chose a demure dress and some shoes from a clothing cupboard. In a drawer he found fresh lingerie and, feeling odd, chose some lace bikini panties. There were no bras in the drawer. He stuffed the lot into a small duffel he found in a locker. He was about to go up the companionway stairs when he stopped and looked around.

Allison Manning was an innocent woman, he was sure of that, but if there was anything incriminating on this yacht, he wanted to know about it. He certainly wasn't going to tamper with evidence, but he needed to know what was here. He set down the duffel and went to the galley. He had no idea what sort of criminal investigation skills were available to the St. Marks police force, but he thought it wise not to leave a lot of fingerprints about. He went to the galley and found a pair of rubber kitchen gloves and put them on. Then he went to the bow of the yacht and started working his way toward the stern, looking at everything along the way. He paid particular attention to the chart table and bookcases, then moved on to the master cabin. He found nothing incriminating. Then he found himself staring at Allison Manning's briefcase.

He was torn between his lawyer's respect for his client's privacy and the cop in him who wanted to know everything. If she was guilty, did he want to know? Probably not. Yes. Finally he made his decision; he laid the briefcase on the large bed and pressed the releases on the locks. Nothing happened. Then he saw the combination locks. Frustrated, he tried changing the last digits one, then two notches in each direction, then he turned the combinations to zero on both sides. The case would still not unlock. "Shit!" he said. Well, it was none of his business anyway. He left the briefcase on the bed, returned the rubber gloves to the galley, picked up the duffel, and went on deck.

He trudged up to the Shipwright's Arms and climbed upstairs to the room over the bar. Nobody ever seemed to lock anything in St. Marks; he walked in, tossed Allison's duffel onto the bed, sat down at the desk, picked up the phone, and dialed Bill Eggers's home number.

"Yeah?" Eggers said grumpily.

"It's Stone, Bill. Wake up; I need you to pay attention."

There was a groan as Eggers apparently sat up in bed. "What are you doing back?" he asked, awake now.

"I'm not back; I'm still in St. Marks."

"Then you must be in jail," Eggers chuckled. "I can't think of any other reason you'd call me from there."

"Close. I have a client who's in jail, and it's very, very serious; a murder charge."

"Did she do it?"

"No, but what does that matter?"

"What do you want from me?"

"She needs an English barrister badly; nobody here will defend her, for political reasons, but it's a former English colony with an English-style court system. I don't know any English barristers; you got any ideas?"

"We deal with a firm at Gray's Inn in London. Let's see, it's . . . six forty-five?! Jesus, Stone; you ever hear of office hours?"

"Bill, I've got a preliminary hearing at ten o'clock. It's what, noon in London? You need to catch these people before they go to lunch."

"Yeah, yeah; what's your number there?"

Stone read it off the telephone on the desk.

"I'll call you back in a few minutes."

Thomas knocked and walked into the room. "Everything you need here?"

"Yes, it's fine, Thomas; I'm just waiting for a call back from New York about an English barrister."

"How about some breakfast?"

"I've had something, but I'd love some coffee."

They sat and drank their coffee together.

"Thomas," Stone said, "there's something I need to know."

"What's that?"

"Is Leslie Hewitt going to be able to get through this hearing without . . . you know?"

"I wouldn't worry about it. Leslie is very sharp when his mind is fully engaged. He'll manage."

"God, I hope you're right." The phone rang, and Stone picked it up. "Hello?"

"It's Bill; I've got you a guy, but . . . has this client of yours got any money?"

"Maybe."

"Maybe won't do it. This guy's fee is a retainer of two hundred thousand pounds sterling against an hourly fee of two hundred pounds an hour, and travel time counts; he wants the retainer in his bank account before he even makes an airline reservation."

"That's a fee of more than three hundred fifty thousand dollars plus more than three hundred fifty dollars an hour. He must be an absolutely fucking wonderful lawyer," Stone said.

"That's what he tells me; what do you want me to tell him?"

"If I had my druthers I'd tell him to go fuck himself, but I guess I'd better ask my client first."

"The fee is not out of line, Stone. After all, you're asking a top-flight barrister to fly halfway across the world on short notice and to stay indefinitely. A top New York man would cost at least that. Oh, by the way, he'll want to bring a clerk with him; that's seventy-five pounds an hour."

"And he'll want to fly first class, too, I suppose."

"Of course."

"Tell him you'll get back to him after I've talked to my client."

"Okay. When will you want him?"

"We'll probably get a trial date set today, and it could be soon; things move quickly here."

"I'll tell him. See you." Eggers hung up.

Stone turned to Thomas. "Well, I hope her husband turns out to have had a hell of a lot of money."

Thomas Hardy pulled into the Government House parking lot simultaneously with Sir Leslie Hewitt, who was driving an ancient Morris Minor station wagon festooned with rotting wood paneling.

"Good morning, Leslie," Stone said, getting out of Thomas's car.

"Good morning, Stone, Thomas," Sir Leslie called back. He reached into the rear of the little car and removed a long plastic garment bag and a small suitcase, then led the way into the building.

They signed in to the jail, were searched for weapons, then were led to a small cell that held a table and four chairs.

A moment later Allison Manning was led into the cell by a black matron. She was pale and rumpled and seemed to have had little sleep. She went to Stone and put her head on his shoulder. "I am so glad to see you," she whimpered.

Stone patted her back awkwardly, then introduced her to Sir Leslie. "Sir Leslie is going to represent you at the hearing and apply for bail," he said.

She shook the barrister's hand. "Thank you so much for being here, Sir Leslie," she said.

"I am happy to represent you," the little man replied. "Please sit down, and I'll tell you what is going to happen this morning." Everyone sat down, and Sir Leslie continued. "This will be a short meeting of the court at which the presiding judge will ask the prosecutor if he has sufficient evidence to bring a charge of murder to trial. Then we will ask for bail, and I'm told you have a yacht which might serve as your security."

"Wait a minute," Stone said. "Won't the prosecution have to present evidence of the crime? I was hoping we might get a dismissal."

"Oh, no," Sir Leslie replied. "The judge will simply take Sir Winston's affidavit that he has enough evidence for trial; it's all very gentlemanly."

"It's all very unheard of," Stone said.

"Stone, you must understand that although our court system is based on English law, over the years, in the interest of efficiency, certain procedures that the court thinks superfluous have been pared away from the process."

"Superfluous? This court thinks that the presenting of evidence in a preliminary hearing is superfluous?"

"I'm afraid so," Sir Leslie said. "I assure you that if Sir Winston wants this to go to trial, it will go to trial, no matter what evidence might be presented, and no matter how we might challenge that evidence."

"Leslie," Stone said, "this crime—I mean the alleged crime—occurred on the high seas, in the middle of the Atlantic Ocean. Can't we ask for a dismissal on jurisdictional grounds?"

"Oh, no," Sir Leslie said. "You see, many of the cases tried in our courts over the past two hundred years were based on crimes that occurred at sea. The local rule is that the defendant will be tried in the jurisdiction of the first port he puts into after the act."

Stone nodded dumbly.

"Now, Mrs. Manning," Sir Leslie continued, "I understand you have a yacht which might be used to secure your bail, is that correct?"

"Yes," she replied.

"What is the value of the yacht?"

"I don't really know," she said. "I'm sure it's expensive."

Stone spoke up. "A minimum of a million and a half dollars American."

"Oh, that should be quite sufficient. And where does the yacht lie?"

"In English Harbour."

"Good, good."

"Leslie," Stone said, "Mrs. Manning will need to live aboard the yacht until this matter is disposed of."

"I'm sure His Lordship would agree to that."

"Who?"

"The judge, Lord Cornwall."

"Oh."

"Stone, did you ever see the film *Witness for the Prosecution?*"

"Yes."

"Well, that is a pretty good model for how court is conducted. I expect you've seen other such films as well."

"Yes, I suppose so. Oh, Allison, I brought you some things." He shoved the duffel across the table. "I couldn't find a . . . I hope these are all right."

Allison held up the dress and looked at it. "Well, at least you didn't bring the sequined cocktail dress."

Sir Leslie opened his garment bag and removed two black robes, handing one to Stone. "You'd better get into this."

Stone stood up and put on the robe; it was ridiculously small on him.

"And this," Sir Leslie said, opening his small case. He handed Stone a wig.

"You can't be serious," Stone said, regarding the thing at arm's length.

"Oh, yes, quite serious," Sir Leslie said. "On second thought, just carry it; don't put it on."

"Good," Stone said. "I'll carry it."

Thomas put a hand over his face and laughed quietly.

CHAPTER

9

Allison was taken away by the matron, and Stone, Sir Leslie, and Thomas left the jail, walked upstairs, and found the courtroom. Thomas took a front row seat, and Sir Leslie led Stone to the defense table. Sir Winston and another man, probably his supporting attorney, were already seated at the prosecution table. Various people milled around the room until the bailiff stood and shouted for all to stand. A moment later a red-gowned, bewigged black man entered from a side door and took the bench. He was middle-aged, tall and thin, with short, graying hair under his gray wig.

"Be seated," the judge said. "Bring up the prisoner."

Stone turned and watched as Allison came up from a hidden stairway and entered the dock. She had pulled back her hair, and in her fresh dress looked quite normal.

"Madam, would you like a chair?" the judge asked.

"Thank you, yes, Your Lordship," she replied, giving him a grateful smile.

That's it, Stone thought, *pour on the charm for the judge; wouldn't be the first time that had worked.*

"Sir Winston," the judge said, "do you have a request for this court?"

Sir Winston stood and handed a folder to the bailiff. "Thank you, Your Lordship, yes. The government petitions this court for the trial on a charge of murder of one Allison Ames Manning, now present in the dock. We certify that we have sufficient evidence to bring this case to trial and to convict the defendant."

The judge accepted the folder, flipped through it for a moment, and addressed the middle distance. "All is in order; who will appear for the prosecution?"

"I will, Your Lordship," Sir Winston replied, "assisted by Henry Porter."

The judge turned to the court reporter. "Write down that Sir Winston Sutherland and Mr. Henry Porter will appear for the prosecution." He looked over at the defense table. "And who will act for the defense?"

"I will, Your Lordship," Sir Leslie said, standing, "and I request to be assisted by Mr. Stone Barrington." He turned to Stone and whispered, "Stand up."

Stone stood, feeling foolish in the tight robe, the wig in his hand.

"I do not recognize Mr. Barrington," the judge said.

"Your Lordship, Mr. Barrington is an American barrister, a prominent member of the New York bar. I request that he be admitted to the St. Marks bar for the duration of this action, so that I might have his advice."

"Will he question witnesses?" the judge asked.

Stone spoke up before Sir Leslie could. "Yes, Your Lordship."

"Mr. Barrington, have you had the experience of defending in a murder trial?"

"I have, Your Lordship, on four occasions."

"And how did you do?" the judge asked impishly.

"They were all innocent, Your Lordship," Stone replied with mock seriousness, "but only three were acquitted."

The judge smiled. "Three out of four acquitted, eh? But then, you have such a lenient judicial system, don't you?"

"On the contrary, Your Lordship, in a lenient system all four would have been acquitted."

The judge laughed. "Very well, Mr. Barrington, you are admitted to the St. Marks bar for the duration of this trial." He turned to the reporter. "Write down that the defense will be represented by Sir Leslie Hewitt and Mr. Stone Barrington."

Sir Leslie leaned over and whispered out of the corner of his mouth, "Put on the wig."

"What?" Stone whispered back.

"Put on the bloody wig!"

Stone put the wig on and stood there, feeling extremely foolish.

The judge smiled broadly. "Very becoming, Mr. Barrington. I'm sure you will do the St. Marks bar proud. You may be seated."

Stone sat down, but Sir Leslie remained standing. "Your Lordship," he said, "the defense requests bail for the defendant to extend through the trial."

"Well," the judge replied, "in a capital case, the bail would have to be substantial. Is the defendant possessed of a substantial sum of cash?"

"Your Lordship, the defendant owns a large yacht moored in English Harbour, which I am assured is valued at in excess of one and one-half million dollars in U.S. currency. I request that the yacht secure her bail, and that she be allowed to live aboard the vessel until these proceedings are concluded."

The judge turned to the prosecution. "Sir Winston?"

"I have no objection, Your Lordship, as long as the defendant has a clear understanding of the terms of her bail."

"Quite right, Sir Winston," the judge replied. He turned to Allison, sitting in the dock. "Mrs. Manning, in St. Marks, bail is more than security, it is a sacred obligation. In order for me to grant bail, you must agree not to leave this island, and you should know that if you should do so, you would not only forfeit bail—in this case, your yacht—but under St. Marks law your departure would be tantamount to a plea of guilty to the charge, and you would stand convicted of murder."

Holy shit, Stone thought.

"Do you understand the terms of your bail?"

Allison stood. "I do, Your Lordship."

"Very well, bail is granted, and the yacht will be secured to the dock." He looked down at his calendar. "Trial is set for Monday next, at 10:00 A.M."

Stone's jaw dropped. "Your Lordship," he managed to say, "that gives us only six days to prepare for trial."

"Quite right, Mr. Barrington," the judge replied. "Any problem with that?"

Sir Leslie spoke up. "The defense is satisfied with the trial date, Your Lordship," he said.

"But we have to get a barrister in here from London to conduct the defense," Stone said. "If it pleases the court."

"Mr. Barrington," the judge said, as if speaking to a backward child, "it is already in the record that the defense will be conducted by Sir Leslie, with your assistance. The record cannot be changed." He stood.

"All rise," the bailiff called out.

The judge turned and left the courtroom.

Stone turned to Sir Leslie. "Leslie, what the hell is he talking about?"

"What?" Sir Leslie replied, packing his wig into his case and removing Stone's.

"I thought you understood that we have a barrister coming from London."

"What?" Sir Leslie asked.

"Leslie, you cannot conduct this trial; you said so yourself."

Sir Leslie turned on him. "To whom do you think you are speaking, sir? I have conducted the defense at five hundred and eighty-three trials in this court! This one will be five hundred and eighty-four! I will discuss my fee with you later." He wheeled and walked out of the courtroom, carrying his robe and his wig.

Stone turned and looked for the first time at Thomas Hardy in the front row.

Thomas sat with his head in his hands, making a moaning sound.

Allison came down from the dock. "All ready to go?" she asked cheerfully.

CHAPTER

10

Thomas drove while Stone sat beside him and Allison took the backseat. For all of Stone's life, extreme worry had caused him to become sleepy, and right now he was having a very hard time staying awake.

"God, but I'm glad to be out of that place," Allison said.

"Were you treated all right?" Thomas asked.

"Well, yes, and contrary to what I've heard about jail, the food was pretty good. I had a cell to myself, and except for the open toilet, it wasn't bad."

"I'm glad to hear it," Thomas replied.

"I had some absolutely fascinating conversations with the woman in the next cell, too; she was in for shoplifting, and it wasn't her first time, so she knew the drill. Stone, I can't thank you enough for getting me out of there."

Stone stirred from his lassitude. "Don't mention it," he said.

They pulled up at the restaurant, and Stone and Allison got out so that Thomas could park the car. An American-looking man was seated at the bar, drinking what looked like a gin and tonic; his suit and briefcase made him look out of place, made him look like an insurance salesman. He seemed to recognize Allison and approached her, handing her a card. "Mrs. Manning, I wonder if I could speak with you for a few minutes."

Stone turned to Allison. "If you don't need me for a moment, I have some phone calls to make."

"Go right ahead," she said to him, then turned to the other man. "Of course," she said, "let's take a table."

Stone went up to his new room over the bar, threw his newly acquired barrister's robe at the wall, and called Bill Eggers.

"Yes, Stone, are we a go for the London man?"

"I'm afraid not, Bill; it seems I've wasted his time and yours."

"Why? What happened?"

"Bill, I hardly know where to begin: I have this perfectly innocent woman for a client who it seems is being railroaded by the judicial system in this godforsaken island country, and unless I can think of something fast they're going to hang her."

"Hang her?"

"I'm afraid so." Stone explained the chain of events thus far.

"That's the craziest thing I've ever heard," Eggers said when Stone had finished.

"I wish I were hearing about it instead of living it," Stone said.

"And your barrister is gaga?"

"At least some of the time; he appeared to be perfectly normal in court, except that he seemed to forget that we were bringing in the London man."

"Well, at least he knows the score down there; that's worth something."

"I hope you're right, but it's Tuesday, and I'm going to have to be prepared to try this case next Monday morning."

"Is there anything else I can do to help?"

"Not right now; believe me, I'll call in a hurry if there is."

"I'm here if you need me," Eggers said, then hung up.

Stone made another call, to Bob Cantor, a retired cop who had been helpful on a previous case.

"Hello?"

"Bob, it's Stone Barrington."

"Hi, Stone; aren't you supposed to be on vacation?"

"I'd rather not talk about that; I'm in big trouble on a case, and I want you to do some things for me. Can you clear the decks for the next week?"

"Sure; I'm not all that busy."

"Good. The first thing I want you to do is to get on a plane for the Canary Islands."

"Where the hell is that?"

"It's a Spanish possession a few hundred miles out in the Atlantic, off North Africa."

"Back up here, Stone; tell me what's going on."

Stone related the events of the past few days.

"That's the craziest thing I ever heard," Cantor said. "They want to hang her?"

"That's right. Now look, their last landfall before St. Marks was the Canaries; they were in Las Palmas, the capital, for some work on the boat, then they stopped on the southernmost island, which is called Puerto Rico, their last night before starting the transatlantic. I want you to go to both places and ask about the yacht, which is called *Expansive*."

"Got that," Cantor said, obviously scribbling.

"Talk to anybody who saw them, talked to them, had a meal with them, saw how they interacted."

"What exactly are you looking for?"

"Straws to grasp at; God knows I've got nothing else. See if you can find me a witness who can, from personal experience, characterize the relationship between Paul Manning and his wife during the last few days they were in the Canaries—ideally somebody who can say he saw a lot of them and that they obviously adored each other."

"Anything else?"

"Anything else you can possibly think of. You understand the situation now and something of what I need. If I'm going to get this woman off I'm pretty much going to have to prove that she didn't do it."

"That's impossible," Cantor said. "There were no witnesses."

"I'm going to have to do it anyway."

"What airline goes to the Canaries?"

"I haven't the faintest idea; call my secretary and tell her to book it for you, tonight if possible."

"Right. Anything else?"

"Yes, I want you to dig up everything you can on Paul Manning for me—library, Internet, credit report, criminal record, military record, anything you possibly can before you leave for Las Palmas. FedEx it to me here." He gave Cantor the address and phone and fax numbers. "If you can think of any other avenue to pursue, pursue it; if you need outside help, hire it; if you have any ideas for me, fax them, okay?"

"I'm on it," Cantor said, then hung up.

Stone called his secretary. "Hi, Alma."

"Hi, Stone. I saw Arrington this morning; why is she still here?"

"Don't ask; she's not coming. I'm going to be busy down here for at least another week, so scrub anything I've scheduled through the middle of next week—reschedule or tell them I'll call as soon as I'm back."

"Okay."

"Any calls or correspondence worth bothering with?"

"Nothing that won't wait until you're back."

"Oh; call one of the judges' clerks and find out where they buy robes, then get one in my size and FedEx it to me."

"You doing some judging down there?"

"I'll explain later. Is Arrington upstairs?"

"She was on the way out when I saw her; a limo was waiting for her."

"I'll call her later, then." He gave her his address and numbers. "You can always leave a message at the bar if I'm not here. I'm still sleeping on the boat; it's all the use I'm getting out of it."

"Okay; anything else?"

"Oh, I almost forgot: Bob Cantor is going to call you in a minute about some travel arrangements. Get him on a plane tonight, if possible, and give him a thousand dollars in cash for expenses. Anything else he needs, get it for him, all right?"

"All right."

Stone hung up. He felt a little better now that he was actually doing something about the mess he was in. He went back downstairs just as Allison was saying good-bye to the businessman.

"Who was that?" he asked.

"An investigator from Paul's insurance company. If we need any cash for legal expenses, it'll be in my bank account in Greenwich shortly."

"Good; we ought to give Leslie Hewitt his fee up front; it's usual in this kind of case."

"He's such a sweet old man," she said. "I just loved him."

"Yeah," Stone said. "Allison," he said, taking her arm and leading her to a table, "you and I have to talk, and right now."

"Sure," she said. "You're looking pretty grim."

"I'm feeling pretty grim, and I'm going to tell you why." He pulled out a chair for her and sat her down, then took a deep breath and started in.

11

S tone sat her down and talked to her. "I don't have time to be gentle about this or pull any punches, so here's your position as I see it. This Sir Winston Sutherland has it in for you, apparently because he thinks it will help him politically. He somehow engineered an open verdict in the coroner's jury, which gave him a legal basis for charging you with Paul's murder. Now you're going to be tried, and there's nothing I can do to stop it."

"Surely any reasonable jury will acquit me," Allison said. "I don't really have anything to worry about, do I?"

"Allison, I don't know if we're going to have a reasonable jury. The judge picks the panel, and no objection from me is going to stand; the jury may be all or mostly black, and they may or may not be more likely to convict a white person, I don't know. All I know is that this is a capital offense."

"You mean I could get the death penalty?"

"Yes, and the way things apparently work on this island, if you're convicted there's no other penalty you could expect to get."

Allison stared at him, her mouth open. "Are you serious?" she managed to ask.

"Perfectly serious. What's more, there's no lengthy appeals

process available; the only appeal is to the prime minister, and he apparently acts on appeals very quickly."

"How quickly are we talking about?"

"The appeal must be lodged within twenty-four hours after the trial ends, and he normally acts on it within twenty-four hours after that."

"Let's look at the worst case," she said. "I'm tried on Monday—how long is that likely to last?"

"The way things are done here, no more than a day, possibly two."

"Then if I'm convicted on Monday, the appeal has to be filed on Tuesday, and the prime minister would either grant or deny it on Wednesday. If he denies it, then I would be . . . How do they do it?"

"Hanging."

"I could be hanged . . . when?"

"The day after the prime minister acts."

She swallowed hard. "So by a week from Thursday I could be dead?"

"Worst case."

She put her elbows on the table and her face in her hands. "What can we do?"

"Put on the best defense we can, in the circumstances. I had wanted to bring in a top barrister from London, but the judge has precluded that by making Leslie Hewitt the counsel and me his assistant."

"Isn't there anything else we can do?"

"There are two ways we can go: I've already said that we have to put on the best defense that we can, and I've got some-body in New York working on that now. He's leaving for the Canaries right away to see what he can find to help us there. Did you make any friends while you were there? Someone who might testify as to your relationship with Paul?"

"No, not really; we pretty much stayed to ourselves. What's the other thing we can do."

"Well, we know that Sir Winston somehow finds it politi-cally desirable to try you on this charge; what we might be able to do is make it politically undesirable for him to convict you, or," if he should, to make it desirable for the prime minister to uphold your appeal."

"How do we do that?"

"By letting the press know about your predicament."

"On this island? What press?"

"Not here; in New York, in London; wherever people read newspapers or watch TV."

"You want me to become famous?"

"Yes."

She shook her head. "I just don't see how that's going to help."

Stone spread a hand as though he were tracking a headline. "BEAUTIFUL BLOND AMERICAN GIRL LOSES HUSBAND AT SEA! CONNIVING POLITICIAN CHARGES HER WITH MURDER IN BACKWATER ISLAND NATION!!! It's called marshaling public opinion; it might bring pressure to bear."

"How do we accomplish this?"

"I'll call New York and get a public relations firm involved. Can you afford that?"

"How much?"

"I'm no expert at this, but I should think fifty to a hundred thousand dollars would go a long way toward accomplishing what we want. Woodman and Weld would hire and instruct them, and you'd have to pay their fees, too. Will the insurance money cover it?"

"Yes," she said, but she looked doubtful.

"What's the problem?"

She shrugged. "I just don't know if I want to be that kind of celebrity. I'm really a very private person."

"Allison, let me put this to you as strongly as I can. If we don't do something you're going to be a very dead private person. In St. Marks, Sir Winston holds all the cards; he's in control. But he can't control the rest of the world. This island subsists mostly on tourism; if he wants to become prime minister he's not going to want somebody telling the world's tourists that if they come to St. Marks they're liable to be arrested, tried, and hanged on spurious charges. That translates into a lot of empty hotel rooms and a catastrophic loss of revenue for the government."

She wrinkled her brow. "Why don't I just get the hell off this island? There must be a way."

"Didn't you listen to His Lordship this morning? If you try that and they catch you, it's tantamount to conviction; they could hang you before the week is out. Even if you made it off the island, they could come after you, maybe extradite you; then you'd be worse off than you are right now; you'd be guilty."

She shrugged and said nothing, but she seemed to be imagining something terrible.

"Will you let me get this PR campaign in gear?"

"All right," she sighed.

"Good. I suggest you get a hundred thousand dollars sent to Bill Eggers at Woodman and Weld as soon as possible. Nobody's going to want to extend credit to you in the circumstances."

"All right; I'll call my bank in Greenwich; the insurance money is supposed to be deposited there soon."

"Allison, speaking of insurance, did you mention to the investigator that you had been charged with the murder of the insured? That might make them reluctant to pay."

"It never came up," she said.

"Hello, Bill, it's Stone."

"What's happening?"

"Allison Manning is sending you a hundred thousand dollars from her Greenwich bank tomorrow."

"How nice! Do I have to do anything for it?"

"I want you to get ahold of the hottest PR firm you can find and have them start a campaign in the media to get Allison Manning released."

"I believe I get the picture," Eggers chuckled. "Barbaric islanders persecuting American blonde?"

"You're a quick study, Bill."

"How much does she want to spend?"

"I told her I thought fifty thousand would do the job; spend more if necessary. By this time the day after tomorrow I want this island overrun with wild-eyed reporters, photographers, and television crews. See if you can get 60 Minutes interested, but tell them they have to move fast; she goes on trial on Monday, and she could be strung up by the middle of next week. It's this Sunday night, or nothing."

"They'll want as much background on her as possible."

"Call Bob Cantor." He gave Eggers the number. "He's researching her husband; tell him to copy you on anything he finds. Paul Manning was a well-known writer, so lots of people should have heard of him. Try to be careful what you release to the PR people; don't let anything unfavorable get into the mix."

"I get the picture."

"The firm has got a lot of Washington connections, right?"

"Right."

"Find out who her congressman is in Greenwich, get ahold of him and both Connecticut senators and tell them they're about to lose a voter. Get them to get on to the State Department and tell them an American abroad is being railroaded. There's no consulate here, but there's bound to be one on a neighboring island. Have them issue the strongest possible protest to the St. Marks government."

Eggers was laughing now. "Why don't we get the president to send a cruiser down there to drop anchor in the harbor, with her guns pointed toward the capitol building?"

"Send a fucking aircraft carrier, if you can."

"Are there any communists in the St. Marks government? That always helps, especially in the Caribbean."

"Let's assume there are, for the moment; we can always apologize later."

"Call me tomorrow."

"Right." Stone hung up and walked downstairs, where Thomas was getting the bar ready for lunch. "Thomas," he said, "you'd better prepare for some business. Maybe we can even make up for the New York blizzard."

"Sounds good to me," Thomas said, laughing.

12

Stone dialed the number and waited. "This is Stone Barrington," his own voice said. "Please leave your name and number and I'll get back to you." "Arrington?" he said into the phone. "Pick up, Arrington." Nothing. He hung up.

He felt he had done all he could for the moment, so he left the room above the restaurant and walked down to his chartered yacht; he was weary and aching, as if he had run several miles. He fell onto his bunk and slept.

A rapping on the hull woke him; a glance through the hatch showed him dusk outside. He poked his head up.

Allison was standing on the pontoon between their boats. "How you doing?" she asked.

"How you doing is a better question."

"I had a little cry; now I feel better. Come over and have some dinner with me?"

"Sure, I'd like that."

She held up a finger. "One condition: no talking about my problems; I've put them out of my mind until tomorrow."

"Agreed. Give me time for a shower? I've been asleep, and I'm a little groggy."

"I hate a groggy date," she replied. "See you in half an hour."

Stone hunted down his razor, then squeezed himself into

the tiny head and turned on the cold-water shower. In St. Marks, it wasn't all that cold.

He rapped on the deck of the big blue yacht and stepped aboard.

"Come on down," she called out from below.

Stone walked down the companionway ladder, which, on a yacht this size, was more a stairway. Allison was at work in the galley, and the saloon table had been set for two, side by side. Whatever she was wearing was mostly concealed by a large apron.

"Can you make a decent martini?" she asked.

"I believe I can handle that."

"The bar's over there." She pointed. "Just open those cabinet doors."

Stone followed her instructions and found a handsome bar setup, nicely concealed. He found a cocktail shaker, two glasses, and ice cubes, then the gin and vermouth. "You sound awfully cheerful," he said as he mixed the drinks. "I don't know how you do it."

"It's a gift," she said. "For my whole life, when faced with something awful, I do as much as I can, then I put it out of my mind. I mean really right out of my mind. Then I find that the next day, things seem clearer."

"That's a great gift," he said.

"You can cultivate it if you work at it."

He handed her a martini. "I'll start right now."

She was sautéing chicken breasts in a skillet on the four-burner gas range, which was large for a yacht.

"When did you find time to get to the grocery store?" he asked.

"I didn't. I provisioned in the Canaries, and I've got lots of cold storage here, plus a large freezer. There won't be a salad, though; sorry about that."

They clinked glasses. "Better times," Stone said.

"I'll drink to that." She took a swig of her martini. "Expert," she said.

"A misspent youth. I tended bar in a Greenwich Village joint one summer, during law school." He leaned against a galley cabinet and sipped his drink. "Tell me about you," he said.

"That's easy," she replied. "Born in a colonial village in Litchfield County, Connecticut, father a country lawyer, mother a volunteer for this and that; went to local private schools, then Mount Holyoke, in Massachusetts; did a graphics course at Pratt, in Brooklyn, worked as an assistant art director for an ad agency in Manhattan, met Paul, married Paul; lived ... well, lived. What about you?"

"Born and raised in the Village, father a cabinetmaker, mother a painter; NYU undergrad and law school. NYPD for fourteen years, eleven of them as a detective."

"Why'd you quit?"

"A very bad boy put a twenty-two slug in my knee, and the force quit me, gave me their very best pension. That's the short version; I won't bore you with the long one, which involves a lot of department politics and a very strange case I worked on. Anyway, once off the force, I crammed for the bar, and an old law school buddy hooked me up with Woodman and Weld."

"How much money do you make?"

The bald question stopped him for a moment, then he recovered. "I made about six hundred thousand last year," he said. "My best year so far."

"You're doing well, then."

"By New York law firm standards that's only middling, but I have a lot more freedom than I would as a partner in a firm. I'm lucky that I can pick and choose my cases. If I want to bugger off to St. Marks for a week's sailing, I can manage it."

She put an oily hand against his cheek. "But you got stood up, didn't you? Poor baby."

"That's me."

"Who is she?"

"Name's Arrington Carter; she's a freelance writer."

"And when the blizzard was over, what kept her in New York?"

"She's writing a *New Yorker* profile of Vance Calder."

"Ooooh, lucky girl."

"I guess. She's known him for a while; matter of fact, she was his date the first time I met her."

"And you won out over Vance Calder? You must be sensational in bed."

He laughed. "You think that was it? I always thought it was my boyish charm."

She gave him a bright smile. "That, too." She opened a sealed packet of smoked salmon and arranged the slices on two plates. "First course is almost ready," she said. "There's a bottle of white on the table; will you open it?"

Stone went to the table, found a corkscrew, and opened a bottle of Beringer Private Reserve '94, then tasted it. "Excellent," he said. "Was Paul a connoisseur of wines?"

"Paul was more of a wino; I'm the authority." She handed him a bottle of red. "For the main course; might as well open it and let it breathe."

"Dominus '87. Very nice."

"You know wines?"

"Enough to stay out of trouble." He opened both bottles.

She set the two plates of smoked salmon on the table and untied her apron. Underneath it she was dressed in a very short skirt and a white cotton blouse, unbuttoned and tied under her breasts.

Stone remembered that the first time he had seen her she'd been wearing that sort of blouse, tied that way.

They finished their smoked salmon, then she whipped up a chicken dish over rice, with a lovely sauce. They were both warm with the wine and laughing easily. Allison cleared the table, then pressed a button and it folded away electrically.

"Very slick."

"Glad you like it." She caught him looking at her breasts. "Any yachtsman should be able to deal with a simple square knot," she said, knocking back the last of her wine.

Uh-oh, Stone said to himself. But he had had nearly a bottle of wine on top of the martini, and he was feeling hurt by Arrington, feeling incautious, and feeling extremely attracted to Allison Manning.

She went to a switch panel and lowered the lights; when she came back the knot in her shirt had been untied. She bent to kiss Stone, and her breasts fell free. "Let's forget about the attorney–client relationship for the night," she said.

Stone had a decision to make, and it didn't take long. "It's forgotten," he said.

She straddled his bare legs, and he found that there was nothing under the short skirt. He shucked off his shorts, and she pulled his polo shirt over his head. A tug at a zipper and a shrug of her shoulders, and they were both naked.

"I don't think I can wait," Stone said.

"I can't wait, either," she said, reaching down and slipping him into her. "We'll wait longer next time."

They were both very quick and very together; they finished, clutching each other and smothering their cries in each other's flesh. When they had both stopped trembling, she stood up, took his hand, and led him toward the aft cabin.

"Now we can start working on the next time," she said, "and we can practice waiting."

13

S tone woke not long after dawn as a shaft of new sunlight fell across his face; it had been a warm night, and they were both lying on top of the bedcovers. She lay on her stomach with her head turned toward him, a strand of blond hair falling to a corner of her mouth and a tiny frown on her face, as if she were trying to figure out something about a dream. The frown lent her the innocence of a little girl.

Stone didn't know what had motivated her to make love to him—maybe the realization that she might have no more than a week to live and the desire to make the most of it; or maybe she was just horny. For himself, he had been disappointed, angry, jealous, drunk, and, oh yes, horny. She was a client, of course, but he was a long way from the Ethics Committee of the New York State Bar Association, and he had never been any good at saying no to women. He reached over and lifted the strand of hair from her face, and, to his surprise, she smiled.

"I was just going to do that," she said.

"Glad to be of service," he replied.

Without opening her eyes, she reached for him and ran her hand down his body until it rested on his crotch. "Speaking of service," she said, "are you in a mood to render a little?"

"I am now," he replied, reaching over and running a finger lightly down the cleft between her cheeks.

She gave a little shudder and pulled herself on top of him.

He took her buttocks in both hands and moved them up until her pelt was in his face, then began using his tongue lightly, teasing her until she became more insistent. She came easily, as she had been doing for most of the night, then she slid down his sweaty body and returned the favor, insisting on hanging on until he was entirely spent. Then she flopped down beside him, and they panted together, laughing. Shortly they were asleep again.

They were awakened by a sharp rapping on the hull.

"Ahoy there, anyone aboard?" A female voice.

"Jesus," Stone said, "what time is it?"

"Half past nine," she replied, checking the bulkhead clock. She raised herself on an elbow. "Who is it?" she called out.

"The *New York Times*," the voice replied. "If you're Allison Manning, I'd like to talk with you."

"I really don't think the *Times* should find us like this," Stone whispered.

Allison grabbed a robe and left the cabin, while Stone lay low. He could hear her climbing the companionway ladder, then the two voices.

"I'm afraid I overslept," Allison was saying. "Could I meet you over at the Shipwright's Arms in half an hour?"

"I'm Hilary Kramer," the woman said. "I'd really like to see your yacht."

"Maybe later in the day," Allison said. "It's a mess right now."

"All right," the woman said, sounding disappointed. "I'll meet you over there in half an hour."

Allison came back to the after cabin. "The *New York Times*! That I wasn't expecting."

"I don't know how she could have gotten here so soon," Stone said. "I wasn't expecting anybody until tomorrow, late this afternoon at the earliest. I'm certainly glad she didn't arrive at dawn."

Allison burst out laughing. "That would have made quite a story, wouldn't it?"

•

"I hope I can sneak over to my boat without being seen."

"You'd better start sneaking."

"I'll be there when you talk to her. Just be yourself, tell your story just as you told it at the coroner's inquest."

"I don't know any other way to tell it," Allison replied.

Stone, showered and dressed, got to the Shipwright's Arms a little before Allison. He walked over to the table where the woman was drinking coffee. "Good morning," he said, "I'm Stone Barrington, Allison Manning's attorney." He stuck out his hand.

"Hilary Kramer," she replied, shaking his hand. "Your name is familiar."

Stone shrugged. "I'm a New York lawyer; I was down here on a sailing charter when Allison sailed into the harbor. I helped her at the coroner's inquest and ... well, ever since." He sat down. "How did you hear about all this?"

"I was vacationing on Antigua, right next door; the story moved last night on the AP wire and the paper called me late; I got a little plane over here this morning."

"Sorry to interrupt your vacation," Stone said.

"You won't interrupt it for long, believe me. I'll file something before noon, then I'll be back on my beach."

Stone looked up. "Here comes Allison," he said.

"She's cute," Kramer said. "How did you know I was here?"

"My boat is moored next to Allison's; I heard talking." He stood up. "Good morning, Allison; I think you've already met Hilary Kramer from the *Times*."

"I did," Allison said, sitting down. She waved at Thomas, who had appeared at the bar. "Can I have some coffee? You, too, Stone?"

"I've already had some," he lied, "but a second cup wouldn't hurt."

"Make it for two," Allison called.

Before the coffee arrived, Hilary Kramer was deep into her interview. She covered all the ground, most of it better than had been done at the coroner's inquest. "So what's your legal position now?" she asked finally.

"Stone can explain it better than I," Allison said, "but as I understand it, they could hang me as early as next week."

Kramer turned to Stone. "They want to hang her?"

Stone nodded gravely.

"And what do you think are their chances of doing that?"

"Off the record, I think that will depend greatly on what the press has to say about this. If enough pressure can be brought to bear in the media, her chances will improve a lot."

"Why is the government doing this, with so little incriminating evidence?" Kramer demanded.

"Still off the record, there is a body of opinion that holds that Sir Winston Sutherland, the Minister of Justice, has an ax to grind."

"What sort of ax?"

"You've got me. Why don't you ask Sir Winston?"

Thomas, who had returned with a fresh pot of coffee, piped up, "Be glad to lend you my car," he said.

"Thank you very much," she replied. "Is there a phone here? I'd like to call Sir Winston's office for an appointment."

"I think you'd have a much better chance of seeing him if you'd just show up at Government House," Thomas said.

"You might get more if he's a little off-balance," Stone chipped in.

Kramer looked around the table at all of them. "Look, this is not some sort of elaborate practical joke, is it?"

"I wish it were," Stone said. "And before you go, I think I should enlighten you a little about the system of justice as it exists on St. Marks—all off the record, of course. If you should quote me, it might react to Allison's detriment."

"Sure, off the record. Shoot."

When he had finished, her mouth was hanging open. "Is there someplace I can get a room for the night?" she asked, finally.

Thomas spoke up. "I have some rooms upstairs," he said. "We had some cancellations because of the snowstorm in New York."

"Great," she said. "Can I borrow that car now?"

"Sure."

"And where can I pick up a toothbrush?"

"There are shops all around Government House."

"I'd like to call my office, too."

"There's a phone on the bar, or in your room," Thomas replied.

Kramer produced a camera from her bag. "I'd like to get some pictures of both of you," she said, beginning to snap them. "Does Federal Express know about this island?"

"They do," Thomas said. "They'll pick up from here; delivery will likely take two days, though."

"Shit," she said. "Allison, are there any pictures of you floating around New York?"

"Paul's agent has one of the two of us together," Allison replied. "Her name is Anne Sibbald; she's at Janklow and Nesbit."

"Know them well," Kramer said, continuing to photograph. "I'll call them right now. Thomas, will you lead the way to my room?"

"Right this way," Thomas replied.

When they had gone Allison turned to Stone. "Did that go well?"

"I think it could hardly have gone better."

"She's suspicious of you and me, though; woman's intuition. We'd better be very correct around her."

"We'd better be very correct everywhere, except in bed," Stone replied. "I'd suggest we give up sex for the duration, but I don't think I could stick to that."

She smiled. "Neither could I."

"Stop smiling at me that way," he said, looking around.

The smile disappeared. "I'll be very correct," she said.

14

Stone had just finished his breakfast when Thomas waved at him from the bar and held up the phone. "Call for you from New York; fellow named Cantor. You want to take it here or upstairs?"

"I'll take it down here," Stone said, crossing to the bar and picking up the phone. "Bob?"

"Yeah, Stone."

"I thought you'd be on your way to the Canaries."

"I'm calling from Kennedy Airport; this morning was the first flight I could make and still do your legwork in the city."

"What did you find out?"

"Almost nothing about Allison Manning, but quite a bit about her husband."

"Shoot."

"First, Allison; she went to some New England women's college, then worked in advertising, then she met Paul Manning, and they got married."

"That much she's told me; anything else?"

"Not yet; I didn't have the time to track down anybody who knows her."

"What about the husband, then?"

"I got luckier there. There was an interview a couple of

years ago in *Publishers Weekly*, the trade magazine, right after he signed his last contract, which was for four and a half million dollars for two books. Not bad, huh?"

"Not bad at all."

"He finished the second book just before they left on the sailing trip. He had done increasingly well over the years, but three books ago he had a big bestseller, and that got him the new contract."

"Pretty rich writer, huh? And I was worried about Allison financing her defense."

"He's a big spender, at least since he signed that contract. He bought the place up in Greenwich; I called a friend of mine who's in real estate in that area, and she remembered the house. Big place—six or seven bedrooms; pool, tennis court, stables, greenhouses; on about eight acres; that's a lot of real estate in Greenwich. He paid two million eight for it, and she says it's probably worth three and a half, four million now. Then he ordered this yacht; I gather you've already seen that."

"Yeah; you find out anything about his debts?"

"He's got a two-million-dollar mortgage on the house—that's about the max you could get at that level—and he owes a million two on the boat. There's some smaller stuff, but not that small; he's got sixty grand in credit card debt and a line of credit secured by the equity in the house—three hundred thousand—and half that is used up."

"Anything about insurance?"

"His credit report shows that Chubb ran a check on him a while back, and that sounds like he's buying insurance."

"I know he had insurance; I just don't know how much."

"I reckon he has a net worth of around five, six million, if you include what's still to pay on the book contract. He's sometimes late on bill payments, but nothing serious, never more than thirty days."

"In short, he lives like a prince, but he's not all that rich."

"That pretty much sums it up."

"Any criminal record?"

"None."

"Ex-wives?"

"One. He was divorced about a month before he married Allison."

"Alimony?"

"I haven't had time to dig out the court records, but the divorce happened before he hit it big, so it's probably not too bad. They were only married a year, and it was a Florida divorce, so there's no community property law."

"What else?"

"Out of college he worked for newspapers, starting in small towns, then working his way up. His last job was on the *Miami Herald*, before he quit to write full time." The sound of notebook pages being turned came down the line. "Graduated from Cornell with a degree in journalism; high school in Olean, New York; born and raised there. He was pretty much the all-American boy. Too young for Vietnam, so he was never in the service; won a couple of awards at the *Herald*; that's about it for now. I gotta run, Stone; it's last call for boarding."

"Get going, then; call me from Las Palmas when you've had a chance to pick up some more." He hung up the phone.

"You getting anywhere?" Thomas asked. "Sorry if I was eavesdropping."

"No problem. No, I'm not getting anywhere. That was just some background stuff on Paul Manning; nothing of any real help."

"Chester called a while ago; he's making special runs starting this afternoon—lots of requests for seats on that little plane of his."

"Sounds as though the press is heeding our call."

"Sounds like it."

"You know, Thomas, I think we might need a little security down at the marina when these people start arriving. I wouldn't like to let them too near Allison's yacht; she's going to need some privacy."

"Uh-huh," Thomas replied. "I've got two brothers on the police; they could help out and round up enough guys to stake it out around the clock, I imagine. How many you want?"

"Say two at a time, around the clock?"

"Shouldn't be a problem."

"How many brothers and sisters have you got, Thomas?"

"Six brothers and four sisters, and a whole bunch of nieces and nephews; I lose count. In those days there was less opportunity in St. Marks; it was before tourism took hold down here. Two more of my brothers left, then came back; the two on the police stayed and did all right. They're both sergeants."

"What did the sisters do?"

"They got married and had babies. Everybody's prosperous, for St. Marks."

"And you most of all, huh?"

Thomas grinned. "You could say that." The fax machine rang, and he turned to receive whatever was coming. "Hang on, this is more likely for you than for me." The machine spat out a single sheet; Thomas glanced at it and handed it to Stone.

It was typed sloppily on his own letterhead. "Dear Stone," she said, "I wanted to let you know that I'm not going to be here when you get back. Vance has to go back to L.A., and we're not nearly finished with the piece, so I'm going with him. I've no idea how long I'll be out there, but it's going to be at least a couple of weeks. I'll call you when you're back in New York. Best, Arrington."

Best. Not love, best. He didn't like the sound of that in the least, and he was suddenly very glad he'd fucked Allison Manning. He would do it again, every chance he had, for as long as he could.

He tore up the fax, threw it into the wastebasket behind the bar, and trudged up the stairs to start working again on Allison's case.

CHAPTER

15

Stone worked on his notes for the trial and tried to come up with new ideas for Allison's testimony, but he was depressed, and depression always made him sleepy. Soon he was stretched out on the bed and dead to the world.

Thomas was shaking him. "Stone, wake up."

"Huh?" He was groggy, and he felt hung over.

"You got two press people downstairs: one from *60 Minutes* and one from *The New Yorker*."

"Jesus, we landed the big ones first, huh?"

"Looks like it."

"I'd better splash some water on my face; tell them I'll be down in a minute."

"Okay."

Stone shook himself awake, washed his face and toweled it briskly to bring back some color, then went downstairs. Two men came toward him, a tall, slim, tanned one in Bermuda shorts and a short, stocky, pasty man in a khaki bush jacket.

"I'm Jim Forrester from *The New Yorker*," the tall one said, shaking hands.

"I'm Jake Burrows, I'm a producer on *60 Minutes*," the bush jacket said, "and I was here first. I want to talk to you before he does." He nodded at his competitor.

"All right, all right," Stone said. "Let's all sit down and discuss this; I mean, you two guys are not exactly competitors."

"That's right," Forrester said.

"Everybody is a competitor," Burrows said.

"Come on, sit down, and let's talk." Stone herded them toward a table. "Thomas, how about some lunch menus?"

"Sure thing," Thomas said.

"I want the first interview," Burrows said; "I was here first."

"Wait a minute," Stone said. "Just listen to me, both of you. Jim, you're not exactly on deadline here, are you?"

"No, I'm not," the writer said. "I'm here to get the whole story; the soonest we could run would be a couple of weeks after the trial."

"Feel better, Jake?" Stone asked.

"A little," Burrows said grudgingly. "I've got a reporter arriving here tonight, and either I get an exclusive interview, or I'm getting out of here right now."

Stone turned to him. "Either it runs Sunday night, or there's no interview."

"I can't promise you that," Burrows said.

"Then you might as well go home, because before the Sunday after that rolls around, my client could very well have been executed, and I'm not much interested in a postmortem feature."

"This week's show is already set," Burrows said. "There's nothing I can do about it."

"I'm sorry, Jake, there's nothing I can do for you," Stone said.

Burrows looked at him incredulously. "Listen to me, Stone, this is *60 Minutes;* do you know what that means?"

"Sure I do," Stone replied. "It means you'd be airing an interview with a dead woman. I thought your show liked saving innocent people from death row, not reporting on the execution later."

Jake Burrows looked at him intently for a moment without speaking. "I've got to make a phone call," he said finally, pushing his chair back.

"Tell them I want it in writing," Stone said.

"If I do this, will you guarantee me an exclusive?"

"I'll guarantee you an exclusive on in-depth TV, but she's going to hold a press conference, where I'll answer most of the questions, and an awful lot of photographs of her are going to be taken. The only way I can save her life is to carpet American TV wall to wall with her face, and that's what I intend to do. Anyway, all that will be great promotion for your interview."

Burrows nodded and went off to find a phone.

"You're going to have your hands full pretty soon," Jim Forrester said.

"I've already got my hands full, just with the two of you. Are you on staff at the magazine?"

Forrester shook his head. "This will be my first piece for them. I was in San Juan doing a travel piece when they called."

"Who's your editor there?" Stone asked.

"Charles McGrath."

"He's number two there, isn't he?"

"That's right."

"What are you going to want?"

"Well, obviously, I want to see Allison again as soon as possible, then I want to cover everything that happens, including the *60 Minutes* interview and the trial. There's nothing I can do to save her life, but if what she says rings true, then I can reinforce her innocence if she survives. That could be important to her, because there is always going to be a question mark hanging over her, even if she's acquitted."

"You're right about that." Stone wrinkled his brow. "What did you mean by seeing Allison again?"

"I've met her before."

"Where?"

"In the Canaries, in Las Palmas and in Puerto Rico. I was there on assignment from *Conde Nast Traveler* when I met Paul at the yacht club in Las Palmas."

"Jesus," Stone said, "I've got a guy on a plane for Las Palmas right now, looking for somebody just like you. We have to talk." He looked up to see Jake Burrows coming toward them.

"All right," Burrows said, "let me lay it out for you: I'll give you a letter on *60 Minutes* letterhead, guaranteeing you air time this Sunday night."

"Guaranteeing me a full segment," Stone said.

"All right, all right. You give me first and exclusive access to Allison first thing tomorrow morning, and you don't hold your press conference until my reporter and I are out of here with our tape."

"Who's the reporter?"

"Chris Wheaton."

"Never heard of him. What happened to Mike Wallace and Morley Safer?"

"Chris is a she, and she's new; this will be her first story. She's already on a plane, and she's all you're going to get."

"This is a full segment, though?"

"I'll put it in writing."

"Okay, but Jim here is going to sit in." He held up a hand before Burrows could object. "He's not going to ask her any questions during your time, he's just going to observe for his *New Yorker* piece. Can't hurt to have your program's name in the magazine, can it? I bet Chris Wheaton will love it."

"Okay, it's a deal. First thing in the morning; Chris won't be in until tonight, and I want daylight, with palms and water in the background."

"How about in the cockpit of her boat?"

"Ideal."

"You go write your letter; Jim and I have to talk."

Burrows went back to the bar, opened his briefcase, extracted a sheet of stationery, and started writing.

Stone turned back to Forrester. "Tell me about your meeting the Mannings," he said.

"We had done a shoot in the yacht club, and I was having a drink at the bar when Paul sat down next to me; I recognized him, so I introduced myself."

"What was your impression of him?"

"Big guy," he spread his hands; "full beard, bearlike; as tall as me, but a good fifty, sixty pounds heavier; laughed easily. He liked it that I knew his work, and he offered to show me his boat."

"What else did you talk about while you were in the bar?"

"The outline of his cruise, where he'd been, et cetera."

"How long were you there?"

"Long enough to finish a piña colada—twenty minutes, half an hour—then we walked down to the marina, and he introduced me to Allison."

"What was your first impression of her?"

"A knockout; she was wearing a bikini, after all."

"Right. I mean, what did you think of her?"

"Bright, charming, funny. I liked her immediately, just as I did Paul."

"How much time did you spend with them?"

"It was late afternoon, and they invited me to stay aboard for dinner. Allison cooked some steaks on an outdoor grill, off the stern, and we drank a couple of bottles of good California cabernet."

"What time did you leave?"

"Must have been close to ten o'clock. I was staying in a hotel in town, and I had an early-morning flight back to New York; I wanted to get some sleep."

"Think back: What was your impression of their relationship?"

"Warm, affectionate; they shared a sense of humor. They seemed to like each other a lot."

"Were they in love?"

"Yeah, I guess they were. I remember I admired how well they got along, especially after spending several months together on a boat. That kind of intense, long-term proximity has ruined more than one relationship."

"Did you ever see them again?"

"Yeah, briefly; when I got back to my hotel there was a message from New York saying they wanted some more shots on Grand Canary, then some on the Canaries island of Puerto Rico. I stayed on in Las Palmas for another day, then flew down to Puerto Rico in the late afternoon of the day after that."

"Did you know they'd be there?"

"They might have mentioned it, but it didn't register. Next time I saw them, I was standing on a stone jetty on the south side of the island, and they motored past on the boat, heading for Antigua. I yelled to them, and they waved back and said they were sorry they missed me, then they were gone."

"What was their mood at that moment?"

"Jubilant, like they were glad to be getting back to sea. They were laughing, I remember; he said something to her that I couldn't hear, then she laughed and slapped him on the ass."

"Jim, will you testify to all this at her trial?"

The writer shrugged. "Sure, if you think it will help."

"I think it just might help; you were apparently the last person besides Allison to see Paul Manning alive."

"Glad to do it."

"One more question, Jim, just between you and me: Do you think that Allison is the sort of person who could have killed Paul?"

Forrester looked astonished. "Of course not. Well, I guess anybody could kill anybody under the right circumstances, but I would bet the farm she had nothing to do with his death. Absolutely nothing I saw in their relationship would indicate that."

"Good," Stone said, relieved to have an objective opinion that reinforced his own. "I'll ask you some form of that question under oath."

"And I'll give you the same answer."

16

The rest of the *60 Minutes* crew arrived at dusk, and Stone had dinner with Jake Burrows and his reporter, Chris Wheaton. They met at the bar of the Shipwright's Arms, got a drink, and found a table. Stone looked over the reporter: she was small, intense, as blond as Allison, and handsome rather than pretty. He thought she would look very good on camera.

"Allison asked to be excused from dinner," Stone told her. "She says she needs a good night's sleep."

"That's okay," Wheaton said, "I don't want to meet her until we're on camera; the interview will be fresher that way. Has Jake told you how we're going to work this?"

Stone shook his head. "We made some ground rules about the air date and the segment, but that's it; you can ask her anything you want."

"Good. I expect we'll talk for at least an hour, maybe a lot longer."

This hadn't occurred to Stone, and it meant that they would be editing the tape to show the parts they liked best, and that might not work entirely to his client's benefit. It was too late to start negotiating again, though, and he'd just have to put a good face on it. "That's fine," he said, "talk as long as you like. If she gets tired or upset, we might have to take a break."

"We'll have to change tape," Wheaton replied. "She can pee or have a cry while we're doing that." She leaned forward. "Tell me, how did you become involved in this? Did she get you down here from New York when she found out she needed a lawyer?"

Stone shook his head. "I was down her for a cruise when she sailed in alone. My girlfriend didn't make it because of the snowstorm, and I went to the inquest for lack of anything else to do. It became obvious that her questioner had some ax to grind, and at the lunch break I offered to advise her."

"Who was the questioner?"

Stone told her about Sir Winston Sutherland and his attitude toward Allison.

"I don't get it," Wheaton said; "why would this Sir Winston guy want to make trouble for this poor widow?"

Stone thought she was being disingenuous, but he didn't call her on it. "I don't get it, either," he said.

"So why isn't some local lawyer defending her?"

"A local lawyer is defending her; I'm second chair."

"Who is he? I want to talk to him."

Stone's stomach turned over. "He's not talking to anybody but Allison and me. Maybe after the trial, we'll see."

Wheaton glanced at her producer.

"I mean that; he's got a lot of work to do between now and the trial, and I don't want him disturbed. He's an elderly man; he only has so much energy to devote to this, and I want Allison to get the benefit of all of it."

Wheaton nodded. "How much are you getting paid to defend her?"

"We haven't discussed a fee."

She smiled. "Uh-huh."

"It just hasn't come up," Stone said lamely.

"Is that how you would operate in New York?"

Stone shook his head. "Of course not, but we're not in New York. She's a fellow American in trouble in a foreign place, and I'm glad to help her if I can. Anyway, I'm not necessarily a very good buy as an attorney in St. Marks, since I don't really know the ropes of the local legal system."

"What is the local legal system like?"

"Bizarre, and I hope you'll bring that out in your piece." He told her about the preliminary hearing and what he had learned about how the court operated.

She laughed out loud. "That's the most outrageous thing I've ever heard!"

"Please make that clear on television. To tell you the truth, I think there's more than one piece in this for you. If you're here for the trial, that ought to be an eye-opener, and I'd certainly be glad to have a camera waiting outside the courtroom."

"Any chance we could get a camera inside the courtroom?"

"You can try; go see the judge. I'd be happy for him to know that the American press is taking an interest."

"Jake, you want to take care of that tomorrow?"

"Sure," Burrows replied. It was the first time he had spoken. "Look, Stone, while I, and I'm sure Chris, have some sympathy for the lady's plight, we're not here to fight your battles for you; you have to understand that."

"Sure I do, but if just doing your job happens to work to Allison's benefit, that's okay with me."

"We understand that," Wheaton said.

The menus arrived, and they ordered dinner. When the food arrived, Chris Wheaton took another tack.

"I used to work local news in New York," she said. "I remember when you were on the force."

"You mean you remember when I left the force, don't you?" Stone said, cracking a crab claw.

"That's what I mean. Your name still pops up now and then."

"Does it?"

"You haven't exactly been press-shy, have you, Stone?"

Stone laughed ruefully. "I've never sought coverage, but sometimes coverage has been thrust upon me by your colleagues in the media."

She found that funny. "Still, your occasional flash of fame must have brought you a lot of cases as a lawyer."

"I've ducked more of that kind of case than I've taken," he replied. "Most of my work has been fairly run-of-the mill."

"Didn't you get a very nice personal injury verdict a while back?"

He nodded. "Got a nice one last year; we even collected." And it had made life a bit easier for him, too, he remembered. "I'm not the sort of lawyer who gets the big cases; those usually go to the big firms, and I'm pretty much an independent."

"But you've done well, haven't you? I seem to remember something about a townhouse in Turtle Bay."

"I inherited that from a great-aunt and did most of the renovation myself. That verdict you mentioned paid off the construction loan, though. That was a relief."

"I'll bet." She was looking at him the way he had once looked at perps in interrogations.

"Chris, have you got something on your mind about me?"

"It just seems odd that you would just happen to be here when Allison Manning came sailing in. Could that be a bit more than a coincidence?"

Stone pointed toward the marina. "If you'll go down to the marina office and check their reservations log, you'll find that I booked my charter nearly three months ago, and since you're from New York, you'll know firsthand about the blizzard. If not for that I would now be south of Guadeloupe somewhere with a rum and tonic in one hand and the girl of my dreams in the other."

"And who is the girl of your dreams?"

"Her name is Arrington Carter; she's a magazine writer, a freelancer."

"I've met her," Wheaton said. "As a matter of fact, I saw her two nights ago in the company of an actual movie star."

Stone nodded. "Vance Calder. She's working on a *New Yorker* profile of him that she was offered after the snowstorm hit; that's why she's not here now."

"Aren't you just a little uncomfortable knowing that your girlfriend is in New York with Vance Calder, instead of here with you?"

"Not really." He smiled. "As a matter of fact, Vance introduced us last fall." This was not quite a lie. "And she's not in New York, she's in L.A. They both went out there today."

"Ah," Wheaton said, sounding disappointed.

I hope I bent that needle, Stone thought, but it irritated him no end that she knew about Arrington and Vance. He hoped it didn't show.

There was a brief silence, then Wheaton turned to her producer.

"Jake, when we're done tomorrow, you take the tape back to New York and do the editing; you can play me the track over the phone later in the week."

"And where will you be?" Burrows asked.

"I'll be here," she said. "I'm staying for the trial, and so is the camera crew. You work it out with Don or whoever."

"Chris, don't you think you're pushing it just a bit on your first assignment?"

"I know a good story when I see one," she said. "You can explain that to them in New York. I think the network might want a feed for the evening news, too. Check on that, will you?"

"Sure."

Stone began to feel good about this. Now all Allison had to do was charm Chris Wheaton out of her socks, and that might not be easy.

CHAPTER

17

After dinner Stone said good night to the *60 Minutes* people and walked back toward the marina. He had no sooner set foot on the dock when he found himself grabbed from both sides by two shadowy figures. He made a point of not struggling.

"Is one of you Thomas Hardy's brother?" he asked the darkness.

"Both of us is," a deep voice replied.

"My name is Stone Barrington; I live on the smaller of the two yachts over there. I'm the one who asked Thomas to find some security." The pressure on his arms relaxed, but he was not let go.

"You got some ID, then?" the voice asked.

"Right-hand rear pocket," he said. "My New York driver's license." He felt some fumbling, and a flashlight came on.

"Okay, then, Mr. Barrington, we'll know you next time."

"Gentlemen . . ." Stone began.

"Henry and Arliss," the voice said.

"Henry and Arliss, I think our purposes would be better served if you stood over there under the lamp by the gate, instead of lurking in the dark. You can do the most good by being seen to be keeping people away from Mrs. Manning."

"I see your point," Henry replied. "You expecting anybody else? Anybody at all?"

"Not until early tomorrow morning, when some people, including a camera crew, will be coming down here. Please keep them at the gate until you've called me. Just rap on the hull; I'll be awake."

"Of which boat?" Henry asked.

Stone decided to pretend there was no meaning in the question. "The smaller one."

"Good night, then, Mr. Barrington."

"Good night, Henry, Arliss; see you in the morning." Stone walked down to his boat and went aboard. The lights aboard the big yacht were out. He undressed and climbed gratefully into his berth, just in time to hear a dim scrambling in the cockpit. A moment later, Allison was crawling into bed with him; she was naked.

"I take it you met Henry and Arliss," she said, snuggling up to him.

"I did, and I hope to God you didn't meet them on the way across the pontoon."

"Nope. They're standing up by the gate now; I could see them."

"Were you naked when you left your boat, or after you arrived on mine?"

"The whole time."

Stone laughed in spite of himself. "Allison, while your craving for my body may be perfectly understandable—even admirable—you have to remember that there is now on the island a camera crew for the most popular television news program in the United States of America, and we don't know yet how powerful their lenses are."

"I'm glad you understand my craving," she said.

"On Sunday night, your interview may be preceded by a shot of you, naked in the moonlight, climbing aboard your lawyer's boat. That might not exactly get the American public behind you."

She turned over and pushed her buttocks into his increasingly active crotch. "Why don't you get behind me?" She reached between her legs, found him, and guided him in.

Stone pushed into her sweet depths. "Oh, God," he breathed. "When this is over, remind me to talk to you about your interview tomorrow morning."

"Shhh," she whispered, helping him.

Stone jerked awake. Sunlight was streaming through the port above his head. He heard voices and footsteps on the dock. "Allison," he said, shaking her, "wake up."

"What is it, baby?" she asked, snuggling her warm body closer.

There was a sharp rap on the hull, and Henry Hardy's booming voice called out, "Mr. Barrington, you up?"

"*60 Minutes* is here," he whispered.

Allison's head came off the pillow. "What?"

He glanced out the port and saw legs standing next to the boat. "I'll try to get rid of them," he said. He got out of bed, tried to rub some color into his face, and brushed his hair back with his hands. He got into his swim trunks, which were lying on a seat next to the berth, went into the main cabin, climbed the ladder, and emerged, waist high, from the hatch. Jake Burrows and Chris Wheaton were standing on the dock next to the bow of his boat. "What time is it?" he asked. "Aren't you a little early?"

"It's seven-fifteen," Burrows said. "We have to set up for our eight o'clock interview."

Stone shook his head. "I haven't finished breakfast yet, and I don't know if Allison is even up." Suddenly he felt a naked body slither between his legs and up the ladder behind him. "Why don't you go back to the Shipwright's Arms, have some breakfast, and come back at eight?" He heard Allison sneaking across the cockpit behind him, then the rattle of his boarding ladder, followed by a tiny splash. He stepped off his boat, crossed the pontoon, hopped into the cockpit of the larger yacht, and yelled down the hatch. "Allison, you up yet?" He pretended to listen for a moment, then looked up at the television crew. "She's up, but nowhere near ready," he said. "Come back at eight."

The disappointed crew turned and began walking back toward the pub. As Stone stood in the cockpit, Allison climbed up the stern ladder into the cockpit and, soaking wet, slipped past him and down the companionway ladder.

"I don't know if I can be ready by eight," she said, laughing.

"You'd bloody well better be," he muttered, refusing to look at her.

"If we hurry, we could get in a quickie before they come back," she said, pulling the hair on his legs.

"Ouch! I'm getting back to my boat right now. You get yourself together." He fled the yacht and went back to his own.

At eight o'clock sharp he emerged, dressed, to find the crew standing on the dock, waiting. "Just a minute," he said, "I'll see if she's ready.

As he spoke, Allison climbed into her own cockpit, wearing a sleeveless cotton dress that showed off her tan, yet made her look like a high school senior. "Good morning!" she cried, delivering a dazzling smile. "I'm Allison; come aboard, all of you."

As the crew climbed aboard, Stone took deep breaths and tried to get his pulse rate back down to normal.

18

I *must be crazy,* Stone thought as the interview began. *I've let this girl go on TV, before an audience of millions and at the mercy of a reporter on her first assignment who would kill for a success, which she might not define as I would, and with no preparation whatever.* He watched from the pontoon as Chris Wheaton tossed Allison a few softball questions to relax her, then tensed as the real questioning began. Jim Forrester from *The New Yorker* had shown up and was sitting quietly beyond camera range, listening and taking notes.

"Allison," Chris Wheaton said, sounding really interested, "when you and Paul left the Canary Islands and set sail for home, how much sailing experience had you, personally, had?"

"Well, I had sailed across the Atlantic and around Europe with Paul, but he had always done the sailing. The boat was rigged for singlehanding, so he took care of that, and I just kept house—or boat, I guess."

"So how was it, after Paul's death, that you managed to sail this very large yacht all the way across the Atlantic all by yourself?"

Allison launched into an explanation of how she had learned enough celestial navigation to find her latitude and how she had managed the sails by using only the main most of the time.

Wheaton seemed fascinated by her reply and satisfied with her answer. Forrester seemed almost to be taking a transcript of the proceedings. Wheaton continued with questions about the sailing of the boat, and Allison grew visibly more relaxed. Then Wheaton changed tack, and Stone knew that the questions were not coming in the order in which they would appear in the edited version of the interview. Wheaton probed the depths of Allison's marriage to Paul Manning, taking her over and over the same ground, looking for what might appear to be a motive for murder. To Stone's surprise, Allison stood up to it beautifully, genuinely seeming to try to answer every question put to her, holding nothing back.

When a halt was called for the first change of tape, Wheaton turned to Stone. "You want a break?"

Stone looked at Allison and she shook her head imperceptibly. "No," Stone replied. "Go ahead."

Wheaton got the signal from her producer; she turned back to Allison. "Allison, how much life insurance did your husband have?"

"Honestly, I don't know," Allison replied. "Ashore, the division of our lives was pretty much the same as at sea. He handled the business, I handled the house. I never made an investment, bought a life insurance policy, or even wrote a check, unless it was for groceries or clothes. Paul had people who handled the business end of his career, and they're sorting out the estate now, I guess, and when they tell me where I stand, then I'll know. I'm told it will be some weeks before it's all figured out. I do know from what Paul said in passing that although he owned an expensive house and boat, they both have large mortgages on them, so I don't know yet what will be left when everything is settled."

"Are you going to keep the big house in Greenwich and this beautiful yacht?"

Allison shrugged. "The house was always too big for even the two of us, since we didn't have any kids, and I don't know if I would want to live there alone; I just haven't thought that far ahead. As far as the boat is concerned, what would I do with it? Anyway, the memories are too painful; I don't think I could ever sail on her again without Paul." She brushed away a tear.

Perfect, Stone thought.

There were two more changes of tape before the interview ended, but Allison kept going. Apart from an occasional sip of orange juice, she never paused. Finally, they were done, and the crew began to pack up their equipment. Allison chatted idly with Chris Wheaton and Jim Forrester, answering questions about her yacht.

"It's nice to see you again, Jim," Allison said. "Paul and I enjoyed your company in Las Palmas, and we were sorry not to know you were in Puerto Rico until we saw you as we were leaving port."

"I was sorry, too, Allison," the journalist replied. "Do you think we could get together later today or early tomorrow for a few minutes? I have some more things to ask you."

"I'm sure we can," she replied. "Let me talk to Stone about my schedule, and I'll get back to you. Where are you staying?"

"At the Shipwright's Arms."

"Good. I'll call you."

Wheaton and Burrows thanked her for her time and, with Jim Forrester, left the boat. As they were walking up the pontoon, Chris Wheaton stopped and spoke quietly to Stone. "That was some performance," she said. "I've never seen anything like it."

"I'm glad it went well," Stone replied. "You should be able to get an awfully good segment out of that."

"You bet I will," Wheaton said, then she looked back at Allison, who was standing in the cockpit, looking out over the harbor, sipping her orange juice. "She's really something," she said. "You won't have any trouble getting her off."

"I wish I could believe that," Stone said, "but from what I've seen so far, I think the odds are heavily against her. Sir Winston Sutherland wants her neck in a noose, for whatever reason, and I don't know if I'm going to be able to stop him."

Wheaton looked at him closely. "Jesus," she said with wonder, "you really think she's innocent, don't you?"

Stone looked at her in amazement. "Of course I do; after all that questioning, don't you?"

"Not for a minute," Wheaton replied. "Listen, over the years I've interviewed a couple of hundred people who were either accused of murder or who had just been convicted or acquitted; I learned to tell the guilty from the innocent, and let me tell you, not more than ten of them were innocent." She pointed her chin at Allison. "And she's not one of them."

"Show me one hole in her story," Stone said.

"There isn't one. But she's guilty just the same. Call it a woman-to-woman thing, if you like, but I look in those beautiful blue eyes and I know."

"Is that what you're going to say on *60 Minutes*?"

"Are you kidding? I'd be fired out of hand. No sir, I'm going to play it straight, let her answers speak for themselves, and ninety-nine percent of the audience is going to be outraged that this beautiful, innocent young woman could be charged with murder. That's what you want, isn't it?"

"Certainly, that's what I want."

"Well, relax, because that's what you're going to get." She paused and looked across the harbor at the boats. "Unless I can dig up something new between now and Sunday." She turned and walked up the pontoon toward the pub. Then she stopped, turned, and walked back. "One more thing," she said. "You seem like a nice guy, Stone, so let me give you some free advice: don't fall in love with her; don't even fuck her, if you haven't already. Allison Manning is a dangerous woman."

Stone was speechless. He watched her walk away.

19

Stone was having lunch with Hilary Kramer from the *New York Times* at the Shipwright's Arms when Thomas Hardy waved him to the bar, pointing at the phone. Stone excused himself, got up, and went to the bar.

"It's somebody named Cantor," Thomas said, handing Stone the telephone. "By the way, Chester called from the airport, too; says he's loaded down with media folk all afternoon."

"Right," Stone said, taking the phone. "I'd like to have a press conference here Friday morning at ten, if that's okay."

"Sure."

Stone spoke into the phone. "Bob?"

"Stone? Glad I caught you; I'm coming home tomorrow."

"That was fast; were you able to cover any ground in such a short time?"

"You bet; I got into Las Palmas early, so I took a connecting flight to Puerto Rico and spent a couple of hours there, then came back to Las Palmas."

"What have you learned?"

"Nothing in Puerto Rico, except they took on fuel and water and spent one night there; more in Las Palmas, though."

"Tell me."

"They were at the yacht club marina for four or five days,

doing odd jobs on the boat and provisioning with fresh fruit and vegetables at the local market. Paul had a drink at the yacht club bar late every afternoon, once or twice with Allison, but apart from the shopping, she kept pretty much to the boat. Boats go in and out of that marina constantly, so I was only able to find one boat still there with people who remembered the Mannings. Apart from their boat, which was big and beautiful, they remembered only a couple of things about them: first, their rubber dinghy was stolen, and Manning apparently had trouble finding the replacement he wanted; finally he had it flown in from Barcelona. Second, the Mannings had a terrific fight late on the night before they left Las Palmas."

"Tell me about the fight," Stone said, lowering his voice and looking around to be sure no one overheard.

"A real knockdown, drag-out domestic dispute. Crockery was thrown, names were called, tears were shed, and the whole thing happened at top volume."

"Did you get any direct quotes?"

"No, but it had something to do with sailing—with their route, or something."

Odd, Stone thought, that Allison would argue with Paul about something to do with sailing the boat. "That's all you could find out?"

"That's it. Apparently the couple did all the usual things that the yachties do when they sail in and out of Las Palmas—repairs, food, and like that."

"Funny, a guy showed up here, a journalist, who says he had dinner with them their last night in Las Palmas. Any mention of a third party there during the fight?"

"Nope, no mention. I'm afraid that's all there is here."

"About the dinghy, what was so special about the one he had flown in from Barcelona?"

"I don't know; apparently the guy was real picky about his stuff. There were other dinghies available here—Avons and Zodiacs, mostly, both good brands, one English and one French. He wanted something called a Parker Sportster, an American model, very expensive. It arrived on their last morning. Can you think of anything else I should be doing here?"

"No, I guess not; go on home."

"Soon as I'm back I'll finish up my research into Manning; there wasn't time to do much before I left."

"Do that, and get back to me soonest. It's Thursday, and the trial is on Monday; I'll need the info fast."

"Right; I'll be in touch."

Stone hung up the phone just as Jim Forrester ordered a drink at the bar. "Just the man I wanted to see," he said.

"What's up?"

"You said you had dinner with the Mannings their last night in Las Palmas, right?"

"Right."

"How late were you with them?"

"I don't know, maybe eleven o'clock."

"Did the Mannings have a fight when you were there?"

"No, not exactly; they did disagree about something, though."

"What was that?"

"It was kind of crazy, when you consider that Allison apparently didn't usually take much interest in the sailing of the boat. We were looking at their route on the chart, and she wanted to sail a direct course from Puerto Rico to Antigua. Paul pointed out to her that the trade winds blow some distance south of the Canaries, and if they wanted to take advantage of the trades, which everybody does who's crossing in those latitudes, they'd be better off sailing south or southeast from Puerto Rico until they picked up the trades, then turning west with a good breeze at their backs. She couldn't seem to grasp that, for some reason. We'd all had a good deal to drink, of course; maybe she was just spoiling for a fight. You know how married couples can be. Anyway, I was a little uncomfortable, so I said my good-byes and left. They were still arguing about it when I stepped ashore."

"Do you recall anything about Paul having a rubber dinghy flown in from Barcelona?"

"Yeah, I do; somebody had stolen his dinghy, and he wanted a new one, something special. It wasn't available in Las Palmas, so he called somebody in Barcelona and had one sent."

"A Parker Sportster?"

•

"Beats me."

"Did he give any reason for wanting that particular dinghy?"

"Not that I can recall. He seemed obsessive about having just the right gear on his boat, I remember that well enough; every item on it seemed to have been chosen with great care."

"Was the one that was stolen a Parker Sportster?"

"I don't know, I guess so."

"Thanks, Jim. Thomas, put Jim's drink on my tab."

Forrester grinned. "You think a *New Yorker* reporter would accept favors from a lawyer in a case he was writing about?"

"You bet I do."

"You're right," Forrester said, raising his glass to Stone, then taking a big swig. He wandered off to find a lunch table.

Stone dialed his office number in New York, and his secretary answered. "Hi, it's Stone," he said. "What's happening?"

"Not a hell of a lot," she replied. "Arrington went to L.A., but she said she faxed you about that."

"Yeah, she did."

"There's a lot of mail, mostly junk and bills; nothing that can't wait until you're back."

"Listen, I want you to do something for me."

"Shoot."

"I want you to call a couple of marine supply houses and see if you can get me some information on a rubber dinghy called Parker Sportster—a brochure or something. Apparently it's a high-end piece of equipment."

"Okay; you want it sent to you?"

"Yeah, FedEx it, priority."

"Anything else?"

"Not right now. Bob Cantor is coming home tomorrow; you can go ahead and reimburse his expenses and pay him for his time; he's always short of money."

"Okay."

Stone hung up and returned to his table. Allison had arrived and was deep in conversation with Hilary Kramer, who was taking copious notes. He sat down and listened to the interview, which included most of the questions Wheaton had already asked her, but in more of a chronological order.

When they had finished talking, Allison returned to the yacht with Jim Forrester, whose turn it was for an interview.

Stone picked at the remains of his lunch. "Hilary, what did you think of Allison?" he asked.

"She's a brave little thing, isn't she?" Kramer replied. "If I had been in her shoes, I don't know if I could have done what she did."

"I'd like your opinion about something that might help me with the trial."

"Sure, go ahead."

"Did you find any holes in her story? Anything that was hard to believe?"

Kramer shook her head. "Not a thing; she's a transparently honest girl; a jury is bound to see that."

"Thanks, I'm glad to have my opinion reinforced," he said. And Chris Wheaton's opinion opposed, he thought.

CHAPTER

20

The first of the media rush began at midafternoon. Stone watched them ask Thomas where to find Allison Manning and be told of the news conference. As six o'clock approached they were still arriving, and he put back the conference until the following morning at ten, much to the annoyance of those who had arrived early. They were not relying on Chester's small airplane now, but chartering out of San Juan and St. Thomas. Stone spoke to Henry and Arliss and had the guard on the marina doubled.

Allison was nervous; she sat in the saloon of the yacht and drank a martini just mixed by Stone.

"Easy," he said. "You don't want to be hung over in the morning. We only have to do this once, and I'll be there to protect you."

"But there are so many," she said. "I had a look through the binoculars, and there must be thirty of them."

"Yeah, they got together and chartered an old DC-3 in San Juan and packed it. I hear the airplane is making another flight, due in early in the morning."

"Are you sure this is good for us?" she asked.

"It can't be bad," Stone said. "When the authorities get wind of what's happening, I hope to see a change in their attitude." At her insistence he mixed her another martini. "Tell you what, I'll cook for you tonight."

She brightened. "No kidding? I've never had a man cook for me."

"Not once?"

"You forget, I'd been with Paul forever, and he wouldn't so much as make himself a sandwich. Once, when I was sick and couldn't cook, I saw him eat beans straight out of the can rather than heat them."

"Let's see what you've got in here," Stone said, rummaging through a cabinet. He found some linguine and a couple of cans of minced clams. "Where's the olive oil?"

"Down below, under the silverware drawer," she said. "I'll find us a nice chilled white wine." She went to a cooler and produced a bottle.

Stone found some garlic, peeled and chopped it, sautéed it in some olive oil, then drained the clam juice into the skillet, seasoning with salt and pepper. "Any parsley?" he asked, adding some of the white wine.

"Only dried; up there in the spice rack."

Fifteen minutes later they were dining on linguine and white clam sauce.

"Excellent," she said.

"Typical bachelor dinner," Stone replied.

"Have you ever been married?"

"Nope."

"So you've had a lot of practice at quickie bachelor dinners?"

"Oh, I can make a few more elaborate dishes, too, if I have time to plan and shop. I don't do it all that often."

"And only early in the relationship, before seduction is assured," she said, grinning.

"You are a cynic."

She laughed. "Nailed you, huh?"

He tried not to smile. "Certainly not."

Stone washed the dishes, then stuck his head up through the hatch for a look toward the Shipwright's Arms. The bar was jammed with people, and their raucous laughter reached all the way to the marina. He noticed that two of Henry's policemen stood near the restaurant, ready to stop any journalist who so much as ventured onto the lawn between the bar and the marina.

"I think we're safe for the evening," he said, climbing back down the companionway.

She met him, tugging at his shirttail. "No safety for you," she said, unzipping his fly.

At ten sharp on Friday morning, Stone, with Allison beside him, began walking across the lawn toward the Shipwright's Arms. Somebody had nailed together a little platform and on it stood a forest of microphones, taped and lashed together, their wires snaking into the crowd of reporters like so many reptiles. There were two ranks of cameras, high and low, and the TV reporters stood by, microphones in hand, for their own comments. The print journalists stood in clutches or sat on the grass, notebooks at the ready, and photographers were everywhere. Stone had never faced anything like this, and he wasn't looking forward to it. The buzz of voices turned to a shout as he and Allison approached.

"Good morning," he shouted over the crowd, taking a sheet of paper from his shirt pocket and waiting for the noise to subside. When they were quiet, he spoke. "My name is Stone Barrington; I am one of the legal team representing Mrs. Allison Manning in the case against her, about which I am sure you have all heard. I will be making a statement, and then I will take questions for thirty minutes. Then Mrs. Manning will make a brief statement and will answer no questions."

There was a roar of outrage from the assembled media.

Stone shouted them down. "I hope you can understand that Mrs. Manning is facing a serious charge in a strange country, and that by answering questions at this stage, she might inadvertently put herself in further jeopardy. I know that none of you would wish to contribute to her difficulties." He began to read his statement, covering events from the time of Allison's arrival in St. Marks, including the coroner's inquest and her questioning by Sir Winston Sutherland. He gave them a brief primer on the workings of the St. Marks criminal justice system, and they listened, rapt and astonished. Finally, he wrapped up his statement and asked for questions, glancing at his watch. "To preserve some sort of order, I will point to a questioner and answer his or her question only. Let's do this one at a time, people." He pointed at a woman television reporter.

"Mr. Barrington, do we understand you to say that in St. Marks, the judge selects the jury, and that the defense may not even question them or object to them?"

"Both the defense and the prosecution may ask the judge to address particular questions to a prospective juror, but the judge will ask the question only if he deems it relevant to the proceedings."

The questions continued, mostly about the legal system and his plans for mounting a defense. When thirty minutes had passed, Stone pulled Allison forward. "Now, ladies and gentlemen, Mrs. Allison Manning will make a statement, and at its end, this press conference will be over. She will take no questions after that, nor will I; I hope that's clearly understood." He turned to Allison and nodded.

Allison stepped forward to the microphones and, with a shy smile, began to speak. "Good morning," she said, and after those words there was complete silence among the reporters. "My name is Allison Manning; I am the widow of Paul Manning, the writer, with whom some of you may be familiar." She recounted their voyage across the Atlantic and their time in England, Spain, the Mediterranean, and the Canaries, then she began her account of their trip back across the Atlantic.

"Ten days out of the Canaries Paul hoisted me to the top of the mast to make a repair." She smiled. "He was too large for me to hoist him." This got a laugh from the crowd. "While I was at the top of the mast I saw Paul clutch his chest and collapse in the cockpit. It took me more than two hours to get myself back down the mast." She pointed at her yacht. "You can see how tall it is. When I was able to reach him, he was dead. Some hours later I managed to bury him at sea and then began trying to sail the yacht the rest of the way across the Atlantic. Somewhat to my own surprise, I was able to manage it. Then, to my astonishment, after I had saved my own life and reached St. Marks, I found myself charged with my husband's murder. Now I must place my faith in Stone Barrington and Sir Leslie Hewitt, who could not be here today, because he is working on my defense. I thank you all for coming here and hearing my story. I hope we will meet again in happier times." She stepped back from the microphones to a hail of shouted questions.

Stone quieted the group. "As I said earlier, Mrs. Manning will answer no questions. Now you may have thirty minutes to photograph her yacht, down at the marina." He pointed to the boat, and most of the crowd sprinted across the lawn. Another clutch of reporters tried to approach Allison and were pushed back by police officers.

Stone hustled Allison upstairs to his rented room. "We'll wait them out here, then go back to the yacht," he said. He walked to the window and looked out. The reporters were swarming over the dock, prevented from boarding the yacht by the police. Then his eye was caught by another sight in the parking lot. Sir Winston Sutherland was standing next to his chauffeured car, watching the reporters, an outraged expression on his face.

Thomas was standing next to Stone. "I predict an explosion," he said, grinning broadly.

21

Stone sat at the little table near the window and watched Sir Winston, who was speaking into a cellular phone. A few minutes later, a bright yellow school bus pulled into the parking lot, and the driver received some instructions from Sir Winston. Abruptly, the bus left the tarmac and started across the lawn toward the marina. When it stopped, a dozen police officers got down from the bus, one with a bullhorn.

"Ladies and gentlemen," the officer was saying, "a press conference by the Ministry of Justice will be held in ten minutes, and I have come to transport you there. Please board the bus immediately, as we are short of time."

Stone watched as the journalists crowded the entrance to the bus, ready to fight to get on, if necessary. Shortly the bus pulled away and, to Stone's surprise, took the road not toward the capital, but toward the airport. "What the hell?" he muttered.

There was a rap on the door and Thomas entered. Allison, who had been dozing on the bed, sat up on one elbow and looked at him.

"What's going on?" Stone asked.

"Half a dozen cops are going through my rented rooms, taking suitcases and clothes belonging to those reporters."

"Sir Winston wouldn't have the balls to arrest that many journalists, would he?"

"I can't see it happening," Thomas replied, "but he's taking them somewhere."

"Let's drive out to the airport," Stone said. "Allison, the coast is clear to the marina; you go back to the yacht and wait for me there." Allison nodded and put her feet over the edge of the bed, rubbing her eyes.

In Thomas's Toyota they drove quickly along the airport road and turned through the gates. In the distance they could see two DC-3s sitting on the apron; one of them already had her engines running. The group of reporters stood in a hangar listening to a young man in a business suit. There was much shouting and shaking of fists going on.

"We'd better not get too close to this," Thomas said, stopping the car. A truck loaded with luggage moved past them toward one of the DC-3s.

The reporters were now being herded onto the two airplanes by uniformed policemen; Stone noted that nobody was being beaten with the truncheons the policemen carried, but their body language told him that the cops were brooking no argument. The truck with the luggage pulled up and suitcases were thrown hurriedly into the luggage compartment of the airplanes.

"Where'd the other airplane come from?" Stone asked.

"It's a government plane, used only by high officials."

"Where do you think they're sending them?"

"I can only hope that they won't be flown out to sea, then chucked overboard," Thomas murmured. "Look, one camera crew and a couple of others are still in the hangar."

The two airplanes were taxiing now, and in a few minutes they were both taking off and heading to the northwest.

"Antigua, do you think?" Stone asked.

Thomas shook his head. "Antigua's due north; they're flying northwest. St. Thomas is my guess; that's the nearest U.S. airport; or maybe even to San Juan."

"That is the most high-handed thing I ever saw," Stone said, grinning. "Those people are going to go absolutely nuts when they get back to their respective news organizations."

"And that pleases you, I suppose."

"You bet your ass it does. If they were aroused by Allison's plight, then they're going to be mad as hell about their own treatment. The press never gets as angry as when their own freedom gets tampered with, and I'll bet half a dozen cameras got the whole thing on tape."

"You think this is going to soften up Sir Winston, then?" Thomas asked.

"When he finds out what they're saying about him in Miami and New York, it just might."

"Don't count on it. Sir Winston and our prime minister are accustomed to dealing with a more compliant press; I doubt if they give a damn about what foreigners think."

"Thomas," Stone said, "I hate to point this out, but this business is not going to be good for your business."

"I already thought of that," Thomas said glumly.

Back at the Shipwright's Arms, Federal Express had delivered two packages for Stone. One was from Bob Cantor and contained a copy of the *Publishers Weekly* profile of Paul Manning. The other package was from Alma, his secretary, and it contained two items: a brand-new black judge's robe and a brochure on the Parker Sportster inflatable dinghy. Stone sat down at a table and read the article on Paul Manning, which featured a photograph of the writer and Allison, arm in arm, in front of a large, handsome house. It was pretty standard stuff about a writer, his lifestyle, and his work, and there was nothing in particular that interested him in the piece. The boat brochure was more interesting.

He spread it out on the table and admired the many color photographs of the craft being rowed, being propelled by an outboard, and, most interesting, under sail. The Parker Sportster, it seemed, came with an aluminum mast, a mainsail, a jib, a rudder, and a centerboard. The brochure claimed it was the only inflatable dinghy so equipped. Stone thought the thing must be good for four or five knots, more if surfing with the wind aft.

Stone left the Shipwright's Arms and walked down to the marina. He stepped lightly aboard *Expansive*, tiptoed down the companionway ladder, and looked into the aft cabin. Allison was asleep on the large bed, her breathing deep and regular.

Stone climbed back into the cockpit and began quietly opening the cockpit lockers. There was the usual tangle of gear found aboard any yacht: fenders, warps, plastic buckets and deck brushes, life jackets, and in a special aft locker, an eight-man life raft. He opened another of the lockers and was greeted with the sight of an inflatable dinghy in its canvas bag; the manufacturer's name was printed boldly on the bag: AVON. Stone's heart began to beat a little faster, as much out of apprehension as discovery. There was one more locker, and he opened it expecting no new information. But there, lying packed and ready for use, was another, larger canvas bag emblazoned with another brand name: PARKER SPORTSTER. It seemed new and unused.

He closed the locker softly and sat down on a cockpit seat, feeling relieved.

22

On Saturday morning Stone fixed breakfast, then woke up Allison, who had been sleeping unusually well. "I've had a message from Leslie Hewitt," he said. "He wants us to come out and see him this morning."

"Okay," she said, rubbing her eyes. "I think a swim will wake me up." She started up the ladder.

"Hang on!" he commanded. "It's broad daylight, and there may be some press still on the island."

"Oh," she said, blinking.

"I enjoy you naked, but I don't want anyone else to," he said.

She smiled. "You're sweet. I think I'll just have a shower; join me?"

"Already had one," he replied, "and breakfast is nearly ready, so hurry."

They walked up to the Shipwright's Arms together, to borrow Thomas's car, and the first person they saw was Hilary Kramer from the *Times*.

"What are you still doing here?" Stone asked. "Didn't you get the bum's rush with everybody else?"

"Nope. I was in the capital, buying some necessities, and when I came back, everybody was gone."

"You missed the press conference, then?"

"I didn't care anything about that. I'd already filed."

"Did anybody else survive the press purge?"

"There's a crew from CNN here who got to stay to provide pool coverage for the TV people."

"How about Chris Wheaton, from *60 Minutes?*"

"Gone with the wind, along with everybody else."

"What sort of attention did your story get at the *Times?*"

"I don't know; I modemed it in, and I'll trust their judgment, but it's a good story. Where are you off to?"

"A visit with my co-counsel."

"Can I come?"

"Sorry, this is strictly business."

Kramer shrugged. "Well, I've got nothing to do but file my story on the ouster of the international press, then it's vacation until the trial on Monday, since Sir Winston won't see me."

"Lucky you; see you later."

They got the car keys and drove out along the coast road to Sir Leslie Hewitt's cottage. They found him weeding his back garden, and Stone was relieved to see that he recognized them. "Morning, Leslie," he said.

"Good morning to you, Stone, and to you, Mrs. Manning."

"Please call me Allison," she replied with a winning smile.

"I thought we might talk about how to proceed at the trial," Stone said.

"Of course we will," Hewitt said, "but I wonder if I could ask a small favor of you before we begin?"

"Of course."

"I'd like to give you some tea, but I'm out of milk. Would you be kind enough to run down to the grocer, about two miles along the coast road, and fetch me a bottle?"

"All right, Leslie," Stone said, and Hewitt insisted on giving him money.

As he turned to leave, Hewitt offered Allison his arm. "May I show you the garden, my dear?" he asked, smiling sweetly.

"I'd be very pleased to see it," she replied, taking his arm. "See you later, Stone."

Stone drove to the grocery with ill grace, annoyed at being dispatched on such an errand when they should have been discussing how to save Allison's life. He was struck by how completely lucid Hewitt was, as compared to their last meeting; the man apparently went in and out of his haze unpredictably. Stone bought the milk and drove back to the cottage, entering through the front door. He went to the kitchen to put the milk in the refrigerator and was surprised to find a full bottle there. *Well,* he thought, *when I'm his age I'll forget the milk, too.* He walked out the back door into the garden and saw Hewitt and Allison deep in conversation on a bench at the bottom of the garden. When they saw him coming, Hewitt had a few more words to say, patted her on the knee, then rose to receive Stone.

"Come into my study, and we'll begin," Hewitt said.

Stone fell in alongside Allison. "What were you two discussing so seriously?" he asked.

"Gardening," she replied.

"Now," Hewitt said, taking his usual seat at his desk and waving Stone and Allison to a sofa. "Here's how it will go on Monday: the judge will select a jury, which should take an hour or so, then the prosecution will make an opening statement, probably a very long and passionate one, if I know Winston Sutherland, and I have since he was a lad. The jury will be very impressed. Then I will make an opening statement, which will be equally passionate, but very much shorter, for which the jury will be grateful, I assure you. That should bring us to lunchtime.

"After lunch, Winston will present his case, which will almost certainly be confined to reading passages from Mr. Manning's journal, or outline for his novel, whichever way you would like to characterize it. I would be very surprised if he called any other witnesses."

Stone interrupted. "Isn't he required to submit his evidence and witnesses to the defense?"

"Oh, no," Hewitt replied. "Nothing of the sort. Then we will call your writer acquaintance, Mr. . . . ."

"Mr. Forrester, from *The New Yorker*," Stone said.

"Yes, quite. I should think it would be best if you, Stone, questioned him. I'm sure you already have a complete grasp of what we must get from him."

"Yes," Stone said. "I want to . . . ."

Hewitt held up a hand. "No need to go into that; I trust your judgment completely."

"Thank you very much," Stone said, "but shouldn't we go into this in more detail?"

"Completely unnecessary, I assure you," Hewitt replied with a big smile. "Then we will put Mrs. Manning on the stand, and I think you should question her as well," Hewitt said. "No need to go over that with me, but I should think that the two of you might go through it once or twice."

"You may be sure we will," Stone said. *Jesus,* he thought to himself, *is this the man's idea of preparation?*

"Then there will be cross-examination and redirect, but I urge you to keep redirect to an absolute minimum, since Lord Cornwall is impatient at such times. Then Winston will make his closing statement, which will be annoyingly like his opening one, then I will make our closing statement, which will move the jury very nearly to tears. Juries always love my closing statements. Then we will wait for the jury to make its decision."

"We have no idea, of course, how long that will take," Stone pointed out.

"Quite the contrary; I would be surprised if they took more than an hour, two at the most. The jury will, like most juries, have already made up their individual minds before the proceedings are finished. They will just need time to chat a bit to be sure they're all in agreement."

"That has not been my experience with juries," Stone said.

"Oh, I am sure that in your country there is extensive deliberation before the jury decides what it has already decided," Hewitt said, chuckling, "but in St. Marks, it is considered rude to keep anyone waiting, especially on so important a matter as Mrs. Manning's life."

"That will be very nice of them," Stone said dryly.

"Of course it will, and we will be spared the suspense."

"I hope we are spared a great deal more," Stone said.

"You may certainly hope," Hewitt said. He looked at a gold pocket watch that he produced from his Bermuda shorts. "Well, I see that time is getting on. We will meet at the court at ten o'clock on Monday morning and all do our very best." He rose and left the room without so much as a good-bye. Stone reflected that Hewitt had not offered them the promised tea, for which he had obtained the unnecessary milk.

Allison turned to Stone. "You know, sometimes I think he's not entirely all there."

Stone certainly could not disagree with her. "What did you two talk about while I was shopping for milk?"

"I told you," she said. "Gardening."

23

S tone was having lunch alone at the Shipwright's Arms when Thomas called him to the phone. "It's Bob Cantor," he said, moving the receiver down to the end of the bar, away from where Hilary Kramer was sitting.

"Hello, Bob," Stone said into the instrument. "You back from the Canaries?"

"I'm home again," Cantor replied, "and a little worse for the wear. The jet lag will kill you."

"I sympathize. You got something new from the Canaries?"

"Nothing at all. I have got something new from here, though."

"Shoot."

"You remember I told you I checked out Paul Manning's credit record?"

"I do, and he had a pretty good one, as I recall; paid everything on time."

"That's right, but I had that information only from a phone call from a friend at my bank. Now I have the printed report, and it shows a lot more."

"Like what?"

"Seems Mr. Manning was living right on the edge. He was pulling in a magnificent income, of course, probably something between a million and two million a year, and closer to two. But he was spending one hell of a lot of money, too."

"That's very interesting," Stone said.

"It gets more interesting. The credit report shows that he was pretty maxed out on all his credit cards and that he was borrowing heavily to make it from paycheck to paycheck."

"Writers don't get paychecks, do they? They get royalty checks."

"Okay, okay, he got paid in widely separated lumps, but they were big lumps. My point is, his credit record shows that he was borrowing heavily from three banks, usually a hundred thousand bucks at a time, then repaying it when his royalty or advance check came."

"Was he keeping up?"

"Just barely. I, ah, did a little unauthorized snooping last night."

"What do you mean?"

"I drove up to Greenwich, got into his house, and had a look through his financial records, which his secretary had neatly filed away."

"Bob, you should check with me before you do things like that."

"If I had checked with you, you wouldn't have let me do it."

"You're right about that. So what did you find out?"

"When he got a check he would pay off the three banks, and there would be only a few thousand left, not enough to get him to the next publisher's payment. Right before he set off on the transatlantic voyage, he got two checks at once from two contracts, and that squared him for a while. But he borrowed while he was away, and now the banks are lined up, waiting for the will to be probated."

"Well, I guess that's going to cut into Allison's insurance money."

"I wouldn't worry about that," Cantor came back. "Manning had twelve million bucks in life insurance."

"Twelve million bucks? Nobody has that much insurance."

"You'd be surprised how many people do. He was paying something like fifteen thousand bucks a month in premiums,

•

113

which is one of the reasons, along with his lifestyle, that he was having to go to the banks to get by. And get this, he also had mortgage life insurance to cover both the house and the boat loans. When Allison pays all the outstanding bills, she's going to have at least eleven million bucks in cash, tax free, plus the house, the boat, the cars—everything—free and clear. Her biggest expense is going to be property taxes, and she won't have those long, because she's already put the Greenwich property on the market. I told you I have a buddy up there in the property business."

"Have you seen the *New York Times* piece on Allison's plight down here?"

"Yep, and you can be sure that the insurance company has seen it, too."

"That means they won't pay unless she's acquitted."

"Wrong; they've already paid. They'd have to sue her to get it back, and they'll have a very hard time doing that."

"Why?"

"Because she's already transferred nearly the whole amount to an account in the Cayman Islands. I found the receipt for the wire transfer."

"Holy shit!" Stone breathed. "Either Allison has some very sharp advice from her lawyer and accountant, or I've underestimated her by a long shot. I've never even seen her so much as make a phone call from down here."

"Well, somebody is, shall we say, acting in her best interests."

"Somebody sure is, and it isn't me."

"Bottom line is, Mrs. Manning's husband could not have kicked off at a better time for her. If Manning had lived and had continued to live as he did, I reckon he wouldn't have been able to afford the life insurance premiums much longer."

"How long had he had the insurance?"

"A little over two years, and if the company had known he was going to sail, two-handed, across the Atlantic twice, he never would have gotten it. Insurance companies frown on that sort of sporting activity."

"I guess not. This information certainly puts a whole new complexion on things, doesn't it?"

"I would say so. I mean, if you were still a cop, you'd now

suspect Allison Manning of helping her husband overboard, wouldn't you?"

"That's one theory."

"The other theory which suggests itself has to do with the very special dinghy Paul Manning had air freighted to him in Las Palmas."

"Right. I got the brochure on the Parker Sportster today. It sails."

"Could it have sailed Manning back to the Canaries from where Allison says they were when he died?"

"Yes, but it wouldn't have had to; Manning could have left the yacht as soon as they were out of sight of land."

"Aha!"

"Except for one thing."

"What's that?"

"The Parker Sportster is still on the yacht."

"Could he have had another dinghy?"

"He did have, but it wasn't sailable, and anyway, that one is still on the yacht, too."

"So it looks as though Manning, when he left the yacht, was either dead or swimming."

"Looks that way."

"Could he have swum back?"

"I think we can discount that possibility; he might have been spotted near shore in the daytime and there are sharks out there; I don't think he would have tried it at night."

"Another boat might have spotted him sailing a dingy, too."

"Not if he sailed at night. That's what I would have done in his shoes, but of course, the point is moot, because the dinghy is still on the yacht."

"Well, pal, good luck with sorting this one out."

"I don't have to sort it out, thank God. All I have to do is think about getting Allison Manning acquitted. I'm not the cops."

"Good point. I'll call you if I find out anything new."

"Thanks, Bob. Take care." He hung up.

"I'm not the cops," Stone repeated to himself. "I'm her lawyer, and if she's guilty, she won't be the first guilty client I've represented." Still, he wanted her to be innocent.

24

Stone hung up the phone and returned to his lunch. He wasn't the cops, granted, but he was still bothered by what he was hearing about Paul Manning's affairs. He was about finished with lunch when Jim Forrester pulled up a chair.

"Mind if I join you?" the *New Yorker* reporter asked, settling his lanky frame and waving to Thomas for a drink.

"Not at all. I wondered what had happened to you; I was afraid my star witness had gotten shipped out with the other reporters."

Forrester shook his head. "Nope. I ducked into the men's room when I saw the cops, and they missed me. My luggage went, though; I've been shopping for the necessities."

"Good; can we talk about your testimony?"

"Sure."

"I don't see any need to rehearse, but I do want to be reassured that you're willing to testify that, on the occasion you met them, they were happy together, affectionate, and glad to be in each other's company."

"No problem with that."

"I think we'll skip the argument they had about their routing later in the evening; it doesn't seem germane."

"I think you're right; I've been married, so I know how those little spats can arise over nothing."

"Yeah," Stone replied, as if he knew what the reporter was talking about. It occurred to him that he and Arrington had never had that sort of spat in their time together. He hadn't heard from her since she had arrived in L.A., and he wondered how she was.

"Let's see," Stone said, "you first met Paul Manning in the bar at the yacht club in Las Palmas?"

"Well, no; I had met him earlier, much earlier."

"You didn't mention that," Stone said.

"Well, it was a long time ago. I went to Syracuse University, and Paul went to Cornell at the same time. The towns are not far apart, and we had an interfraternity basketball league. I played against Paul two or three times. I just knew him to speak to, though; at the time, I don't think we ever had a conversation that didn't involve who fouled who."

"I guess we can use that; it gives you some sort of history with Paul, however slim. What were your impressions of him in those days?"

"Pretty much the same as in Las Palmas: cheerful, outgoing, good company."

"Not the sort who might commit suicide?"

"No, absolutely not. In Las Palmas he was enthusiastic about getting back across the Atlantic; said he had an idea for a new novel based on their trip, and he was anxious to get started on it."

"That we can use," Stone said. "He apparently kept some notes in a leather-bound book; did he mention that at all?"

"He said he had made a lot of notes; he didn't say anything about a leather-bound book."

"That will be helpful, nevertheless. Sir Winston is taking Paul's notes as complaints about Allison; it's the most damning evidence he has."

"Look, I don't want to get you into some sort of ethical quandary here, but if you want me to mention the leather-bound book, I'll be glad to do it. It's not as though the other side is playing anything like what we would call fair."

●
117

"I think it's best to play this straight," Stone said. "The difference in the effect of your testimony would be small, and anytime you start deviating from the straight and narrow, you open yourself up to getting caught lying. I wouldn't want to end up with a perjury charge against you."

"Neither would I," Forrester said. "God knows what the penalty for perjury is on this island."

"Can you think of anything else during your evening with the Mannings that might help us at the trial?"

Forrester looked uncomfortable. "Can we talk off the record for a minute?"

"Sure."

"I certainly don't want to bring this up at the trial, but it's the kind of thing that I can't ignore when I come to write my piece."

"Shoot."

"You remember we talked about this dinghy that Paul had flown in from Barcelona?"

"Yes, the Parker Sportster."

"I didn't mention this before, but that dinghy can be sailed. I read something in a magazine about somebody sailing one from Norway to Iceland."

"I'm aware of the dinghy's sailing capability."

"Does that suggest anything to you?"

"What does it suggest to you?"

"That Paul Manning could have conceivably sailed the thing back to the Canaries and faked his own death, for whatever reason."

"That occurred to me, but it's not possible."

"Why not?"

"Because the Parker Sportster is still in a cockpit locker of *Expansive*. I found it there, unused."

Forrester took a deep breath and let it out. "Boy, am I glad to hear that. I didn't want to think that Allison could be mixed up in something like that, but . . ."

"I understand. While we certainly won't bring this up at the trial, I think it might be very helpful to Allison if you mentioned it in your piece. There will always be people who would think the worst, and it might help her."

"I'll certainly do that. It's the kind of detail that will make the piece more interesting. By the way, I talked with my editor, Charles McGrath, and in light of all the publicity Allison's story has gotten, they're more interested than ever in the piece."

"I'm glad for you."

"You should be glad for Allison, too; this kind of long, detailed piece will satisfy the curiosity of a lot of people. I know it's going to be tough for her when all this is over."

"I know it is, though I haven't talked about it with her yet. I think she's got enough on her mind at the moment."

"I'm sure she has."

"Have you talked with her at length yet?"

"Twice. She's remarkably open and forthcoming; sometimes I think she doesn't really have a grasp of what she's facing."

"I know what you mean," Stone said, "and I don't see how it would help to make her more aware. She's been told all the facts and the risks, and if she chooses to be in denial, then who's to say she shouldn't be? Certainly not I. If her attitude helps her get through this, that's fine with me."

"Let me ask you something for the record, Stone, and I'd appreciate the frankest answer you can give me. Your answer won't appear until well after the trial, and I'll hold it in confidence until then."

"What would you like to know?"

"Right now, at this moment, what do you estimate her chances are of getting out of this?"

Stone sighed. "I don't really know how to answer that. There are so many variables here, most of which I have no control over, that the situation is entirely unpredictable."

"Do you think there's really a chance she could hang?"

"Yes, I do."

"No kidding, really?"

"Really."

"Jesus Christ."

"Yes."

"It just doesn't seem possible that this sort of thing could happen in this day and age. I mean, if she'd fetched up in the United States, she'd be walking around scot free, wouldn't she?"

"I believe she would. I don't think a prosecutor could get past a preliminary hearing in the United States. I'd blow him out of the water. With Paul's medical records, his note-taking habits, your testimony, and above all, with Allison's testimony, I don't think any judge would buy a murder charge for a minute. I sometimes wonder what would have happened if she'd fetched up in Antigua or Guadeloupe."

"I wonder, too."

The two men sat silently, each contemplating the worst for Allison Manning.

25

Stone sat talking with Jim Forrester. As they chatted he saw a taxi pull up outside and a woman get out. She seemed middle-aged, was tall and fashionably thin, and was wearing a wrinkled silk dress and a straw sun hat. The driver got two suitcases out of the trunk, took some money from her, and drove away. Thomas Hardy saw her, too, and went out to help with her bags.

"Well," Jim Forrester said, "I'm going upstairs for a nap." He got to his feet. "I think I might be coming down with something." He ambled off toward the stairs.

Stone watched as Thomas set the woman's bags down by the bar and reached for the registration book. The woman signed it, then seemed to be asking Thomas some questions. Thomas's eyebrows suddenly went up, and he beckoned to Stone.

Stone got up and walked across the restaurant toward the bar, getting a closer look at the woman as he walked. She was, at the very least, in her early forties, he reckoned, and she had on more makeup than suited her.

"Stone," Thomas said. "This is someone you might want to meet."

The woman turned toward him. "Are you Stone Barrington?" she asked.

"Yes, I am," Stone replied.

She held out her hand. "I'm Allison Manning," she said.

"How do you do," Stone said. Then the name sank in. "Who did you say . . ."

"I'm Paul Manning's widow," the woman said, "and I'm not very well, if the truth be told. However, I expect to be a lot better quite soon."

Thomas went upstairs with the bags, leaving Stone alone with the woman.

"I suppose you're with the press," Stone said wearily.

"I'm not with anybody," the woman replied. "I used to be with Paul Manning, but I understand he's dead. Can you confirm that?"

"Yes, I can," Stone replied. "Why don't we sit down?" he indicated his table. "You seem to have been traveling; would you like a drink?"

"Oh, God, yes," she breathed and headed toward a chair. "A very dry Gibson would be lovely."

Thomas came back down the stairs, and Stone ordered her drink. When they were settled at a table, Stone said, "I'm afraid you have me at something of a loss, Miss . . ."

"Mrs.," she said. "Mrs. Manning. And yes, I suppose you are at something of a loss. You're representing her, aren't you?"

"I'm representing Allison Manning," he said. "Why don't you tell me what's going on here?"

"What's going on, Mr. Barrington, is that I've come to claim my husband's estate."

"You're speaking of Paul Manning, the writer?"

"I am."

"And you claim to have been married to him?"

The woman opened a large purse, extracted an envelope, and handed it to Stone. "I believe this will answer your question," she said.

Stone opened the envelope and took out a single sheet of paper. It was a photocopy of a marriage certificate stating that Paul Manning and Elizabeth Allison Franklin had been married in Dade County, Florida, some fourteen years before.

"And you are Elizabeth Allison Manning?"

"Call me Libby; everyone does."

"May I see some sort of identification, please?"

She opened her bag again and handed over an American passport.

Stone examined it, and it confirmed her identity. He handed it back. "Thank you," he said. "And when were you and Paul Manning divorced?" he asked.

"Never," she replied. "Paul and I were never divorced; we were married until the day he died."

"I see," Stone said. He didn't see at all. "And what brings you to St. Marks?"

"I read of Paul's death in the papers," she replied. "I told you, I've come to claim his estate."

"And how do you propose to do that?" Stone asked.

She opened her bag again and produced another document. "This is a copy of Paul's will," she said, "leaving everything to me."

Stone looked it over. It was short and to the point and dated the day after the date on the marriage certificate. He handed it back to her. "Mrs. Manning," he said, "I'm afraid you've come a long way for nothing."

"Oh? How's that?"

"Paul Manning's estate is being handled in Connecticut, and there is another, more recent will leaving everything to another, more recent Mrs. Manning."

"Oh, I know all about her," the woman said. "Paul was never married to her, not really, no matter what he told anybody. I am the only woman he was ever married to."

"Can you give me a little background on all this?" Stone asked, trying not to sound plaintive, though he was feeling very plaintive indeed.

"Of course. Paul and I met when we were both working for the *Miami Herald*, some fifteen years ago. We fell in love, were married, and . . ."

"And lived happily ever after?"

She smiled sourly. "Not exactly. He ran out on me some years later."

"How many years later?"

•

"Four years later, four and a bit. But we never bothered to get a divorce. Paul continued to support me, though. He sent a check every month."

"And when was the last time you saw Paul?"

"When he left. After that, I dealt with his lawyer, in Miami."

"Do you still live in Miami, Mrs. Manning?"

"Libby; please call me Libby; everyone does."

"Libby, do you still live in Miami?"

"No, I live in Palm Beach. Well, near Palm Beach."

"And you never remarried?"

"Never."

"What sort of work do you do, Libby?"

"I write a society column for a local paper in Palm Beach. Doesn't pay very much, really, but it gets me to all the parties."

"So you live on the monthly check from Paul?"

"That's right. Only it didn't arrive this month, and when I saw the papers, I knew why. I called the lawyer in Miami, but he said he had received nothing from Paul's office this month. So I figured I'd better get down here and take charge of things."

"I see."

"You're a lawyer, right?"

"Yes, in New York."

"Well, I guess I'm going to need a lawyer. You want to handle this for me?"

"I'm afraid I'm otherwise engaged," Stone said.

"Then I'll just have to find somebody else, I guess."

"Mrs. Manning ... ah, Libby, I'm afraid that getting a lawyer in St. Marks won't help you in dealing with Paul's estate. As I said, that is being handled in Connecticut, in Greenwich."

She stared at him blankly. "You want me to go to Connecticut?" she demanded.

"It's not a matter of what I want, and I don't want you to think that I'm giving you legal advice, which I'm not, but it seems logical that the solution to your problem, if there is a solution, is not in St. Marks." He wanted desperately for her to be anywhere else in the world but St. Marks.

"Well, shit," she said disgustedly.

"I take your point."

She stood up. "Right now," she said, "I'm going to get into a hot bath, and after I've had some dinner and a good night's sleep I think I might just get a second opinion on what you've told me."

Stone stood up. "If there's anything else I can do . . ."

"I thought the gist of what you told me was that there's nothing you can do," she said.

"That's pretty much it," he admitted, trying desperately to think of something to say to her that might make her go back to Palm Beach.

"Well, tomorrow's another day, and then I guess I'll see what I can find out about this murder trial. Who's the DA?"

"It's being handled by the, ah, local government," he replied.

"Right. I guess I can talk to them. See you around, Stone." She picked up her purse and headed for the stairs.

Stone went straight to the bar, picked up the phone, and dialed Bob Cantor's number.

"Problems?" Thomas asked, ambling over.

"You wouldn't believe me if I told you," Stone replied. He got Cantor's answering machine. "Bob," he said, "you mentioned earlier that Paul Manning had been divorced in Florida. Do whatever you have to do to find a copy of the decree and fax it to me at the earliest possible moment, please. I've got another Allison Manning on my hands." He hung up.

"Another Allison Manning," Thomas repeated, chuckling to himself.

"Thomas, please do whatever you can to keep that woman from ever hearing the name of Sir Winston Sutherland," Stone said.

Thomas laughed aloud. "Right!"

26

Stone marched over to the marina, jumped aboard *Expansive*, and went below. The saloon was empty. He went aft to the owner's cabin, and found Allison sound asleep. "Wake up," he said, patting her on the shoulder.

Allison opened her eyes slowly. "Oh, hello," she said, reaching for him.

Stone took her hands in his. "Not now, Allison; we have to talk."

"Talk? What about?"

"Come into the saloon." He handed her a robe and went ahead of her.

She came in, tossing her hair and rubbing her eyes. "What is going on?" she asked.

"Tell me about Paul's first marriage," he said.

"What?"

"Paul was married before he married you; tell me everything he told you about that."

She took a bottle of mineral water from the fridge, uncapped it, took a long swallow, and settled onto the sofa beside him. "He was married, that's all. It didn't work out."

"When did he get married?"

"When he was a lot younger, in the early eighties, I think."

"How long was he married?"

"Three or four years. What's this all about?"

"Do you know exactly when he was divorced?"

"No, not exactly."

"Have you ever seen a copy of his divorce decree?"

"No."

"Not even when you went to get your marriage license?"

"I don't think so."

"Normally, if you've been married before, you have to produce a divorce decree in order to get a license. Where were you married?"

"In New York, at the courthouse, by a judge."

"You went with Paul to get the license?"

"Yes, but I don't remember anything about a divorce decree."

"Swell."

"Stone, if you don't tell me what this is about . . ."

"The first Mrs. Manning has just checked into the Shipwright's Arms."

Allison's face fell. "Libby?"

"Yes."

"That bitch!" Allison hissed. "What the hell is she doing here?"

"She says she's come to claim Paul's estate."

"Hah! That's a laugh! She's not getting a penny."

"Allison, let me see Paul's will."

"She's not in it."

"I want to see the will. It's in Paul's briefcase, isn't it?"

"How would you know that?"

"I'm just guessing. Is it in the briefcase?"

"Yes."

"You'd better let me see it right now."

"Oh, all right." She got up, went into the aft cabin, and came back a couple of minutes later with a document. "Here," she said ill-humoredly, handing it to him.

Stone read through it quickly. There were a number of small bequests to organizations—the Author's Guild Fund and PEN—and to two clubs to which Manning had belonged, and the rest was left to Allison. No mention of his first wife.

"See?" Allison said. "I told you he left her nothing."

"Did you know he had been sending her monthly checks?"

"Yes."

"How much?"

"Three thousand dollars a month."

"Alimony?"

"I suppose."

"Was it dictated by a divorce decree?"

"I don't know; Paul called it alimony, though."

"It's not a lot of money for someone in Paul's income bracket."

"Paul didn't make any real money until after they were divorced; he was just a newspaper reporter."

"Let's see, if they were divorced ten years ago—do you know if there was any time limit on the payments?"

"No, I don't. Is this really going to be a problem?"

"Maybe; it depends on the decree, if there is one."

"What do you mean, if there is one? There must be one, somewhere."

"I've got somebody looking into that now. Do you know where they were divorced?"

"In Miami, I guess; that's where Paul lived at the time. Stone, what's the worst this could mean?"

"Well, the absolute worst, legally, would be if they were never divorced. In that case, she might have some sort of rights as the wife in either Florida or Connecticut—I'm not familiar with the domestic or estate laws in either. On the other hand, if they were legally divorced and we can get hold of the decree, it shouldn't be much of a problem. Let's say the judge gave her three thousand a month for life, or until she marries; then she'd be entitled to claim that much from the estate. Or he might have put a time limit on it. It doesn't seem likely that the payments were pegged to his income, since he was paying her only three thousand a month; they would have gone up as he became more successful. Did Paul seem to feel any great obligation to her?"

"Not really. He never complained about writing the checks, though."

"He didn't leave her any money, either."

"Right," Allison said, brightening. "How can she make any claim at all?"

"She can easily enough, if she has a court order, and that's what a decree is. But she's claiming they were never divorced, and if that's true, there wouldn't be a decree."

"Stone, this doesn't sound like the greatest problem in the world. Just tell her to call my lawyer in Greenwich, and if she doesn't like that, then tell her to go fuck herself."

Stone shook his head. "We can't do that."

"Why not?"

"Because she's here, don't you understand?"

"So what?"

"She's a completely unknown quantity. Worst case, suppose Sir Winston gets his hands on her and charms or frightens her? Suppose she turns up at your trial and testifies that Paul told her that he was afraid you were going to murder him?"

"That's ridiculous."

"I did say it's the worst case; people will do strange things when there's a lot of money at stake. The thing is, I don't want her hanging over our heads. She's a loose cannon, and she could turn out to be very dangerous."

Now Allison had grown quiet. "So what do we do?" she asked finally.

"I think we have to get her off the island as quickly as possible."

"Maybe one of Thomas's many brothers could kidnap her or something."

He looked at her sharply. "Don't even joke about that."

She held up her hands. "Sorry. So how do we get her off the island?"

"How much money have you got in your Greenwich bank account?"

"Well, I'm not sure, exactly."

"Allison, this is no time to fuck around. How much?"

"A little over a million dollars."

"In your checking account?"

"Well, it's an interest-bearing account."

"Oh, great."

"Are you suggesting I should pay her a million dollars?"

"No, but you're going to have to let me negotiate something with her."

"How much of a something?"

"Whatever it takes, if we want to get rid of her in a hurry, and we certainly do."

"Do you think we could get rid of her for half a million dollars?"

"I think a reasonable person would accept that, but I have no idea how reasonable she is."

"If she wants more than that I'll shoot her myself," Allison said.

"Goddammit, I told you not to talk like that!" he practically shouted.

"All right, all right, just deal with her. I'll trust you to handle it as you see fit."

"God, I wish I had that decree," Stone said.

"But you don't; just do the best you can."

"Give me your checkbook," Stone said.

She found her handbag, dug out the checkbook, and handed it to Stone.

He ripped out a check. "Sign it," he said.

"A blank check? Are you nuts?"

"Sign it."

Allison signed the check.

Stone ripped it out and tucked it into a pocket. "Now find two blank pieces of paper, and sign them."

She went to the chart table, found some paper, signed two sheets, and handed them over. "You see how I trust you," she said.

"I'll be back as soon as I can," he said, and left the yacht.

27

S tone strode toward the Shipwright's Arms. Dusk was falling, and the first customers were arriving for dinner. He looked around, saw no sign of the other Mrs. Manning, then went to the bar. "Give me a rum and tonic, Thomas," he said.

Thomas complied. "Seems like you got something of a mess on your hands," he said.

"Tell me about it. Will you ring Mrs. Manning's room, please?"

"She left orders not to be disturbed."

"Disturb her."

"Stone," Thomas said gently, "if you're going to handle this lady, don't you think you'd better do it gently?"

Stone took a deep breath and exhaled. "You're right," he said. "I'll wait for the lady to make her appearance for dinner." He picked up his drink. "I'm going upstairs for a few minutes; if she shows up tell her I'd like it if she'd join me for dinner."

"I'll tell her."

Stone went up to his room, switched on his computer, and began to type. When he had finished he printed out the document on the blank page over Allison's signature, slipped it into an envelope, and started to leave. Then he stopped, picked up the phone, and dialed Bob Cantor's number again, and once more got his answering machine. He swore and slammed down the phone, then composed himself and went downstairs.

Libby Manning was sitting at the bar, sipping a martini; he wondered if she were a drunk. If so, he'd better get moving. "Good evening," he said to her, managing a smile.

"Good evening," she said. "I accept your invitation to dinner."

"I'm glad," he replied. "Thomas, may we have a table?"

"Right this way," Thomas said, picking up a pair of menus.

"Something quiet," Stone whispered as he passed.

Thomas showed them to a corner table with a view of the harbor, then he brought Libby Manning another martini and Stone a rum and tonic.

She raised her glass. "Better days," she said, smiling.

"I'll drink to that," Stone said, sipping his drink. "So, Libby, tell me something about yourself. Are you a Florida girl?"

"Born and bred," she said. "Went to Dade County High and the University of Miami, majored in journalism, went to work for the *Herald*. How about you?"

"Born and bred in New York, NYU law school, a time with the NYPD, then retirement and the practice of law."

"What kind of law?"

"Whatever comes along."

"I thought most lawyers specialized these days."

"Most do. Whatever my clients need done, I specialize in."

"And how did the lovely Allison come to hire you?"

"Well, when she sailed in alone on that boat, I was the only game in town, I guess."

"Were the papers right? Is she going to hang?"

"Not if I can help it."

"Can you help it?"

"That remains to be seen."

"The trial is next week?"

"That's right."

"And if they hang her, it'll be pretty quick, will it?"

"Libby, you are a pessimist." Or maybe an optimist, he thought to himself. "Let's order." They chatted idly until their food came, and ate mostly in silence. She was waiting for him to make the first move, he reckoned. Then, as they ate, another couple was shown to a table a few yards away. Stone looked up and gulped.

Libby leaned forward. "Who is that extraordinary-looking black fella?" she asked.

"His name is Sir Winston Sutherland," Stone replied, keeping his voice down, "and he is the worst nightmare of any white woman traveling alone in this country."

Her eyes widened. "How do you mean?"

"His greatest pleasure seems to be finding innocent American girls, charging them with capital crimes, and hanging them without much of a trial. Allison is his most recent victim."

"He's the one who's prosecuting her?"

Stone nodded. "Take my advice, Libby; avoid him at all costs, and whatever you do, don't let him find out who you are."

Libby downed the rest of her martini and started on the wine. "Why should I be afraid of him?"

"Well, another rich American widow might be a tempting target."

"Rich? Me?"

"Well, Paul was fairly rich, wasn't he? Sir Winston knows all about that."

"Jesus, Paul was only sending me ten thousand dollars a month."

"Three thousand," Stone said, sipping his wine.

"Well, I'm sure he must have provided for me in his will."

Stone took the document from his envelope and handed it to her. "I think you'd better read his will."

She dug some glasses out of her handbag and read quickly. "That shit," she said under her breath. "That utter and complete shit. I'll get a lawyer and sue his estate."

"On what grounds?" Stone asked.

"Oh, a lawyer will come up with something."

"Libby, the kind of lawyer who would take your case would bleed you dry before the court even ruled, and then you'd get nothing."

"I'd still get my alimony," she said.

"Maybe. I won't know that until I see your divorce decree. A copy is being faxed to me from Miami tomorrow morning."

She blinked rapidly, but said nothing.

"Libby, if you should sue the estate, it will upset Allison very badly, and right now, she holds the purse strings. She'll stop paying your alimony until a court rules otherwise, and that could take a long time. Are you prepared to get by on the salary from your newspaper column in Palm Beach until it all gets sorted out? It could take years."

"Oh, I'll get by all right; don't you worry," she said, smiling, but she was still blinking rapidly.

"Let me make a suggestion," Stone said.

"Go right ahead."

"Suppose Allison gave you, say, ten years of alimony, all at once. That would be three hundred and sixty thousand dollars in your bank account, right now."

"Right now?"

"The minute the check clears."

Libby stared at him for a moment, then shook her head. "No, sir; I want a million dollars."

"Allison has authorized me to offer you four hundred thousand dollars," Stone said, "and not a cent more." He took the check out of his pocket, filled in her name and the amount, and handed it to her.

Libby put on her glasses again and looked at the check. "Yeah," she said, "and as soon as I'm out of here she'll stop payment."

"No, she won't do that," Stone replied, handing her the document he had written a few minutes before.

She began reading.

"You see, it says that if she stops payment, you can sue her. And four hundred thousand dollars, wisely invested, should give you an annual income that represents a substantial raise over what you're getting now. And you'd always have that nest egg to fall back on." He took the document, filled in the amount, and handed it to her. "Allison's signature is already at the bottom, and her signature is on the check."

She looked up at him, obviously tempted.

"If you demand more, Allison will fight you, and she's the one with all the money. All you have to do is sign both copies of that document, have Thomas witness it, then go upstairs, get a good night's sleep, and take the first plane back to Miami tomorrow morning. The reservation has already been made."

Still, she hesitated.

"The money can be in your bank account within three business days, if you ask your bank to rush it."

"Suppose Allison gets hanged next week? What then?"

"The money's still yours. But if she hangs and you sue her estate, then you'll have to fight Allison's heirs, and they're going to care even less about you than she does. At least she's trying to do the right thing, even though she doesn't have to."

Libby Manning stood up and walked over to the bar, clutching the documents, with Stone right behind her. "Thomas," she said, "will you witness my signature, please?"

"Of course," Thomas said, watching her sign the documents, then signing them himself.

She handed Stone his copy and tucked her copy and the check into her handbag. "What time is the first flight out tomorrow morning?" she asked him.

"Chester flies at eight o'clock sharp. Would you like me to drive you to the airport?"

"Thank you, yes," she said. She held out her hand to Stone and shook his. "Thank you for your assistance, Mr. Barrington," she said, then she turned and marched upstairs.

Thomas looked at Stone. "I take it the matter is settled?"

"It is. Call Chester and get her on that plane, no matter who he has to throw off."

"Right."

"And kill her telephone; I don't want her talking to anybody tonight. Oh, and send her a bottle of good champagne on me; I want her to sleep well."

Thomas smiled broadly. "Right."

Stone walked toward the door. As he did, Sir Winston Sutherland smiled at him and raised a hand. Stone smiled broadly and returned his salute. Then he glanced out of the restaurant toward the marina and saw something he did not wish to see. Allison was walking fast across the lawn toward the inn, her arms pumping, and she had an angry and determined look on her face. Stone, without actually running, went to head her off.

He met her thirty yards from the inn and grabbed her arm, spinning her around. He tucked her arm in his and started steering her back toward the marina.

"Let go of me!" she erupted, struggling to free her arm.

"Shut up, Allison, and keep walking toward the boat," he said through clenched teeth.

She continued to struggle. "I'm not giving that bitch a thin dime!" she hissed. "Let go of my arm!"

"Allison, you and I cannot have a wrestling match on the lawn; Sir Winston Sutherland is up there having dinner with his wife. Don't make a scene!"

That stopped the struggle, but did nothing for Allison's temper. "I'll kill her!" she hissed.

"Shut up! That's all we need is for somebody to hear you say that. It would make very interesting testimony at your trial!" He stopped walking. "Now, I want you to go back to the yacht and calm yourself. I'll be there in a few minutes, and I'll explain everything to you."

"Oh, all right," she said and stalked off toward the marina.

Stone watched to see that she went all the way, then he walked back to the bar and ordered another drink. He wanted to be sure that Sir Winston left the restaurant without running into Libby Manning.

CHAPTER

28

Stone smelled cooking as he boarded *Expansive.* He found Allison below, with lamb chops on the stove. "Smells good," he said.

"Want some?" she asked. Her fit of temper seemed to be over.

"No, thanks. I had something to eat with the former Mrs. Manning." He poured himself a glass of wine from an open bottle on the saloon table.

"So how did it go?" Allison asked, looking anxious.

"If I tell you, do you promise not to go up there and kill her?"

"I promise; I'm sorry about the way I behaved. I just got to thinking about the avaricious bitch, and it got the better of me."

"She accepted your offer."

Allison groaned. "And how much did I offer?"

"Four hundred thousand."

"Jesus. Did she sign something?"

Stone handed her the document and watched as she read it. "Don't worry, it's ironclad."

Allison threw her arms around him. "And you saved me a hundred thousand dollars!"

"That's one way of looking at it," Stone said.

"Well, I had expected to pay half a million."

"Then I saved you a hundred thousand dollars." He sat down at the table and sipped his wine. "Funny, I feel bad about it, for some reason."

"You sure you don't want a lamb chop?"

"I'm happy with my wine."

She sat down across from him and dug into her dinner. "Why would you feel bad?"

"I felt sorry for her, I guess."

"I don't; why should you?"

"Well, she's been struggling along for the ten years since her divorce on not a hell of a lot of money from Paul, plus whatever she got for writing some column for some local paper in Palm Beach, and that's not the cheapest place in the world to live. She said the column didn't pay much, but it got her to all the parties. I just have this vision of her growing old in Palm Beach with nothing."

"She's got four hundred thousand dollars," Allison said, savaging a lamb chop. "I don't call that nothing."

"You're right; I guess she's better off than she was before she came down here. I hope she doesn't blow it all on high living."

"If she does, it would serve her right, taking all that money from a poor widow."

"A very rich widow."

"Not very rich."

He felt unaccountably exasperated with her. "Come on, Allison, you're fixed for life—not like poor Libby."

"And how do you know I'm fixed for life?" she said, pausing in her attack on the chop.

"I have my sources," Stone said.

She cocked her head and looked at him with mock suspicion. "Stone Barrington, have you been checking up on me?"

"Checking up on people is a big part of my work," he said.

"And just what did you find out?"

"That you're who you say you are, and Paul was who you say he was, and you're very rich, that's all. You could easily afford the four hundred grand."

"I hope you didn't find out anything bad about me," she said, resuming her dinner.

"No, I didn't. Is there something bad about you I should know?"

"Only in my own mind, I guess."

"You been thinking bad thoughts about yourself?"

"Well, I seduced you, when I knew perfectly well that you had a girl."

"I wouldn't feel too badly about that; I knew what I was doing. I was mad at Arrington for not showing up down here and even madder at her for running off to California."

"With Vance Calder."

"Yeah, with Vance Calder. I have to admit, that didn't sit too well."

"So I just got lucky and caught you in a weak moment?"

"There wasn't all that much luck involved," Stone said ruefully. "I have a lot of weak moments."

"You mean you weren't faithful to Arrington, even before you met me?"

"Oh, yes, I was faithful to her, but not out of trying to be; we were just together all the time, and I was content, and I didn't give much thought to other women."

"Were you living together?"

"Yes."

"I sometimes wish I'd lived with somebody before Paul. Maybe I would have had a better idea of what it was like to be married." She was uncharacteristically quiet as she took her dishes to the galley.

"Is something else bothering you?" he asked.

"I guess I've been feeling a little guilty about how much fun we've been having. The sex, I mean; that's the only fun I've had lately. I mean, Paul's only been dead for a short time, and I confess, I've already been looking forward to a new kind of life." She smiled at him. "In addition to inordinately enjoying your body." She sat down beside him and held his hand.

"And I yours," he said, smiling. "And I don't think you have anything to feel guilty about. What happened at sea wasn't your fault; you did the best you could in the circumstances. You go right ahead and look forward to that new life." *If you have one,* he thought. *If I can somehow pull off an acquittal.*

"Are you going to be in this new life of mine?" she asked.

"That remains to be seen," he said. "I do have some unresolved issues to take care of."

"When they're resolved, I'd like to know about it."

"I think I can promise you that. But you're going to be a very popular lady, you know. Men are going to come out of the woodwork. They'll all want your money; you'll have to be careful."

"I will be. You want to go to bed?"

"If you don't mind, I think I'll sleep on my boat tonight."

"Going off me?" she asked, pouting.

"Not in the least." He kissed her lightly. "I'm awfully tired, though; the negotiation with Libby seems to have taken a lot out of me, and I ought to write to Arrington. She probably thinks I'm sulking."

"Okay, you do that; I'll see you in the morning."

He got up. "By the way, you should fax the Libby document to your lawyer and have him let your banker know that check is coming through. It's a very large amount, and it will make him nervous if he's not expecting it. And whatever you do, don't have second thoughts and stop payment. All hell would break loose."

"I'll write him a note and take it over to Thomas tonight," she said.

He kissed her again, and left her yacht for his own.

He wrote Arrington what was, for him, a long letter; the longest he had ever written anybody—two pages. He apologized for being incommunicative and told her about Allison's case, though he knew she would have seen the papers. Then he got romantic—unusual for him—and by the time he had signed the letter, he began worrying about faxing something so personal to her L.A. hotel; he didn't want some clerk reading it. Then he had a better idea. He would take care of it in the morning.

Some time after he had fallen asleep he stirred, hearing footsteps on the dock; Allison returning from the inn, he guessed. Then he fell asleep again and heard nothing else.

29

When Stone woke it was seven-thirty, and he jumped out of bed and into some clothes; he didn't want to miss Libby's departure, still harboring a lingering fear that she might not, after all, leave. He grabbed the letter to Arrington and ran toward the inn, zipping up his trousers. He arrived at the bar in time to see Thomas disappear around a corner, going toward the parking lot with some suitcases. "Thomas," he called, "where do you keep the Federal Express packaging?"

"Under the bar," Thomas called back. "See you later; I've got to get Mrs. Manning to the airport. We're running late."

"Just give me a minute to address . . ." But Thomas was gone. Stone grabbed a FedEx envelope and ran after him. Thomas was pulling out of the parking lot when he flagged down the car and jumped in the backseat. "Morning, Libby," he said. "I'll come to the airport with you, if you don't mind."

"Sure, why not?" she said. She was wearing the straw hat in which she had arrived.

"Thomas, have you got a pen?"

Thomas handed one back to him.

"Libby, I'd appreciate it if, when you get to Miami, you'd drop this into the nearest Federal Express bin for me. I want it to be in California tomorrow."

"Sure, glad to," she replied.

"Nothing you can fax?" Thomas asked.

"No, I want it delivered." He sealed the letter into the envelope and handed it to Libby, who put it into her large handbag. "You're sure this is no trouble?"

"Of course not; it's like mailing a letter—they have those bins all over the airport."

"I appreciate it," Stone said.

"Do you always drive this fast?" Libby asked Thomas, fastening her seat belt.

"No, but we're running late, and I don't want Chester to leave you behind. He has to keep to a schedule."

"We were half an hour late arriving in St. Marks," she said. "Chester owes me. Besides, if you hadn't been delivering breakfast to somebody or other, we wouldn't be late. I was on time."

"I didn't know you offered room service, Thomas," Stone said.

"I took Jim Forrester up some food; took him his dinner last night, too, but he couldn't keep it down."

"He's sick?"

"As a dog. I tried to get him to let me call the doctor, but he said he'd be all right. He did look a little better this morning, but not much."

"He said something yesterday about not feeling well."

"At least he cleaned up after himself," Thomas said. "The maids hate it when folks get sick all over the place."

"Is there a bug going around?"

"He ate some conch from one of those street vendors in the capital yesterday. Don't you ever do that, Stone, not unless I point out the good ones."

"I promise."

They raced into the airport and across the tarmac, where Chester was waiting next to his airplane with the baggage compartment standing open. There was one other passenger, a black woman, already aboard. Thomas hustled Libby's bags into the airplane and locked the compartment, then shook hands with Libby.

"You come back when you can stay longer," he said.

Stone shook her hand, too. "You find yourself a good broker and invest that money conservatively," he said to her. Her answer

•

142

was drowned out by an engine starting. He helped her into the airplane, got her seat belt fastened, and closed the rear door.

Libby held up the Federal Express envelope and gave him a thumbs up, then she stuck it back into her handbag. The airplane began to move, and Stone stepped out of its way.

Thomas turned toward the car. "Let's go," he said; "I want to get back to work."

"Hang on just a minute, will you, Thomas?" Stone replied, watching the airplane. "I just want to be absolutely sure she's really gone."

Thomas laughed. "Glad to have her off the island, huh?"

"I can't tell you how glad." He pointed at the airplane. "Look, Chester must really be in a hurry; he's not even doing his runup check." The little twin was already rolling down the runway.

The two men stood and watched as Chester roared off the runway and got the landing gear up. The airplane turned north toward Antigua, visible in the distance across the channel separating the two islands. The early morning sun glinted on the water.

"There goes a happy woman," Stone said, waving. "Goodbye, Libby!" He turned toward the car. As he did, he noticed a change in the sound of the engines, and he looked back at the airplane. "What was that?" he asked.

Thomas looked at the airplane, now out over the water. "He's just reducing power after takeoff. It's only a few minutes' flight, and he has to start slowing down if he wants to make Antigua on the first pass." Thomas frowned. "What's that?" he asked, pointing. Smoke was trailing from the airplane's left engine.

"Looks like Chester's got a problem," Stone said. "He must have already shut down the engine."

"I see flames," Thomas said.

Stone shielded his eyes from the morning sun. "So do I," he said. The airplane began a rapid descent toward the water.

"Why doesn't he return here?" Thomas asked.

"He's trying to blow out the fire," Stone said. "When I was training for my license, that's what I was taught to do with an engine fire, a power-on descent, to blow it out." The airplane seemed to be headed straight down into the sea, and then it leveled off. "The fire isn't out," Stone said. "He's going to ditch in the water."

"Jesus help him," Thomas said.

"If the engine doesn't blow and he can get the airplane down, they've got a good chance." He looked at the wind sock; it was standing straight out. "There's going to be a chop on the surface, though. Put her into the wind, Chester."

The airplane was flying level, just off the surface of the water now.

"Why doesn't he put her down?" Thomas asked. "He's still flying."

"He's bleeding off air speed; he'd built up a lot on the descent. He wants to touch down right at stall speed, as slowly as it will still fly. Look, he's raising the nose now; he'll be down in a second."

"I hope he's got a raft," Thomas said. "It's going to take a while to get to him."

"Surely he has; he'd have to. Here comes touchdown; don't stall the thing, Chester!"

The nose came up some more and the airplane headed toward landing. Then a wing dropped, touched the water, and the airplane cartwheeled, breaking into pieces.

"Oh, shit," Stone said, watching as the wreckage scattered over the water.

"Come on," Thomas called, running for the car. "I know a man with a boat."

Stone jumped into the car and Thomas, driving like a madman, headed out of the airport and along the coast road. "There's a little fishing settlement along the coast, right near where Chester went down," he said.

"Thomas," Stone said, "nobody on that airplane is alive; don't kill us in the bargain."

Thomas slowed a little. "Somebody might have made it," he said.

"They might have if he'd gotten the thing down in one piece," Stone said quietly. "But when it broke up, that ended it. Anybody alive would be unconscious, and anybody unconscious would have drowned by now."

"Still," Thomas said. He threw the car into a left turn and careened down a short dirt road, screeching to a stop at a small dock. A man was already taking in the lines on a fishing boat. "Henry!" Thomas yelled, "wait for me!" He and Stone jumped onto the moving boat. "You saw the plane?" Thomas asked the skipper.

"Everybody saw the plane," Henry replied. "We're goin', but cain't be nobody alive out there. How many folks was on it?"

"Three, including Chester."

"Chester gone," Henry said. "They all gone."

Twenty minutes later they saw the first piece of wreckage— a wing tip, floating on the surface; then smaller bits of flotsam.

"Look," Thomas said, pointing to some woven straw in the water. "That's Libby's hat, I think."

"There somebody is," Henry called out, pointing and changing course. "Peter, get the boathook!" His crewman got the tool and ran forward as Henry slowed the boat. "It's Chester," Thomas said.

"He's missing an arm," Stone said quietly.

It took fifteen minutes in the swells to get a line around the body, and Stone was feeling a little queasy from the motion. He had seen enough bodies as a cop to be unruffled by the sight of Chester. The body aboard and covered, they patrolled the area for another two hours, but, except for the floating wing tip, which they brought aboard, found nothing larger than Libby's hat. A police boat joined them.

"I reckon we go in now," Henry said.

"How deep is the water out here?" Stone asked.

"Deep. We outside the hundred-fathom line." He pointed to their position on his chart.

"How much of a search will there be?" Stone asked.

"You're looking at it, I expect," Thomas replied. "I reckon the two women must still be in the fuselage, but there's no National Transportation Safety Board to go after the wreckage and the bodies, not down here in the islands. They're gone." They headed back toward the dock with their grisly cargo.

Stone thought about Libby Manning and her newfound wealth, which she would never spend.

30

Stone poured himself some orange juice and sat down at a table. After a moment, Hilary Kramer from the *New York Times* came downstairs.

"Morning, Stone," she said. "May I join you?"

"Please do," Stone replied.

Thomas came over with menus. "What can I get you folks?" he asked quietly.

Kramer ordered bacon and eggs. "I'm hungry this morning," she said.

"Stone, you want something?" Thomas asked.

"Just toast and coffee; I'm not very hungry."

"You're looking kind of grim, Stone," Kramer said. "Something else go wrong with your case?"

Stone shook his head. "Plane crash this morning. Thomas and I saw it."

Kramer dipped into her handbag and came up with a notebook. At that moment, Jim Forrester joined them, looking not very well.

"Morning, Stone, Hilary," he said.

"Morning, Jim," Stone said. "You want some breakfast?"

Forrester shook his head. "Thomas was kind enough to bring me something in my room this morning."

"Oh, yes," Stone said. "He said you were ill; you're looking better."

"Guess I got it out of my system," the journalist said. "Hilary, take my advice; stay away from the street vendors in the capital, especially the ones selling conch. For a while there, I thought I was going to die."

"Apparently someone did, only this morning," Kramer said. "Stone was just about to tell me about it."

"Yeah," Stone said. "Chester's plane went down; two passengers aboard; everybody died."

"Jesus," Forrester said. "In that plane we all came over in?"

"That's the one."

"It looked in pretty good shape," Forrester said.

"Thomas and I watched them take off," Stone replied. "Chester didn't do a runup before he leapt off."

"What's a runup?" Forrester asked.

"With piston engines, you rev up to a couple of thousand rpms, then test the magnetos and the propeller and look for low oil pressure or other problems. It's the last thing you do before takeoff, and it's a very important check."

"Any idea what happened?" Kramer asked.

"Engine fire; we saw the flames. He dived to try and blow out the fire, and when he couldn't he ditched in the water, but he stalled and cartwheeled. We saw the airplane come apart. We went out in a boat and found Chester's body, but the two women apparently went down with the fuselage."

"Who were the two women?" Kramer asked, scribbling in shorthand.

"One was a local lady; don't know her name; the other was Elizabeth Manning of Palm Beach. She stayed here last night."

"The lady in the straw hat?" Forrester asked.

"That's the one."

"Any relation to Allison Manning?" Kramer asked.

"Not really; she was Paul Manning's ex-wife."

"What was she doing here?"

"I think she had some idea of claiming part of Manning's estate," Stone said. "But that's all being handled in Connecticut, so she went home."

"Did she have some legitimate claim?" Kramer asked.

"Not that I'm aware of," Stone said. He was skating close to a line here, but he hadn't quite crossed it.

"Palm Beach, you said?"

"That's right."

"What did she do there?"

"She said she wrote a society column for one of the local papers."

"That's all you know about her?"

"That's it," Stone said.

"Is there going to be some sort of investigation of the accident?" Kramer asked.

"Beats me," Stone said, "but the airplane went down in water deeper than a hundred fathoms, so I doubt if they could find much of it, even with a load of experts, which they don't seem to have around here."

"That's over six hundred feet," Forrester said. "No diver could go that deep; they'd need some sort of submersible, I think."

"Something the St. Marks Navy, if there is one, probably doesn't have," Kramer chipped in. "Do you know if she had any family?"

"She didn't say, but I got the impression she was unmarried. Her passport was still in the name of Manning, and they had probably been divorced for a good ten years."

"How long had Manning been married to Allison when he died?"

"Four years."

"Did the two women know each other?"

"They never met."

"You think the other Mrs. Manning just came down here in the hope of money, then?"

"Seems that way, but please don't quote me as having said so."

"Is somebody notifying next of kin?"

"I suppose the local police will handle that."

"Stone," Forrester said, "do you think she might have been some sort of help to you at Allison's trial?"

Stone shook his head. "I can't imagine how. I don't think she had seen Paul since the divorce."

"Did Sir Winston Sutherland know she was here?" Kramer asked.

Stone shrugged. "I don't think so. He was here for dinner last night; she was sitting with me, and they didn't speak."

"I take it you didn't introduce them," Kramer said dryly.

"I'm not the social director around here," Stone said with a straight face.

Kramer laughed. "Can't say I blame you."

"I suppose it will make an interesting footnote to my piece," Forrester said.

"I haven't seen you taking any notes," Kramer observed.

"I have a very good memory," Forrester said. Then he frowned, placed a hand on his belly, and stood up quickly. "Uh-oh," he said, then ran for the stairs.

"I guess he wasn't feeling as well as he thought," Kramer said.

"I guess not," Stone agreed.

"Stone, you've answered all of my questions, but why do I have the feeling there's something you haven't told me?"

"About what?"

"About this Elizabeth Manning?"

"I never saw the woman before yesterday; never heard of her, either."

"Did she demand money from Allison?"

Not until after her lawyer had made her an offer, Stone reflected. "No," he replied.

"Was she headed for Connecticut to pursue something with the estate?"

"Not to my knowledge," he said.

"If she had, would she have had a claim?"

"There's no mention of her in Paul Manning's will."

Kramer closed her notebook. "Well, I'll phone this in after breakfast."

They ate their food in silence, then Thomas waved some papers at Stone, and he went to the bar.

"Fax for you," Thomas said.

Stone took a stool and read through Libby Manning's divorce decree, then he laughed out loud.

"What?" Thomas asked.

"Nothing," Stone replied. "By the way, did Libby Manning make any phone calls last night?"

"Nope; no calls on her bill. Anyway, you told me to unplug her phone."

"Right." Stone was looking at Libby's divorce decree, at the instructions for alimony. "Plaintiff shall pay to the defendant the sum of three thousand dollars a month on the first day of every month," he read, "beginning immediately and continuing for a period of ten years." He checked the date on the decree. Libby Manning's alimony had run out three weeks earlier. She must have been desperate, he thought, but she had been cool enough to shake down Allison for four hundred thousand dollars, with his help.

He walked away shaking his head.

31

As Stone walked back toward the marina he could not stop thinking about Libby Manning. He was depressed, and he felt guilty, though he could not think why. Certainly a human being was dead, one he had known; but not one he had known well or had come to care about. So why couldn't he shake the feeling? He boarded *Expansive* and went below. Allison was putting something away in a cupboard.

"Libby Manning is dead," he said.

"Come again? I don't think I heard you right."

"Libby is dead. Chester crashed shortly after takeoff this morning, and Libby and a local woman were killed, along with Chester."

She stood, staring at him for a long moment. "Dead," she repeated tonelessly. "No chance she might still be alive?"

"The airplane went down in at least six hundred feet of water. Chester's body was recovered, but nobody else."

Allison sank onto a sofa, looking as if the wind had been knocked out of her. "How could this have happened?" she asked.

"There was an engine fire, but nobody knows why, and my guess is that nobody is going to know. In order to figure out what made an airplane crash, you need the airplane, or at least a lot of it, and a wing tip was all that was recovered."

"Some sort of mechanical problem, then?"

"Apparently."

"What could cause such a problem?"

"A fuel leak, maybe. I have no idea what sort of rules a pilot like Chester would operate under on this island, but my guess is he was pretty much on his own. He'd have had the manufacturer's service requirements to go by, but I doubt if there was anybody looking over his shoulder." He looked at her. "Are you feeling all right?"

"I'm fine," she said, but she didn't sound it. "I'm just shocked, I guess. Three people dead."

Stone sat down beside her. "It is pretty depressing," he agreed.

"Maybe I shouldn't be depressed," Allison said. "After all, her death saves me four hundred thousand dollars."

"Maybe," he replied.

"Maybe? Why maybe? Didn't our agreement and my check go down with her?"

"I suppose so."

"Then why maybe?"

"Strictly speaking, that money was hers, and her heirs are entitled to it."

"Heirs? Libby had heirs?"

"I've no idea, but let's say, for example, she had a sister, and she left a will leaving everything to her. She'd be entitled to the four hundred thousand. Even if Libby died intestate, that is, without a will, her next of kin would be in line for it."

"But there's nothing. The check and the agreement went with her."

"Suppose she called this putative sister last night and said, 'Guess what? I just got four hundred grand, and I'm going to give you some.' And she told her sister where and how she got it. Suppose she mailed a copy of the agreement, or the agreement itself, to the sister. Then the sister would come after you, because she'd have evidence of an agreement to pay, but no payment."

"But you don't know if there is a sister."

"No, and Libby didn't make any phone calls last night, according to Thomas, who would have a record of it if she had. She didn't mail anything this morning either, as far as I know."

"So I'm safe."

"If you want to be."

"What do you mean by that?"

"I mean, the proper thing to do would be to search out Libby's executor, if she has one, and pay him the money. Then he could distribute it to any heirs or family she may have had."

"And suppose she didn't have any heirs or family?"

"Then it would go to the state of Florida, which is where she resided."

"So you're suggesting I should give the state of Florida four hundred thousand dollars in Libby's memory? So they could, maybe, put a statue of her in front of the state capitol?"

"No, but I could have a search for heirs or family done. Then, at least, you'd know."

"I don't want to know," Allison said. "I think that in the circumstances, that's a ridiculous idea."

"If it will help, I'll add to the circumstances," he said, handing her a document. "That's Libby and Paul's divorce decree. The judge gave her ten years of alimony, and the ten years expired earlier this month."

Allison read the paragraph. "So she was bluffing?"

"Looks that way."

"She had no claim to the estate whatever, and she had the gall to come down here and extort four hundred thousand dollars out of me?"

"She didn't extort anything; she responded to an offer, an offer I made her, with your permission, because of circumstances she knew nothing about."

"So you're saying she just got lucky; that she happened to be at the right time and at the right place to come into four hundred thousand dollars of my money."

"I think that's accurate. And while you're at it, you might remember that it was I who advised you to pay her off."

"Stone, I understand why you gave me that advice and, in the circumstances, I think it was the right advice. I'm not angry with you, I promise."

"I'm glad you understand all that," Stone replied, "because I think I gave you the right advice, too."

"And now you're advising me to search out Libby's relatives and give them the money."

"I'm not really giving you advice now; I'm just pointing out to you the legal and ethical burdens of your situation."

"But if I just forget about Libby and the agreement and the check, and if I tell you, my lawyer, to forget about it, then . . ."

"Then you can keep your four hundred thousand dollars, and the ethical requirements of the attorney-client relationship would prevent me from disclosing any of this to Libby's heirs."

"Did you tell anyone else in the world about that agreement?"

"No. Thomas witnessed it, though."

"Did he read it?"

"No. If someone subpoenaed him and questioned him in court, he could testify that he witnessed a document, but he could not say what it contained."

"Then from a legal point of view, my position is airtight, isn't it?"

"I'll put it this way: if someone, a relative, an heir, a lawyer, turned up here or in Greenwich and tried to press a claim against you or the estate, he would have no grounds on which to proceed. No grounds that I'm aware of, anyway."

"So I have no legal obligation to Libby's heirs?"

"Yes, you do have such an obligation, but it is unknown to anyone outside the attorney-client relationship, and if it were known it would very probably be unenforceable, unless someone had a copy of the agreement. You also have a moral obligation, but whether or not you meet it would depend on the condition of your morals."

"So you're advising me to pay the money to her heirs, if they exist."

"As your attorney, I am required to make you aware of your obligations under the agreement that you signed."

"But you can't make me meet those obligations."

"No, I can't. Probably no one can."

"The condition of my morals," she said, thinking about that. "What about the condition of your morals?"

Stone blinked. "What?"

"You've got a woman back in New York, or in L.A., or wherever the hell she is, and you're supposed to be in love with her, but you come down to the islands and jump the first widow you lay eyes on, right?" She didn't wait for him to answer. "And

you're a lawyer who's fucking his client, not that I'm complain-
ing. Is there some canon of legal ethics that covers that?"

Stone felt his ears getting hot. "Not the first part of your
contention," he said, aware that he was sounding legalistic and
officious, but unable to help himself, "but as to the second part,
as far as I'm concerned, there is no ethical requirement for me
not to fuck you, unless my fucking you would somehow react
to the detriment of your legal position."

She burst out laughing.

"I don't think that's particularly funny," he said, knowing
how ridiculous he must have sounded.

"Oh, yes, it is!" she shrieked. "It's the funniest thing I ever
heard in my life." She began to get herself under control again.
"It's also very sweet," she said, wiping the tears from her cheeks,
"and I love you for it." She moved closer to him and placed a hand
on his face. "I know now, if I didn't before, that I have the most
legally and ethically proper attorney in the world." She kissed
him. "And you just cannot imagine how that turns me on."

She continued to kiss him, then she showed him how turned
on she was.

Later, when Allison was asleep, Stone walked back to the
Shipwright's Arms and called Bob Cantor.

"Hello."

"It's Stone. Thanks for the divorce decree."

"No problem."

"I'd like to dig up some more information on Elizabeth
Allison Manning. It's probably going to be best to find a reliable
PI in Palm Beach and let him spend a day on it."

"Okay; what, specifically, do you want to know?"

"Next of kin, other relatives."

"Has Ms. Manning clutched her chest and turned blue?"

"Worse. Plane crash, this morning."

"I see."

"Don't break the news to anybody you find; we'll let the
official channels do that."

"Gotcha."

Stone hung up, walked back to the marina, undressed, and
crawled into bed with Allison, who was glad to see him.

CHAPTER

32

Stone sat in his rented room over the Shipwright's Arms, staring at the screen of his computer, trying to write an opening statement for Allison's trial, even though he knew that Leslie Hewitt intended to open himself. He felt that he had to be ready with something if Leslie should suddenly veer off into one of his lapses. He had nearly finished a draft when there was a knock on the door.

"Stone," Thomas's voice called from the hallway.

"Come in, Thomas."

Thomas opened the door. "There're two policemen downstairs wanting you; they wouldn't tell me what it was about, but they took my guest registration forms for the past week."

Stone saved his document and shut down the computer. "Let's see what they want," he said. He followed Thomas downstairs to the open-air bar where two starched and pressed black officers waited. "I'm Stone Barrington, gentlemen," he said. "What can I do for you?"

The taller of the two nodded at an elderly Jaguar in the parking lot. "You must come with us, Mr. Barrington," he said.

"Where are we going?" Stone asked.

"In the car, please."

"Am I under arrest?"

"Get in the car," the man repeated.

Thomas spoke quietly. "Do it; I'll find out where they take you."

Stone walked toward the car without another word. The shorter officer held the rear door open for him, closed it after him, and got into the driver's seat; his tall companion sat up front, too. The car pulled out of the lot and headed inland, toward the capital.

"Where are we going?" Stone asked.

"Government House," the tall officer said. "You in a lot of trouble, man."

Stone remembered that the jail was in the basement of Government House. "What kind of trouble?"

"You see pretty quick," the man said.

The remainder of the journey passed in silence. Stone wracked his brain for some notion of what they could be arresting him for, but the only motivation he could come up with was that he was representing Allison Manning. Perhaps in St. Marks that was enough.

Eventually, the car entered the little city and drove to its center, passing the front door of Government House and going to the side, to the jail door. Stone got out of the car and, with an officer on each side of him, walked to the door. The booking desk was dead ahead. He wondered what, if anything, Thomas could do about this.

"This way," the tall officer said.

Stone turned to his left and found the officer holding open a door that led to a flight of stairs. He followed the man up two stories, with the short officer bringing up the rear. They emerged into a long, broad hallway, cooled by a row of ceiling fans and open to the air at each end, a tribute to the British desire to remain cool in hot places. The building seemed deserted. They marched to the opposite end of the hall, through a set of double doors, and into a waiting room.

"Wait here," the tall officer said, then went through another door.

Stone looked around him. It was a large room, furnished with well-worn leather furniture, and on the wall was a large portrait of the prime minister, a benevolent-looking man who, Stone guessed, had been in his mid-seventies when he had sat for the portrait. He wondered how long ago that was.

The inner door opened, and the tall officer braced just inside. "This way," he commanded.

Stone walked into a large office, and the officer stepped outside and closed the door behind him. Stone was quite alone in the room. A huge desk dominated the office; a single visitor's chair sat before the desk. In a corner were a round conference table and eight chairs, and the walls were decorated with oils and watercolors, island scenes of a high quality. From somewhere came the muffled sound of a flushing toilet, then, a moment later, a door opened and Sir Winston Sutherland emerged, rubbing his hands briskly with a towel. He was dressed in white linen trousers and a rather loud short-sleeved sport shirt. He discarded the towel and strode toward Stone.

"Ah, Mr. Barrington," he said, extending a huge hand. "How good of you to come."

Stone shook the hand. "It wasn't good of me at all," he said. "I didn't have a choice."

"Oh, I hope the two officers were not officious," Sir Winston said, sounding genuinely concerned.

"Am I under arrest?"

Sir Winston looked shocked. "Of course not, my dear fellow, of course not. This is merely a pretrial meeting between opposing counsel." He walked to a set of French doors and opened them wide, revealing a large balcony that stretched across the rear of the building. "Please come outside, and let's have some lunch."

Stone followed the big man onto the balcony and found a table set quite elegantly for two. A uniformed waiter stood at a loose parade rest to one side.

"Let me get you some refreshment," Sir Winston said, waving a hand at a bar.

"Nothing for me," Stone said.

Sir Winston snapped his fingers, bringing the waiter to stiff attention. "Mr. Barrington and I will have some champagne." He turned to Stone. "Surely I can tempt you with a glass?"

"Oh, all right," Stone said. "Just a glass."

Sir Winston indicated a chair at the table, and Stone took it. A moment later, the waiter was pouring Veuve Clicquot into two crystal flutes.

"Your health," Stone said, sipping the wine. It was perfectly chilled. He looked out at the vista, which was over the better part of the town, with green hills beyond and the sea shining in the distance. "Lovely," he said.

Sir Winston sat down opposite him. "Yes, we are fortunate on our island," he said. "God has given us great beauty on all sides."

Perhaps not on the side of town harboring the slums, Stone thought. "Oh, yes," he said. The champagne was absolutely perfect.

"Bad crash—Chester's airplane," Stone said.

"Yes, a terrible thing," Sir Winston said, not sounding too sad. "I suppose we'll have to find someone else to start a ferry service to Antigua."

"I suppose," Stone said. "Have the police found any reason for the crash?"

"They're looking into it," Sir Winston said. "I trust you are enjoying your stay with us?"

"I would be enjoying it a great deal more if my original plan of cruising could have been implemented," Stone said.

"Ah, yes, and perhaps the company of the young lady who was to have joined you."

"Quite," Stone replied, beginning to feel slightly British, or at least colonial, in the surroundings.

"I understand she was detained in New York by the unfortunate weather," Sir Winston said sympathetically.

"That is correct," Stone replied, "and then she had to go to Los Angeles on business."

"Leaving you alone to deal with Mrs. Manning's problems."

"As it turned out."

"Tell me, did you know Mrs. Manning prior to coming here?"

"No."

"Or her late husband?"

"No. I'd heard of him, though; he was quite a well-known author."

"Did she seek you out while at sea, then?"

"She didn't seek me out at all," Stone replied, sipping more champagne. "I had scheduled my cruise some weeks before the Mannings set sail from the Canaries. And I didn't know them."

"No professional connection? No mutual friends who might have referred you to Mrs. Manning?"

"None. I was just sitting on my chartered boat when she sailed in. At that time there was still some hope of my companion joining me."

"And how did you happen to appear at the coroner's inquest?"

"I had nothing else to do," Stone said. "It was the only entertainment available."

Sir Winston smiled broadly. "Entertainment, eh? I like that: a coroner's inquest as entertainment."

"Tell me, Sir Winston, how did you happen to attend the inquest? Wasn't it perhaps overkill for the minister of justice to participate in such an event?"

"We are a small island, Mr. Barrington," Sir Winston replied smoothly. "But enough of this chat," he said, taking a slip of paper from his pocket and unfolding it. "Tell me—who, exactly, is, or perhaps I should say was, Elizabeth Allison Manning?"

Stone took a long swallow of his champagne. *Oh, shit,* he thought.

CHAPTER

33

Sir Winston stared across the table at Stone, waiting for an answer. Stone thought fast, but there was not much he could do in the way of obfuscation. Sir Winston had seen him at dinner with Libby Manning and had, no doubt, noticed the passing of documents between them. He decided to follow Mark Twain's advice: when in doubt, tell the truth.

"Elizabeth Manning was the first wife of Paul Manning," Stone said.

Sir Winston's eyebrows went up. "Ahhhh," he breathed. "Not a sister or a cousin, but an ex-wife?"

"Yes."

"Tell me, Mr. Barrington, how many ex-wives did Paul Manning have?"

"Just the one, to my knowledge."

"And what brought the first Mrs. Manning to our beautiful island?"

"Your beautiful island, I expect; and, perhaps, some curiosity about the death of Paul Manning. She'd read about it in the American papers, you see, and she wondered if she could be of any assistance."

"Ah, yes," Sir Winston said, an edge in his voice. "It seems a great many people read about Mr. Manning's death in the

American papers. I have heard from a number of them, including Senators Dodd and Lieberman of Connecticut."

"Yes, I believe Mr. Manning was a very substantial contributor to the Democratic Party," he lied, "and a personal friend of the President and Mrs. Clinton." The champagne was taking effect now, and he had trouble keeping a straight face.

"Indeed?"

"Yes, I've heard that the president is an avid reader of Mr. Manning's books." He stopped himself from adding that Paul Manning was also an investor in the Whitewater real estate venture and a financial advisor to the First Lady.

Sir Winston cleared his throat loudly. "To return to the first Mrs. Manning, what business did you and she discuss during her visit?"

Stone wondered if, somehow, Libby's copy of the agreement had been found. "Sir Winston," he said, "I am sure you understand that I am bound by the confidentiality strictures of the attorney-client relationship, but I think it would not be untoward for me to tell you that Elizabeth Manning, who was not a wealthy woman, had some notion of participating in her former husband's estate. He had been paying alimony to her during the past ten years, a requirement of their divorce decree which had recently expired."

"And did she participate in Mr. Manning's estate?"

"Elizabeth Manning was disappointed to learn that she had not been mentioned in Mr. Manning's will, and, the requirement for alimony having expired, she was entitled to nothing further."

"So why were you and Mrs. Manning exchanging documents at dinner the other evening?"

"I can tell you only that the second Mrs. Manning, being of a kind nature, felt moved to improve the reduced circumstances of the first Mrs. Manning."

"Improve to what extent?"

"I'm afraid that client confidentiality prevents me from saying more."

Sir Winston stared at him for a long moment, then nodded at the waiter, who disappeared and came back with two platters of lobster salad. Sir Winston ate his lobster, sipped his champagne, and stared out to sea.

Stone ate his lunch, too, grateful for the opportunity to collect his thoughts. Clearly, Sir Winston had believed that he might turn the presence, or perhaps even the death, of Elizabeth Manning to his advantage in court. Stone was happy to disappoint him.

Sir Winston finished his lobster and sat back in his chair. "What else do you know of Elizabeth Manning?" he asked. "There is the matter of notification of next of kin, you see, and lacking her passport or other documents, we are somewhat at a loss as to how to proceed."

"I know that Elizabeth Manning made her home in Palm Beach, Florida . . ."

"But you said that she was not a wealthy woman," Sir Winston interrupted. "I should think that living in Palm Beach would be a very expensive matter. I have visited that city, you see."

Stone shrugged. "Every American city, even the wealthiest, has neighborhoods that house those who are employed by the wealthy. I do not have Mrs. Manning's address, but I am sure that she must have lived in such a neighborhood. She told me that she was employed by a small newspaper to write a column about Palm Beach society. It gave her a sort of entree to social events, but I imagine that her nose was very much pressed against the shop window of that society."

"Mmmm," Sir Winston mused.

"I should think her address would be on her hotel registration card," Stone said, "and that the nearest American consulate could be of assistance in tracing her next of kin."

"Of course," Sir Winston replied. "That is all being taken care of."

"If I can be of any further assistance in making inquiries, let me know."

"No, no; that won't be necessary."

Coffee and petit fours appeared on the table, and both men helped themselves.

"Tell me, Stone, if I may call you that?"

"Please do."

He smiled broadly. "And you may call me Winston, of course. Tell me, just what is in all this for you?"

"In all what?"

"The trial, your, ah, services to the second Mrs. Manning."

"We have not discussed a fee, Winston," Stone replied. He had no doubt of what Sir Winston meant by "services."

Sir Winston allowed himself a small smile. "But, I take it, you have accepted a retainer of sorts?"

"I'm afraid I don't know what you mean," said Stone, putting on his best poker face.

"I'm reliably informed that the second Mrs. Manning has taken you into her . . . confidence."

"I am her attorney; she would be foolish not to take me into her confidence."

Sir Winston smiled again. "While I do not wish to be indelicate, reports have reached me that you have been seen entering and leaving Mrs. Manning's very beautiful yacht at, shall we say, odd hours."

Stone tried to appear confused. "I'm sorry, I don't know what this has to do with my representing Mrs. Manning."

"Then I will be blunt," Sir Winston said, clearly out of patience, "I believe that you have been providing services to Mrs. Manning which are above and beyond those which might be construed as legal."

Stone, cornered, decided to tack. "Winston, where did you attend law school, if I might ask?"

Sir Winston pulled himself up to his considerable full height. "I read law at Oxford," he said.

"At Oxford University, in the town of the same name, in England?" Stone asked, sounding surprised.

"The very same."

"Then, with such an illustrious legal background, perhaps you could provide me with some precedent for a prosecutor— let alone a minister of justice—indulging in such conjecture with a defense attorney."

"Sir," Sir Winston said, leaning forward, "you are fucking the lady, aren't you?"

•

164

"Is that why I was brought here?" Stone demanded. "To indulge your prurient curiosity?" He stood up. "Sir," he said, "neither my sex life nor hers is your proper concern. Rather, you should be concerned with this extremely strange prosecution of an innocent and bereaved woman for a crime which she could never have committed." He threw down his napkin and left, in the highest dudgeon he could manage.

"You listen to me, Barrington!" Sir Winston called after him, following him through the large office and the reception room into the hallway. "When this trial is over—and maybe even before—you are going to come to a reckoning with me!" His voice echoed down the long hallway.

Stone kept his eyes straight ahead, down the hall and the stairs into the street, expecting to be arrested at any moment. He flagged a cab and dove into it. Not until he was a block away did he allow himself to look back to see if he was being pursued.

CHAPTER

34

Stone directed the taxi out to the coast road and Sir Leslie Hewitt's house, then asked the driver to wait for him, hoping that Hewitt might have some explanation for the meeting he had just attended. He knocked at the open door and called out, but no one answered. He walked through the little house to the rear garden and there found Leslie Hewitt at lunch with Allison Manning. He stopped and stared at both of them; this seemed even weirder than his own lunch with Sir Winston.

"Ah, Stone," Hewitt called out, waving him over. "Come and join us, have some lunch."

Stone sat down. "Thank you, Leslie, but I've already had lunch. What's going on?" he asked Allison as much as Hewitt.

"I thought I might discuss some of the finer points of the case with my . . . excuse me, our client."

"It's very kind of you to include me in the possessive pronoun, Leslie, but may I remind you . . ." He stopped himself. "Allison, do you think I could have a few minutes alone with Leslie?"

"Of course," she said, standing up. "I was just going to the little girls' room, anyway."

"How did you get here?" he asked.

"I took a taxi."

"I've got one waiting; we'll be leaving in just a minute."

"I'm not sure I'm ready to leave," she said.

"I said, we're leaving," he said, trying to hold his temper.

She turned and, without another word, walked into the house.

"Leslie," Stone said, "what is Allison doing here?"

"I invited her to lunch," Hewitt said. "Is there something wrong with that?"

"Leslie, may I remind you that I am Allison's attorney, and you are a consultant on the case, hired to help me with the local judiciary at the trial. You are not the lead attorney, and I must ask you not to have meetings with my client from which I am excluded."

"Of course I'm the lead attorney," Hewitt said. "You vouched that to the court yourself."

"Only because local law requires a local attorney," Stone said. "I am still making the decisions in this case."

Hewitt shrugged. "As you wish," he said blandly.

"Thank you. By the way, I have just come from a command lunch with Sir Winston Sutherland."

"Oh, you must have lunched very well indeed," Hewitt said. "Winston always lays on a good spread with the taxpayers' money." He looked at Stone. "What did he want?"

"I was hoping you, with your knowledge of the locals, could tell me. We ended up shouting at each other."

"Stone, I must tell you that in St. Marks, we place the highest possible value on civility among members of the bar. You should not have shouted at Winston."

"I'm sorry, but he shouted first . . . sort of."

"Winston is not a man to be dallied with," Hewitt said.

"I didn't dally with him."

"He could be a very dangerous man to insult. I hope you did not insult him."

"I tried not to, but he really began to get up my nose."

"I sincerely hope he does not decide to retaliate," Hewitt said sadly. "It could be the end of Allison."

"Oh, Jesus, Leslie, don't tell me that," Stone moaned.

"Tell you what?" Hewitt said.

"Tell me . . ." He looked closely at the old man. His eyes had taken on that glazed look again. "Oh, never mind."

Allison came out the back door and came to the table.

"I'm afraid that was as long as I could take in the powder room," she said. "I did everything I could think of."

Stone stood up. "We have to be going," he said.

"Oh, don't go," Hewitt cried. "Please introduce me to this beautiful young woman."

Allison turned and looked closely at Hewitt. "What?"

"Leslie," Stone said, "thank you for your hospitality, but we have to go now. We'll see you soon." He took the protesting Allison by the arm and steered her through the house. In the cab he leaned back and wiped his face with his handkerchief.

"What was that all about?" Allison demanded. "What did he mean, introduce me? Doesn't he know who I am anymore?"

"Allison, please be quiet until we get to the yacht," Stone said through clenched teeth, pointing at the driver. They made the rest of the trip in silence.

Back aboard *Expansive,* Allison practically stamped her foot. "Now tell me, what was that all about?"

"You first," Stone said, getting himself a beer from the fridge. "What were you doing at Leslie's house?"

"He invited me to lunch," she said, "and sent a taxi for me."

"Allison, I don't want you ever to meet alone with Leslie again."

"And why not? Isn't he representing me?"

"He is a consultant; I am representing you. Leslie is not . . . the man he once was."

"Is that why he didn't seem to recognize me?"

"Yes."

"You mean he's . . . gaga?"

"At times."

"I'm being represented by a lawyer who's gaga?"

"You're being represented by me. Leslie is simply advising me on the local judicial system."

"Well, he was talking to me as if he were my only lawyer in the world," she said. "He made me go through the whole story again, and in the greatest possible detail."

"I'm sorry that happened, but you should not have gone to see him without me."

"And speaking of you, where the hell were you?"

"Two policemen showed up this morning and dragged me to Sir Winston Sutherland's office."

"Why?"

"I'm not sure; I think he was fishing for something he could use. He asked a lot of questions about Libby."

"And what did you tell him about her?"

"The truth, but without the financial details."

"God, how could you do that?"

"Why shouldn't I answer his questions? We've nothing to lose by telling him the truth about her. Believe me, this is no time to start lying to the local authorities."

"What did he want to know?"

"Mostly, he wanted to know about next of kin. I think he's having trouble notifying someone about her death."

"Well, that's not our responsibility, is it?"

"I told him where she was from and suggested he get in touch with the nearest American consulate."

"He couldn't figure that out by himself?"

"Apparently not."

"What if he starts talking to her relatives?" she asked.

"What if he does? That doesn't matter to us, does it?"

She didn't reply.

"Does it? Allison, is there something you haven't told me about Libby?"

"No, certainly not," she said.

"Because this is no time to start withholding information from your lawyer. I need to know everything there is to know."

"You do. I mean, I've told you everything I know about her."

"I certainly hope so, because I don't want to get into that courtroom tomorrow and have Sir Winston raise something I've never heard about. You do understand the necessity of my being fully prepared, don't you?"

"Of course I do," she cried. Now she was really getting upset; there were tears in her eyes.

•

"All right, all right, don't cry," he said. He hated it when women cried; he didn't know what to do. "Everything will be all right, as long as I know everything I need to know." He put his arms around her.

"I wouldn't lie to you," she sobbed. "Why don't you believe me?"

"I do believe you, really I do," he whispered. "It's going to be all right, don't worry." He hoped that was the truth, because he was very, very worried himself.

CHAPTER

35

Having placated Allison, Stone returned to the Shipwright's Arms to continue working on his opening statement for the trial. As he entered, Thomas beckoned.

"Bob Cantor called you," he said.

"I'll call him from my room," Stone said, then ran up the stairs, let himself in, and dialed the number.

"Cantor."

"Bob, it's Stone."

"Thanks for calling; I've got some stuff on Elizabeth Manning, but I didn't think you'd want me to fax it."

"What is it?"

"A guy I know is on the Palm Beach force, and he did a little moonlighting for me. Elizabeth Manning is, rather was, something of a gadfly in the town—a hanger-on, sponger, whatever you want to call it. She writes this column for a newspaper—an advertising sheet, really—and she practically lives on the food she gets at parties."

"Any family?"

"A mother."

"Did your man find out anything about her?"

"She's a widow in her early seventies; name is Marla Peters, a former actress, ill much of the last ten years with MS. She lives on Social Security and what she earns playing the piano in a hotel lobby at tea time for tips, plus what her daughter brought in. The two of them shared an apartment."

"Nobody else at all? A brother or sister?"

"Nobody. My guy is sure of that; he talked with the mother."

"He didn't tell her anything about the crash?"

"Nope; I didn't tell him. He told her he needed some information about some society type from her daughter, asked her to have Elizabeth call him when she got home."

Stone sat, thinking about the woman, imagining her taking requests from other old ladies for dollar tips in some faded Palm Beach hotel, scraping by on Social Security.

"Stone, you still there?"

"Yeah, Bob; I'm sorry, I was lost in thought there for a moment."

"Anything else you need?"

"No, not at the moment; I'll call you if I do."

"Sure; see you later."

Stone hung up, depressed. Before he could move, the phone rang again. "Hello?"

It was Thomas. "Stone, there's somebody named Harley Potter on the phone; says he's a lawyer, wants to talk to you."

Now what? "Okay, put him through."

"Hello?"

"Good afternoon, Mr. Barrington; my name is Harley Potter of the law firm of Potter and Potter, of Palm Beach, Florida." The voice was elderly, courtly.

"What can I do for you, Mr. Potter?"

"I understand you are the attorney for the estate of Paul Manning."

"No, that's incorrect. I represent Mr. Manning's widow in . . . another matter. I believe the estate is being handled by a firm in Greenwich, Connecticut." He gave the man the name of the firm.

There was a long silence.

"Is there something else I can do for you?"

"I wonder, Mr. Barrington, have you, during the past few days, had occasion to meet a Mrs. Elizabeth Manning?"

"Yes, I have. She arrived in St. Marks the day before yester-day."

"Ah, good; I wonder if you could tell me where she's stay-ing?"

"Do you represent Mrs. Manning?"

"I represent her mother, who is an old friend. Usually, when Libby travels, she keeps in close telephone contact with her mother, but nothing has been heard from her, and Mrs. Peters—that's her mother—is concerned."

"Mr. Potter, I'm afraid I have some very bad news. Mrs. Manning was killed yesterday in an airplane crash. She was on her way home to Palm Beach."

"Oh, dear God!" the man cried, more upset than Stone would have expected an attorney to be. "Are you absolutely positive? Could there be any mistake?"

"I'm positive. In fact, I witnessed the crash. It was a light, twin-engined airplane that flies people to Antigua, where they make airline connections. There was an engine fire; the pilot tried to ditch in the water, stalled, and the airplane disinte-grated. All three people aboard, Mrs. Manning among them, were killed instantly. I believe the local government has been trying to notify Mrs. Manning's next of kin, but apparently they've not yet contacted Mrs. Peters."

"No, I'm sure they haven't; I spoke with her not ten minutes ago. This is just terrible; Libby's mother is so dependent upon her."

"I suggest you get in touch with the minister of justice in St. Marks, whose name is Sir Winston Sutherland, at Government House in the capital city."

"I shall certainly do that. I will want to make arrangements to bring the body home for burial."

"I'm afraid that two of the three bodies, including Mrs. Manning's, went down with the fuselage of the airplane in deep water. I should think that it is unlikely in the extreme that it will ever be recovered."

"Oh, how terrible."

"Mr. Potter, do you know if Elizabeth Manning had any life insurance?"

"Why do you ask?"

"It occurs to me that you might need an affidavit to establish death. I can supply that, having been a witness, and there was another witness, who I'm sure would be glad to do the same."

"Oh, good. Yes, there was a small insurance policy, little more than enough to cover the burial expenses. You are an attorney, you said?"

"Yes, I practice in New York."

"I suppose there will be an inquest."

"Yes, I should think so."

"I wonder if you would undertake to act for this firm in the matter of obtaining a death certificate and any other legalities which might arise. I'm afraid that Mrs. Peters could not afford to send me down there, and in any case, I would find it physically impossible to make the trip."

"I'm leaving St. Marks to return to New York the middle of next week, but until that time I would be happy to handle any details that might come up, including the death certificate."

"Let me give you my address and phone number."

Stone wrote down the information.

"You may send your bill here."

"I would be glad to render this small service as a courtesy to Mrs. Peters," Stone said.

"You are very kind, sir. Ah . . ." He paused as if unwilling to mention something. "Mr. Barrington, Libby spoke with me before she left, and I was under the very distinct impression that she expected to realize some financial benefit from the estate of her former husband. Are you aware of any such benefit? Even a modest sum would mean the world to Mrs. Peters."

Stone winced. "I am aware that there was no mention of the first Mrs. Manning in Paul Manning's will," he said, "and that the alimony required by his divorce decree had expired."

"Yes, I'm afraid that is correct," Potter said. He sighed deeply. "No bequest, eh?"

"I'm afraid not, but I will raise the subject with Mr. Manning's widow."

"Would you? I would be so very grateful. Mrs. Peters's

health is not good, and I'm very much afraid that without her daughter's help she will be unable to afford to stay in her apartment, and I don't know where she would go."

"I'll speak to Mrs. Manning about it," Stone said, "and I'll be in touch with you on my return to New York next week."

"Good. I won't mention this to Mrs. Peters until I hear from you; I wouldn't want to get her hopes up, you know."

"I understand," Stone said.

"One other thing, could you learn the name of the insurance company representing the owners of the airplane? If it crashed because of a mechanical problem, Mrs. Peters might be eligible for a payment from the policy."

Stone was anxious to get off the phone before he was saddled with any other duties. "Yes, yes, I'll inquire about that."

"I'll look forward to hearing from you, then."

"Good-bye, Mr. Potter."

Stone hung up and lay back on the bed. It was worse than he could have imagined, and he didn't know whether Allison would honor her agreement. He went back to work and tried not to think of the old lady at the piano in Palm Beach.

36

The inquest was held in the same village hall that had been used for the inquest into the death of Paul Manning, the coroner was the same, and the jury was indistinguishable from the first one. The only difference was the absence of Sir Winston Sutherland, who, apparently, could see no political advantage in attending.

Stone and Thomas gave their testimony, and then the mechanic employed by Chester's air taxi service was called and questioned by the coroner.

"State your name," the coroner said.

"Harvey Simpson," the mechanic replied. He was black and appeared to be in his early forties.

"Mr. Simpson, are you a fully qualified aircraft mechanic?"

"Yessir, I am. I done my training in Miami, and I worked in Fort Lauderdale for eight years before I come home to St. Marks."

"How long had you done mechanical work on Chester Appleton's airplane?"

"For eleven years."

"The same airplane?"

"No, sir; Chester bought this one six years ago."

"Was the airplane in good condition?"

Harvey Simpson straightened in his seat. "Yessir, it certainly was. I did an annual inspection on the airplane last month; I always kept it right up to snuff."

"What about the port engine?"

"That was the newest of the two. I installed it eight months ago, and it only had five hundred and ten hours on it."

"How long is an engine good for?"

"That one was rated for two thousand hours."

"So Chester had only used a quarter of its expected life?"

"That's right, sir."

"At the time of the annual inspection, did you find anything wrong with the engine?"

Harvey Simpson opened a plastic briefcase and removed a book. "I got the engine logbook right here," he said. "There's a list of what I done to it."

"My question was, did you find anything wrong with the engine?"

Simpson consulted the logbook. "I found two exhaust brackets broken. That's a common fault; vibration weakens the metal. I replaced both brackets. The compression on all the cylinders was in the high normal range; that's a pretty good indicator of the health of the engine. All the airworthiness directives and service bulletins were up to date on it."

"We have heard testimony that the engine caught fire; can you think of anything that might have caused this to happen?"

"No, sir," the man said emphatically. "I did a fifty-hour inspection on the engine three days before the crash—that includes an oil change—and there wasn't nothing wrong with it."

"What, in your opinion, could cause an engine fire in that airplane?"

"Leaking fuel would be about the only thing, sir, but I checked all the fuel connections during the fifty-hour inspection, and they was all tight."

"Nothing else could have caused the engine fire?"

"Well, a bad exhaust leak, maybe, but there wasn't no exhaust leaks, either."

"So you have no explanation for the engine fire?"

"No, sir, I don't, and believe you me, I've done some considerable thinking on the subject. If I had the engine back and could inspect it, I might be able to tell you what caused the fire, but . . ."

"Quite," the coroner said. "Does any member of the jury have any questions for Mr. Simpson?"

A tall black man stood up. "I've got a question," he said.

"Go ahead and ask it," the coroner replied.

"Harvey, Alene Sanders, who got killed in that crash, was my wife's sister-in-law. What I want to know is, who's going to pay for killing her?"

Simpson shook his head. "I don't know, Marvin. Chester didn't have nothing but that airplane and his house."

"What about insurance?" the man demanded.

Simpson shook his head again. "Chester stopped paying the insurance last year. Said it was too much, it was going to break him."

The man shook his head and sat down. Stone shook his head, too. That answered Harley Potter's question.

"All right, then," said the coroner, "the jury can retire to consider their verdict. I won't recess for another fifteen minutes, because I don't think it's going to take long."

The jury retired, and everyone stood up to stretch. Stone turned to find Hilary Kramer of the *Times* and Jim Forrester of *The New Yorker* in the row behind him.

"What brings you two here?" Stone asked.

"Nothing else to do," Kramer replied. "Not until your case begins. I'll file a short piece on the crash. You happen to know anything about the Manning woman, Stone?"

"As a matter of fact, I had a call from a lawyer in Palm Beach. She left an elderly mother—no other family."

"No insurance for the mother, either," Kramer said, jotting down some notes. "Got the mother's name?"

"Marla Peters; a widow and retired actress."

"Address?"

"No idea."

"The lawyer?"

"Harley Potter of Potter and Potter." He looked at Forrester. "I don't see you taking any notes, Jim."

Forrester grinned. "I'll clip Hilary's piece; it'll all be in there. It'll be no more than a marginal reference in my piece."

"I guess not," Stone agreed.

"What was Elizabeth Manning doing down here?" Kramer asked.

"She wanted to know if she was mentioned in Manning's will. She wasn't."

"I heard you and she were looking over some documents in the Shipwright's Arms," she said. "What were they?"

"Paul Manning's will; she wanted to see it."

"When were they divorced?"

"Something like ten years ago, I think."

"When were they married?"

"I don't really know."

"You're a font of information, aren't you?" Kramer said suspiciously. "Is there something you don't want me to know?"

"Hilary," Stone said, "why would I keep information from you?"

She was about to reply, but the jury was returning.

The coroner waited for everyone to be seated, then spoke. "Have you gentlemen reached a verdict? If so, read it."

A man stood up. "We find that Chester Appleton, Alene Sanders, and Elizabeth Allison Manning met their deaths by misadventure," he said, then sat down.

The coroner rapped sharply on his table. "A verdict of death by misadventure having been found, these proceedings are closed."

Stone made his way forward and introduced himself to the coroner.

"Oh, yes, Mr. Barrington, I remember you from an earlier inquest."

"That's right. A law firm representing the next of kin of Mrs. Elizabeth Manning has asked me to act for them in St. Marks. They have requested a copy of the death certificate, so that Mrs. Manning's estate may be probated."

"Of course," the coroner said. "I'll give you an original." He sat down, took a pad of blank certificates from his briefcase, wrote one out, signed it, and handed it to Stone. "There you

•
179

are," he said. "Nice that this inquest is so much simpler than the last, isn't it?"

"Yes, it is."

He smiled a little. "Not as interesting, though."

Stone smiled with him. "No, I guess it isn't." He shook the man's hand and left the hall. To his relief, the two journalists had disappeared.

Back at the Shipwright's Arms, a fax was waiting for him.

Dear Stone,

Just a quick note to let you know I'm not dead. My research is going well. I've been spending all my time with Vance, who has been a dear. I've been staying at his house, which is very beautiful, and I've met many friends of his. The life out here is really wonderful.

Oh, Chip McGrath at the New York Times Book Review *has asked me to review a big new book on the history of Hollywood and the studios—front page of the review, if you can believe it. It's a nice showcase for me.*

I might stay out here for a week or two when I finish the piece. This California living gets under your skin.

Got to run. We're off to dinner.

Love,
Arrington

Stone was hurt. After all he'd said to her in his letter, she hadn't even referred to it. Then it hit him: his letter had gone down with Chester's airplane, in Libby Manning's purse. She had never received it. He swore at himself for not remembering that before now. *I'll write her tomorrow,* he thought. *First thing.*

CHAPTER

37

S tone returned to *Expansive* with some trepidation. He was not looking forward to talking with Allison about this, partly because she did not need additional problems while facing a trial for murder, and partly because he did not relish a scene with her, and he had come to know that she was adept at scenes.

To his surprise, he found her packing.

"Oh, hi," she said, stuffing things into a duffel. There were two others, already full, on the aft cabin bed.

"Going somewhere?" he asked. He really wanted to know.

"Sure," she said, "next week. I didn't have anything to do, so I thought I would get some things together, and then when the trial is over I can get out of here pronto!"

"I don't blame you for wanting to get out of here," he said. "What will you do about the boat?"

"Oh, I don't know; probably take your advice and sell it in Fort Lauderdale. I don't want to think about the boat; I'm sick of it, and once I'm out of here I never want to see it again."

He could understand that, too. "We have to talk for a minute," he said.

"What about?" She kept packing.

"Could you stop that for a minute? I need your full attention."

She stopped packing and sat down on the bed. "Okay, shoot."

He sat down beside her. "I had a call from a lawyer in Palm Beach who represents Libby's mother."

Her eyes widened. "How the hell did he know to call you?"

"Libby told him where she was going, and why; also, he watches television, I guess."

"What did he have to say?"

"He was looking for Libby; her mother hadn't heard from her. He didn't know about the crash."

"Did you tell him?"

"Of course. Sir Winston hadn't been able to find a next of kin. It was the proper thing to do."

"What's this about a mother?"

He sighed. "It's bad. She's in her seventies, and she's had multiple sclerosis for years. She lives on Social Security and what little she makes playing the piano in a Palm Beach hotel, for tips."

She remained expressionless. "Go on."

"She relies on Libby for support. They share an apartment, and the lawyer thinks the old lady will have to move, and he doesn't know where she'll go." He waited for a response.

There wasn't one. Allison continued to stare at him.

"I told you something like this might come up. Her mother is entitled to her estate."

"She has an estate?"

Oh, God, he thought; this was going to be hard. "The lawyer asked me some questions about any financial arrangements Libby might have with Paul's estate." This was true.

"So you think she might have sent him a copy of the agreement?"

"It's possible." Just. "She could have sent him the original."

"You said she didn't make any phone calls or mail anything."

"I said I didn't know that she did."

"So the lawyer might come after me for the money?"

"That's a possibility; a certainty, if he has the agreement."

"It would cost a lot of money to sue me for it, wouldn't it?"

"Maybe not; you wouldn't have much of a defense; it would be cut and dried." This was not entirely truthful, he thought, but that interpretation might legitimately be placed on the situation.

She put a hand on his knee. "Stone, I know you're worried about this, but I don't want you to be. I'll deal with this after the trial, all right? Don't worry, I'll do the right thing."

"Allison, I'm glad you feel that way, but . . ."

"But what if the trial goes wrong?"

He nodded.

"Well, then, her lawyer can make a claim on my estate, can't he?"

"Yes, I suppose so. It would just be simpler to . . ."

"Not now," she said, and she said it emphatically.

Stone nodded. "By the way, do you have a will?"

"Yes, it's with the lawyer in Greenwich."

"Do you want to make any changes to it? I could draft something for you."

She thought for a minute. "No, I don't think so; it still reflects my wishes. I gave it a lot of thought at the time."

"All right." He stood up. "I'd better get up to my room at the Shipwright's Arms; I've got some work to do." There was a folder lying on the dressing table, the folder he had given Allison containing her copy of the agreement with Libby. He took a step toward it.

"Excuse me," she said. She stepped past him, picked up the folder, and stuffed it into a duffel. "See you later."

He left the boat and started up the dock. As he did, a very modern, fast-looking motor yacht entered the harbor and made for the marina. He stood and watched her. She must have been on the order of eighty feet, and she looked as if she'd do a good fifty knots in the open sea. As he watched she moved into a berth a few yards down, and two smartly dressed crewmen hopped onto the pontoon to make her fast. She was flying a yellow customs flag, and the officer on duty stirred himself from his shack and ambled down to the marina.

Stone continued toward the Shipwright's Arms, and when he was nearly there, he stopped and looked back. The skipper of the yacht, which was called *Race*, was sitting in the cockpit, going over documents with the customs officer. A thought occurred to him; a bad thought. *No*, he said to himself, *Allison wouldn't do that*.

He picked up some Federal Express materials at the bar, stuffed the death certificate into the envelope, addressed it, and left it on the bar, then went up to his room and dialed the law offices of Potter & Potter. An elderly-sounding secretary put him through.

"This is Harley Potter."

"It's Stone Barrington, Mr. Potter."

"Ah, yes, Mr. Barrington; do you have some news for me?"

"Nothing very earthshaking, I'm afraid. The inquest was held this afternoon, and a verdict of death by misadventure was reached."

"I see."

"I obtained a death certificate from the coroner, and it will go out to you by Federal Express."

"Well, that's a relief," Potter said.

"An employee of the man who owned the airplane gave testimony that the airplane and a house were the man's only possessions, and that he had let his insurance lapse last year. I'm afraid there won't be anything to go after."

"I see. You're certain about this?"

"As certain as I can be without conducting a thorough investigation, and I'm afraid I don't have time to do that."

"That will be very bad news for Mrs. Peters," he said.

"I know it will; I'm sorry."

"Have you had an opportunity to speak with the second Mrs. Manning about . . ." He let the sentence die.

"Briefly. She won't be giving the matter any thought until her return to Greenwich next week. I expect she will want to consult her attorney there. Perhaps you'll hear something then; I'll give her your number."

"Won't you be representing her?"

"No, my work will be finished when I leave here next week."

"I see."

"I will be in touch if any further information comes my way."

"Thank you, Mr. Barrington, for your kindness," Potter said. "Good-bye."

"Good-bye, Mr. Potter," Stone replied, then hung up.

He felt sick to his stomach, but there was nothing else he could do in the circumstances. But yes, there was something he could do, he reflected. He telephoned his bank in New York, spoke to an officer he knew.

"I've got a CD maturing about now, haven't I?"

"Yes, Stone, it matured earlier this week. I sent you a notice, and your secretary called to say you were out of town. You want me to roll it over?"

"No, cash it and deposit it in my trust account."

"I'll take care of it right away."

Stone thanked the man, then hung up and called his secretary at home.

"Hi."

"Hello there."

"Anything happening?"

"Nothing I can't handle."

"Something I'd like you to do."

"Shoot."

"Tomorrow, I want you to write a check for twenty-five thousand dollars on my trust account, made payable to the estate of Elizabeth Allison Manning, and send it to a law firm in Palm Beach." He gave her the address. "Cover it with a letter saying that the money was sent at the direction of Mrs. Allison Manning."

"Pursuant to what?"

Stone thought for a minute. "Just say what I told you; nothing else."

"Okay, but we don't have a lot more than that in the trust account."

"I made a twenty-five-thousand-dollar deposit."

"That CD of yours that came due this week?"

"Right."

"We're going to need to pay some bills the first of the month."

"Woodman and Weld owes us some money; call Bill Eggers and rattle his cage. Tell him we need it right away."

"I'll do it."

"Take care, then."

"When you coming home?"

"Next week; I'll let you know when."

"You going to get that lady off?"

"Jesus, I hope so. If I don't we can kiss that twenty-five grand good-bye."

He hung up feeling both better and worse.

38

Stone finished up his work feeling thirsty, and he headed down to the bar for something cold. A young man in whites and shoulder boards was having a drink, looking bored. Stone sat down a stool away and ordered a rum and tonic, then he turned to the young man.

"You the skipper of the yacht that just came in?"

"Yep," he replied, "she's called *Race*."

"There must be a reason," Stone said. "What sort of speeds will she do?"

"Sixty knots in reasonable seas; seventy in a raging calm."

"Whew! Who builds them?"

"She's a one-off, designed by a guy out of Miami who does racing boats and built at the Huisman yard in Holland."

"What brings you into St. Marks?"

"Picking up a charterer."

"Anybody I know?"

"Beats me; name of Mr. and Mrs. Chapman; they haven't shown up yet. We're supposed to be out of here by midnight. She's being refueled now."

"Where you bound for?"

"Way up the chain of islands; St. Thomas is our first call after we leave here."

"The first U.S. port, huh? That's a long passage. Can I buy you a drink?"

"Thanks, yes."

"Thomas, bring another round to . . ."

"Sam's my name," the young man said, sticking out a hand.

"I'm Stone."

"First name, or last?"

"First." Stone clinked glasses with the skipper, and they both drank. "Where's this charterer coming from?"

"Beats me. They're supposed to fly in this evening, and we leave as soon as they get here."

"A night passage, huh? They must be in a hurry."

"That's why we're refueling; the boat eats up gas at any kind of speed."

"Can you make it to St. Thomas at speed without refueling?"

"It's at the outer limits of our range, but we can do it with no headwind, and down here the trades will be on our beam. We'll be in the lee of the island chain, so it will only be rough once in a while."

"Where is the boat based?"

"Fort Lauderdale."

"I've got a client wants to sell a yacht up there pretty soon; can you recommend a good broker?"

"Sure," Sam said, taking a card from his shirt pocket. "Crockett and Smith; they handle all our charter work. They're good people."

"So if I wanted to charter *Race*, I'd get in touch with them, not you?"

"That's right; we're in constant touch. You really in the market?"

"Maybe next winter," Stone said. "How much red tape is there in that sort of charter?"

"Not much. You'd put down a fifty percent deposit, and pay the rest thirty days in advance."

"That what this guy Chapman did?"

Sam shook his head. "This one was on short notice, so he'd have to wire-transfer the money right away. The deal only got made a couple of days ago. We had just dropped off a party in Guadeloupe, so we were nearby. This charter works out really well for us, too, since it will take us back to U.S. waters. My next charter is out of San Juan, so it's perfect; we don't have to

•

187

deadhead all the way and burn up a lot of the owner's fuel."

"What does she cost, by the week?"

"Fifty-five grand, dry, sixty-five all in, booze and everything."

Stone laughed. "Forget my interest in chartering; that's out of my range."

"Don't feel bad; it's out of just about everybody's range."

"Think I could get a look at her interior while you're here? I have a client or two who might be interested in chartering."

"Sure thing," Sam replied, tossing down the rest of his drink. "How about right now?"

"Great; let's go."

The two men walked out of the Shipwright's Arms and across the lawn toward the marina.

"What's her length?" Stone asked.

"Sixty-seven feet overall; draws six feet, so we can cruise the Bahamas."

"How many cabins?"

"Four; one big one for the owner, and three pretty good-sized ones. She has a little less volume than most boats her length; that's because of the speed designed into her."

They walked down the pontoon and went up the boarding ladder. Sam led the way, showing off the bridge and the navigational gear, then the saloon, complete with bar and entertainment center, featuring a big-screen television and video library. The owner's cabin was, indeed, luxurious, and the other cabins, although smaller, were equally plush.

"I'm impressed," Stone said as he descended to the pontoon again. He stuck out his hand. "Thanks for the tour, and good luck." He walked back up to the Shipwright's Arms and found Thomas.

"Thomas, I've never seen many airplanes out at the airport besides Chester's; do you get many outside aircraft in here?"

"Not many," Thomas replied. "Chester had the only license to land here any time he liked. Charter services from the other islands have to phone the airport office and get permission to land, usually twenty-four hours in advance. It's nothing but red tape, really."

"Do you think you could find out if any aircraft are expected in today or tonight?"

"I can call the guy who runs the airport," Thomas said.

"Thanks."

Thomas used the phone and came back. "Nobody coming in today or tonight," he said.

"What would happen if an airplane landed without prior permission?"

"Big fine, for sure, and they might even confiscate the airplane if they got mad enough, but no airplane from the islands would try that. All the charter services know the score. What's up, anyway?"

"The skipper of the big motor yacht that came in this afternoon says he's meeting a charter client who's flying in today."

"Well, that's going to come as a big surprise to the folks out at the airport."

"Yeah," Stone said. "See you later." He walked back down to the marina and boarded *Expansive*. "Hello, below," he called out.

"Stone, is that you?" Allison's voice called back.

"Sure is." He started down the companionway.

"I'm not feeling very well," she called out. "Would you mind coming back later this evening?"

Stone stopped halfway down the steps.

"Stone?"

"I have to talk to you right now," he said and started down again.

"Please don't!" she cried, but he was already in the saloon. There were half a dozen packed duffels piled near the steps, and Allison had a safe open behind the navigation station. "Dammit," she said, "are you deaf?"

"What time are you planning to leave?" he asked.

"I don't know what you're talking about," she replied, closing the safe and putting some papers into her late husband's briefcase.

"What time?" he asked again.

She began going through the drawers next to the chart table, apparently looking for something.

Stone walked into the aft cabin and looked around. He opened a closet door and found only a few things hanging there, along with a lot of empty hangers. He walked back into the saloon. "What time are you leaving?" he asked a third time.

She looked at him for a long time without expression. "Sometime after midnight," she said finally.

39

S tone sat down on the sofa opposite the chart table. "You can't do it," he said. "You know the penalty if you're caught running. You'll be judged guilty without even the formality of a trial, and they'll hang you."

"They're going to hang me anyway," she said.

"Not if I have anything to say about it."

"Stone," she said. "Can't you see the way this is headed? They've stacked the deck against me in every possible way. The jury will probably be stacked against me, too. Sutherland wants my hide on his wall, and he's going to get his way."

"Allison, listen to me. We've got a shot at an acquittal, really we have."

"And if I'm not acquitted?"

"Then we turn on the pressure on the prime minister. Sutherland has already heard from both Connecticut senators and God knows who else. If they try to hang an American citizen under these circumstances, the world will fall on them. The pressure on the prime minister will be unbearable; he'll have to cave in."

"These people can do whatever the hell they want," she said. "They're in this insular little world of theirs, and nobody has ever cared about what went on here."

"Until now. Do you know that you're already very nearly world famous? Every television station on the planet has run a story about you. On American television you're right up there with Princess Di for air time."

"I'm the flavor of the week, that's all," she sighed. "And probably half the people who heard about it think I'm guilty. Anyway, there would only be forty-eight hours between a conviction and an execution. That's not enough time to build outrage and get some sort of intervention. Don't you think I've thought about this? I've hardly thought of anything else."

"But if you run and are caught, you'll appear guilty and you'll lose all that support. People will say, 'Well, she killed her husband and she got what she deserved.' Is that what you want?"

"I'm not going to get caught. That boat over there is the fastest thing afloat between here and Miami. We'll be in international waters fifteen minutes after we leave the harbor. They don't have anything that can stop us."

"Sutherland will go after you and extradite you."

"I can fight that in the American courts."

"And by the time the lawyers are finished with you, all the money will be gone. All of it, Allison, the house, the yacht, and the twelve million in insurance money will have gone right down the legal drain. Then, even if you win, you can never travel abroad. The minute you arrive in another country, Sutherland can start extradition proceedings all over again. You'd be hounded for the rest of your life."

"I'm hounded now; what's the difference? At least I'll have a life. They won't catch me, Stone; they'll have to find me first."

"So you're going to change your identity and hide out somewhere, give up who you are and worry every day about being caught. You don't want to live as a fugitive, Allison, believe me."

This seemed to have an effect. Tears welled up in her eyes, and when she reached for a tissue her hands trembled. "It's better than dying on this godforsaken island," she managed to say.

"They'll think I helped you," Stone said. "I'm an officer of the court, you know; I'm obliged to prevent you from committing another crime, and to attempt to escape is a crime."

•

"You'll talk your way out of it, Stone. After all, you didn't suspect anything until now."

"They won't know that. They'll know that I had a drink in the bar with the captain of that yacht and that we talked for quite a while, and that I went down and took a tour of the yacht."

"Come with me, then; we'll both get out of here."

Stone shook his head. "I'm not going to become a party to a crime for you or anybody else, and I'm certainly not going to become a fugitive." He stood up.

"Where are you going?" she asked, alarmed.

"I'm going to get as far away from you as I possibly can, although, in the circumstances, that's not very far."

"You're going to turn me in, aren't you?" she asked.

"Of course not; I'm not going to be the instrument of your death. I'm trying to save your life." He turned to leave.

She stood up and grabbed him, turned him to her, and put her arms around his waist. "Don't go," she said. "Stay here with me; I'm so frightened."

Stone disentangled himself from her arms. "I'm leaving right now. We won't be seeing each other again, Allison." He turned and started up the companionway before she could speak again.

He was furious. The stupid girl was jeopardizing them both, herself most of all, and there was not a damn thing he could do about it. At the top of the steps he looked toward the Shipwright's Arms and saw three policemen striding across the lawn toward the marina. "Oh, shit!" he moaned, and ran back down the steps.

"What is it?" Allison asked.

Stone looked around the cabin for some place to hide her luggage. They'd look in the after cabin. "Quick, fix us a drink; the cops are coming." He opened the door to the engine room and started tossing duffels down the steps.

Allison ran to the bar, got two glasses of ice, and poured some brown whiskey into both of them.

There was the sharp rap of a nightstick on the deck. "Ahoy, *Expansive!*" a deep voice called.

"Answer him!" Stone whispered, closing the engine room door and diving for the sofa.

"Hello!" Allison called back. She was halfway to the sofa with the drinks when the first policeman appeared on the stairs.

"Good afternoon," the man said. "I am Colonel Buckler of the St. Marks police." Two other officers crowded the companionway behind him.

"Good afternoon, Colonel," Allison replied smoothly. "We were just having a drink; can I get you something?"

"No, ma'am, thank you," the colonel said.

Stone stood up. "Colonel, I am Stone Barrington, Mrs. Manning's lawyer. Is there something we can do for you?" He took a drink from Allison and sat down. Allison sat next to him. "Please," he said to the policeman, "be seated."

The policeman sat down gingerly at the chart table. "I understand Mrs. Manning has made some travel plans," he said.

Stone looked at him blankly, then at Allison.

"Come again?" Allison said.

"I believe you have recently chartered a yacht," the colonel said.

Allison waved an arm about her. "Colonel, I already have a yacht; why should I want to charter another one?"

"Colonel," Stone said, "perhaps you could explain yourself?"

"Of course, Mr. Barrington," the policeman replied. "Earlier this afternoon a very fast yacht berthed here and cleared customs, stating his intention of picking up a charter passenger. And you were seen, not half an hour ago, having a drink at the bar of the Shipwright's Arms with that yacht's captain, and then going aboard her."

"That's quite true, Colonel," Stone said. "I met the man, whose name I believe is Sam, at the bar. I expressed an interest in his boat, and he was kind enough to offer me a tour. He said his charterer was a Mr. and Mrs. Chapman."

"Come, come, Mr. Barrington, you are being disingenuous," the policeman said.

"I assure you, I am not," Stone replied firmly.

"Colonel," Allison piped up, "why do you think I have anything to do with that yacht?"

"Yes, Colonel, why?" Stone asked.

"I am not a fool, Mr. Barrington," the man said.

"Of course you aren't," Stone agreed. "But what, specifically, causes you to believe that Mrs. Manning has chartered the yacht? Have you spoken with the captain?"

"Not yet," the man admitted.

"Well, when you do, I'm sure he will tell you what he told me, that someone else has chartered his yacht."

"Oh, I will speak to him, Mr. Barrington; you may be sure of that." He stood up. "In the meantime, Mrs. Manning is confined to this yacht and to the Shipwright's Arms."

Allison shrugged. "I've hardly left this yacht since I came to St. Marks, except at the insistence of Sir Winston Sutherland," she said. "I don't know why I would want to leave it now. You see, Colonel, I am quite looking forward to my trial and acquittal."

"She is not to go to the airport or anywhere else on the island or to board any other yacht," the colonel said, continuing to address Stone, "on pain of immediate arrest and close confinement."

"I quite understand, Colonel," Stone said, "and believe me, Mrs. Manning will follow your instructions to the letter."

The policeman saluted them smartly and, herding his colleagues before him, went up the companionway.

Stone followed them partway and watched as they marched off toward the *Race.*

CHAPTER

40

Stone sat back down on the sofa and took a large swig of his drink. It turned out to be straight rum. "Jesus," he said, coughing, "I was expecting Scotch or something."

"I grabbed the first thing I saw," she said, sitting beside him. "That man frightened me very badly."

"I'm glad you still have the capacity for being frightened by something," he replied. "He was on the point of jailing you, you know."

"I believe you. What do I do now?"

"We've got to get that motor yacht out of English Harbour, that's what. How did you go about chartering it?"

"I found an ad in an old yachting magazine we had aboard, and I called them. The money was wire-transferred from my Greenwich account."

Stone looked at her in amazement. "And how the hell did you accomplish all that? You've hardly left this yacht, and I've never seen you use a phone."

She got up, went to the chart table, opened a cupboard behind it, took out what looked like a laptop computer, and set it on the chart table.

Stone looked at the thing. "What is it?"

She opened it and displayed a telephone handset.

•
195

"A telephone?"

"A satellite telephone. The antenna is at the top of the mast."

"It works?"

"It certainly does. Would you like me to demonstrate?"

"Yes, please; call the broker and get that yacht out of here."

She plugged the unit into a jack near the chart table, switched it on, and waited. "It will seek a satellite," she said. A moment later, it beeped three times. She picked up the handset, consulted her address book, dialed a number, and pressed a button.

"Like a car phone," Stone said.

"Exactly, except it will work almost anywhere on the face of the earth." She put the phone to her ear. "Hello, Fred? It's Allison Manning; I'm sorry to bother you at home. I have some new instructions for you. Yes, the yacht arrived, and now I have to get it out of here, for the moment."

"Tell him to have them leave around nine this evening," Stone said. "No sooner."

"Please call the yacht and have them depart the harbor at nine o'clock this evening. Tell them to go back to Guadeloupe and wait for my call. It may be a few days. What? Fred, you've already been paid. If I want the yacht to go to Guadeloupe and wait, then that's what they'll do. Right. Thank you so much." She pressed another button, breaking the connection. "There, it's done."

"And they have one of these on the other yacht?"

"Yes, or something like it."

Stone shook his head. "Technology is passing me by."

"Why nine o'clock?" she asked.

"Because you and I are going to be having dinner at the Shipwright's Arms at that time, in view of the whole world, or at least all St. Marks. We are going to appear relaxed and happy and unconcerned about the yacht's departure. Do you have a local phone directory?"

She fished one out of the chart table.

Stone looked up a number and showed it to her. "Dial that for me, will you?"

She dialed the number and handed him the handset.

•

"Hello, is that the St. Marks airport? Good. My name is Chapman; my wife and I are meeting a chartered yacht there, and I was told that I would have to get permission for my airplane to land at your airport; is that correct? Well, we plan to land around nine this evening, so I hope the runway is lit. What? Twenty-four hours? Why, that's outrageous! I can land at any other airport in the world on no notice at all! Well, in that case, I'll meet my yacht in Guadeloupe, and St. Marks will lose the money I would have spent there. No, no, don't apologize, I no longer wish to land at your airport. Good-bye!" He broke the connection and turned to Allison. "There, maybe that will give us some cover."

They waited until eight, then, freshly scrubbed and changed, they walked over to the Shipwright's Arms, exchanging pleasantries with the two police officers now permanently established at the dockhead of the marina, with a full view of all the yachts there. They had a drink at the bar and chatted with Thomas for a while.

"Trouble down at the marina this afternoon?" Thomas asked when he was far enough away from the other patrons.

"A bit," Stone replied. "A Colonel Buckler showed up with two other cops and accused Allison of chartering the new yacht down there in order to escape the island."

"Buckler got a call here a little later," Thomas said. "From Government House. I heard the name Chapman mentioned."

"Ah, Mr. Chapman; I'm told that he is the actual charterer of the yacht."

"I gathered from what I overheard that Mr. Chapman had tried to get permission to land his jet at the airport tonight and was turned down."

"Did you get that impression?" Stone said.

"I did. Buckler seemed confused. Buckler and his wife are at a table a few yards behind you, having dinner."

"Oh, good," Stone said.

"Why is that good?" Thomas asked.

"Because he'll get to see the yacht steam out of English Harbour, and he'll see Allison here with me. That might make him feel better."

"Good evening, Sir Winston," Thomas said suddenly. "Your table is ready."

Stone and Allison turned to see the minister of justice and his wife standing behind them.

"Good evening, Mrs. Manning," Sir Winston said. "Mr. Barrington."

"Good evening, Sir Winston," they both replied.

"Such a lovely evening," he said. "You wouldn't want to leave us on such a lovely evening, would you, Mrs. Manning?"

"Of course not," Allison said. Then she looked pointedly over his shoulder.

Sir Winston and his wife turned to follow her gaze. They saw the yacht *Race* back out of her berth and turn toward the entrance to English Harbour. She gave a couple of blasts on her horn.

"Such a beautiful yacht," Sir Winston said; then he turned to his wife. "Shall we be seated, my dear?" They followed Thomas to their table.

Stone looked at his watch; a quarter to nine. "A little early," he said, "but perfectly timed."

"Look," Allison said, "Colonel Buckler sees her, too."

"I believe he does," Stone said with satisfaction.

Thomas returned to the bar. "He asked me if you'd made any phone calls from here since this afternoon."

"I'm glad you were able to tell him the truth," Stone said.

"I try always to tell Sir Winston the truth," Thomas said, "except when I lie to him."

"I hope you haven't had to tell too many lies for us, Thomas," Allison said.

"None that I didn't enjoy telling," Thomas replied with a grin. "Would you like to sit down now?"

"Please," Allison said. "And not too near Sir Winston, if you please."

"I have a lovely table for you, one with a fine view of English Harbour."

"Perfect," she said.

They followed Thomas to their table, passing that of Colonel Buckler on their way. Allison gave him a smile, and Stone nodded pleasantly.

"Did the phone call from Chapman work?" Allison asked when they were seated.

"Maybe," Stone said. "Although Colonel Buckler has not offered to change the terms of your confinement."

"I don't mind," Allison said. "I'm as happy here as anywhere on the island."

"Just see that you don't get onto any other boats, not even mine," Stone said. "And for God's sake, don't go anywhere near the airport."

"I'll be good," Allison promised.

CHAPTER

41

They took their time over dinner, talking like old friends and lovers. They had champagne with their fish, and, as always, the wine was an exhilarant, making them laugh easily. They emptied the place, outlasting Sir Winston and Colonel Buckler, as well as the rest of the crowd. Thomas brought them cognac at the end of the meal, and they nursed it past midnight.

There was a lull in the conversation, and Stone asked a question. "Allison, what are you going to do with yourself when this is all over?" He regretted it immediately, but to his surprise, she answered him as if she would not be on trial for her life in a short time.

"Gosh, I really haven't looked all that far ahead," she said. "I've sold the house—it's under contract now—so I guess the first thing I'll do is go back to Greenwich and start getting ready to move out."

"Where do you think you'll go?"

"Oh," she murmured, "I was thinking maybe New York. Would you be glad to see me there, conveniently located, as it were?"

He felt a little stab in the chest; after all, Arrington would soon be back from California. "Of course I'd be glad to see you," he said, after perhaps too long a pause.

"Oh, yes, there is the other woman, isn't there? What are your intentions, sir, if I may ask?"

"I don't honestly know," he replied, and it was the truth.

Allison leaned forward on her elbows. "Do you think she's fucking Vance Calder?"

Stone shrugged. "She's had the opportunity before, and she says she never did, never thought of him as anything but a friend."

"I would be," Allison said.

"Would be what?"

"Fucking Vance Calder."

"Oh. Well, if she is, then that would make life easier for me, in a way."

"Oh, Stone, you're the perfect old-fashioned man."

"How's that?"

"You'd leave Arrington for fucking Vance Calder, but you wouldn't want her to leave you for fucking me."

"What I meant was, if she left me for Vance, I wouldn't have to make a decision, she'd have made it for me. Also, I'd have some things to tell her."

"You mean about me?"

Stone nodded. He hadn't allowed himself to think about it until now, but he knew he would tell her.

"For God's sake, why?"

"I guess I'm not as old-fashioned as you think—not your idea of old-fashioned, anyway."

"Why, Stone, I believe you're an honorable man."

He felt his ears turning red, and he wondered why he was embarrassed. "If I were as honorable as you think, why would I be fucking you at all?"

She smiled. "It's not your fault," she said. "I simply made myself irresistible."

"That you did."

"Women can do that, you know—make themselves utterly irresistible."

"Some women."

"Thank you, kind sir. Do you know when I decided to seduce you? I mean, the very moment?"

"When?"

"When I was on the stand at the inquest."

"Nonsense."

She shook her head. "No, really. I was sitting there, and Sir Winston was making me absolutely furious, and I caught a glimpse of you sitting there."

"You never looked at me."

"I did. You were looking at Sir Winston. You see, after Paul's death, I was alone for another two weeks, and I had a lot of time to get used to being a widow. I had a friend once who lost her husband; she was in her forties at the time. It took her months just to accept the idea that he was actually dead. She'd walk into his study, expecting to find him sitting there reading the newspaper. It wasn't like that with me. I wasn't distracted by a funeral, or by friends and relatives coming to call or by all the details of settling the estate. I was all alone, right there, in the place where he had been for so long, and he was dead. I think that after the first week I had accepted that completely. Then I started to get horny."

Stone smiled. "I was angry with Arrington for not being here."

"And that gave you an excuse to crawl into the sack with me."

He nodded. "I guess it did."

"You are the best lover I've ever had," she said. "Not that I've had all that many, but I had the years between puberty and the time I met Paul, and I enjoyed myself. But you are the very best."

"That's high praise," he said, satisfyingly flattered.

"Do you know why?"

He shrugged.

"It's not because you're a beautiful man, though you are, and it's not because you're experienced and inventive, though God knows you are: it's because you're so considerate. I know when we're fucking that you really care that I'm enjoying it as much as you. It makes me want to please you even more."

"And you do, believe me."

"I know I do; I can tell. I think you like me best when I'm

wanton, when I do the things a proper Greenwich, Connecticut matron isn't supposed to enjoy, and when I do them well."

He smiled, but said nothing.

"Take me back to the boat," she said.

"Yes, ma'am," he said.

They walked past the two policemen on guard and boarded the yacht, and as they started down the companionway, she began undressing. So did he. She led him to the after cabin and threw off the bedcover, then made him lie on his back. She began slowly, kissing him here and there, using her tongue, but staying away from his genitals until he was completely erect, which didn't take long. Then she spent several minutes bringing him to the edge and backing off, playing him as if he were a musical instrument.

Stone then found himself in a condition where he knew he could resist coming for as long as he liked but still remain rigidly erect. Finally she rolled over on her stomach, took him in her hand, and guided him home. Then, after a while, she let him slide out.

"Now here," she said, guiding him into a different place. She let him ride her for a short time, then turned on her back and reinserted him in the same place. Then, without parting from him, she rolled him onto his back and sat astride him, moving slowly up and down, making little noises. Half an hour had passed before she said to him, "Now. Come for me."

And he did.

They passed the night alternately sleeping and making love, as the mood took them.

She woke him at dawn and made him do it again, then they slept for another hour.

"Want some breakfast?" she said, yawning.

"Sure."

"Oh," she said, "all my stuff is packed. Will you bring me the smallest duffel? It's got my toothbrush in it."

"Sure." He rolled out of bed and stretched.

She kissed him on the belly. "You were perfectly wonderful last night."

"You were way beyond wonderful. I don't think I've ever had a night like that. I'm exhausted."

"You'll live." She slapped him on his naked buttocks. "Now get me that duffel."

Stone went forward to the door of the engine room, under the companionway. He opened it, walked down two steps, and looked around the small compartment, which contained the two engines and a small workshop. It was as clean and neat as the galley, he thought. On the bulkhead behind the workbench, all the ship's tools were arrayed in motion-proof brackets. He picked up a wrench and saw that each tool had been traced in black paint. He marveled at the time Paul Manning had spent ordering his ship. He turned and looked at the other equipment. There was a wet suit, hung neatly on a hanger, and a pair of diving tanks resting in custom-made stainless steel holders fixed to the bulkhead.

Then, in a sudden, sickening flash, Stone became a cop again.

He saw something that, in an earlier day, would have made his heart leap in triumph, but now made him feel sick with revulsion.

Next to the tanks, fixed to the bulkhead and outlined in black paint like all the tools, was a spear gun for underwater fishing, with brackets for the gun and three spears. One of the spears was missing, its outline empty. That would have given him pause, but it was something else that immobilized him. The spear gun was there, but it had been taken down and awkwardly replaced backward in its brackets, the opposite of its painted outline.

Stone knew in an instant that Paul Manning would never, never have replaced the gun in anything but its proper position. It had been put there by someone else, of course, but the third spear had not been returned to its place.

The third spear, he knew beyond a doubt, was still in what was left of Paul Manning's body, out there in the depths of the cold, cold ocean.

42

Stone placed the small duffel on the bed in the aft cabin and looked at Allison, who was sitting on the little stool in front of the vanity, brushing her hair. She looked, he thought, like something out of a Degas oil. He was having a lot of trouble. It wouldn't be the first time, he thought, that he had represented a client whom he knew to be guilty; that was part of his job. It was the first time, however, that he had represented a guilty client with whom he had been enthusiastically making love— one he had grown very fond of—was nearly in love with. It was also the first time he had represented anyone charged with a capital crime. He was trying very hard to ignore his cop's instincts and keep her innocent in his mind.

"Allison," he said absently.

"Yes?"

"After Paul died, why didn't you use the satellite phone to call for help?"

"Two reasons," she said without hesitation. "First, I couldn't get the damned thing to work. I've never been very good at reading manuals, and I just couldn't get it to lock onto a satellite, so I gave up. After I got to port I got it to work the first time; maybe it was because the boat wasn't moving anymore, or maybe it was the crossword syndrome."

"What's the crossword syndrome?"

"You're working on the crossword, and there's a big patch of it you just can't solve. So you put the thing down for a while—maybe until the next day—and you pick it up and immediately get all the words. Maybe it's like that with following directions in a manual."

"I've had that experience," Stone agreed. "What was your second reason for not calling for help?"

"First of all, I did call for help, but on the VHF radio. I didn't know how to work the high-frequency unit—still don't—but I tried calling 'any ship' on channel sixteen, but I never got an answer. I never even saw a ship or a yacht the whole trip. Second, I would have been ashamed if somebody had come to my rescue."

"Why ashamed?"

"Well, I had a perfectly good yacht under me, and I had some idea of how to sail it, so my sense of self-reliance would have been punctured if I'd had to ask somebody else to do it for me. Anyway, in the end, I proved I could sail her." She looked at him in the mirror. "Why did you want to know about the satellite telephone?"

"I thought the police might have seen it during their search and that Sir Winston might ask the question at the trial. If he does, stick with the answer about not being able to get the phone to work, and calling for help on the VHF; don't mention that business about your sense of self-reliance. I'm not sure how it would play with the jury."

"Okay."

"Later, I'll go through your testimony with you, and we'll fine-tune it."

"You mean you're going to rehearse a witness?"

"You bet I am. Oh, I'm not going to tamper with your story; I just want to shape it in a way that will tell the jury, in a simple and straightforward way, that you're innocent."

"Okay. What are you going to do the rest of the day?"

"I have to go out and talk to Leslie Hewitt about the trial. I've made some notes that I want to give him."

"I'll be here all day," she said, "or as long as the cops are."

"You don't have some other escape plan up your sleeve, do you? Because if you do, I beg you not to try it."

"Relax, Stone; I've learned my lesson about escaping."

"I hope to God you have."

Stone borrowed Thomas's car and drove along the coast road to Leslie Hewitt's house. He turned down the dirt road to the cottage and parked out front, next to Hewitt's Morris Minor station wagon, and got out, taking a file folder with him. The front door of the house stood open, and Stone stepped inside. "Leslie!" he called. "You home?" There was no response. "Leslie!" he called again. He looked in the little study and in the kitchen, but the barrister was not in the house.

Stone walked out the back door and into the garden, but there was still no sight of Hewitt, not even down at the beach. He walked a few steps more, looked around, then turned to go back into the house. As he turned his eye drifted to his left and there, behind a low hedge, lay the inert form of Sir Leslie Hewitt, clad only in faded Bermuda shorts. He was lying on his stomach, his head turned away from Stone; a bucket of hand gardening tools lay next to him and a trowel was near his right hand.

"Leslie!" Stone cried, turning him over on his back and brushing dirt from his face. He slapped Hewitt's face lightly and peeled back an eyelid. The pupil was contracted; thank God for that.

Suddenly Hewitt coughed, then opened his eyes. "Oh, good morning," he said, sitting up and rubbing his eyes with a fist. "I must have dozed off."

"Leslie, are you all right?" Stone asked. "You were out like a light."

"Young man, when you are my age, you will take the occasional nap, too, believe me." With Stone's help, he got to his feet. "Well now, what brings you to see me?" he asked.

Stone wasn't sure that Hewitt recognized him, and he didn't want to ask. "I brought you some material to read in preparation for the trial," he said. "Do you feel up to reading it?"

"Of course," Hewitt replied. "Come into the house, Stone."

Stone breathed a sigh of relief and followed him into the study.

Hewitt arranged himself behind his desk. "Now, what is it?" he asked, in the manner of a man who didn't have much time for whatever Stone wanted of him.

Stone placed the file folder before him. "Leslie, I know you plan to give the opening and closing statements, but I put some thoughts together on how you might proceed, and I'd appreciate it if you'd read the two statements I've prepared. There might be something there you can use."

"Of course I'll read them," Hewitt replied. "Now if you'll excuse me, I'd like to get back to my garden."

"Do you think you could find time to read them now?" Stone asked. "You might have some questions for me."

"No, no, not now," the man said. "I'll read them this afternoon after my nap; I'm more alert then. Now, I'll see you in the courtroom." He walked out of the room, leaving Stone standing there alone.

Stone followed him as far as the back door and watched as Hewitt knelt down and began digging in the earth behind the low hedge again, seemingly oblivious to Stone's presence. Finally, Stone shook his head and returned to the car. As he was about to turn toward English Harbour, he had another thought and turned left instead, toward the airport.

He drove through the gates and down the approach road, with the runway and the single hangar in full view. He pulled up in front of the hangar and got out. The mechanic who had testified at the inquest was working on an engine of the DC-3 that belonged to the St. Marks government. Stone couldn't remember his name, but he walked over to the airplane.

"Excuse me," he said to the man. "I'm Stone Barrington; I heard you testify at the inquest."

"Righto," the man said. "You're the lawyer fellow, aren't you? The one who's defending that lady?"

"That's right. I wonder if I could talk to you for a minute. What's your name again?"

"Harvey Simpson," the man said, turning away from the airplane and wiping his hands with a cloth. "What can I do for you?"

"I was just noticing that the hangar has an overhead door,

like a garage," he said, pointing at the ceiling, where the door was retracted.

"That's right; there it is," Simpson said, following his gaze.

"Do you close that every night and lock up?"

Simpson shook his head. "Not unless the weather looks like it's turning bad. That door is a pain in the ass; sticks all the time. I keep meaning to do something about it, but I never seem to get around to it."

"Was the hangar door closed the night before Chester's crash?"

Simpson thought for a minute. "No, we haven't had no bad weather for a while now."

"So anybody could have come in here where Chester's airplane was?"

"That's right, I guess."

"How about your tool cabinet over there," Stone said, pointing to a large, double-doored cupboard. The doors were open, exposing an array of spanners, screwdrivers, and socket wrenches.

"I never lock it," Simpson said.

"Don't your tools get stolen?"

Simpson shook his head. "Everybody who might steal them knows that my tools are American gauge, for working on the American-built airplanes. All the cars on the island and all the other machinery are metric gauge, so my tools wouldn't be worth much to anybody."

"So somebody could have come in here the night before the crash, taken some tools out of your cabinet, and done something to an engine?"

Simpson gazed into the middle distance for a moment before answering. "Yessir, I guess somebody could have done that. But there isn't no one on this island who would want to do that to Chester."

"How about to his passengers?"

"I can't speak for the white lady, but I knew the black one well, and everybody liked her. Anyway, if somebody wanted to kill her, he wouldn't kill Chester doing it."

"Is there anybody on guard out here at night?"

Simpson shook his head. "Nope. There's a couple of people

in the airport office, through there," he said, pointing at a door that led from the main part of the hangar to the offices, "but they wouldn't be out here at night. The runway lights are pilot-operated, you see. The approaching pilot just tunes in the local frequency and clicks his mike three times, and the lights come on."

"I see," Stone said.

"Mister, this is not the first time I've thought about this," Simpson said. "I been over it in my mind a few times. I thought about how it was the morning of the crash, and everything was just like I left it."

"Did Chester make it a habit of doing a runup before takeoff?"

"Well, he made it a habit sometimes, and other times he didn't," Simpson said. "If you know what I mean. Chester been flying that Cessna a long time; he didn't have much use for checklists no more."

He didn't have much use for runups, either, Stone thought. A runup might have saved his life and those of his passengers.

"Chester was a good pilot, though," Simpson said. "A natural-born pilot."

"Right," Stone said. Chester had been a cowboy; Stone had flown with him in the right seat when he had come to St. Marks, and the man was strictly a seat-of-the-pants pilot—no checklists. Stone walked over to the tool cabinet and looked at the array of tools inside; then he saw something familiar on the cabinet door. He touched it lightly. Fingerprint powder; he had seen enough of it in his time. "The police have been here?" he asked.

"Sure have; looked at everything, asked a lot of questions, took my fingerprints."

Stone nodded. "Well, Harvey, thanks for your time." He shook the man's oily hand and walked back to the car thinking, *I'll never fly an airplane off a runway without doing a runup first. Not as long as I live.*

He got into the car and headed back to English Harbour. He didn't want to think about Allison right now; he tried thinking about Arrington instead and found that he missed her. He still hadn't rewritten his letter to her; he would do it before the day was out.

43

Stone parked Thomas's car in its usual place and left the keys in it, as Thomas often did. His business with Leslie Hewitt apparently concluded for the time being, he wanted now to talk with Jim Forrester again, and he was lucky enough to find him at the bar, talking to Thomas.

"Hi, Jim; have you got a few minutes for me?"

"Sure, Stone, what's up?"

"I want to go through your testimony with you; make sure we're both on the same page."

"Great, let's get a table."

Thomas held up an envelope. "Fax for you," he said to Stone.

"Thanks, Thomas," he said, stuffing the envelope into his pocket. He'd read it when he was through with Forrester. He followed the reporter to a table, and they got comfortable. "Jim, I'll just ask you some questions, the way I will at the trial, and you answer them as you see fit. If I don't like the way you answer a question, we'll talk about rephrasing."

"Okay, shoot."

"Have you ever testified in court before?"

"No."

"They'll ask you your name for the record."

"Right."

"Now I'm on my feet in my robe and my wig, and . . . "

"Wig? You have to wear a wig?"

"I'm afraid so. You'll have to try not to laugh; it wouldn't look good for me in front of the jury."

"I'll do my best, but I'm not promising anything."

"All right, Mr. Forrester, what is your occupation?"

"I'm a magazine writer."

"And what brings you to St. Marks?"

"I intend to write an article about this trial for an American magazine."

"I see. Now, were you acquainted with Paul Manning?"

"Yes, I knew him in college."

"Tell us how you met him."

"We were on the same basketball team."

"Hang on, Jim; I thought you told me you played against him."

Forrester shook his head and raised the glass from which he was drinking. "I'm sorry, Stone; the booze must be going to my head."

"Let's start again; tell the court how you and Mr. Manning first met."

"We went to college in nearby towns—he to Cornell, I to Syracuse."

"Spell it out for them; say Cornell University and Syracuse University in New York State."

"Okay."

"Go on."

"We were both members of the same fraternity, Sigma Alpha Epsilon, and we had an interfraternity basketball league that included both universities."

"Just say club, and don't bother with the Greek; this jury isn't likely to know much about American college fraternities. In fact, just say you played in the same league."

"Right. Paul Manning and I both played on basketball teams, and we sometimes played against each other."

"And how well did you know him?"

"Fairly well, but we were not close."

"Just say fairly well, don't say you weren't close. Sir Winston may worm that out of you on cross-examination, though. Don't lie about it."

"Right. I knew him fairly well."

"How would you describe his personality?"

"He was friendly and outgoing. We got along well."

"Did there then pass a number of years when you did not meet?"

"Yes; I didn't meet him again until recently."

"Please tell the court of those circumstances."

"I was in the Canary Islands, working on a magazine piece, and I met him at the local marina."

"Not the yacht club?"

"Right, the yacht club; it has its own marina."

"Start again."

"I ran into him at the bar at the yacht club in Las Palmas, and we renewed our acquaintance."

"Had he changed much in the years since you'd seen him?"

"Well, he'd gained a lot of weight, but he was still the same friendly guy."

"Did he mention his wife while you were at the bar?"

"Yes, he said he was married to a beautiful girl that he was crazy about."

"You didn't mention that before," Stone said. "That he was crazy about her."

"Sorry; there were words to that effect."

"Good, that will help. Now, how much time did you spend with him on this occasion, at the yacht club bar?"

"We were there an hour or so, and then he invited me to dinner on his yacht."

"Did you accept?"

"Yes."

"Did you then go down to the marina and have dinner on his yacht?"

"Yes."

"Did he introduce you to Mrs. Manning?"

"Yes. She was already on the yacht, cooking dinner."

"How long did you spend with them that evening?"

"Oh, I guess four or five hours."

"And on that occasion did you form an opinion of the sort of relationship these two people had?"

"Yes."

"How would you describe that relationship?"

"They were good together; they obviously loved each other. They touched each other a lot, and always with affection."

"Good, I like that, the part about the touching; remember to say it."

"Okay."

"Would you say these people were happily married?"

"Yes, I would. Very happily."

"And how long was it before they sailed across the Atlantic?"

"I believe they sailed the next day for another island, then started across the Atlantic the day after that."

"Did you see them again?"

"Yes. I went to another island called Puerto Rico, and I happened to see them as they sailed out of the harbor into the Atlantic."

"Did they see you?"

"Yes, they waved and shouted good-bye."

"Were they in good spirits?"

"Yes, they were laughing and smiling."

"Did they still seem to be the happy couple you had met only two days before?"

"Very much so. They were holding hands."

"Great!" Stone said. "I like that as a memory to leave the jury with."

"What do you think Sir Winston will ask me on cross?"

"Oh, he may play up the fact that you didn't know them intimately. I can't think what else he might ask you. He may not cross-examine at all."

"Good. The sooner I'm off the stand, the better."

Stone stood up. "Don't worry about it, you'll do fine. I've got to go over Allison's testimony with her."

"See you later, then."

Stone walked down to the marina, greeted the two policemen on guard, and boarded *Expansive*.

"That you, Stone?" Allison called from the aft cabin.

"It's me."

She came into the saloon, wearing her usual tight shorts and shirt tied under her breasts.

She couldn't be a murderer, he thought; *she just couldn't be.*

"Are we going over my testimony?"

"Ready when you are."

"Would you like a beer?"

"Sure, why not."

She went to the fridge and got them both a cold bottle of Heineken.

Stone remembered that he had a fax in his pocket. He pulled it out, opened the envelope, and unfolded the sheet of paper. He thought it was odd that Thomas had put the fax in an envelope; he had never done that before. He read the letter.

"Stone," Allison said, concern in her voice, "what's wrong? You look awful."

He felt more numb than awful. He handed her the fax.

44

Stone took the fax from Allison and read it again, slowly this time, letting the words sink in, trying to make some sense of it. He might have seen this coming, he thought, but he hadn't; it was a bigger surprise than he was ready for.

Palm Springs

Dear Stone,

I didn't want to write this letter. When I saw what was happening, I wanted to sit down with you and tell you, face to face. Circumstances prevented that, of course, and I'm sorry. This letter will have to do.

Vance and I were married yesterday in Needles, Arizona. We flew there in Vance's airplane, just the two of us, and a justice of the peace performed a simple ceremony, with his wife and daughter as witnesses. Then we flew here, to Palm Springs, where Vance has a house. We'll spend our honeymoon here, and we hope the press won't discover us.

I can't explain to you how this happened, but it did. I had always liked Vance, and during the time we spent together working on the New Yorker *profile, I fell in love with him.*

You might wonder how I could so quickly fall in love with

*another man when you and I have been so close, living
together these past months. I wonder, too. I think I was more
vulnerable to someone else than I had been willing to admit to
myself. Although it wasn't a conscious thought, I think I had
come to know that you would have the greatest difficulty
making a permanent commitment to me, and I know now that
permanence is what I wanted most. I had meant to talk
seriously with you about this while we were on the sailing trip
to St. Marks, to see if we could work through it. I dreaded
bringing it up, hoping for a long time that you would do so.
When you didn't, I planned to make the try.*

*But fate and the weather were against us, and I have to
admit to you that when I couldn't go, I felt relieved. I think
that later, if I had thought you were pining away for me, I
would have gone, but then you became involved in the Allison
Manning business, and I knew from what I read in the press
and saw on television that you had your hands full.*

*I want children, and Vance does, too; that's a big part of
this. But I'm making it sound logical and carefully planned
when, really, it was entirely spontaneous, growing day after
day, until it overwhelmed us both. The only flaw in my
happiness is that I could not resolve my relationship with you
before this happened. I certainly did not wish to cause you pain.*

*I know you have your own very independent life to live and
over the long haul, I know that I couldn't have fit into it without
changing the things I loved about you most—your spontaneity,
your love of your life, and your singularity as a man.*

*I hope that you and I can remain friends, and that you can
wish Vance and me well. We truly are deliriously happy. After
some time has passed, and when we're in New York again, I'll
call you, and perhaps we can have lunch and talk about
things. Vance was very impressed with you when you met,
and he would like to know you better.*

*I hope this time hasn't been too bad for you and that you
get that poor woman off. From what I've heard she is so
obviously innocent and those people down there are
prosecuting her for their own ends. I know you'll do your very
considerable best.*

Until I see you again, I remain your good friend and feel nothing but affection and admiration for you.

Arrington

Stone folded the letter and put it into his pocket.

"Are you all right?" Allison asked. "You look as though you've had the wind knocked out of you."

"I suppose I have," Stone replied. "I have to admit, I wasn't expecting this."

Allison sat down beside him and took his hand in hers. "I'm sorry you're hurt, but you really should have seen it coming. I did."

Stone looked at her, incredulous. "You did? How could you? You hardly knew anything about it."

"I knew just enough to read the signs. No girl who was really in love would have passed up a week in St. Marks with you, not even for Vance Calder. You're really not very perceptive about women, you know."

"Well, if I didn't know that, I do now," he said, sighing.

She went to the bar and mixed him a rum and tonic, then brought it back to him. "Drink that; you'll feel better in a while." She went into the aft cabin and left him alone in the saloon.

Stone sipped the drink and thought about the last few days. If his letter had reached Arrington in time, would that have mattered? Probably not, he realized. It wouldn't have healed the problems in their relationship. Presently, he did feel better. The defense mechanisms were clicking into place now, and the ego's own anesthesia was numbing the parts of him that hurt most. He took some deep breaths, and something inside him unclenched. Now, he thought, he must bring himself back to the present, because he had a lot to do.

45

H e sat her down across the saloon and told her to get comfortable. "Comfort is the first thing," he said. "I don't want you squirming on the stand. No, don't cross your legs, cross your ankles, and fold your hands together. Comfortable?"

"Fairly."

"Find a position early on and be still. If you have to change, do it slowly and deliberately, and remember not to cross your legs."

"I think I got that part about the legs."

"Good. Now, your attitude is going to be important. When I question you I want you to think hard and tell me exactly the way things happened. I want the jury to see that you're trying to be honest."

"All right."

"When Sir Winston's turn comes, I want you to keep exactly the same demeanor; don't use defensive body language like crossing your arms. Don't be petulant; don't show anger; above all, don't raise your voice. Take his questions very seriously, and try to answer them honestly, unless it appears that he's asking a question merely for effect, a rhetorical question, then you can look disappointed."

"Disappointed, not angry," she repeated.

"All right, are you ready?"

"Ready."

"Mrs. Manning, what was your motive for killing your husband?"

She stared at him, and her eyes grew hard.

"Sorry, I didn't tell you I was going to be Sir Winston, did I?"

"No, you didn't."

"You have to be ready for surprises. He may come right out of left field with something, but you can answer it immediately, because you're relying on the truth, not subterfuge."

She shook her shoulders and tried to relax her body. "Okay, who are you this time?"

"I'm your attorney. Mrs. Manning, did you love your husband?"

Allison looked as if she might weep. "Oh, yes, I loved him."

"Don't overdo it; this isn't a soap opera."

"Isn't it?" she asked archly.

"Mrs. Manning, what reason might you have had to kill your husband?"

"I had no reason whatever," she replied firmly.

"Now you're getting it right," he said.

"Mrs. Manning, how much life insurance did your husband have?"

She frowned and began thinking.

"Don't hesitate, tell the truth. If he asks you such a question, it's because he already knows the answer."

"Aren't you going to have some sort of structure to this questioning?"

"In court, yes; but not now. I'm deliberately throwing curves at you, because I want you to be ready for anything. Don't worry about structure right now, or even if I'm Sir Winston or me; just answer each question truthfully."

"All right, all right," she said irritably.

"If you think this is hard, wait until the trial starts. I'll tell you again, rely on the truth, because it really can set you free. If you start striking poses the jury will know it immediately. Try to think of these people as your friends, friends you wouldn't lie to, friends on whom you're depending to do right by you, friends you trust."

"Who are these people likely to be?"

"They could be this island's aristocrats, or they could be cab-drivers and shopkeepers; we won't know until they're there, facing you. Don't look at me or Sir Winston all the time when you're being questioned; look at the jury, not as a group, but as individuals. Share your answers with them, one at a time; suck them into your story, each man of them."

She nodded. "All right."

"Mrs. Manning, what is the net worth of your husband's estate?"

"I believe it will be around fifteen million dollars, but I won't know for sure until all the debts are paid."

"Good! Mrs. Manning, why would your husband have twelve million dollars in life insurance?"

"Paul had never saved much money, although he earned a lot from the sale of his books. He knew he was a candidate for a heart attack, because his doctor had told him so, and he wanted me to be secure if he should die suddenly. Buying so much insurance was sort of a way of saving, of forcing himself to save, so there would be support for me if he died."

"Good! Answer that way—fully and completely always."

"Of course," Allison replied with assurance.

"Mrs. Allison, have you ever fired a scuba diver's spear gun?"

She reacted as if struck. "Ah, I . . . no."

"That's a lie. If I can spot it, so can the jury. Answer the question."

She took a deep breath and exhaled it. "Yes, of course. Paul and I went diving whenever we were near a good reef."

"Have you ever struck anything with a harpoon fired from a gun?"

She smiled ruefully. "I'm afraid not. Paul was a good shot, but I would always miss."

"Good, get a laugh out of them. How far were you standing from Paul when you fired the spear gun at him?"

Her face collapsed into disbelief. "What?"

"Where did the spear strike him?"

"Are you crazy?"

"In the chest? In the neck? Did he fall overboard immediately, or did you have to help him?"

"Stone, goddammit!"

"Did he bleed a lot? Did sharks come when they smelled the blood?"

"Stop this!"

"Answer the questions!!!"

"I never fired a spear gun at my husband, never!" she cried, furious now. "I would never have done anything to harm him!"

"Now that's better," Stone said. "That's a good time to get angry, when he does that to you."

"You said not to get angry."

"I misled you."

"You son of a bitch."

"No, I'm the sweetest guy in the world; Sir Winston Sutherland is the son of a bitch, and he'll do anything he possibly can to get you to come apart on the stand. He already knows about the spear gun."

"How do you know that?"

"Because the police searched the yacht, remember? You think they wouldn't notice a lethal weapon hanging on a bulkhead in plain sight?"

"Oh," she said.

"What about the other weapons?"

"What other weapons?"

"What did they take from the boat? A pistol? A shotgun?"

"We didn't have any weapons on board; Paul was very anti-gun."

"What about the spear gun? That was a weapon."

"It was a tool; it was used for fishing," she said calmly.

"What didn't they find? A nine-millimeter automatic? A riot gun? What?"

"There were no weapons aboard!" she cried. "None!"

"How many knives were aboard the yacht?"

"I don't know how many . . ."

"Think! Count them in your head!"

She thought for a moment. "Maybe eight or ten, maybe a dozen."

"Enumerate them."

"Let's see, in the galley, there was a chef's knife, a bread knife, a boning knife, and two paring knives."

"How long was the chef's knife?"

"About eight inches. I could never handle the big ones."

"Is that what you used on your husband? An eight-inch chef's knife? That would do the job."

"I never harmed my husband," she said quietly.

"What other knives were aboard?"

"There were a couple of rigging knives; we kept one by the main hatch and one strapped to the mast, for deck work. Paul wore another one in a scabbard, along with a marlin spike."

"Did you take the knife from his belt and stab him with it?"

"No! I never harmed him."

"So you just gave him a shove when he was pissing overboard, huh?"

"I did not!"

"Was he wearing the scabbard with the knife and marlin spike when you rolled his body overboard?"

"No, I removed the belt first."

"So, you did roll him overboard!"

"Yes, I did; some hours after his death."

"Did you search his pockets, Mrs. Manning, for money or spare change? Was there anything you wouldn't take from him?"

She locked her eyes onto Stone's, and when she spoke she was begging him to believe her. "Please, I never, ever harmed Paul. He was dead when I buried his body at sea." Tears rolled down her cheeks.

Stone went and took her in his arms. "All right," he said. "That's my girl; that's my star witness; that's my innocent victim of perverted justice."

She looked up at him and laughed. "Gotcha, didn't I?"

Stone buried his face in his hands.

CHAPTER

46

Stone strode across the lawn toward the Shipwright's Arms, thinking hard about Arrington. He thought of writing to her, maybe even calling her; then he remembered that she was at Vance Calder's Palm Springs house. He didn't have any of Calder's addresses or numbers, so there was no way to get in touch with her until she got in touch with him.

He was almost to the bar when he stopped in his tracks. A man in a seersucker suit was sitting at the bar, drinking something and talking to Thomas. He was big, over six feet, and better than two hundred fifty pounds; that was obvious even when he was seated. Stone had seen only one photograph of Paul Manning, but the man seemed to look very like him, except for the absence of a beard, and he had no idea what Manning would look like without the beard. Stone suddenly had the strange feeling that the whole business was some sort of dreadful error, that Paul Manning had simply fallen overboard near the Canaries and had swum ashore, and now he had shown up in St. Marks to save Allison's life. He approached the bar with some trepidation and sat down. "Thomas, could I have a beer?"

Thomas set a Heineken on the bar, and the big man turned and looked at him. "You must be Stone Barrington," he said.

"That's right," Stone replied.

The man stuck out a hand. "I'm Frank Stendahl."

Stone shook the hand. "How do you do?"

"Very well, thanks. Been seeing a lot about you on television the past week."

"I expect so. Where have you come from, Mr. Stendahl?"

"I'm a New Englander," he said. "The Boston area."

"And what brings you to St. Marks?"

"Vacation," the man said. "I seem to be about the only tourist around here."

"Well, first there was the blizzard in the Northeast, then we were pretty choked up with press, and then, I guess, the bad press made St. Marks an unpopular destination."

"Funny, the publicity somehow made it more attractive to me. I understand you've got a trial starting soon."

"That's right."

"I wonder if I could attend? Could you arrange it for me?"

"I'm afraid not; I'm out of my own bailiwick here, you see."

Thomas chimed in. "It's open to the public," he said. "I expect if you were there an hour before the trial you'd get a seat."

"Thanks, Thomas," Stendahl said. "Well, Stone—if I may call you that—what's your trial strategy going to be?"

"I don't think I can discuss that," Stone replied, sipping his beer.

"Of course not; that was silly of me. The lady seems to be innocent, though; you going to get her off?"

"I'll do my best."

"Well, how will . . ."

Stone cut him off. "I said, I can't discuss it."

Stendahl held his hands up before him. "Hey, my fault; didn't mean to dig."

"That's all right."

"Well, now that I've cooled off, I think I'll get up to my room and change into something more tropical," Stendahl said. The man got down off his stool and lumbered toward the stairs.

"What's his story?" Stone asked Thomas.

Thomas shrugged. "He used a credit card with the right name on it, but . . ."

"But what?"

"There was a moment when I thought he might be a cop," Thomas said, "but after I talked with him a while, I didn't think so anymore."

"What did he want to talk about?"

"Allison, the trial, the press, anything he could find out. He was really pumping me."

"And you still don't think he could be a cop."

"A cop would have done it differently," Thomas said. "More subtly. This guy just charged straight ahead."

"You think he's just an interested tourist?"

"He doesn't feel like a tourist, either."

"What does he feel like?"

"I think he's got an agenda, but I'm damned if I know what it is. Besides, what would an American cop be doing down here?"

"I don't think I ever saw a cop wear a seersucker suit," Stone said.

"Me neither."

"What sort of luggage did he have?"

"Hartmann leather, a suitcase and a briefcase, matching."

"That doesn't sound like a cop, either; too expensive. That's a businessman's luggage."

"I would have thought so."

Stone shrugged. "Well, I guess businessmen take vacations."

"Usually with their wives; he's alone."

"Bachelor? Divorced?"

"I guess he could be."

Frank Stendahl reappeared, wearing casual clothes, exposing pasty white arms. "Think I'll walk down to the marina and have a look at the boats," he said to no one in particular.

Stone and Thomas watched him as he strolled across the lawn and came to a stop at the marina gate, confronted by the two police officers on guard there. He chatted with them for a minute or so, then turned and walked back toward the inn. Halfway, he changed his mind and walked back toward the water at an angle chosen to take him to the harbor's edge beyond the marina. A moment later, he disappeared around a point of land.

"Where will that walk take him?" Stone asked.

"To the mouth of the harbor, eventually," Thomas replied.

"I've got some work to do upstairs," Stone said. "If he comes back, see what you can find out about him, will you?"

"Sure, glad to. You think he's up to no good, Stone?"

"Right now, all I think is that he's a tourist, like he says; maybe the sort of guy who turned up at the O. J. Simpson trial. I can't think of any other reason for him to be here, can you?"

Thomas shrugged.

"See you later." Stone hopped off his barstool and headed upstairs. After what he'd been through with the press, Stendahl didn't seem to be much of a threat.

47

An hour later, Stone came back downstairs. Stendahl was back at the bar, sucking on a piña colada, and across the room, Hilary Kramer of the *Times* and Jim Forrester of *The New Yorker* were sharing a table. He walked over to them. "Mind if I join you?" he asked.

"Not at all," Hilary replied. "Sit down."

"Jim," Stone said, "did you by any chance get a good look at the man at the bar?"

Forrester looked that way. "The big guy? Nope."

"I wonder if you'd do me a favor."

"What?"

"Go over there and strike up a conversation with the guy, then come back and tell me what you think. Shouldn't be too difficult; he seems to be pretty outgoing."

Forrester shrugged. "Okay." He walked over to the bar, ordered a drink, and in a moment was engaged in conversation with Stendahl.

"What's that all about?" Kramer asked.

"I just want to know who the guy is," Stone replied. "He seems to have come down here just to attend the trial."

"A camp follower?"

"Maybe, but whose camp?"

"Well, Jim will worm it out of him; he's endlessly curious, a typical reporter—asks hundreds of questions, answers few."

"I haven't found him to be particularly close-mouthed," Stone said. "He doesn't talk much to you, huh?"

"Maybe he's gay," Kramer said.

"Doesn't seem so, but I guess you never know for sure. Have your charms been wasted on him?"

She smiled. "Let's just say that I've told him a lot more than he's told me. I envy him one thing, though."

"What's that?"

"He's got the best memory of any reporter I've ever met. Either that, or he's just too sloppy to take notes."

"Well, he's a magazine writer, been doing travel stuff," Stone said. "He's not the died-in-the-wool *Front Page* type, like you."

"Like me?" she asked, surprised.

"You're a regular Hildy Parks," Stone said.

She laughed again, then she looked at him sharply. "Stone, while I'm in my Hildy mode, did you really just stumble into the Allison Manning mess, or is there something more to it?"

Stone raised his right hand. "Stumbled, honest."

"You were just down here all on your own?"

"Wasn't supposed to be that way."

"How was it supposed to be?"

"Want me to cry in your beer?"

"All you want; I'm a good listener."

"This isn't for publication, not even for a mention."

"It's nothing to do with the trial, then?"

"Nothing; purely personal."

"Cry away."

"My girl was supposed to meet me at the airport; we were coming together. She missed the flight because of a meeting at *The New Yorker*—she's a magazine writer, like Jim—and before she could get on the next day's flight, the blizzard happened."

"That was bad luck."

"It gets worse. The subject of her piece was Vance Calder. She went to L.A. with him for more interviews."

"Uh-oh."

"You said it."

"She's not your girl anymore?"

"Worse; she's now Mrs. Vance Calder. They were married yesterday; I got a fax."

"Hoo! Well, at least you lost her to somebody spectacular."

Stone shrugged. "I wonder if that's better than having her run off with a CPA?"

"What's her name?"

"Arrington Carter."

"Jesus; I know her." Kramer shook her head. "Well, a little, not much. She is very beautiful."

"Don't rub it in."

She started. "Does anybody know about this?"

"Just you and me."

She looked at her watch. "I wonder if I can still make tomorrow's paper."

"Oh, no you don't," Stone said.

Kramer fell back into her chair. "Oh, shit, I promised, didn't I?"

"You promised. Anyway, it's not your kind of story, is it?"

"No, but it would have been nice for the Chronicle column, which is the nearest thing the *Times* has to gossip, and nobody would have believed that I could get the beat on the story."

"Leave the Calders in peace," Stone said. "They're holed up, hoping that somebody like you won't find them until they're ready to spring the news themselves."

"Well, that's the last story I expected to get in St. Marks." She looked up. "Here comes Jim."

"Don't mention Arrington to him."

"Okay."

Forrester ambled up and sat down, tossing a business card onto the table. "Well, thanks a lot, Stone; you got me into a conversation with a life insurance salesman."

Stone looked at the card. "Frank R. Stendahl, Boston Mutual," he read.

"I barely got away with my shirt. You owe me a drink."

Stone waved at Thomas and pointed at Forrester, then made a drinking motion. "So, Jim, you think he's for real?"

"You want his whole story?"

"You bet."

"He's divorced, with two teenage kids; he lives in Lynn, Massachusetts—that's near Boston—his wife got the house and nearly everything else, and he makes the million-dollar round-table every year. I believe that, too: I told him I was getting a divorce, hoping that would keep him off the subject of insurance, and he had ten reasons ready why a born-again bachelor would need another million in coverage!"

"I owe you two drinks," Stone said.

"You owe me dinner," Forrester replied.

"Okay, okay; probably not tonight, but before we leave."

"I want to debrief you after the trial anyway; maybe we can do that over dinner."

Kramer spoke up. "Only if I can be there, too."

Forrester laughed. "It's a good thing you and I aren't direct competitors."

"Jim," Stone said. "Does Stendahl remind you of anybody?"

Forrester looked toward the bar. "Remind me of anybody?"

"Maybe of Paul Manning, a little?"

Forrester looked thoughtful. "Well, they're about the same size and build, but apart from that they don't really look alike."

"Even taking the absence of a beard into account?"

Forrester shook his head. "Very different in manner and accent, and not at all the same face, even without the beard. What, did you think he might not be dead after all?"

"It crossed my mind for a fleeting moment. My life would certainly be a lot simpler if Paul Manning walked in here and sat down at the bar."

"Well, put your mind at rest, pal; I mean, maybe Manning's out there swimming around somewhere, but that ain't him at the bar."

"And you're the only one here who knew him," Stone said, sighing.

"Allison knew him; give her a look at Stendahl and see what she has to say."

Stone shook his head. "I wouldn't put her through that."

Forrester looked sympathetic. "That would solve a lot of

•

231

problems for you, wouldn't it? I mean, if Stendahl were Manning."

"It certainly would," Stone agreed.

Kramer spoke up. "It would get Allison off, but Stendahl would sure be in a lot of trouble."

"Yes, he would," Stone said. "Although I'm not sure what they might charge him with in St. Marks."

Forrester laughed. "It would be funny, wouldn't it? Stendahl/Manning stands up in court and says, 'I am the deceased; let my wife go!' I can just see Sir Winston's face."

They all had a good laugh.

48

Ⅰt was their last night before the trial. "Want to go to dinner at the inn?" Stone asked.

She shook her head. "I don't want to be on display. I would much rather cook dinner for you aboard."

"Why don't I cook dinner for you instead?" he asked.

"No, that would have too much of the condemned's last meal about it."

"Come on, I don't want you to worry about the trial."

"I am serene," she said, and she certainly seemed that way. "I'd just rather do something normal, like cooking. In fact, I've already thawed a chateaubriand in anticipation."

"Sounds wonderful. Can I make a Caesar salad?

"Oh, all right, but just the salad. There's some romaine lettuce in the supplies Thomas sent down."

"And I need fresh eggs, olive oil, garlic, some Dijon mustard, and a can of anchovies."

"All in the galley. I'll get the meat started and make some béarnaise sauce first. You can make me a martini."

"Pffft! You're a martini!"

She groaned.

"One martini, coming up." Stone mixed the drink, shook it,

dropped an olive in, strained the crystal liquid into a large martini glass, and set it on the galley counter.

She sipped it. "Mmmm. Just right."

Stone mixed himself a rum and tonic and watched as she
unwrapped the beef, the center of the tenderloin, pounded it to
about an inch and a half of thickness with a meat mallet, dusted
it liberally with salt and pepper, and laid it on the gas grill.
Then she diced some shallots and sautéed them with some tarragon, vinegar, and white wine. While this mixture was reducing she separated half a dozen egg yolks, heated some butter,
then put the yolks into the Cuisinart, turned it on, and poured
hot butter into the chute. Moments later she had hollandaise,
which, when mixed with the reduced shallots and tarragon,
became béarnaise. She dipped a finger into the sauce and held it
up for Stone to taste.

"Wow!" Stone said. "You made that look easy."

"It is easy," she replied, turning over the beef. "Now you
can make your salad.

Stone rinsed the romaine leaves and left them to drain. He
crushed a couple of garlic cloves and some anchovies into the
wooden salad bowl, then separated two egg yolks and dropped
them into the bowl as well. Then he whipped the mixture with
a whisk while adding olive oil until the consistency was perfect.
He added a teaspoon of mustard and a little vinegar, some salt
and pepper, and gave her a fingerful to taste.

"Absolutely perfect," she crowed, hoisting the meat onto a
cutting board and slicing it deftly with a sharp knife.

Stone put the lettuce into the bowl with the dressing and
tossed it until each leaf was thinly coated, then set the bowl on
the saloon table alongside the beef.

Allison dug out a bottle of red wine. "You do the honors,"
she said, holding it out with the corkscrew for him.

"Opus One, '89," he said, reading the label. "I'm impressed."

"It's the best bottle on the boat."

"And it will need decanting. You have a seat." He poured
the wine gently into a decanter, watching for the sediment to
creep up the bottle's neck, stopping when it did. Then he sat
down and poured them both some.

Allison raised her glass. "To the best last meal a girl ever had," she said.

Stone raised his glass. "To the last meal's arriving about seventy years from now."

She laughed. "I'll drink to that."

They ate hungrily, wolfing down the tender beef and taking the marvelous wine in large sips, then served themselves seconds of everything.

"I won't have room for dessert," Stone said.

"I'm dessert," she replied. "And you'd better have room."

They lay together in the aft cabin, kissing and stroking each other tenderly. They both had things to forget, Stone thought—he, Arrington; she, that he might be the last man she'd ever have. There was a moon filtering through the portholes, and in its light, with her fair hair and skin, she was as white as marble. Stone bent over her and his tongue found its way through the soft, blond pubic hair into the warm sweetness beneath. He was gentle, not pressing her, and she ran her fingers through his hair, encouraging and directing him until she shuddered and came quietly.

Then she reversed their positions, taking him into her mouth, caressing him with her tongue and fingers, drawing him to his fullest—teasing, tempting, but never allowing him to climax. Finally, when he was nearly mad, she mounted him and pulled him into a sitting position. They were mouth to mouth, nipple to nipple, he deeply into her. She brought her feet behind him so that she could pull him even farther inside her.

They stayed that way for what seemed like hours, then Allison began moving more rapidly. Stone moved with her, and, locked tightly together, they came noisily, finally toppling over onto the sheets.

"If that has to be my last time," she panted, "I won't have any complaints as to how well it went. I honestly don't think sex can be any better than that."

"You won't get an argument from me," Stone panted back.

They lay in each other's arms for a while, then she surprised him by bounding out of bed. "Come with me!" she cried.

He followed her into the saloon, then up the companionway

and into the cockpit, oblivious of the two startled guards on the dock. She flung herself over the lifelines and into English Harbour, with Stone right behind her, matching her stroke for stroke.

She stopped and treaded water. "Do you think they think I'm making a break for it?" she asked.

"I think they're too astonished to think," Stone replied, laughing.

They swam out into the harbor, the moon sparkling on their wake, then back to the yacht, climbing aboard again. Then they went back to bed and started over.

CHAPTER

49

The drive to Government House, with Thomas at the wheel, was silent. Stone sat in the front, reading the opening statement he had written, merely for something to occupy his mind. Leslie Hewitt would probably ignore it anyway. He glanced occasionally at Allison, who sat in the backseat, gazing absently out at the St. Marks landscape, seemingly calm and self-possessed. Her hair was pulled back tightly into a bun, at Stone's request, and she wore a mostly blue, floral-printed silk dress. She looked about twenty-one, Stone thought.

They arrived in the official parking lot nearly simultaneously with Sir Leslie Hewitt's ancient Morris Minor station wagon. Everyone got out and shook hands, smiling, attempting good spirits. With Hewitt in the lead they entered the building through the police door and climbed the stairs to the second floor, passing through a short corridor to the door used by guards, lawyers, and defendants. To one side was a small robing room, and Stone and Hewitt donned their robes and wigs. Once again, Stone felt foolish.

They entered the courtroom. Stone had forgotten that Allison would have to stand in the dock, several feet behind the defense table; he would not be able to confer with her when court was in session. He felt very much out of his element. In

New York he would have been at home in any courtroom and in at least partial control. Here he felt like an intruder, and he worked hard at not letting Allison know it.

Spectators were filing into the gallery, which was raised in tiers like a college lecture room or, more aptly, London's Old Bailey. The room was not paneled, simply painted, and the paint had begun to fade and peel. Stone saw Frank Stendahl, the insurance salesman, enter and take a front-row seat not far from the dock.

At the front of the room, elevated above the defense and prosecution tables, was the bench; to the judge's right was the witness box, and beyond that, the jury would sit. Stone and Sir Leslie sat down at the defense table. A moment later Sir Winston Sutherland swept into the courtroom, his robes flowing, followed by his assistant.

"Leslie," Stone asked "did you have an opportunity to study the opening and closing statements I wrote?"

"I read them," Hewitt replied.

"There were a number of very important points, particularly in the opening statement, that I thought should be included in your opening."

"I'm aware of that, Stone," Hewitt said, arranging his robe. "Please don't concern yourself with my opening."

Stone sighed and tried to make himself comfortable in the hard wooden chair.

A moment later, the bailiff entered, stood at attention, and cried, "Hear ye, hear ye, all rise for the Lord Cornwall."

All rose, and the judge, resplendent in red robes, his black face contrasting sharply with the whiteness of his long wig, entered and sat down at the bench in a high-backed, ornate leather chair, with a gilded crown set at the top, a remnant of Her Majesty's rule. "Good morning," the judge said.

Hewitt was on his feet. "Your Lordship," he said, "a small request before we begin."

"Yes, Sir Leslie?"

"We have a long day ahead of us; I wonder if the prisoner might have a chair?"

Stone's stomach lurched at hearing Allison so described.

"Of course, Sir Leslie. The bailiff will provide a chair for the prisoner." The bailiff found a chair and set it in the dock for Allison, who thanked him sweetly, eliciting an unexpected smile.

Stone hoped that was a harbinger of things to come.

"The court will come to order," the judge said. "I will hear from the minister of justice."

Sir Winston stood, cleared his throat, and spoke. "Your Lordship, today we hear the case of the people of St. Marks against the prisoner Allison Manning, on a charge of murder. We are ready for Your Lordship to select the jury." He sat down.

"Call the first juror," the judge said.

"Call the first juror!" the bailiff cried.

A door opened at the rear of the courtroom and a man entered. He was elderly and thin and he was wearing a three-piece wool suit that fit him very well. He took the first seat in the jury box.

"State your name and occupation," the bailiff said.

"I am Charles Kimbrough," the man said. "I am a tailor by trade, and I am recently retired."

"Mr. Kimbrough," the judge said, "are you in good health and of sound mind?"

"I believe I am, Your Lordship."

"Are you acquainted with the prisoner or any members of the court?"

"I am acquainted with Sir Leslie Hewitt and yourself, Your Lordship, as I have made suits for both of you in the past."

"Anyone else?"

"I know Sir Winston, though I have never had the pleasure of his custom."

"Yes. Have you heard anything about this case?"

"Oh, yes, Your Lordship," the man said. "I have read all about it in the newspapers."

"Have you formed an opinion of the prisoner's guilt or innocence?"

"Well, Your Lordship, I think she might have done it, but then again, she might not have."

"He's okay with me," Stone murmured.

•

"Keep your seat, Mr. Kimbrough," the judge said. "You're the foreman of this jury."

Kimbrough sat down, and another man was brought in. He was not so finely dressed, but he was clean and neat. He was a bartender at a local hotel, and he was soon seated. He was followed by a taxi driver, an apprentice shoemaker, who could not have been more than twenty, a street vendor, and a white merchant, all of whom were briefly questioned and rapidly seated.

"We have a jury," the judge said.

"Only six?" Stone asked Hewitt.

"It is all we need," the barrister replied.

Stone was dissatisfied with only the taxi driver, who looked at Allison with something like contempt, as if he had seen her kind before, but only in his rearview mirror. But on the whole, he thought, he had tried cases before worse juries.

"The foreman is good for us," Hewitt whispered. "He is a very kind man and will not hang a woman lightly. The others will respect his opinion because he is so well dressed."

Stone hoped so.

"The bailiff will read the charges," the judge said.

The bailiff stood and read from a single sheet of paper. "The prisoner, Mrs. Allison Manning, is charged with murder, willfully taking the life of Mr. Paul Manning, her husband, on a date unknown between January first of this year and the present day, on the high seas, having departed the port of Puerto Rico, in the Canary Islands, a Spanish possession, and not yet having arrived at the port of English Harbour, in St. Marks. Be it known to all present that the crime of murder is a capital offense in St. Marks, and that if convicted, the prisoner will suffer death in the prescribed manner, which is hanging." He sat down.

Short, but not very sweet, Stone thought.

"Now," the judge said, addressing the jurors, "I will explain how we will proceed in this courtroom. The prosecuting barrister, Sir Winston, will make an opening statement of his case, then he will be followed by Sir Leslie, who will make an opening statement in defense of the prisoner. Thereafter, Sir Winston will call witnesses and question them, followed by a cross-examination by Sir Leslie. When the government has completed its case, Sir Leslie may call witnesses and question them, and Sir Winston may cross-examine them. Items may be entered in evidence by either side. When the defense has concluded its case, Sir Leslie will make a closing statement, followed by a closing statement from Sir Winston. When he has concluded I will charge the jury, and the jury will retire to the jury room to consider their verdict, which must be a majority verdict. While we are in the courtroom the bench will make all rulings on the admissibility of statements and other evidence, and the decision of the bench will be final in all matters. Is there any one of you who does not understand what will take place?"

No member of the jury moved, let alone spoke.

"In that case, we will begin with the opening statement of the people of St. Marks, who are represented by Sir Winston Sutherland. Sir Winston?"

Sir Winston rose, smoothed his robes, adjusted his wig, shot his cuffs, cleared his throat, and began to speak.

50

Sir Winston bowed to the bench, and his voice boomed over the courtroom, stentorian and didactic. He might have been instructing the jury without waiting for the judge to do so. "Gentlemen of the jury," he began, though he was looking at the packed gallery rather than at the jurors, "we come here this day to avenge the death of a human being. Paul Manning was a gentleman in the prime of life who had made for himself a successful career, becoming famous and rich. He owned a large house; he owned an expensive yacht; he owned a life insurance policy with a death benefit of twelve million dollars. It was for this wealth that he was murdered by his wife." He gestured dramatically at Allison in the dock.

"You might not think that she looks the part of the murderess, being demure in appearance, but we will show today how she took the life of her husband, how she cruelly and heartlessly consigned him to the depths of the ocean and watched him die as his yacht sailed away from him. You will hear Paul Manning speak from the grave," he intoned, and the apprentice shoemaker's eyes became large and round. "His words recorded in his own handwriting." He held up the leather-bound diary, and the juror looked relieved.

"You will hear how she plotted his death over many months,

biding her time until the moment came when he was helpless, and then she took his life." He paused and looked witheringly at Allison, as though his eyes were sufficient to punish her. Allison returned his gaze and shook her head slowly.

Good girl, Stone thought.

"When you have heard the evidence against Allison Manning," Sutherland continued, "you will reach the only verdict that the evidence will permit: you will find her guilty of willful and deliberate murder." Sir Winston bowed to the bench and sat down.

The judge turned toward the defense table. "Sir Leslie Hewitt will make the opening statement for the defense," he said.

Stone turned and looked at Hewitt. The little man appeared to be dozing. "Leslie!" Stone whispered sharply.

Hewitt's eyes popped open. "Eh?"

"Do you want me to give the opening statement?"

"Certainly not," Hewitt replied, looking around the courtroom. He rose to his feet and bowed to the bench, then, ignoring the gallery, turned his full attention to the jury. "Good morning, gentlemen," he said pleasantly. Two or three of them nodded in response. "I trust Sir Winston has not clouded your minds," he said with a chuckle. "The defense has quite a different view of his so-called evidence, as you might imagine, and as you will come to see during the course of this trial."

He indicated Allison with a warm smile. "Here we have a young woman who, with her much-loved husband, set off on the adventure of a lifetime, sailing across the Atlantic from America to Europe, just the two of them. This is not the act of two people who do not love each other—to be confined for weeks at a time at sea with only each other for company. This was a positive act, showing that these two people were happy together. You will hear from her own lips how they enjoyed their adventure and how, on the voyage back to the Americas, her husband suddenly fell ill and died, struck with an illness about which he had been warned by his doctors, but which he had taken none of the prescribed steps to prevent. You will hear how his death endangered the life of his young wife and how with courage and fortitude she managed to sail a large yacht alone across the sea, to make landfall on our island."

Sir Leslie cleared his throat and rearranged his robes. "Finally," he said, "when this trial has been concluded, you will see how this charge of murder is spurious and should never have been brought." He gestured toward Sir Winston. "You will wonder at the motives of the prosecution in bringing it. And you will have the opportunity to set things right, to return this dear young woman to freedom and her native country, to live out her life as best she can without the sorely missed companionship of her beloved husband." With a flourish he bowed to the bench, returned to the defense table, and sat down.

Not bad, Stone thought, for a periodically senile old man who had recently been asleep in the courtroom. While it may not have been all he had wished, Hewitt's opening was at least the equal of Sir Winston's, maybe even a little better. He was relieved that Sir Winston had not mentioned any witnesses or evidence in his opening statement that the defense didn't know about. The playing field was level, and that was as much as he could wish for at this point.

The judge turned to the prosecution table. "Sir Winston, call your first witness."

Sir Winston rose and spoke. "Call Mr. Frank Stendahl," he said.

Stone sat up straight. "What the hell?" he said aloud.

The judge looked at him sharply.

Stone tried to look ashamed of his outburst. He turned to look at the gallery as Stendahl left his seat and walked toward the witness box. He caught a glimpse of Hilary Kramer and Jim Forrester watching him, looking as puzzled as Stone was.

Stendahl stood in the witness box.

"Take the book," the bailiff said, offering a Bible and a card, "and read from the card."

Stendahl grasped the Bible and read, "I swear by Almighty God that the evidence I shall give in this court will be the truth."

The bailiff relieved him of the Bible and the card.

Sir Winston turned to the witness box. "State your name, address, and occupation for the record," he said.

"Frank Stendahl, 1202 Old Brook Road, Lynn, Massachusetts, U.S.A. I am the chief claims investigator for the Boston Mutual insurance company."

"Oh, Christ," Stone whispered to himself, earning a rebuking glance from Sir Leslie. He hadn't seen this coming.

"Mr. Stendahl, did your company, Boston Mutual, insure the life of Paul Manning?"

"Yes, we did."

"In what amount?"

"In the amount of twelve million dollars."

There was a stir in the jury box and raised eyebrows among the men who sat there.

"Is this, in your experience, a large sum of life insurance?"

"Indeed it is," Stendahl replied. "In fact, it is the largest policy my company has ever written on an individual life."

"And how old is your company? Was it recently formed?"

"Boston Mutual was founded in 1798."

"And in the nearly two hundred years since its founding, it has never written a policy as large as this?"

"Not on an individual life, when the individual was himself paying the premiums. We have had corporate policies that were larger, when a company was insuring the life of, say, its chief executive."

"What steps did your company take before insuring the life of a person for such a large sum?

"We did what we do for any large policy, that is, we investigate the background, the reputation, and the net worth of the applicant, and we have him examined by a doctor of our choosing. I personally conducted the background investigation of Mr. Manning."

"And what did you learn about Paul Manning during your investigations?"

"I learned that Mr. Manning was an important author with a large income; that he had an excellent credit record; and that he was known to be a person of good reputation in his community."

"And what did the medical evaluation of Mr. Manning reveal about his health?"

"May I consult notes?"

"Yes."

Stendahl took a sheet of paper from his inside pocket and read from it. "I quote from the report: 'Paul Manning is a forty-year-old writer who is in excellent health and who does not have any history of cancer, heart disease, diabetes, or any other serious illness. Neither is there any history of serious disease in either of his parents, both of whom died accidentally in their sixties, in an automobile accident."

"What was Mr. Manning's height and weight?"

He consulted his notes. "Six feet, two inches, two hundred and nineteen pounds."

"Did the examination include a test for serum blood cholesterol and triglycerides?"

"Yes, it did."

"What was the result?"

Stendahl checked his notes again. "His cholesterol count was one hundred ninety-nine, and his triglycerides were one hundred forty-seven."

"Did your company consider these to be within the normal range for a man of Mr. Manning's size?"

"Yes. We would expect the cholesterol count to be under two hundred and twenty, and the triglycerides to be under one hundred and fifty, in order to be insurable. Mr. Manning qualified on both counts."

"Did your company's medical examiner think of Mr. Manning as a heart attack waiting to happen?"

"Certainly not. If he had thought that, we would never have insured him."

"Mr. Stendahl, has your company paid the death benefit of the insurance policy?"

"Yes, we have."

"In full?"

"Yes."

"Without investigation?"

"Oh, we investigated, all right; we'd never pay a sum that large without an investigation. We sent a man down here to talk to Mrs. Manning last week."

"And he found all was in order?"

"He did, but there was something he didn't know until later."

"What was that?"

"That Mrs. Manning was about to be tried for the murder of her husband."

"She didn't tell your investigator that?"

"No. He learned about it from the newspapers, but by that time we had already paid the money into Mrs. Manning's bank account."

"And is that money still in her account?"

"I am advised that it is not."

"Where is that money now?"

"I am advised that it was wire-transferred into an account in the Cayman Islands, so by now it could be in any bank in the world."

"I have no further questions for this witness, Your Lordship," Sir Winston said, then sat down.

The judge turned to the defense table. "You may cross-examine."

Stone stood up. "Your Lordship, may I have a recess for a few minutes in order to consult with my client?"

The judge stifled a yawn. "You may not."

Stone looked at Allison, who sent him a sympathetic glance. He was going to have to wing it with this witness.

CHAPTER

51

Stone took some papers from a file folder and rose to address the witness. "Mr. Stendahl, how long ago did Paul Manning undergo the physical examination for his insurance policy?"

Stendahl consulted his notes. "Two years ago last week."

"And did your company's doctors see Mr. Manning after that date?"

"Not that I'm aware of."

"Had they seen him before that date?"

"Not that I'm aware of. He had no earlier policies with us."

Stone was getting into shallow water now, and he hoped he would not run aground. "Did he have any earlier policies with any other company?"

Stendahl consulted his notes. "None."

"Mr. Stendahl, when you are investigating an applicant for life insurance, is there a central record of health history you can consult?"

"Yes. If the applicant has had medical problems, we can usually find out about them."

"But if he hasn't had health problems, and if he hasn't previously applied for life insurance, there would be no record of his height, weight, or blood studies, would there?"

"No."

"Did you find any earlier medical records of Paul Manning?"

"No."

"So you don't know what occurred with regard to Mr. Manning's weight and various blood studies either before the examination or between the date of that examination and the date of his death?"

"No."

Stone breathed easier. He held up the documents for the bailiff. "May the witness read from these, Your Lordship?"

"He may."

The bailiff took the documents and handed them to Stendahl.

"Mr. Stendahl," Stone continued, "what are the documents you have just been handed?"

Stendahl flipped quickly through them. "They appear to be the results of another physical examination taken by Mr. Manning."

"On what date?"

"A year after our company's doctors examined him."

"Would you read the first paragraph, which has been high-lighted?"

Stendahl found the paragraph. "'Paul Manning is a forty-year-old author who has come in for a physical examination prior to an extensive sea voyage. Mr. Manning has no com-plaints, but he is desirous of being examined and taking a copy of his medical records on his journey. Mr. Manning is six feet, two inches tall and weighs . . .'" Stendahl paused.

"Go on, Mr. Stendahl."

"'. . . weighs two hundred and sixty-one pounds, rather too much for a man of his frame. The results of blood tests show a serum cholesterol count of three hundred twenty-five and serum triglycerides are four hundred and ten. These are both dangerously elevated, the high end of normal being two hun-dred and twenty for cholesterol and one hundred and fifty for triglycerides. Because of these numbers, in conjunction with Mr. Manning's lack of regular exercise, I have advised Mr. Manning to immediately undertake a program of exercise, a diet low in

•

cholesterol and other fats, and to bring his weight down to a maximum of two hundred pounds.'"

"Does this sound like the man your doctors examined?" Stone asked.

"No. It would appear that Mr. Manning changed his eating habits after our exam."

"Do you think it possible that Mr. Manning might have lost weight and watched his consumption of fats prior to your examination, so that he would have been insurable, then reverted to his old ways after the exam?"

Sir Winston was on his feet. "I object, Your Lordship. This calls for a conclusion on the part of the witness."

"Sustained," the judge said.

"Let me put it another way, Mr. Stendahl," Stone said. "Would you think that the man described in this later exam was, and I quote, 'a heart attack waiting to happen'?"

Sir Winston was up again.

"I withdraw the question, Your Lordship," Stone said, cutting him off. "We would like the medical examination report to be Exhibit Number One for the defense." Now he had to wade further into shallow water, violating the rule of every trial attorney: He was going to ask a question he didn't know the answer to. "Mr. Stendahl," he said, "was there a provision in Mr. Manning's insurance policy covering double indemnity?"

Stendahl hesitated a moment, then answered, "Yes, there was."

Thank God, Stone thought. "Would you explain to the court the meaning of the term 'double indemnity'?"

"It means that if the insured suffers accidental death, then the death benefit is doubled."

"So if Paul Manning had died accidentally, the death benefit would have been twenty-four million dollars?"

"That is correct."

"Now, Mr. Stendahl, I ask you to imagine the circumstances surrounding Paul Manning's death: he is alone with his wife in the middle of the Atlantic Ocean. Let us say, merely for the purposes of argument, that Mrs. Manning has decided to kill her husband. Having done so, would it not then be very profitable for her to claim that he had died as a result of an accident at sea?"

"Yes, I suppose it would."

"Profitable to the extent of an additional twelve million dollars?"

"Yes."

"But instead, she has asserted that he died as the result of a heart attack, has she not?"

Sir Winston was up. "Objection; no testimony to that effect thus far."

"Sustained," the judge said.

"Let me put it this way, Mr. Stendahl. In your experience as an insurance investigator, would a person who had decided to murder an insured do so under conditions of maximum profitability?"

"Yes."

"Not under conditions which would pay only half the available money?"

"No."

"Then, as an experienced investigator, when determining the facts of this case, would you say that Mrs. Manning is more likely or less likely to have murdered her husband?"

Stendahl sighed. "Less likely."

"One final question, Mr. Stendahl," Stone said. "As a witness in this trial, you are not entirely objective, are you?"

"I beg your pardon?"

"What I mean is, you have an ax to grind in this case, do you not?"

"I don't know what you mean." But he looked as though he knew exactly what was meant.

"Mr. Stendahl, can a person murder another, then collect on his life insurance?"

"No. A murderer is not legally entitled to benefit from his crime."

"So if Mrs. Manning should be convicted in this court, what would be the next action of you and your company?"

The ax fell on Stendahl. "Ah, we would of course endeavor to recover the money already paid."

"So, you and your company have a twelve-million-dollar ax to grind, do you not?"

"I, ah, see your point," Stendahl said softly.

"I'll take that as a yes. Thank you, Mr. Stendahl; no further questions." Stone sat down and gripped the edge of the table so that his hands would not be seen to tremble. Now the playing field was better than even; it was tilting his way.

Sir Winston had no redirect. He was not looking happy. He called his next witness. "The prosecution calls Captain Harold Beane of the St. Marks Constabulary." A well-starched officer took the stand and the oath.

Now, Stone thought, *we find out what, besides the diary, the police might have found on the* Expansive.

52

Sir Winston shuffled some notes, then addressed his witness. "Captain Beane, in the pursuit of your duties did you have occasion to visit the yacht *Expansive* at the marina in English Harbour?"

"I did."

"For what reason?"

"I received a call from the customs officer at English Harbour saying that a death had occurred on a yacht which had just sailed into the harbour."

"What did you find when you arrived at the marina?"

"I found Mrs. Allison Manning alone on the yacht. She told me that her husband had died aboard while they were en route from the Canary Islands to St. Marks."

"Did she mention a cause of death?"

"She said he had died of natural causes; she strongly suspected a heart attack."

"Did you later have occasion to search the yacht?"

"I did, after the preliminary questioning of Mrs. Manning."

"Did you find any evidence aboard the yacht to support Mrs. Manning's contention that her husband had died of natural causes?"

"No, I did not."

"Did you find any evidence aboard the yacht to suggest that Mr. Manning might not have died of natural causes?"

"I did."

Sir Winston held up the leather-bound diary for the jury to see, then handed it to the officer. "Did you find this book?"

"I did."

"After comparing it with other documents aboard the yacht, did you find the book to be in the handwriting of Paul Manning?"

"I did. Mrs. Manning confirmed that."

"In what form is the book written?"

"In the form of a diary."

"A diary written in the hand of the murder victim?"

Stone was on his feet. "Objection; no evidence has been offered to indicate that a murder took place."

Sir Winston turned on him. "The man is dead, isn't he?"

The judge intervened. "I am sorry, Sir Winston, but Mr. Barrington is right. The objection is sustained."

Sir Winston nodded, then turned back to his witness. "A diary written in the hand of the deceased?"

"Yes."

"Captain, would you turn to page three and read the passage marked, please?"

The officer found the page. "'They had been on the boat together for months now, and she had been the perfect bitch. She had always had a temper, but now she frightened him with the intensity of her anger.'" He looked up from the book.

"Now please turn to page seven and read the marked text."

The officer found the passage. "'They argued one day as she was making lunch. She had a chef's knife in her hand, and for a moment, he thought she might use it on him. He slept badly that night, waking often, expecting to feel the blade in his back.'"

"Thank you, Captain," Sir Winston said, taking back the book. "Your Lordship, we wish the diary to be recorded as Exhibit Number One for the prosecution. Now, did you find on the yacht any weapon that might be used to commit a murder?"

"There were no firearms, except a flare gun which had

never been fired," the officer replied, "but there were many knives aboard—several in the galley and two on deck in scabbards, secured to parts of the yacht."

"Was any of these knives of sufficient size and strength to be used to kill a man?"

"They were, all of them."

Sir Winston paused dramatically and looked at the jury as he asked his next question. "And did you find any other weapon?"

"Yes, I did."

Sir Winston reached into his briefcase, brought out an object, and held it up for the jury to see. Without taking his eyes from the jury, he addressed his witness. "Did you find this item?"

"I did," the officer replied.

Sir Winston handed it to the bailiff, who handed it to the witness. "And what did you determine this object to be?"

"It is a spear meant to be fired at fish by a gun operated by compressed air."

"Could this spear be fired out of the water?"

"Indeed it could."

"With sufficient force to penetrate and kill a man?"

"Yes, indeed. I believe it would be effective from a distance of as much as twenty feet."

"Is any particular strength or skill required to load and fire such a spear gun?"

"No."

"Could a woman do it?"

"A child could do it."

Sir Winston produced a spear gun from his briefcase. "Would you demonstrate the weapon for the court?"

"I would be glad to."

Sir Winston turned to the judge. "May the witness leave the box for the purpose of a demonstration, Your Lordship?"

"He may," the judge replied.

The captain stepped down from the box, and another officer entered with a sheet of plywood, leaning it against a wall. The captain loaded the spear gun, aimed it at the plywood, and fired. The spear buried itself solidly into the wood with a loud thunk. There was a stirring in the jury box as the members imagined the spear entering Paul Manning's body.

"The defense wishes the spear recorded as Exhibit Number Two for the prosecution," Sir Winston said. "I have no further questions for the witness at this time."

"Mr. Barrington?" the judge said.

Stone rose. He wanted to address the spear first. "Thank you, Your Lordship. Captain Beane, have you had occasion to go aboard other yachts at English Harbour?"

"On many occasions," the officer replied.

"Did any of them have knives aboard?"

"Oh, yes."

"Did all of them have knives aboard?"

"I suppose so."

"Did any of them have spear guns aboard?"

"Yes, I suppose so."

"So knives and spear guns are quite common, if not universal equipment aboard yachts, are they not?"

"Yes, they are."

"Did you find any specific evidence that the spear or any of the knives aboard the yacht *Expansive* was used in the commission of a murder?"

"Well, no."

"No blood on the spear or any of the knives?"

"No."

"No blood on the decks?"

"Well, blood could have been washed off."

"Did you find any evidence that blood had been washed off anything?"

"No."

"Then what made you conclude that a murder had taken place at all?"

"Oh, the diary," the captain replied. "I found the diary very incriminating."

"Have you read the diaries of any other men besides Paul Manning?"

"One or two."

"Were they written in the third person?"

"I'm sorry?"

"Mr. Manning's diary was written to say, 'He did or she did,' not 'I did,' is that not so?"

"That is so."

"So it was written in the third person?"

"Ah, yes, I see. Yes, the third person."

"Were any of the other diaries you read written in the third person? Or were they written in the first person, where the diarist describes himself as 'I'?"

"They were written in the first person."

"In your experience as a police officer, would you say that diaries are generally written in the first person?"

"Generally, I suppose."

"Are you aware of how Mr. Manning earned his living?"

"Yes, he was a writer."

"Do you know what his specialty was as a writer?"

"No."

"We have heard evidence that he was a writer of thrillers and mystery stories. Did you know that?"

"No, I didn't."

"Have you ever before seen the notes a writer makes before he begins writing a book?"

"No."

"Can you understand how a writer might write notes and scenes that he might later incorporate into a book?"

"Yes, I suppose."

"Has it occurred to you that this so-called diary might not be a diary at all, but a collection of notes for Mr. Manning's next book?"

"Ah, no."

"Now that you have been enlightened as to a writer's working habits, don't you think it possible that the book might be Mr. Manning's preliminary notes?"

"I suppose it could be," the captain admitted.

"Is it not likely that the book is his notes?"

Sir Winston was up. "Objection; calls for a conclusion."

"Your Lordship," Stone said, "the captain has already reached a quite different conclusion, with the help of Sir Winston, based on no real evidence at all; why can he now not change his mind and possibly reach another conclusion?"

"Overruled," the judge said. "Answer the question, Captain."

The officer looked very uncomfortable. "I suppose it might be likely that the book is Mr. Manning's notes."

"Thank you, Captain," Stone said. "No further questions."

Sir Winston stood up. "Captain Beane, how long have you been a police officer?"

"For twenty-one years," the officer said, looking grateful to be back on familiar ground.

"Is it, after thorough investigation, your professional opinion that the spear gun might have been used as a murder weapon?"

"Yes, it is," the captain said, smiling broadly.

"No further questions," Sir Winston said, sitting down. "The prosecution rests."

Stone was flooded with elation. He turned to Sir Leslie Hewitt and whispered, "Is that it?"

"It appears to be," Hewitt whispered back.

"Good," Stone said, feeling relieved.

The judge produced a gold pocket watch from a fold of his robe. "We will break for lunch now," he said. "Court will reconvene in one hour."

CHAPTER

53

tone stood up and waved at Allison. "Want some lunch?" But a police officer was already escorting her from the dock. "Can't she have lunch with us?" he asked Leslie Hewitt.

"I'm afraid not," Hewitt replied. "Her bail was automatically revoked when the trial began. Don't worry, they'll feed her."

They walked out of the courthouse, and Hewitt led Stone to a small restaurant across the street. "Everyone from Government House has lunch here," he said.

Stone took a seat with the barrister at a small table, then remembered that he was still clad in robe and wig. He removed the wig and placed it on the table next to him.

"Put it back on," Hewitt said. "Bad form to remove it as long as you are robed."

Stone put the thing back on, and as he did he saw Sir Winston and his assistant at the other end of the narrow room, both still robed and wigged.

"What would you like?" Hewitt asked.

Stone didn't see a menu. "Whatever you're having."

"They make a very nice seafood stew here; it's the speciality of the house."

"That will be fine."

Hewitt ordered for both of them, and the waitress brought them cold bottles of beer.

"Well, we have a decision to make," Stone said.

"What is that?" Hewitt asked.

"Whether to call Allison to the stand."

"Of course we must call her," Hewitt said.

"But why? Sir Winston has no case at all, as far as I can see. We should simply rest our case and move for an acquittal, and I think we'd get it."

"We shall certainly move for an acquittal, as a matter of form," Hewitt replied, "but it is unlikely in the extreme that we would get it."

"Even when the prosecution has offered thin evidence, and that evidence has been refuted in court?"

"I can see where you might not wish to call Allison, coming from the American legal tradition, as you do."

"She's not required to testify, is she?"

"Not legally, no; she has a right to forgo questioning by invoking her right against self-incrimination. But unlike in America, in St. Marks the jury may consider that an indication of guilt."

"Oh."

"What's more, if we didn't call Allison, Sir Winston would reopen his case and call her himself, you see."

"I see."

"In any case, Allison is her own best witness, don't you think?"

"Yes, I do think that, but it troubles me that Sir Winston has brought this case with no more evidence than he has."

"You must understand that in our legal tradition, although the presumption of innocence is given lip service, in fact even the insinuation of guilt must be answered in order to convince a jury that the accused is innocent beyond a reasonable doubt. Even the term 'reasonable doubt' has a different meaning here, as you will learn when the judge charges the jury. It more or less means that if a juror, after hearing the evidence, thinks the prisoner is probably guilty, then he votes that way. Only if he seriously doubts guilt will he vote for acquittal. I know you think all this is very quaint, but that is the way the law has developed here in the years since the British left. Of course, it has been steered that way by the likes of Sir Winston, the prime minister, who was a barrister and a judge, and Lord Cornwall. The system is very much more comfortable if it is easier to find the accused guilty instead of innocent. And, of course, they have no written constitution or Supreme Court looking over their shoulders."

"That's just wonderful," Stone said glumly. He began to feel a real longing for the vagaries of the American system of justice.

Their food came and they ate slowly, not talking much. The seafood stew was, indeed, good, Stone thought. "What do you suppose they're giving Allison for lunch?" he asked.

"Oh, the food is better there than you might imagine, since the prisoners prepare it themselves in their own little kitchen. They give the warden a grocery list, and he gets them whatever they want. Since they're not paying a cook, it's cheaper letting them cook for themselves, no matter what they're cooking."

"I haven't heard much about the prime minister," Stone said. "What is he like?"

"He is exactly my age, which is eighty-nine, if you were wondering, and in better health than I."

"How long has he been prime minister?"

"Since 1966, when the British left."

"That's rather a long time in office, isn't it?"

"The people have always liked him. He is not in the way of being oppressive, and he has never been too corrupt."

"Just a little corrupt?"

"Oh, well, you know how government officials are. They are paid very little, really. Do you think Sir Winston pays for his Savile Row suits from his meager salary?"

"I thought perhaps his beautiful wife had money."

"She does, in fact; her father held Sir Winston's job for more than twenty years."

Stone laughed aloud.

"I know you may think our country amusing, Stone, but it really does work very well, you know. Mostly we live and let live, and if some of us live better than others, well, that's the way of the world, isn't it? Sometimes I think we are able to be viable as a country because of our climate."

"Your climate?"

"It's warm year-round, you see, and hot in the summer. When people are warm in winter, they tend to think that they are not so badly off. There are fish in the sea and work in the hotels and bars, and clothing, if one is not a member of the governmental or managerial classes, is rudimentary—a length of cloth, a shawl, a bandanna, a pair of shorts will dress one well enough for most St. Marks occasions."

"This country has not been so good to you, Leslie," Stone said. "I understand that you come from some wealth."

"That is true. When I was younger I was something of a firebrand in the legal system. I would have much preferred the American definition of reasonable doubt to our own; I would have preferred better-paid and unimpeachable officials and a more frequent change of prime minister. I was not popular."

"If your prime minister is eighty-nine, then there must be a change of power in the offing."

"That is true," Hewitt said, "and Sir Winston is one of two or three who might succeed the present occupant of that office. If he wins a conviction in our case, that will probably give him a distinct advantage."

"Why?"

"Because he will be seen to have prevailed over a wealthy white American with a white American lawyer."

"Would he really have Allison put to death in order to obtain a political advantage?"

Hewitt smiled sadly. "My dear Stone, you are naive. Men have put whole peoples to death for such power. Don't believe that because we are an insignificant country, political power here is deemed to be insignificant. Remember, if Sir Winston becomes our next prime minister, he will have, for all practical purposes, a lifetime job at the very pinnacle of our governmental and social heap, such as it is on this small island. If he went to England and worked as a barrister, he might make a living, in spite of his race, perhaps even a fine living. But here, on his home island, he can be the closest thing we have to a king."

"A big fish in a small pond?"

"In England, he would be a minnow in the sea."

"So his ambition makes him dangerous."

"Indeed it does—most immediately to Allison, but eventually to us all on this island."

"Is any of the other candidates to succeed the prime minister a better man than Sir Winston?"

"Both," Hewitt said. "One of them could be very good indeed. He has Sir Winston's intelligence without his venality or his vanity, especially that. It is his vanity as much as his ambition that makes him dangerous. If we can defeat him in court today, we will have struck a blow, perhaps a fatal one, to his political dreams. That is why I am taking part in this case. A new prime minister, whoever he is, will not reappoint Sir Winston as minister of justice. He will be back depending on his skill as a barrister and his wife's money. That would give me great satisfaction." Leslie Hewitt smiled sweetly.

54

Court reconvened after lunch, and Sir Leslie Hewitt rose and addressed the bench. "Your Lordship, normally at this time the defense would move for a dismissal of the charges on the grounds of insufficient evidence. Certainly, the evidence submitted by the prosecution has been almost laughable and quite easy for us to refute. But the defense will not request a dismissal of charges, because we want the jury to hear our client, Mrs. Allison Manning, tell her own story, so that they will know from her lips that she is an innocent woman." He sat down.

The judge nodded sagely. "Mr. Barrington, please call your first witness."

Stone stood. "Your Lordship, the defense will, of course, call Mrs. Manning to testify, but before we do, we wish to call one other witness, Mr. James Forrester."

"Call James Forrester," the judge said.

The bailiff called out the name, and Jim Forrester took the witness stand and was sworn, giving a New York City address and styling himself as a journalist.

"Mr. Forrester," Stone began, "were you the last person, apart from Allison Manning, to see Paul Manning alive?"

"I think I may very well be, along with anyone else who was standing on the quay when their yacht left the Canary Islands."

"Good, now let's begin at the beginning. How long did you know Paul Manning?"

"I first met him during our university years, more than twenty years ago, when we played on opposing basketball teams."

"How well did you know him?"

"While we were not close friends, we had a very cordial relationship, and I knew him fairly well."

"How would you describe Paul Manning?"

"I always found him to be a pleasant and friendly person, very bright, and a good athlete."

"After your graduation from university, did some years pass before you saw him again?"

"Only two or three years passed before I saw him the first time," Forrester said. "I ran into him in a restaurant in Miami, Florida. He was working as a journalist for the *Miami Herald*, and I was working for a travel magazine in New York."

This was information new to Stone, and he wondered why Forrester had not brought it up before. "Did you renew your acquaintance on that occasion?"

"Yes, we had dinner together."

"And when did you next see him?"

"At a baseball game in New York City, some five or six years later. Paul was covering sports for the *Herald,* and I visited the press box with a reporter friend."

"And did you renew your acquaintance on that occasion?"

"Yes, we had dinner again after the game."

"And when was the next time you saw Paul Manning?"

"Only a few weeks ago, in Las Palmas, in the Canary Islands."

Stone felt relieved to be back on familiar ground. "And how did you come to meet him?"

"I was doing a travel story on the Canaries, and we were taking some photographs at the Las Palmas yacht club. I ran into Paul at the bar late in the afternoon."

"And did you renew your acquaintance on that occasion?"

"Yes, we talked for an hour or so, and Paul invited me to have dinner with him and his wife aboard their yacht."

"Did you detect any change in Paul Manning from your previous knowledge of him?"

"Only that he had grown much heavier and was sporting a full beard. Otherwise, he seemed the same happy person I had always known."

"Did you, in fact, dine with Mr. and Mrs. Manning aboard their yacht?"

"Yes, I did."

"How long did you spend in their company that evening?"

"I didn't return to my hotel until nearly midnight, so I suppose I must have been there five or six hours."

"What was your impression of the Mannings as a married couple?"

"They seemed very happy together; it was obviously a very successful marriage, by almost any measure."

"Did they express affection for one another?"

"Almost constantly. They frequently held hands or kissed. I was impressed that they prepared the meal together and enjoyed doing so. I've not known many husbands and wives who could share the galley of a yacht successfully."

"Did Paul Manning make mention of beginning to write a new novel?"

"Yes, he said he was making notes for a new book, and he planned to begin the writing as soon as they were home in the States. He said he planned to call it *Dead in the Water.*"

This was news to Stone, something else Forrester hadn't mentioned. He decided to mine this vein. "Did he mention that he was keeping notes in a book?"

"Yes, he showed me a leather-bound book that he had bought in a shop in Las Palmas."

"Would the bailiff kindly show Prosecution Exhibit Number One to the witness?"

The bailiff handed Forrester the book.

"Is this the book Paul Manning showed you?"

Forrester leafed through the early pages. "Yes." He held up the open book. "You see, he wrote the title, *Dead in the Water,* at the top of the first page."

"Mr. Forrester, you are a professional writer. Please look

through the text of the book and tell me if what you read might correspond with the sort of notes a writer might make prior to beginning to write a book. Take your time."

Forrester read several pages while the courtroom waited. "Yes," he said finally, "this seems very much to me to be a set of notes, though an incomplete one."

"Does it appear in any way to be a diary?"

"Certainly not. It does not describe the relationship between man and wife that I saw in Las Palmas."

"After the Mannings sailed from Las Palmas, did you see them again?"

"Yes, on the island of Puerto Rico, to the south."

"Would you describe the occasion, please?"

"We were there gathering information for my article, my photographer and I, and I saw the yacht in the marina there. Paul asked me on board for a drink and told me that they were sailing almost immediately."

New information again. Stone wished that Forrester would stop elaborating on what he had said earlier. "Was Mrs. Manning present?"

"Yes, she was."

"Had anything in their relationship changed that you could observe?"

"No, they still seemed to be the same happy couple I had seen a couple of days before."

"Were you present when they left the harbor?"

"Yes, I was standing on the quay, watching them."

"Did they still seem to be a happy couple?"

"Yes, they were laughing as they sailed past the quay. They waved and called out a good-bye."

"Did anyone but Allison Manning ever see Paul Manning after that?"

"No. I believe I was the last to see him."

"You have interviewed Mrs. Manning extensively about their experiences after leaving Puerto Rico, have you not?"

"Yes, I have."

"Did you question her closely about the events that occurred on the occasion of Paul Manning's death?"

"Yes, I did."

"Did Allison Manning say anything to you about those events that you found to be inconsistent with the impression you had formed of the couple in the Canary Islands?"

"No, she did not. Everything she told me had the absolute ring of truth."

"Thank you, Mr. Forrester; no further questions."

"Sir Winston?" the judge said.

"Thank you, Your Lordship. Mr. Forrester, do you consider yourself to be an expert on marriage?"

"No, hardly."

"Are you not presently involved in a divorce from your own wife?"

"Yes, I am."

"So do you think that, on the basis of two brief meetings, you could pronounce their marriage a happy and successful one?"

"That was my impression."

"I ask you again, do you think you are qualified to judge the Mannings' marriage, one way or the other, after meeting them for only a few hours?"

"Well, I'm certainly no marriage counselor, but . . ."

"Mr. Forrester, I ask you again: are you qualified to judge the state of their marriage?"

"Well, I'm certainly no marriage counselor."

"Answer the question: are you qualified? Yes or no?"

"No," Forrester admitted.

"Did you ever see the couple again after they sailed from the Canaries?"

"No, just Mrs. Manning."

"You were not aboard the yacht with them when it sailed, were you?"

"No, I wasn't."

"So you have no personal knowledge of what occurred aboard that yacht when Paul Manning died?"

"I have Mrs. Manning's account."

"But you have no personal knowledge of these events, do you?"

"No."

"I have no further questions of this witness." Sir Winston sat down.

Stone stood. "Your Lordship, I have a brief redirect."

"Proceed."

"Mr. Forrester, you saw Mr. and Mrs. Manning together in the Canaries, didn't you?"

"Yes, I did."

"And you were the last person alive to see them together?"

"Yes, I was."

"Relying on your judgment as a journalist and as a human being, do you believe them to have been happily married?"

"I certainly do."

"Do you believe Allison Manning's account of her husband's death to be true?"

"Yes, I certainly do."

"Thank you, Mr. Forrester, I have no further questions."

"You may step down, Mr. Forrester," the judge said. "Mr. Barrington, do you wish to call any other witnesses?"

"Yes, Your Lordship. The defense calls Mrs. Allison Manning."

Stone watched Allison as she left the dock and walked to the witness box. She seemed relaxed, serene; she certainly looked beautiful. *If I can just get her through this,* he thought, *and if she stands up under cross without losing it, I can win this case.*

Allison took hold of the Bible and swore to tell the truth.

55

S tone waited while Allison arranged herself in the witness chair and recited her full name and address. He began questioning her slowly about her family background and education, letting her settle down and deal with easy questions. She was following his instruction, making eye contact with the jurors as she answered. Then he began to get to the meat of the matter.

"Mrs. Manning, when and how did you first meet your husband, Paul?"

"It was a little over five years ago," she said. "I was working as an art director with an advertising agency in New York, and I was invited to dinner at the home of my boss. Paul was a guest, too."

"Did you hit it off immediately?"

"Yes, we did. Paul took me home in a taxi and asked me out for dinner that weekend."

"And did you begin to see him on a regular basis after that?"

"Yes, we began seeing each other two or three times a week, and before long, we were spending most of our time together."

"Was Paul working as a writer at that time?"

"Yes, he had given up his newspaper career and was writing his third novel when we met."

"Was he a very successful writer at that time?"

"No. He was earning a modest living at his craft, but he had not yet begun to sell books in large numbers."

"After you had been seeing each other for a time, did the subject of marriage come up?"

"The subject came up very early in our relationship," she said, "although we didn't actually set a date until we had been seeing each other for several months."

"And when did you marry?"

"A few weeks after that—about four and a half years ago."

"In what circumstances were you married."

"I gave up my tiny apartment and moved into Paul's. It wasn't much bigger; it was a three-room flat in Greenwich Village, a fourth-floor walkup."

"Would you describe it as a modest apartment?"

She smiled. "I would describe it as less than modest. We painted the place ourselves, but that didn't make the heating or the plumbing work any better."

"After you were married, did Paul's career as a writer become more successful?"

"Yes. His third novel became a bestseller, and that allowed him to get a much better contract for his next book. It also meant that his income increased sharply."

"Did your circumstances improve after that?"

"Oh, yes. We bought a house in Greenwich, Connecticut, a large, comfortable house. Greenwich is near enough to New York City that Paul could spend the day in town visiting his publisher and still be home by dinner."

"In what other ways did Paul's success change your lives?"

"Well, we both drove expensive cars, we ate out in restaurants a lot, and we entertained at dinner parties. I bought better clothes, and so did Paul."

"And did there come a time when Paul decided he wanted a yacht?"

"Yes. He had a small boat—a twenty-five-footer—when we married, and we used to sail that a lot. Then, after the success of his fourth novel, Paul ordered a larger yacht to be built at a yard in Finland."

"How long did it take to build the larger yacht?"

"About a year and a half."

"Is this the yacht which is now moored at the English Harbour marina?"

"Yes."

"Was there anything unusual about this yacht, apart from its larger size?"

"Well, it had the best equipment Paul could find, and it was designed to be sailed singlehanded."

"By singlehanded, do you mean by one person alone?"

"Yes. When we were aboard together, Paul did all the sailing, and I did all the domestic chores—cooking and so forth."

"When the new yacht was delivered, did you and Paul decide to sail it to Europe?"

"Yes; in fact, that was Paul's intention when he ordered the boat."

"Please tell us about the trip."

Allison outlined their route across the Atlantic and their stops in various ports in England, France, Spain, and in the Mediterranean, finishing her account with a description of their departure from the Canary Islands for Antigua.

"Before you left the United States, how would you describe your relationship with your husband?"

"We were extremely happy—euphoric, really. You know how newlyweds are." She said this directly to a juror, who blushed.

"And when you began your voyage across the Atlantic, did your relationship change?"

"Only in that we became closer. When you spend a lot of time with a person on a boat, you really get to know him."

"Did this constant proximity wear on your marriage?"

"On the contrary, I think it made our marriage stronger."

"You are aware that not all couples do as well at sea."

She smiled. "Oh, yes; we met a number of couples in our travels who were sick of each other. On the other hand, we met a lot more who enjoyed being alone together on a boat."

"You were nearly fifteen years younger than your husband, Mrs. Manning; did that become a problem in your marriage?"

"Never at any time. We were both very comfortable with the age difference."

"When you sailed from the Canaries for Antigua, was your marriage still a good one?"

"I would say that it was better than ever. We talked about that, and Paul felt the same way. We both felt very grateful for each other."

"Take us back, now, Mrs. Manning, to your departure from the Canaries, and tell us, with as much detail as you can, what happened in the days after that."

Allison devoted her attention entirely to the jury. She told of their start across the Atlantic and how, after ten days, it had been necessary for her to be hauled up the mast to retrieve the top swivel of the headsail reefing system. She explained this carefully to the jury, and they seemed to understand what the problem was. She told then of looking down and seeing her husband, apparently ill, and of his collapse and her fear of being stuck at the top of the mast. Tears had begun to roll down her cheeks, and she dabbed at them with a tissue. When she told how she had buried her husband at sea, she wept openly, and the judge had to call a brief halt to her testimony while she recovered herself. Stone was delighted; she hadn't cried at the coroner's inquest, but the tears flowed freely now, and a glance at the jury revealed how affected they were. Finally, she stopped crying, and the judge nodded at Stone to continue with his questions.

"Mrs. Manning, did you know how to sail the yacht after your husband's death?"

"Only in the most general sense. The deck of the boat was laid out so that Paul could easily handle it without my help. The only time I had any real job to do was handling the bowline when we docked."

"So, alone in the middle of the Atlantic Ocean, you had to learn how to sail the boat?"

"Yes, and to navigate, as well. There was a book aboard on celestial navigation, and from that I learned to take a moon sight to establish our latitude. From then on, I just tried to keep the boat on the same latitude. I was off a little, though, when we made our landfall. I was aiming at Antigua, but I fetched up in St. Marks."

"When you say 'we,' to whom are you referring?"

"To the boat and me. I began to think of the boat as my partner in survival."

"Mrs. Manning, has everything you have told the court today been the truth, the whole truth, and nothing but the truth?"

"Yes," she said firmly. "As God is my witness it is the truth."

Stone turned to Sir Winston. "Your witness," he said, then sat down.

Sir Winston rose slowly and looked contemptuously at Allison for a good half minute before he began. "Your Lordship, I will be brief," he said. "Mrs. Manning, why did you kill your husband?"

"I . . ." she began, but Sir Winston cut her off.

"Was it for the millions he had earned?"

"I . . ."

"Was it for the *twelve million dollars* in insurance?"

"Sir Winston . . ."

She was beginning to grow angry now, and Stone had warned her against that.

"Was it because you had learned to hate him while you were confined with him aboard the yacht for protracted periods?"

"Sir Winston!" she shouted. "I did not kill my husband!"

"Oh, but you did, Mrs. Manning," he replied. "There were many times aboard the yacht when Mr. Manning was vulnerable, weren't there?"

"Vulnerable?"

"Times when a small shove would have put this large man overboard. Weren't there such times?"

"I did not push him overboard!"

"Answer me, Mrs. Manning! Were there not opportunities?"

"If that was what I wanted, I suppose so. But . . ."

"As when your husband stepped outside the lifelines to urinate, holding on to the yacht with only one hand?"

"Perhaps, but I didn't . . ."

"You could have stabbed that one hand with a knife, couldn't you?"

"No. I . . ."

"You could have *bitten* that hand, couldn't you?"

"I didn't!"

"That hand that had fed and clothed and given you every luxury!"

"I did not do that!" Tears were streaming down her face again.

"Oh, yes, you did, Mrs. Manning. This jury can look into those angry eyes and see that you did!"

"You're mad!" she screamed at him. "Completely mad!"

"But not as mad as you were with your husband. So mad that you could abandon him to his fate in the middle of a huge ocean."

"I did not!" she bawled. "As God is my witness . . ."

"Yes, you did!"

Stone was on his feet. "Your Lordship, Sir Winston is badgering the witness, not offering evidence."

The judge held up a hand to quiet him. "Sir Winston . . ." he said.

"I am finished with this witness, Your Lordship," Sir Winston said, looking at her once again with contempt. "I think the jury can see through this performance." He sat down.

Allison sat in the witness chair, sobbing.

"You may step down, Mrs. Manning," the judge said quietly.

The bailiff helped her down and back to the dock, where she continued to weep.

56

The judge looked up at the jury. "Gentlemen, we will now move to closing arguments. Sir Winston, may we have your closing?"

Sir Winston Sutherland rose and faced the jury, offering Stone and Sir Leslie Hewitt his back. "Gentlemen," Sir Winston said. "Today you have seen evil incarnate in the form of a pretty woman, not the first time the devil has used this form. You have heard how Paul Manning, a successful writer, gave his wife everything—a big house, expensive cars and clothes, a dream trip on a glorious yacht—and how she showed her gratitude by ending his life so that she could have all his money for himself.

"Think of it, gentlemen: a yacht filled with the utensils of death—knives, harpoons, and, no doubt, other weapons since disposed of at sea."

Stone was halfway to his feet, but Sir Leslie put out a hand and stopped him. He held a finger to his lips, and Stone sank back into his chair.

"Was there a pistol aboard the yacht?" Sir Winston continued. "Was there a shotgun? Probably, but the Atlantic Ocean is a very large rubbish bin, so we shall never know. Instead, we must put ourselves aboard that yacht and see what certainly happened there—how Paul Manning was, one way or another, consigned to the sea; how he may have watched the yacht sailing away without him, leaving him alone with the sharks and other creatures that would devour the evidence of his murdered corpse.

"Allison Manning thought she could get away with it, but she had not counted on the will for justice in St. Marks, and she had not counted on you—a jury of honest men who would see through her protestations and her tears to the truth—that she coldly and maliciously and with malice aforethought murdered her husband. Not even when he suspected her motives, as his diary shows he did, could he be on guard every second of the day and night, to protect himself from his evil wife. No, his fate was sealed as soon as he sailed from the Canary Islands. At that moment, he was a dead man.

"In St. Marks we do not placidly accept the murder of human beings. We have constructed a system of justice which has no tolerance for murderers and which rids us of them with dispatch. Today, you are the instrument of that justice, and your island nation expects of you that you will swiftly reach a verdict of guilty and allow His Lordship to pronounce the sentence that follows from such guilt.

"Gentlemen," he said slowly and gravely, "do your duty!" He turned and sat down.

Stone leaned over to his co-counsel. "I hope you will speak longer than that," he said.

Sir Leslie looked at his pocket watch and shook his head. "I must be finished soon or appear to insult the jury by requiring them to attend this trial for another day. That would not rebound to our client's benefit."

The judge was staring harshly at the defense table. "Sir Leslie, will you close now?"

Hewitt stood up. "Yes, indeed, Your Lordship." He left the defense table and walked closer to the jury. "Gentlemen," he said softly but clearly, "today you have been treated to a demonstration of what happens when too much power collects in too few hands."

"Sir Leslie!" the judge barked.

"My apologies, Your Lordship," Hewitt said. "My remarks were not directed at the court but at the prosecution."

"Nevertheless . . ." the judge said, then sank back into his chair.

Hewitt turned again to the jury. "Gentlemen, my remarks were not intended to be of a personal nature but merely to comment on how the ministry of justice is operated by the whim of one man. Only in such a ministry would this case ever have been brought to trial."

"Sir Leslie," the judge said, "I will not warn you again. You do not wish to incur my wrath."

Hewitt turned and bowed solemnly to the bench, then turned back to the jury. "Gentlemen, the prosecution has not presented one whit of convincing evidence today—no evidence that a murder even took place, let alone that my client committed it. To call the prosecution's case circumstantial would be to elevate it to the realm of possibility, and the events aboard the yacht as Sir Winston has described them are not even remotely possible.

"He would ask you to believe, on the basis of no physical evidence, no witnesses, and no common sense, that this lovely woman deliberately caused her beloved husband's death—and for money. As weak as his case is, I will address the points he has attempted to make. First, the so-called diary has been convincingly shown to be notes for Mr. Manning's next novel; second, the presence of knives and harpoons aboard the yacht has been made out to be sinister, but does not each of you have a kitchen where a number of knives reside? And are you murderers because of it? Of course not. You are no more murderers than is Mrs. Manning. Sir Winston has said that Mrs. Manning must be a murderer because she had the opportunity, but each of us has opportunities to kill every day, and we do not kill. Neither did Mrs. Manning.

"The very last person to see Paul Manning alive other than Mrs. Manning, Mr. Forrester, someone who knew Mr. Manning well, has testified that he witnessed a happy marriage in the days before the couple sailed from the Canaries. Not one witness has been brought forward to testify to the contrary, because there is no such witness. If there were, Sir Winston would have found him, believe me.

•

"But the greatest proof of Mrs. Manning's innocence is Mrs. Manning herself. You have heard her describe her life with her husband, their delight in his success, their wonderful sailing adventure which they both enjoyed so much. You have heard her words, and every man of you can surely recognize the truth when he hears it. The prosecution has offered nothing but bluster and posturing to refute her patently truthful testimony, because the prosecution has nothing else to offer.

"Each of you, when his duty is done in this courtroom, will return to his daily life, and each of you will have to live with himself every day after that. Do you wish to spend the rest of your days in the knowledge that you convicted an honest woman on no evidence? Of course not! When you have declared this woman innocent you can walk from this courtroom with your heads held high, knowing that you have done right in the eyes of God and man, and no one can take that from you, not even Sir Winston and his ministry. Go, gentlemen, and do right!"

Sir Leslie returned to the defense table and sat down.

"Well done," Stone whispered to him.

The judge spoke up. "I will now charge the jury. Gentlemen, you have heard a case presented by the prosecution and the defense. There can be no doubt that a man is dead and that it is the province of this court and, specifically, of this jury to decide how he met his death and who is to blame for it. Sir Winston and Sir Leslie have each presented their arguments, and now you must decide, beyond a reasonable doubt, if Mrs. Manning is guilty of the murder of her husband. Your verdict must be a majority verdict. You may now retire to the jury room and consider your verdict. When you have reached it, ring for the bailiff." The judge stood and left the courtroom.

The jury filed out of their box and through a nearby door, which the bailiff closed behind him.

"That's it?" Stone asked. "That's a charge to the jury?"

"I'm afraid so," Sir Leslie answered, glancing at his pocket watch. He beckoned the bailiff over. "May our client join us here at the table while we wait?"

The bailiff nodded stiffly, then went and brought Allison and held a chair for her.

"You were wonderful, Leslie," she said, patting his arm.

Hewitt permitted himself a small smile.

"How do you read the jury, Leslie?" Stone asked.

Hewitt shrugged. "The foreman, my old tailor, is our best hope; the young boy will do whatever he thinks the others want him to; the views of the others will depend on their relationship, if any, to Sir Winston, and their vulnerability to his whim."

"After all this, that's where we are?" Stone said. "That most of the jury will act because of their vulnerability, or lack of it, to Sir Winston?"

"I'm afraid so," Hewitt said.

"Why has no one left the courtroom?" Stone asked.

Sir Leslie looked at his watch. "Because everyone knows that in living memory, no St. Marks jury has ever been late for their dinner," he said.

57

Stone looked up and saw Hilary Kramer and Jim Forrester beckoning from the gallery; he walked over and shook hands with them. "I'd be interested to have your opinion of how things went."

"I'd say you're well on your way to an acquittal," Kramer replied.

"Both you and Sir Leslie did a brilliant job," Forrester chimed in. "How can you possibly lose?"

"I'm astonished," Kramer said, "that this case could even have been brought to court with so little evidence, and I intend to say so in my coverage. This could never have come to trial in an American court."

"Unfortunately, we're not in an American court," Stone said.

"Nobody's left the courtroom," Forrester said. "Are you expecting an early verdict?"

Stone nodded. "Leslie says St. Marks juries don't like to be late for dinner. An early verdict would normally be in our favor, but in this case, I don't know what to think. Leslie says that the relationship between individual jurors and Sir Winston is going to be the deciding factor."

"Relationship?" Kramer said. "They have a relationship with him?"

"It's a small island," Stone said. "If one of them has something to fear from Sir Winston, he's unlikely to vote our way."

"That would be grounds for appeal in the States," Forrester said.

"The appeal here is to the good nature, or perhaps the whim, of the prime minister, who's eighty-nine," Stone said.

"Do you think some of the pressure brought to bear on the government will have some effect on the outcome?" Kramer asked.

Stone shook his head. "I don't know what that pressure could mean to any of the jurors. I'd hoped we wouldn't have to go to trial." He looked back to the defense table, where Hewitt and Allison were deep in conversation. "Leslie was wonderful, wasn't he?"

"He sure got in his digs at Sir Winston," Forrester agreed.

"Apparently he's spent his life digging at the government," Stone said. "Well, I'd better get back and reassure Allison. Will you both be staying for the verdict?"

"Sure we will," Kramer said.

"See you later, then." Stone walked back to the defense table and sat down. "What have you two been talking about?" he asked.

"I've just been telling Leslie what a wonderful job both of you have done," Allison said, smiling. "After what I've heard here today, I'm very optimistic."

"So am I," Stone said, though he knew he would be uneasy until the jury came in.

"The important thing to remember," Hewitt said, "is that even if the verdict goes against us, it's not over. We still have the opportunity for appeal, and I think our position would be excellent."

"I hope it doesn't go that far," Stone said.

"So do I," Allison echoed.

They became silent, each wrapped in his own thoughts.

It was growing dark outside, and the bailiff rose from his desk and began turning on lights in the courtroom.

Sir Leslie Hewitt looked at his watch. "Almost nine o'clock," he said. "I must say, I'm encouraged; I've never known a jury to stay out this long, so they must be deliberating very diligently."

Most of the spectators had given up and gone home, but the reporters from the *Times* and *The New Yorker* still sat in the gallery, waiting.

"I'm hungry," Allison said.

"I wish we could go out to dinner," Hewitt said, "but I'm afraid the bailiff wouldn't allow it. If you want to eat now, I can see that you're fed in a cell."

"No, I'll wait," Allison sighed.

Stone was hungry, too, but he hadn't thought about it until now.

Then, from somewhere beyond the courtroom, a bell rang, something like a big brass schoolyard bell. The bailiff rose and left the room.

"They're coming in," Hewitt said. "Perhaps now we can all have dinner together." He smiled at Allison.

The bailiff returned to the courtroom and escorted Allison back to the dock. A moment later, the jury filed in.

"All rise!" the bailiff called out, and when everyone had stood, the judge entered and took his seat.

"Gentlemen, have you reached a verdict?" he asked the jury.

The retired tailor rose. "We have, Your Lordship," he said, handing a sheet of paper to the bailiff.

The bailiff took the paper to the judge, who read it without expression. "Read the verdict," he said to the bailiff.

The bailiff held up the paper and read it once to himself, then out loud. "We, a jury of freemen of St. Marks, have considered our verdict in the case of the Government of St. Marks versus Allison Ames Manning. After due deliberation, we unanimously find the prisoner guilty of murder."

The courtroom erupted in gasps and whispers; there was even a little scattered applause. Stone felt as though all the air had been sucked out of the courtroom. He turned to Allison and mouthed the words, "Don't worry."

Allison was as white as marble. She sat rigidly, expressionless, looking straight ahead of her but, apparently, not focusing on anything before her. Finally, she turned and looked desolately at Stone, who mouthed his message again. She nodded, then looked down at her lap.

"Sentence will be pronounced immediately," the judge said, nodding at the bailiff.

Sir Leslie Hewitt was on his feet, in his hand a white envelope sealed with a blob of red wax. "Your Lordship, the defense has prepared an appeal, which we request be sent to the prime minister's residence without delay, and that sentence be postponed until we have heard from the prime minister."

The bailiff took the envelope and delivered it to the judge, who glanced at it and returned it to the bailiff. "Deliver this personally as soon as court has adjourned," the judge said to him, then looked up at Hewitt. "I see no reason to reconvene court at some later time," he said. "Sentence will be pronounced immediately." He nodded to the bailiff.

The bailiff went to a small cabinet under the bench and unlocked it with an old brass key. From the cabinet he removed a fringed cushion that supported a black cloth. He walked around the bench, climbed the few steps, and presented his burden to the judge. The judge took the black cloth from the cushion and placed it atop his wig. "All rise to hear the sentence!" the bailiff called out.

Stone struggled to his feet, along with the rest of the court.

The judge looked at Allison. "The prisoner will rise," he said.

Stone looked over his shoulder at Allison, who was still seated. Her head jerked up, and slowly, she got to her feet. There was fear written across her face.

"Allison Ames Manning," the judge intoned, "you have been found guilty of the crime of murder by a properly constituted jury of St. Marks freemen. Do you have anything to say before sentence is pronounced?"

Allison looked bleakly at him. "I am innocent," she said, her voice breaking.

The judge nodded, then continued. "By the power vested in me by the people of St. Marks, I now direct that on the morrow, at the hour of sunset, you be taken from a cell in this building to the inner courtyard, where a scaffold shall have been erected, and be hanged by the neck until you are dead. May God have mercy on your soul."

Allison looked briefly at the wall above the judge; then her eyes rolled up in her head, and she collapsed backward, sending her chair skittering across the floor.

"Court is adjourned," the judge said, then left the bench.

Stone and the bailiff ran for the dock.

CHAPTER

58

Stone reached Allison simultaneously with the bailiff, and a moment later, a court aide appeared with a folding canvas stretcher and placed it on the floor beside the inert woman. Stone slapped her cheeks lightly, but she did not respond. "Please get a doctor," he said to the bailiff.

"I'm sure that won't be necessary, Mr. Barrington," the bailiff said. "Let's get her onto the stretcher."

Together, the two men lifted Allison and set her gently on the stretcher. The bailiff and the court aide each took an end and carried her from the courtroom. Stone and Sir Leslie followed them down the stairs and past the front desk of the jail into a corridor, then to the last cell before the hallway ended in a stout wooden door. By the time they had laid her on the cell's bunk, Allison was stirring. Stone put a pillow under her head and felt her neck for a pulse. It was rapid, but strong.

"What is this place?" Allison asked weakly.

"The jail," Stone replied. "You fainted; how do you feel now?"

"Weak," she said.

"I'll get her some food," Sir Leslie said, then disappeared.

"Did I dream it all?" Allison asked.

"No, but don't worry about it; your appeal has already gone

to the prime minister. We should hear something tomorrow sometime."

Allison nodded. "I'm sorry I fainted," she said. "I'm usually better under pressure."

"I don't blame you," Stone said. "I still can't believe it myself. An American jury would have acquitted you in minutes."

"I'd like to sit up," she said. As she did, with Stone's help, a woman in a denim shift came into the cell, bearing a bowl of something hot.

"Here you are, dear," she said to Allison, setting the tray on her lap. "This'll do you good; I made it myself."

Allison began eating the stew. "It's good," she said. "Lots of fish in it."

From the direction of the inner courtyard, the sound of hammering came through the window high over the outside door.

"What's that?" Allison asked.

"Oh, just some work being done," he lied. "Ignore it." He knew exactly what that hammering meant.

Stone sat beside her on the bunk, and Sir Leslie returned with a chair.

"I don't want you to worry," Hewitt said. "Your appeal will be in the prime minister's hands in just a few minutes." He reached into his briefcase and retrieved two sheets of paper, handing them to Stone and Allison. "Here's a copy for you."

"I'm sure it's wonderful," Allison said, continuing to eat the stew.

"Would you like me to read it to you?"

"I'll read it later," she said.

Stone put his copy into his pocket. Apparently Hewitt had not been as sanguine as he about the outcome of the trial, since he had written the appeal in advance. He looked at his watch: half past nine. "I have some important telephoning to do," he said to Allison. "You're going to have to stay here tonight; would you like me to bring you some things?"

"Thank you," she said. "A cotton dress, some underwear, and my cosmetics case."

Stone stood up. "Thomas is outside, I'm sure; he'll drive me. I'll be back as soon as possible." He left the cell and walked down the hall to the front desk, where he found Hilary Kramer and Jim Forrester waiting.

"Is she all right?" Kramer asked.

"Yes, she just fainted; she's having some dinner now."

"I don't blame her for fainting," Kramer said. "I would have, too, under the circumstances."

Jim Forrester looked almost as pale under his tan as Allison. "When do you expect to hear about the appeal?" he asked.

"Probably not until tomorrow."

"Any way to gauge her chances?"

"None that I know of. I'm about to make some phone calls to muster as much support as possible." He looked at Forrester. "Jim, you look awful; are you feeling all right?"

"I'm okay. I guess I wasn't expecting a conviction; you don't get much of this sort of thing in the travel-writing business."

"Speaking of travel writing, do you think you could call some of your travel editors and get them to send telegrams of protest to the prime minister first thing in the morning? If he thinks hanging Allison is going to hurt his tourist trade, maybe that'll help."

"I'll call a couple of people tonight," Forrester replied.

"Good, now I've got to run back to the marina, make some calls, and get some things for Allison."

"Stone," Kramer said, "give me one good quote for my piece."

"The defense is absolutely shocked at this outrageous verdict. In the United States this case would have been dismissed out of hand, and now we face the prospect of St. Marks executing an innocent American woman who has already been devastated by the entirely natural death of her husband. If this happens, no American will ever be safe in St. Marks again. I urge every American who cares about justice to wire or fax the prime minister of St. Marks in protest."

"Great!" Kramer replied.

"Hilary, I know it's late, but this piece isn't going to do Allison any good if it runs the day after tomorrow. Is there any way you can get it into tomorrow's edition?"

"I may have to break some legs, but I'll get it done."

"Thanks; I have to go now."

Thomas was waiting at the door. "How is she?"

"Much better; she's eating, anyway. Can you run me to the marina, then let me borrow your car to get back here?"

"Of course; let's go."

As they pulled up at the marina, Stone saw the fast motor yacht that Allison had previously chartered pulling into a berth.

"What's that doing back?" Thomas asked.

"It's been in Guadeloupe waiting for a call from Allison to pick her up. Would you tell them that Mrs. Chapman has been delayed and to stick around until tomorrow? I hope she'll be here to go aboard."

"Sure." Thomas handed over his car keys, then walked off toward the big motor yacht.

Stone went aboard *Expansive* and ran down below. In a moment he had the satellite phone up and running and a call in to Bill Eggers's home.

"Hello?"

"Thank God you're there," Stone said.

"Stone! What's up? How did the trial go?"

"She was convicted."

"What?"

"I'm not kidding, Bill, and we've got less than twenty-four hours to save her life. Here's what I want you to do."

"I've got a pencil; shoot."

"Start with the State Department: call the duty officer and ask him to alert the Caribbean desk that an innocent American citizen is about to be hanged in St. Marks. Demand that they call the secretary of state and have him bring to bear every ounce of influence he can muster. No, wait—first call the chairman of the Senate Foreign Relations Committee—it's Jesse Helms, God help us—and get him to call the secretary of state. Call Senators Dodd and Lieberman of Connecticut and get them onto him as well. Hell, tell them to call the president."

"You think they'll do that?"

"They might; we have to try. Call both Phil Woodman and Max Weld and see if you can get them to make some calls. Then call your PR people and tell them to start calling reporters at home and the wire services. We need an all-out mobilization between now and tomorrow morning. Everything should be directed to the prime minister of St. Marks; it's all in his hands now. Tell the PR people to call travel editors, too; we've got to let them know that hanging Allison will kill their tourist business. Jim Forrester is calling a couple of them."

"Who?"

"Forrester is down here doing a piece for *The New Yorker*, but he's done a lot of travel writing."

"Okay. Anything else?"

"Anything you can think of, Bill. I'm absolutely desperate, and we don't have a minute to waste. I want the prime minister to wake up tomorrow morning to the sound of his phone ringing; I want his fax machine flooded with indignant letters; I want to scare the living shit out of him."

"I'm on it." Eggers hung up the phone.

Stone switched off the satellite phone and started getting Allison's things together.

It was nearly midnight when Stone drove up to the jail door and found it locked. He rang the bell for three minutes before a sleepy, barefoot cop opened the door. "What do you want, mister?" he demanded.

"My name is Barrington; I'm Mrs. Manning's lawyer. I want to see her."

"You can't do that, man; we're shut down for the night. Anyway, she's asleep; you don't want to wake her up, do you?"

Stone shoved the duffel through the door. "Will you see that she gets these things, then?"

"Okay, I'll do that first thing in the morning."

"Thank you, and will you tell her I was here? Tell her not to worry; everything is going to be all right."

The man looked surprised. "You want me to tell her that? Everything ain't going to be all right, you know."

"Just tell her what I said, please."

"Okay, okay. Good night now." He closed the door and shot the bolt.

Stone got back into Thomas's car and drove back to the marina, worried, exhausted, and barely able to keep his eyes open.

CHAPTER

59

Stone got five fitful hours of sleep aboard *Expansive*, then threw himself into a cold shower so that he would be fully alert. He made some coffee, ate a muffin, and started making lists of things to do. At 7:00 A.M. he called Bill Eggers.

"Where are we?" he asked.

"Okay, here's a rundown. I couldn't get to Senator Helms, but I did get to one of his staff; I told him the prime minister was a suspected communist."

"Good going."

"Woodman and Weld were also going to call him. I talked to the duty officer at the State Department and he put me through to the head of the Caribbean desk at home. He promised to try to get permission to send a cable in the secretary of state's name. I'll call him back after nine to see how he did. Oh, Woodman called the president last night; he was unavailable, but he did get the White House chief of staff on the line, which is almost as good. He had seen the *60 Minutes* report and promised to get some sort of protest out first thing this morning."

"That's wonderful, Bill. Anything else?"

"The PR people have been on it all night; they'll report to me at the office at nine. I'm afraid we're going to miss a lot of morning editions, but they think we'll make some of them."

"Hilary Kramer promised me she'd get us in the *Times* this morning."

"Hang on," Eggers said, "I'll see." He was gone for a moment, then returned. "She made the front page, lower right-hand corner, continued inside. It's good stuff, Stone, and she quoted you about every American sending a wire."

"Thank God we made that one."

"I'm sure we'll be all over the morning television shows, too; you want to be interviewed over the phone?"

"I'm going to be too busy; you do it."

"If they'll talk to me."

"Tell them you're Allison's attorney, too."

"Okay. I'd better get on that right now; they're already on the air." He hung up.

Stone switched on the television and, over the satellite dish, got the *Today* show. An hour later he heard Katie Couric interviewing Eggers and Eggers reading out the prime minister's fax number.

"Yes!" Stone screamed. He got into some clothes, jumped into Thomas's car, and headed for Government House. The jail door was open this time, and after searching him, they let him into Allison's cell. He held her close for a moment, then looked at her. She seemed surprisingly normal. "How are you holding up?"

"I'm nervous as a cat," she said, "but I got some sleep last night, amazingly enough."

"I was here late last night, but they wouldn't let me in."

"I got the things this morning," she said. "Thank you so much."

From the window over the heavy wooden door outside the cell came a loud noise—a creaking of hinges, a slap of wood against wood, and another sound that made chills run up Stone's spine.

"What's that?" Allison asked.

"Who knows? I want to tell you what's being done at home." He sat down on the bunk with her and filled her in on what had happened overnight. "That thing on the *Today* show is going to have half the country up in arms," he said. "And rightly so. By this time the St. Marks government has got to be up to its ass in faxes."

"Good morning," a voice said from the corridor. The door was unlocked, and Leslie Hewitt walked in with a basket. "I brought you some fresh croissants and a thermos of coffee," he said.

"Oh, thank you, Leslie," Allison replied, kissing him on the cheek. She poured herself some coffee and sipped it.

"Have you heard anything at all?" Stone asked him.

"Not exactly. I called the prime minister's residence this morning and spoke to his secretary. He sounded rather odd; I gather the prime minister has been receiving a lot of telegrams, faxes, and phone calls. He's locked himself in his study with my appeal. I hope we'll hear something this morning."

"Good, good."

They sat with Allison until a guard came and made them leave. "You can come back at four this afternoon," he said.

"Allison, is there anything I can send you?" Stone asked.

"I'm all right, I think. There are some books available here; I'll try and read."

"We'll be back at four," Leslie said. "I hope we'll have some news by then. I'll call here if I hear anything before that time."

Allison kissed and hugged them both, then they left the cell.

Outside the jail, Stone brought Hewitt up to date on what he had done, then asked, "Do you have any idea what's going to happen?"

"I hope all these calls and faxes will have an effect," Hewitt said. "I don't think the prime minister has ever experienced anything quite like this."

"Is he the sort of man who responds to pressure?"

Hewitt shrugged. "It's hard to say. He's always been a stubborn fellow, ever since he was a little boy. I just hope he doesn't dig in his heels."

"If we went to the residence, do you think he would see us?"

Hewitt shook his head. "No, that would be unheard of; we'd be damaging our own case. Do you want to come back to my place and wait?"

"I'd better go back to the marina and handle any calls that come in. Leslie, they've built a scaffold in the inner courtyard, and they've been testing it, I think."

"I know; I heard them."

"Have you ever been through anything like this with a client?"

"Once."

"What happened?"

"They hanged him."

"Oh."

"Let's meet back here at four o'clock, and if we haven't heard anything we can wait with Allison. We can't give up until . . ."

"Right," Stone said. "I'll meet you here at four."

Back at the marina, Stone called Eggers again. "Anything to report?"

"We got on the *Today* show."

"I saw it. You did good."

"I hope we stirred up something. Oh, somebody finally got to Helms; he promised to call the secretary of state."

"Has the president had anything to say?"

"Not publicly, but Woodman got a call back from the chief of staff's secretary, saying that they were putting together a cable."

"Great!"

"How's the woman holding up?"

"Like a champ. I'd be a gibbering idiot in her place."

"So would I."

"I think we're going to pull this off, Bill; I don't see how the prime minister can stand in the wind that's blowing now."

"I think you're right, Stone."

"I'll call you again later. Oh, let me give you the satellite phone number; you can dial it just like a regular phone." He dictated the number, then hung up.

Half an hour later, the calls started coming in—the wire services, reporters who recorded interviews, and, amazingly, the president's secretary, who wanted a report. She told him that a cable had already been sent by the secretary of state. He thanked her profusely.

He had some lunch at the Shipwright's Arms and took some more phone calls. Then everything went quiet. No phone calls, no press. Just a quiet afternoon with Thomas.

"How often does somebody get executed here, Thomas?" Stone asked.

"We get one every two or three years, I guess. Then they knock the scaffold apart and put it together again when another one comes up."

"I know; I heard them working on it this morning. I don't think Allison realized what the noise was; I hope she doesn't, anyway."

"You ever lose a client like this?" Thomas asked.

"Not yet."

"I hope you don't lose this one."

"Me, too."

60

At four o'clock Stone met Leslie Hewitt at the jail door. "What have you heard?" he asked the barrister. "Is there any word at all?"

"Nothing," Hewitt said, shaking his head. "The prime minister's secretary won't even talk to me now. A policeman answers the phone and says that everyone is too busy to talk."

"Well, at least we've made them busy."

"I had hoped to get some sort of hint from the secretary, at the very least, but there's only silence. He didn't return my phone call."

"You look more worried than I've seen you, Leslie," Stone said.

"I confess, I am worried. I really expected some sort of word by now. We have only until sundown."

"What time is sundown?"

"Seven fifty-nine; I checked. And they always do these things on the minute."

"I've never been through anything like this," Stone said.

"Neither has Allison," Hewitt replied.

They went into the jail and found Hilary Kramer and Jim Forrester waiting at the desk, both looking tense.

"Have you heard anything from the prime minister?" Hilary asked Hewitt.

"Not yet," he replied. "But I expect to soon."

"Are you going to see Allison now?"

"Yes," Stone replied.

"Will you come out and let us know how she's doing? And ask her if she'll see me."

"Maybe a bit later. You, too, Jim?"

Forrester shook his head. "No, I don't want to see her." He turned to Kramer. "I guess I'm not much of a reporter."

Stone and Hewitt were searched, then were walked down the corridor of cells. Stone looked at the stout door at the end, with the small window a good fifteen feet above it. At least the sounds from the inner courtyard had stopped; thank God for that.

Allison was sitting on her bunk, her hair pinned up, wearing a denim prison shift that exposed her neck. Stone kissed her on the cheek. "How are you?"

"They took away my things," she said. "Even my underwear." She seemed very calm.

"You'll get them back later," Hewitt said. "Don't worry."

"Haven't you heard anything from the prime minister?" she asked.

He shook his head. "Sometimes it's like this," he said, glancing guiltily at Stone. "We might not hear anything until the last minute."

They all sat down—Hewitt in the single chair and Stone and Allison on the bunk. She held up a copy of *David Copperfield*. "The most exciting thing they had to offer," she said. "It's good, though. I haven't read it since the eighth grade; I'd forgotten how good it is."

"I've had many calls from the press," Stone said. "The prime minister's office is under a lot of pressure."

Allison nodded, but said nothing. Nobody said anything. They sat quietly, each with his own thoughts, for more than an hour.

A jailer appeared at the cell door. "Can I get anything for anybody?" he asked.

"I'd like some water," Allison said.

"I'm sorry; you won't be able to eat or drink from now on. I thought you might like some magazines."

"No, thank you," Allison said, and the man left. "Why won't they let me eat or drink?" she asked.

"I don't know," Hewitt said, before Stone could speak. "They have their silly rules, I suppose."

Another long period of silence ensued, until Stone began to attempt small talk.

"What are you going to do when you get home?" he asked Allison.

"Get the estate wound up, I suppose. I don't really have any plans beyond that. I find it difficult to think about the future right now."

"The fast motor yacht came back and is waiting for you at the marina."

"Good. I certainly don't want to waste any time here when this is over."

He fell silent again, and so did she. Suddenly there was the scrape of a key in the cell door's lock. They had not heard anyone approach down the corridor. A tall black man in a gray suit and a priest's collar stood in the open door.

"Good afternoon, Mrs. Manning," he said gravely. "I am the Reverend John Wills; I thought you might like to speak with me. Are you a Christian?"

"I'm an Episcopalian," she replied. "Yes, do come in."

"Gentlemen," the priest said, "will you excuse us for a while?"

"Of course, Reverend," Hewitt said, then left the cell, motioning for Stone to follow him.

The two men went outside and sat on a bench against the stone wall. "I thought she should be alone with him," Hewitt said.

"Yes," said Stone. He could not think of anything else to say. The sun was lower in the sky now. Stone looked at his watch. "Leslie, it's nearly seven o'clock; could you call the prime minister's residence again?"

"Of course," Hewitt said. He got up and went back inside the jail. As he entered, Hilary Kramer and Jim Forrester came out.

"Stone," she said, "have you still heard nothing?"

"Nothing," Stone replied. "Leslie has gone to phone the prime minister."

They joined Stone on the bench. "This is driving me crazy," Forrester said.

"It's seven o'clock," Kramer said, looking at her watch. "What time is sundown?"

"Seven fifty-nine," Stone replied. "I'm told they do these things on time."

"They're not really going to hang her, Stone, surely," Forrester said, sounding distressed. "This is just some sort of torture."

"I don't know what's going to happen," Stone said. "I'm afraid to hope."

Hewitt came back outside.

"What?" Stone said.

"It's very odd," Hewitt replied. "No one is answering the phone."

"Not even an answering machine?"

"Nothing; it just rang and rang. I must have let it ring twenty-five times, then I called again and got the same result."

"Maybe they're on the way over here," Forrester said hopefully.

Nobody cared to address that possibility.

"Did they make you two leave Allison alone?" Kramer asked.

"A priest is with her," Stone replied. "We thought it best to leave them."

As if on cue, the priest came out the door. "Mr. Barrington?"

Stone looked up.

"Mrs. Manning would like to see you and Sir Leslie now."

"How did you leave her, Reverend?" Hewitt asked the man.

"I think her mind is relieved," he replied. "We had quite a good talk, although I don't think she had met with a clergyman for quite some time. She seems resigned now."

Resigned, Stone thought. He wasn't resigned. Why the hell didn't the prime minister's office call and at least put them out of their misery?

The priest spoke again. "Are you Miss Kramer and Mr. Forrester?" he asked the two reporters.

"Yes," Kramer replied.

"She'd like to see you both for a moment; I spoke to the jailer, and he will allow it."

They all got to their feet and went inside, the priest bringing up the rear. The jailer searched Kramer and Forrester, then conducted the group down the corridor.

Forrester stopped. "I can't do this," he said. "I just can't."

"Wait for us outside," Stone said, and Forrester went back down the corridor.

Allison was sitting on the bunk, reading a Bible that the priest must have given her. She looked up, saw Kramer, and smiled.

"Thank you for coming," she said to her, shaking her hand. "I wanted to tell you how grateful I am to you, Hilary, for the reporting you did in the *Times*. It meant a great deal to me." She looked toward the door. "Where's Jim?"

Stone spoke up. "He wasn't feeling well; he asked that you excuse him."

Allison nodded.

"You will have to go now," the jailer said to Kramer.

The reporter left, leaving Stone, Hewitt, and the priest with Allison. Stone looked at his watch: seven thirty-five.

Finally, Hewitt spoke. "A phone line at the main desk will be kept free," he said, then he was quiet again.

"Stone," Allison said, "they asked me to fill out a form, giving next of kin and so forth. I gave them your name to handle any formalities."

"Of course," Stone said, "but that's not going to be necessary."

She smiled slightly. "It seemed like a good idea at the time." She smoothed her skirt. "I've also left some instructions with Leslie," she said. "To be opened . . ." She let the sentence trail off.

"Everything will be done, Allison," Leslie said. "I feel that I have let you down, you know."

"Don't you believe that for a moment," she said. "Both you and Stone have been perfectly wonderful. I could not have been better represented. I really mean that." She put her hand in Stone's.

There was the sound of footsteps in the front hall. Someone, more than one person, had come into the jail. Then it was quiet again. Stone willed himself not to look at his watch, but it was growing dark in the cell. Suddenly, the single bare bulb came on, making them blink.

Then, from down the hall, came the sound of men marching in step. Stone looked up to find four policemen standing outside the cell. One of them unlocked the door. At that moment, Stone heard the telephone ring. The policeman closed the door, turned his back, and leaned on it, nodding to another officer, who strode back down the hall. He was gone for half a minute, then returned. He looked at his senior officer and shook his head.

No, Stone thought, *no, this can't be. That must have been the prime minister.* He stood up. "The phone call? . . ."

The senior policeman opened the cell door. "Not related to these events," he said. "Mrs. Manning, please step out into the corridor."

Stone made to follow her, but an officer stepped between them. Behind him, another officer was tying Allison's hands behind her back.

"Say your good-byes," the senior officer said to her.

She looked at Stone, panic in her face.

"Allison . . ." he began, then stopped.

"Good-bye," she said. "You have all been very kind to me." She was trembling, but she did not cry.

Then, simultaneously, a policeman opened the big door to the inner courtyard while another closed the cell door and locked it, with Stone, Hewitt, and the priest still inside.

"I want to go with her," Stone said, but the officer shook his head.

"No farther," he said.

Stone looked out the door and saw a corner of the scaffold in the gloomy light. He tried to speak, but nothing came out.

An officer stood on either side of Allison, took her arm, and marched her into the courtyard. The senior officer slammed the stout door shut behind them.

Stone turned to Leslie Hewitt. "Is there nothing we can do?"

Leslie looked at the floor and shook his head slowly. "We have done all we can."

Stone looked at the priest, who avoided his gaze. Then, sooner than Stone had expected, he heard the sound of the trap flying open, followed by a thunk, then silence. He leaned his forehead against the bars; he felt like weeping, but he could not.

The outside door opened, the senior officer and one other stepped inside, and the door closed behind them. The cell door was unlocked and the three men were waved out and marched down the corridor to the front desk.

Allison's duffel sat on the desk, and an officer waited, pen in hand, for Stone to sign for her belongings. Stone signed. "What about the body?" he asked the man.

"The body will be cremated and the ashes scattered at sea," the officer said. "It's how we do things here."

"It is so," Hewitt said.

Stone picked up the duffel and walked out of the jail into a lovely St. Marks evening. Hilary Kramer and Jim Forrester were sitting on a bench next to the outside door. Kramer jumped up. "What's happening? Did you hear from the prime minister?"

Stone shook his head. "No."

Forrester stood up, too. "For Christ's sake, Stone, tell us what's happening?

"Allison was hanged five minutes ago."

Both reporters seemed struck dumb. Kramer's mouth was working, but nothing came out. Forrester turned, leaned against the building, and vomited.

"You can quote me as saying that a monumental injustice has been done," Stone said.

CHAPTER

61

The priest shook hands with both men, then got into his car and drove away. Stone leaned against Thomas's car, which was parked next to Leslie's ancient Morris Minor. "This is completely surreal," he said.

"I know," Hewitt replied, "I feel the same way."

"Leslie, about your fee . . ."

"It has already been paid."

Stone looked at him, surprised. "By Allison?"

The barrister nodded. "She didn't want any loose ends." He took a thick envelope from his briefcase and handed it to Stone. "She asked me to give you this. She said you were to open it aboard her yacht."

Stone accepted the envelope; it felt as though it contained half a dozen sheets of paper. "All right," he said. "I guess I'll go back there now."

Hewitt held out his hand. "Stone, when you remember St. Marks I hope you will think of more than what has happened today. In ways that you cannot now know, you have helped to make sure that something like this will not happen again."

"How?" Stone asked, puzzled.

"You'll hear from me," Hewitt said. "I'll keep you posted on events here."

"I hope so," Stone said, then looked at the little man closely. "Leslie," he said, "there isn't a senile bone in your body, is there?"

Hewitt burst out laughing. "Let's just say that it helps if certain people believe there are a few such bones."

"You're a crafty man and a fine lawyer. It has been a privilege to work with you."

"Thank you, Stone. I can wholeheartedly say the same of you. I hope that in a little while you will not think badly of me."

"Never," Stone said, then embraced the barrister. Then they got into their cars and drove away.

Stone drove on automatic pilot, slowly, feeling numb and drained. He parked the car behind the Shipwright's Arms and left the keys at the bar, but Thomas was not there.

Stone arrived at the marina in time to see the fast motor yacht making her way out of the harbor, her lights reflecting on the water. The news must have reached her skipper, he thought. He boarded *Expansive,* dropping Allison's duffel on a saloon couch and switching on the light over the chart table. The rest of the saloon was in shadow, the desk light reflecting off the gleaming wood. He switched on the satellite phone and dialed Bill Eggers's home number.

"Eggers," the voice said.

"It's over," Stone said.

"Stone? What do you mean, over? Did our tactics work?"

"I'm afraid not. She was executed less than an hour ago."

"Oh, shit. I'm sorry, I know how you must feel."

"Yeah. Will you do a press release? I don't have the energy to talk to anybody."

"Sure. I'll call the PR people and get it on the wire services tonight."

"Is Allison's estate going to owe the firm any money?"

"I think we'll have a surplus to return to the executor."

"We'll talk about it when I'm back."

"When are you leaving?"

"Tomorrow morning."

"You know about Arrington and Vance Calder?"

"I got a fax from her."

"I'm sorry about that, Stone; she was a great girl."

"Still is, no doubt; just not mine."

"Let's have dinner later this week."

"Sure; I'll call you."

"Good night, then."

"Good night, Bill. Thanks for all your help." He hung up, thinking he had never been so tired. His body cried out for sleep; Allison's will would have to wait until tomorrow. He didn't think he could make it back to his own yacht, so he went into the after cabin, shucked off his clothes, and collapsed into the bed. Not until then did he allow himself to weep. He wept for Allison and for himself.

CHAPTER

62

Stone dreamed that he and Allison were making love. Then, just as he was about to come, she vanished, and the bed was empty. He stirred and turned over, kicking off the covers. Cool fingers brushed the damp hair from his forehead. He opened his eyes.

"You were dreaming," Allison said.

Stone blinked rapidly. "I still am." He closed his eyes and tried to recapture the dream.

"Stone," she said, quietly but insistently.

Stone jerked as if he had received an electric shock. "Whaaat!" he yelled, sitting up and pushing away from her. He seemed to go from deep sleep to maximum adrenaline in a fraction of a second. His heart hammered against his rib cage, and he made himself look at her. She seemed perfectly normal.

"It's all right, Stone," she said. "Really it is. You're awake; I'm here; I'm alive."

Stone took a deep breath and tried to stop shaking. A moment ago, he had been making love to this woman, and now he was frightened and confused. "Tell me," he said, then took another deep breath.

"I'm sorry to have put you through this," Allison said, "but it had to be done this way. I didn't know for sure myself when they marched me into the courtyard and I saw the gallows. I thought it hadn't worked, that I was done for."

"That what hadn't worked?" Stone panted.

"Leslie's plan."

"What plan?"

"He insisted that I shouldn't tell you; he wanted absolute secrecy."

Stone was recovering from his shock now. "Allison, what the hell are you talking about?"

"We bribed the prime minister."

"You what?"

"Leslie didn't think you would let him do it; that's why we didn't tell you."

"Well, if he had suggested that, I suppose I would have been against it. I would have thought it very risky."

"He told me what we had to do that day out at his cottage, when he sent you for the milk."

"The milk he didn't need," Stone said, half to himself.

"Yes, that milk. While you were gone, Leslie told me what he had in mind."

"And what did he have in mind?"

"He said that the only thing that worked with these people was money and not even that would work with Sir Winston Sutherland—he was already too committed to a conviction. The prime minister, though, was another matter. He was retiring, and there was always the chance that he hadn't stolen enough to make him happy, Leslie said."

"And how did Leslie go about this?"

"He said nothing to Sutherland; in fact, he said nothing to anybody. When Leslie handed the appeal to the judge, there was a cashier's check for a million dollars in the envelope, along with the appeal document."

"Jesus Christ."

"That's pretty much what I said. It seemed awfully risky, until you consider that at that moment, I had already been convicted and that the prime minister had no motivation to overturn the appeal."

"Didn't the flood of faxes and telephone calls from the States mean anything at all?"

"Merely a nuisance to the old man. He knew he wouldn't be around all that much longer, and that he wouldn't have to deal with any consequences. Sir Winston is, apparently, his hand-picked boy, and he could deal with the aftermath."

"Does Leslie know he succeeded with his bribe?"

She nodded. "When he made that last phone call to the prime minister from the jail, he was given the word, but he couldn't tell me, because you and the priest were there."

"What about Sir Winston?"

"What about him?"

"Does he know about the deal?"

"He knows nothing. That's why I have to get out of here now and why you can't say anything to anybody, either here or in the States. Does the press know about the hanging?"

Stone nodded. "Bill Eggers, in New York, had a press release sent out."

"Good; let's leave it that way."

"For how long?"

"I don't know. Until I let you know it's okay."

The rush of adrenaline was gone now, and Stone was sagging. "What happened after they took you into the court-yard?"

"They whisked me out of the building and into a car and delivered me here, to the motor yacht."

"But I saw it leaving earlier this evening."

"I was already aboard. I made them stop outside the harbor and bring me back in the tender. I had to see you and explain." She looked at him oddly. "Aren't you at all glad to see me?"

He put his arms around her and held her close. "You bet I am," he whispered.

"I'm so sorry to have put you through all this, but there just wasn't any other way."

He held her back and looked at her. "You can read your obituary in the *Times* in a couple of days, I expect."

She smiled. "Well, that will be fun. I'd just as soon be dead for a little while. I have a lot to do, and I can do it better without a lot of reporters and cameras around. Promise me you'll keep my secret until you hear from me."

"I think that comes under the heading of attorney-client confidentiality."

"Don't tell even Hilary Kramer and Jim Forrester. They'd spill the beans."

"As you wish."

She looked at her watch. "I have to get going; I've got a long way to travel."

He got out of bed and walked into the saloon with her, switching on the chart table light. "Your duffel is over there," he said, indicating the sofa.

She went and picked it up. "Thanks; a girl can't get far without her makeup."

He picked up the envelope on the chart table and began to open it, but she took it from him and put it back.

"Not now," she said. "You can do that when I'm gone. Right now, you have to kiss me good-bye." She put her arms around his waist, pressed her body against his, and kissed him for a long time.

"You sure you have to rush off?" he breathed in her ear.

"I wish I didn't, but I do. I'll make it up to you later."

"I'll hold you to that."

"Stone," she said, an uncertainty creeping into her voice, "that envelope contains my last wishes; I want you to promise me that you'll honor them in every respect, as if I really were dead."

"All right, I promise."

She kissed him again. "The days and nights I spent with you on this boat were among the happiest of my life. Remember that, too."

"How could I forget it?"

She kissed him again, grabbed the duffel, and ran up the companionway stairs.

He followed her on deck and watched her get back into the Boston Whaler, which putted slowly away from the yacht. He didn't hear the engine rev up until it was out of sight around a corner of the harbor.

Stone went back below, went to the bar, and poured himself a brandy. His heart was still beating very fast, and he was going to have to wind down a bit if he expected to get any sleep that night. He sat down at the chart table and picked up Allison's envelope, ripping it open. Inside were a letter, some papers, and a U.S. Coast Guard yacht document. He picked up the letter.

Dear Stone,

With any luck, there should be a happy ending to all this. Don't be mad at Leslie; I swore him to silence. I've paid his fee, and yours is in the envelope with this letter.

I will be very angry if you feel I'm being foolish, and I don't want to hear a word about it from you. This all feels very right to me.

The yacht, Expansive, *is yours now, to do with what you will. Unfortunately, Libby's dear old mother is yours, too, and you can handle that situation as you see fit.*

Whatever happens, wherever I go, I will always be grateful to you for the time we spent together and for all your hard work. I hope next year you can have a better sailing vacation.

With great affection,
Allison

Stone put down the letter and went through the other documents. There was one conveying the yacht to him as his fee for legal services, and the Coast Guard, U.S. Customs, and State of Connecticut documents were all signed, notarized, and in perfect order.

Stone took a stiff gulp of brandy. Now he would never get any sleep on this night.

63

S tone managed a couple of hours' sleep, but he was up at dawn, looking over his new yacht. He went through all the cockpit lockers, making a mental inventory of the gear aboard, then he walked fore and aft, checking the way the lines led and what each was for. He thought that for such a large yacht, she would really be very simple to sail. The mainsail had been repaired, and he hauled it back to the cockpit. It took him the better part of an hour to get it bent on. Then he hauled on the line that rolled the mainsail up into the mast like a giant window shade.

Finally, he unreefed the roller-reefing genoa and hauled it down. Paul and Allison had had problems with the top swivel separating into two pieces, and he wanted to think about repairing it. To his surprise, he found that it had already been repaired, and very elegantly. Someone, in an impressive display of seamanship, had seized it together with fine whipping wire. It looked as though it was better than new. He hauled the sail up, then reefed it around the forestay. *Expansive* seemed pretty shipshape, he thought.

"Stone!" The cry came from the lawn, and Stone looked up to see Thomas Hardy running toward him. Behind Thomas, traveling more slowly, came Leslie Hewitt, back in his accustomed shorts and T-shirt. Thomas jumped aboard and turned to give Leslie a hand up.

"What's up?" Stone asked. "You both look very excited."

"You tell him, Leslie," Thomas said.

"I've had a call from a friend at Government House. When Allison . . . when her case was resolved, the yacht, as her bail bond, reverted to her . . . estate. But my friend says that Sir Winston Sutherland has filed a petition with the Admiralty, which administers maritime affairs, claiming the yacht for the Ministry of Justice, supposedly to defray the costs of Allison's trial. It's just a naked grab of someone else's property, but he can probably bring it off."

Thomas grinned. "I hear you are a boat owner now."

"Well, for a few hours, anyway," Stone said. "Leslie, how much time have I got?"

Leslie looked at his watch. "It's just past ten. Lord, I don't know; Winston could be here with an order any minute."

"Thomas, can you put together a week's provisions for me in a hurry?"

"I'll see to it," Thomas said. He jumped down from the deck and sprinted back toward the Shipwright's Arms.

Stone looked at Leslie Hewitt. "Well, Leslie, I hear that my co-counsel hasn't been absolutely frank with me about the way Allison's case was conducted."

"What? What do you mean? I surely . . ."

Stone held up a hand. "Don't bother; Allison came to see me last night."

Leslie looked embarrassed, but he managed a grin. "Well, perhaps I wasn't entirely candid with you, Stone, but all's well . . ."

"That ends well," Stone said. "It did end well, I suppose; you're just lucky I didn't die of a heart attack last night."

"Myself as well," Leslie said. "I was frantic when I couldn't get anyone on the phone at the prime minister's residence or in his office. I was nearly as much in the dark as you, right up until you asked about the disposition of the body, and the policeman gave you that malarkey about cremation. There's no crematorium on St. Marks, so I figured I must have brought it off after all."

"You certainly did, but you aged me ten years in the process."

"Well, I'm glad it came out all right. I got a lovely fee, the prime minister got his, ah, pension fund, and you got a very fine yacht."

"If I can hang on to it," Stone said, laughing. "I'd better get the engine started." He went aft to the cockpit, switched on the ignition, and prayed that the thing would start. The starter ground on for a good ten seconds before the engine caught and ran smoothly. He looked up and saw Thomas running across the lawn again, carrying a cardboard box and followed by an employee carrying a second one.

Stone checked the fuel gauges. Full. He hoped to God the water tanks were full, too.

Thomas and his man ran down the dock and set their boxes aboard, then Thomas ran back down the dock, untied a dingy with an outboard, pulled it to *Expansive,* and tied it to the stern. "Come on, I'll give you a hand getting out of the harbor," he called.

Stone embraced Leslie again, then lifted him over the lifelines and set him on the dock. "Good-bye, old fellow!" he called out. "Let go our lines, will you?"

Leslie and Thomas's employee untied the lines and tossed them on board, then gave the big yacht a shove away from the dock. Stone put the engine in reverse and began backing out.

"Look up there," Thomas said, pointing with his chin, "but pretend you don't see."

Sir Winston's elderly Jaguar had pulled into the inn's parking lot, and the minister of justice was striding toward them, a piece of paper in his hand. They could hear a faint shout over the engine.

Stone shoved the gear lever to forward and spun the wheel to port; *Expansive* accelerated quickly through the smooth water of the harbor. They were about to turn past a point of land when Stone looked back and saw Sir Winston on the dock waving his piece of paper and shouting. He made a show of cupping his hand to his ear and shrugging, indicating an inability to hear, then they were around the point, and the harbor entrance lay ahead. "Thomas, you take the helm, and I'll get some sail up," he called.

Thomas tossed the mooring lines into the cockpit and took the wheel. Stone unreefed the headsail first, and when it was full and drawing, he unwound the big main from the mast. He went aft and switched off the engine, and everything grew quiet, except the fresh breeze in the rigging and the burble of water slipping past the blue hull. He stowed the mooring lines and went below, wrote Thomas a check, then came back on deck.

"I guess that's it," he said, handing Thomas the check.

"You are too generous, Stone," Thomas said, looking at it.

"You've gone to an awful lot of trouble, Thomas, and I'll never forget it. When you come to New York, stay at my house, and we'll do some serious dining and wining."

"That's an offer I can't refuse."

"Are you going to have any problems with Sir Winston?"

Thomas shook his head. "Nah; he's got nothing on me. And even if he did have, I've got enough relatives on this island to turn him out of office."

"I think Leslie has something like that in mind; why don't you talk to him about it?"

"I'll do that."

They were nearly to the mouth of the harbor now. Stone gave Thomas a big hug, then watched as he jumped into the dinghy, untied the painter, and yanked the cord on the outboard. The little engine buzzed to life, and Thomas kept pace with the yacht for another hundred yards. Then, as the smooth water of the harbor met the swell of the sea outside, he gave a big wave and turned the little boat back into English Harbour.

Stone watched him go. He reflected for a moment that he had not made many friends as good as that one, then he bore away around the point and headed for the open sea, a lump in his throat. There would be time later to sort out charts and courses, but right now, he wanted to sail his boat.

That night, sailing north with the autopilot on, Stone fixed himself some supper, opened a bottle of wine, sat down in the cockpit, and began thinking about the events of the past days. There were anomalies in what he had seen and heard, and he wanted to think about them.

He slept in snatches of a few minutes, scanning the horizon often for ships and other yachts and boats. He saw little traffic. The next day, at midmorning, he fired up the satellite phone and got it working. He called his secretary and informed her of his new travel plans, then he called Bob Cantor.

"Hello, Stone; I heard the news on television this morning. I'm sorry. Is there anything I can do for you?"

"There is, Bob. I want you to take a trip up to Ithaca for a couple of days and do a little research for me."

"Sure; what do you need?"

Stone told him in some detail. Finally, he hung up the phone and sat down with his charts. He plotted a course up the leeward side of the islands, then between Hispaniola and Puerto Rico and then to the northwest, leaving the Turks and Caicos and the Bahamas to starboard, and on to Fort Lauderdale. It had not taken him long to figure out that he could not afford to own the yacht; what with dockage, repairs, and insurance, it would break him, unless he sold his house, and he wasn't about to do that.

He sailed on, thinking about what had happened to him and what to do next. He made other calls, the last of them to Sir Winston Sutherland, who was surprised to hear from him, but extremely interested in what he had to say.

By the time he had reached Fort Lauderdale, he had done all he could do. Except wait.

Two Months Later

Stone sat in his Turtle Bay garden on a lovely early spring morning, breakfasting on eggs and bacon and orange juice. When he had finished, his Greek housekeeper, Helene, took away the plates and poured him a mug of the strong coffee he loved. He looked through the *Times* idly, checking for any mention of Allison. He had heard nothing from her, and when he had called the Greenwich house, the number had been disconnected. He had thought of calling her Connecticut lawyer, but had decided just to wait for Allison's call.

Alma, his secretary, came out to the garden with the morning mail. "There's one from the broker in Fort Lauderdale," she said.

Stone opened that first and found a check for one million eight hundred thousand dollars and change. He smiled broadly.

"I take it we're not broke for a while?" Alma asked.

"We certainly are not," he said, endorsing the check and handing it to her.

Her eyes grew wide. "I had no idea it was worth so much."

"The broker reckoned it had cost close to three million to build and equip. Still, after his commission, that's a good price."

"What shall I do with it?" Alma asked.

"Write a check for, let's see"—he began scribbling numbers on his newspaper—"three hundred seventy-five thousand to that law firm in Palm Beach, for the account of Libby Manning's mother. I want that off my conscience."

"Right," said Alma.

"Then send a check for five hundred and forty thousand to the Internal Revenue Service." He groaned. "God, how proud I am to be an American and pay my taxes!"

"Right. That leaves eight hundred and eighty-five thousand."

"Send my broker a check for two hundred thousand, and tell him to call me about where to invest it."

"We're rich!" Alma squealed. "What about the rest?"

"I was thinking about buying an airplane," Stone said.

Alma's face fell. "Oh. We're not rich anymore. Well, it was fun while it lasted." She got up and trudged comically back into the house.

Stone had a thought: he could afford a car now. He got up, went into the house, and walked through the kitchen into a store-room, then through another door. This had been a garage at one time, and there was still a folding door to the street, though he hadn't opened it for a long time. He waded through the stacked boxes and old lawn furniture to the door, which was made of heavy oak. He turned the lock, thinking, *I'll have to install an automatic garage door opener if I'm going to use this space.* He tugged at the door, which moved six inches and stopped. He tugged again, and got it open three feet. Then, with all his strength, he moved the door up all the way, until it was standing wide open. He found himself face-to-face with a tall man.

"Morning, Stone," the man said. "I was going to ring the front bell, but . . ."

"Morning," Stone said. "What brings you around to see me?"

"Oh, just a social call," Jim Forrester said. "Got a few minutes?"

"Sure." Stone dragged two lawn chairs over, made a pass at dusting them, and sat down. "Take a pew."

The two men sat, ten feet from the street. Forrester seemed a little annoyed at not being asked into the house. "How about some coffee?" he said.

"Sorry, coffee's off the menu," Stone replied. "What do you want?"

"Oh, I was just passing by."

"Were you? Say, whatever happened to your *New Yorker* piece? I haven't seen it."

"Oh, they take a long time to edit anything, you know. My editor . . ."

"That would be Charles McGrath?"

"Right."

"Chip McGrath left *The New Yorker* a couple of years ago to become editor of the *New York Times Book Review*."

"Ah, right; I'm working with another editor now. Say, what do you hear from Allison?"

"You must think I'm a medium," Stone said, expressionless.

"I inquired about the disposition of the body at Government House. They didn't seem to know what I was talking about. I began to think that Allison might not be dead after all."

"The police told me that their policy was to cremate the body and scatter the ashes at sea," Stone said. That was certainly what they had told him. "By the way, have you been to any alumni reunions lately?"

Forrester looked at him, puzzled. "No, not for years. Why do you ask?"

"I did a little checking upstate. There was no James Forrester at Syracuse, not since the class of '38, and I think that was a little before your time."

"Must be some mistake," Forrester said.

"No, but there was a Paul Manning, at Cornell, of course."

"Yes, that's where Paul went. Why were you checking on me at Syracuse?"

"When I've been had, I like to know why and by whom."

"Had?"

"Manning did play basketball for his fraternity, as you said he did. In fact, I've got a copy of the yearbook for his senior year, and there's a very good photograph of him in it. He looks very different—thinner and no beard. Would you like to see it?"

Forrester looked at his nails. "It doesn't interest me," he said.

"I guess not," Stone agreed. "Tell me, where are you living these days?"

"I've been living here in the city, but I think I'm going to do some traveling now."

"I'm not surprised," Stone replied.

Alma walked into the garage from the house. "Oh, there you are. Bill Eggers is on the phone; he wants to know if you want to have lunch."

"Tell Bill I can't make it today, but I'll call him later," Stone said. "Oh, and call Dino and tell him to pick me up in five minutes and to bring his friends. I've got some stuff I want to give to the Salvation Army."

"Okay," Alma said, then left.

"Stone," Manning said," I really came to see you to find out if you would represent me as my attorney."

"No, I won't."

"Why not?"

"Because you're looking for attorney-client confidentiality, aren't you?"

"In part."

"Well, you won't get it from me, pal."

"Stone, I don't understand . . ."

"Sure you do, Paul. By the way, I got a check for your yacht this morning. It brought a million eight after the broker's fee."

His face flushed. "I should have thought it was worth a good deal more."

"Oh, I know you paid more, but what with the market and all . . ."

Paul Manning looked at his nails again. "When did you figure it out?"

"Oh, I was very slow. It didn't all come together for me until I was sailing the boat from St. Marks to Fort Lauderdale. No, a little earlier, I guess, when I saw the repair you'd made to the headsail reefing swivel."

"What else do you think you've figured out?"

"The dinghy was never stolen in Las Palmas."

"Wasn't it?"

"You just made some noise about it, replaced it, then sailed the old one back to the Canaries after *Expansive* was over the horizon."

"If you say so."

"What did you do about clothes and papers? You couldn't use your own passport."

Manning looked at Stone for a long moment, then apparently decided it didn't matter anymore. "All right, I left a car on the south coast of Gran Canaria with some clothes."

"How long did it take you to lose the weight?"

"I started dieting the minute we left the States," Manning said. "Losing weight has never been easy for me, but I had some time; I lost a pound or two a week. By the time we got to Las Palmas, I was as slim as I am now."

"Careful you don't gain it back, Paul; somebody might recognize you."

"Not where I'm going."

"And where would that be?"

"You figure it out."

"It's going to be tough without the money, isn't it?"

"Damn Allison!" Manning said suddenly, and with some venom.

"Wasn't the money in the Cayman Islands account? Didn't you have access to it?"

"The money was moved to a different account the day before Allison's trial."

"I thought it might have been."

"I'd like to get my hands on her."

"I'll bet you would, but it's going to be a little difficult, isn't it?"

"She's not dead, is she?"

"Suppose she's not? I doubt if you could find her. After all, you must have given her lessons in how to obtain a real U.S. passport, how to establish new identities, and all that. All the research you did for your books, and for your own use."

"All that insurance money—tax free—the money from the sale of the house and the cars; it's all gone," Manning said bitterly.

"And even if you could find it, you've no way to get at it, have you?"

"Sir Leslie Hewitt showed me the will he drew for her, leaving everything to the Girl Scouts of America!"

Stone burst out laughing. "Paul, you've made my day, you really have."

"And she gave the goddamned boat to you," Manning said through clenched teeth.

"That's right, pal, but your heart will be warmed to know that Libby's mother got four hundred thousand of the proceeds."

"Shit!"

"So you killed Libby for nothing, didn't you?"

"What do you mean?"

"Come on, Paul; you had the skills to screw up that airplane engine. You'd flown with Chester; you knew he never did a runup, that he'd never notice his fuel problem until he was already in the air. You killed Chester, too, and that other poor woman who was aboard."

"You can't prove that," Manning said.

"You know, right up until the moment that plane crashed, this was all just a lark, a bit of insurance fraud. But when that plane went down, you became something else entirely. You became a murderer—not just three times, but four. You stood there in that jail in St. Marks and let Allison walk out to the gallows. I'll bet she thought until she was standing over that trap door with the rope around her neck that you would step forward and save her. You could have at any time; all you had to do was to tell Sir Winston that you were Paul Manning. He couldn't prosecute her for a murder that hadn't taken place. But you didn't do that, did you? You thought all that money was safe in the Caymans account, and it would all be yours. But Allison outsmarted you."

"I can't figure out why she did it," Manning said, looking dejected.

"Because she knew you. At first she thought you'd save her, but finally she knew you'd never turn yourself in, even to save her. If you had turned yourself in, you'd have had all that money to buy your way out of the business in St. Marks, but you decided to go for broke, to keep it all for yourself, and now you're just that—broke."

"I want the money you got for my boat," Manning said. "And I want all of it."

Stone laughed aloud. "I took the boat as payment of my fee; it was all legal and aboveboard. Why should I give it to you?"

"Because I'll kill you if you don't," Manning said calmly.

"You're not going to kill anybody, Manning." Stone stood up, drew back his hand, and brought the back of it across Manning's

•

321

face, spilling him out of the lawn chair. "That's for Allison, you miserable son of a bitch. You cooked up the scam, and she went all the way with you, then you let her hang." Stone looked up and saw a car stop in his driveway. Dino Bacchetti got out. "Hi, Dino," he said.

"Stone, how you doing?"

"Just great. I want you to meet the late Paul Manning."

"How you doing, Paul?" Dino said, grinning broadly.

"Just great," Manning said, wiping away some blood from the side of his mouth.

"Dino and I used to be partners," Stone said. "He's still a cop; he runs the detective squad at the Nineteenth Precinct."

"What is this?" Manning said, alarmed.

"Dino's going to put you in jail," Stone said.

"I haven't committed any crime in the United States," Manning said.

"It's like this, Paul," Dino said. "I'm arresting you for the homicide of your wife, your ex-wife, the pilot, and the other passenger on that airplane you sabotaged."

"I didn't murder my wife or anybody else," Manning said, "and nobody can prove that I did. Anyway, I don't believe she's dead."

"Well, there are a lot of fine legal points in this case," Dino said. "I mean, in addition to the four homicides, there's the insurance fraud. It all gets very complicated, doesn't it?"

Manning smiled, showing blood on his teeth. "Yes, it does. In fact, I expect to be a free man again before the day is over. I've already retained a lawyer, and you'll never be able to hold me."

"I know this is going to come as a big disappointment, Paul," Dino said, "especially since you worked so hard to figure it all out, but I've got some really bad news for you."

"What do you mean?" Manning asked.

Dino pulled a document from his pocket. "This is for you," he said. "Consider yourself served."

"What is it?"

"It's an extradition warrant. You're going back to St. Marks for trial."

"You can't do that!" Manning said, trying to read the warrant.

"Sure I can. Of course, you'll fight extradition, but eventually you'll go back. And then you can prove to them that your wife is still alive."

Manning's jaw dropped. "How can I prove she's still alive?"

"I doubt if you can," Stone said, "but there's more bad news."

"What?"

"The St. Marks police went out to the airport after Chester crashed, and they dusted everything, and I mean everything, for fingerprints, and you know what? They found some prints on the tool cabinet in the hangar that don't match anybody else's at the airport. I had a phone conversation with Sir Winston Sutherland, and he told me all about it. Of course, they never thought to check the fingerprints of the *New Yorker* writer, Jim Forrester. So when Dino gets you back to the precinct, he's going to fingerprint you, and then he's going to fax your fingerprints to Sir Winston, in St. Marks, and if they match the prints on the tool cabinet—and you and I both know they will—then Sir Winston is going to have a real good case against you for those three homicides. And even if they don't match, there's Allison."

"She isn't dead, is she?" Manning asked. "Come on, Stone, you know she isn't."

"I don't think Sir Winston will adopt that view, Manning. After all, he convicted her and had her hanged himself."

Manning looked as if he wanted to run, but now there were two more detectives standing in the driveway.

Stone continued. "You saw how they tried Allison, how they convicted her with hardly any evidence at all. My prediction, Manning, is that before the year is out, you're going to have your neck stretched in St. Marks."

Dino motioned the two detectives forward, and they handcuffed Paul Manning. He stared at Stone, apparently speechless.

"Good-bye, Manning," Stone said. "I'll be a witness at your trial; I'll tell the court how you admitted your identity to me and that you told me how you faked your death. Funny thing is, without our conversation today, they might not have been able to prove who you really were. So I'll see you in St. Marks." He smiled broadly. "And there won't be any attorney-client confidentiality."

The cops put Manning into their car.

"How about some dinner tonight?" Dino asked.

•

"Absolutely; we'll celebrate."

"Elaine's at eight-thirty?"

"That will be great," Stone replied.

Alma appeared in the garage. "Is everything all right?"

"Everything is all right," Stone said.

Late that night, Stone and Dino sat over the remains of their dinner at Elaine's.

"All in all," Stone said, "it's been a very satisfying day."

"Glad I could help," Dino said. "That guy from Boston, the insurance dick, was in my office this afternoon. He's a very happy man."

"Why?"

"Because he's going to get at least some of his money back from Allison Manning's estate."

"He'd better not count on it."

"Why not?"

"Because, unless I miss my guess, that money has disappeared into the worldwide banking system and will never be seen again. Allison moved it the day before her trial."

Dino looked at Stone sharply. "What was that stuff said about his wife not being dead?"

"I think Manning is still in denial."

"Is she dead?"

Stone was still trying to figure out how to answer Dino's question when Elaine came over to the table.

"Phone call for you, Stone," she said, pointing at one of the two pay phones on the wall nearby.

"Excuse me, Dino," Stone said. He got up and went to the phone. "Hello?" he said, sticking a finger in the other ear to blot out some of the noise.

"Stone?"

"Yeah? Who's this?"

"Stone, this is Vance Calder."

That stopped Stone in his tracks for a minute. "Hello, Vance," he was finally able to say. "How'd you find me here?"

"There was no answer at your house, and I remembered that Arrington said you were at Elaine's a lot. I took a chance."

"How is Arrington, Vance?"

"That's what I'm calling about, Stone. Arrington has disappeared."

"What do you mean, disappeared?"

"Just that; she's vanished."

"When?"

"The day before yesterday."

"Have you been to the police?"

"I can't do that; the tabloids would be all over me. I need your help, Stone."

"Vance, you'd really be a lot better off going to the police; there's nothing I can do about this."

"You can find, her, Stone; if anybody can, you can. I want you to come out here."

"Vance, really . . ."

"The Centurion Studios jet is at Atlantic Aviation at Teterboro Airport right now, waiting for you. You can be here by morning."

"Vance, I appreciate your confidence in me, but . . ."

"Stone, Arrington is pregnant."

Stone felt as if he'd been struck hard in the chest. He could count.

"Stone? Are you still there?"

"I'll be at Teterboro in an hour, Vance."

"You'll be met at the Santa Monica airport."

"Write down everything you can think of, Vance; we'll have a lot to talk about."

"I will. And thank you."

"Don't thank me yet," Stone said, then hung up. He returned to the table. "You're buying dinner, Dino," he said. "I'm off to La-La Land."

"About what?" Dino asked.

"I'll call you," Stone said.

"You didn't answer my question about Allison Manning."

"That will have to wait, I'm afraid." He kissed Elaine on the cheek, then walked out of the restaurant and started looking for a cab.

Key West
February 10, 1997

ACKNOWLEDGMENTS

I am grateful to my editor, HarperCollins vice president and associate publisher Gladys Justin Carr, and her associate editor, Elissa Altman, for their hard work, and to my literary agent, Morton Janklow, his principal associate, Anne Sibbald, and all the people at Janklow & Nesbit for their careful attention to my career over the years. I must also thank my wife, Chris, who is always the first to read a manuscript, for her keen eye and sharp tongue, which help keep my characters in line.

AUTHOR'S NOTE

Stone Barrington first made his appearance in *New York Dead* and came back for *Dirt* and now *Dead in the Water*. He will next appear in *Swimming to Catalina,* which will be published by HarperCollins in the spring of 1998. I apologize to those few readers who have complained about his sexual nature, but he doesn't seem to be able to control himself.